# THE CAT'S PAW
# MURDERS

## FRANK L. GERTCHER

Wind Grass Hill Books

Terre Haute, IN

*The Cat's Paw Murders* is the fourth book in the Caroline Case Jones mystery series. In 1930, Caroline and her enigmatic husband Hannibal become paid espionage operatives for the French government. Over the period 1930-34, they meet fascinating historical characters, experience newsworthy events, provide intelligence reports and solve murders in Paris, Berlin, Vienna, Rome, Riccione, Tripoli, Mogadishu and other ancient cities and towns in Europe and North Africa. However, any similarity of the key storyline characters in this novel to persons living or dead is purely coincidental and not intended by the author.

*The Cat's Paw Murders* © 2022 Frank L. Gertcher

Hard cover EAN-ISBN-13: 978-1-7351459-7-6

E-book EAN-ISBN-13: 978-1-7351459-9-0

Paperback EAN-ISBN-13: 978-1-7351459-8-3

Cover design by Phil Velikan

Cover art: 1920 flapper silhouette ©Incomible/Shutterstock.com; window view by Phil Velikan

Packaged by Wish Publishing

Printed in the United States of America

10 9 8 7 6 5 4 3 2 1

*This Caroline Case novel is dedicated to my wife Linda. She shares in my many adventures and patiently edits my books. Without Linda, my heroine Caroline would not be possible.*

## ALSO IN THE CAROLINE CASE MYSTERY SERIES

Meet Caroline Case, a plucky madam in the 1920s who transforms herself into a budding detective when she starts investigating the death of her friend Alec. Full of historical detail and great storytelling, this book is sure to delight mystery lovers. *"Surprisingly and pleasantly lighthearted for a tale involving prostitution, bootlegging and murder. Detailed descriptions of developments in forensic techniques and equipment add a historical bonus."* — **Kirkus Reviews.**

Published 2019 • $29.95 • ISBN: 978-0-9835754-4-3

The year is 1928 and prohibition is the law of the land. Caroline Case now owns her own detective agency, and she finds herself caught up in the world of intrigue in Al Capone's Chicago. Mystery lovers will enjoy this romantic and exciting glimpse into the roaring 20s. *"There is plenty of fuel for a high action drama, and Gertcher does not disappoint. Like the series opener, the novel is enjoyably lightened by humor and a strong protagonist. Caroline is smart, confident, and spirited...A fun murder-and-mayhem detective story enhanced by historical details and a sturdy female lead."* — **Kirkus Reviews.**

Published 2020 • $29.95 • ISBN: 978-0-9835754-6-7

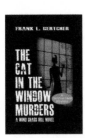

In 1929, beautiful and independently wealthy Caroline Case Jones and her enigmatic new husband Hannibal sail to Europe on the luxury ship SS *Isle de France*. While at sea and in war-scarred France, our intrepid pair become embroiled in social turmoil and political upheaval. Solving murders is the name of the game. *"Frank L. Gertcher is adept at capturing the atmosphere of both P.I. work and Europe of [1929-30]. He also injects moral and ethical conundrums [that] spice the story and give it a three-dimensional feel too often lacking in P.I. procedurals. This [book] will reach newcomers and prior readers alike with a mystery that isn't just a singular production, but a multifaceted journey through bygone times."* — **Midwest Book Review** *"Mystery, history and well-paced excitement in a fun read."* — **Kirkus Review**

Published 2021 • $29.95 • ISBN: 978-1-7351459-3-8

# ACKNOWLEDGEMENTS

My thanks to my wife Linda and the very talented Katherine Garretson. Both provided valuable comments and edits for the entire text of this book and the texts of my other books in this series. Linda also shared my adventures with regard to European and Middle-Eastern country roads, storied waterways, vast cathedrals and museums, dark and sinister city alleys and out-of-the-way eateries with indescribable menus. The contributions provided by Linda, Katherine and others were, I'm sure, factually accurate. Any remaining errors in this book are strictly my own.

## AUTHOR'S NOTE

The cat's paw concept was taken from a fable about a monkey who tricked a cat into using its paw to retrieve chestnuts from a fire.

A cat's paw is a person or organization used by another as a tool to achieve some end, especially in a duplicitous or cynical manner. For example, an espionage agent may become the cat's paw for a government in secret conflict with a foreign power.

# THE CAT'S PAW
# MURDERS

# PROLOGUE

*I am Caroline Case Jones, and this is the fourth volume of my diary.*

What a fascinating evolution! I began with adventures as an amateur sleuth in the Wabash Valley and progressed to action as a full-time private detective in Al Capone's Chicago. Now I live in Paris, and solving murders is still the name of the game.

In addition to murders, I'm ready for new adventures. Hannibal and I will train to be espionage agents for the French Government. Training will take nearly a year. When we finish, we will begin field operations. According to Capitaine Inspecteur Pierre Soucet, we will gather information about the intentions, methods and organizations associated with Adolf Hitler and Benito Mussolini.

Since we arrived in France in 1929, I have educated myself to appreciate and understand modern European art. As wealthy, expatriate Americans, our art-collecting efforts will provide a perfect cover for espionage. We will associate with the rich, the famous and the infamous denizens of aristocratic European society, buy beautiful works of art and spy on the bad guys. How exciting!

We will work for the Deuxiéme Bureau, the French intelligence agency, which is under the Sûreté. The Sûreté reports to the French Minister of the Interior. However, our director and key contact will continue to be Capitaine Inspecteur Soucet from the Sections de recherche de la Gendarmerie Nationale. Soucet reports to the Minister of War.

9

According to Soucet, "Politicians and senior bureaucrats scheme and have mixed agendas with regard to foreign relations, and they often ignore the analysis and the advice of intelligence experts." With a sad expression, he concluded: "Trust no one, except my designated colleagues and me." Who are the bad guys, really?

# 1

## THE MISSION

Saturday, November 2, 1929

Espionage training begins in two months. I will evolve from sleuth to spy. The metamorphosis seems natural, I have proven talents for detailed observation, critical analysis of evidence, deductive reasoning and being sneaky.

According to Capitaine Inspecteur Soucet, Hannibal and I will undergo a rigorous training program at a secret facility near Paris. The location sounds great. We can continue to live in our Paris townhome.

I can still shop at Paris fashion houses when I am not training or doing homework. Weaving shopping into my schedule will be tough, but someone has to keep the fashion industry in business. I also want to explore the art world; I just love impressionist paintings.

Soucet said that Hannibal and I will take courses in French and German. French class will be a refresher for Hannibal. German will be new for both of us. We both already have reasonable skills in Italian. After language training, we will learn how to kill with a variety of weapons.

I have qualms about learning new techniques for killing. The veneer of civilization is not very deep over my primitive inner self, and on several occasions, I have demonstrated unrelenting, hardened talents with regard to subduing villains. However, I know that a killing experience, even if it's gratifying at the time, would trouble my dreams forever.

## Thanksgiving Evening, November 28, 1929

Dawn this morning brought clouds and sleet mixed with snow. Burrr! Hannibal and I decided to celebrate Thanksgiving indoors in our townhome on Rue du Champ de Mars.

Hannibal bought several French, British, Italian and American newspapers on Wednesday evening, and we spent this morning catching up on world events. Somber reading, but good preparation for our espionage activities.

Lynette, our cook, and Susanne, our maid, served breakfast. We had a traditional dinner late this afternoon.

After breakfast, Hannibal and I ensconced ourselves in the parlor. For a while, we observed the Eiffel Tower in the distance out our bay window. The view was occasionally obscured as the wind blew faded leaves and swirls of snow just outside. We had hot coffee, a cozy fireplace and each other.

Minutes passed in comfortable silence. I began the conversation. "As you predicted, the Wall Street stock market crashed last month. Thank goodness our wealth was protected."

Hannibal smiled briefly. His expression turned serious, and he responded: "The effects are already showing up in Europe, especially in Weimar Germany. According to the *London Times*, German exports are falling and unemployment is rising."

I picked up the *Times* and looked through to the end of the article. "Economic troubles, war reparations, loss of territory and French occupation of the Rhineland," I replied. "I can see why the Germans resent the victorious Allies, especially the French."

I put the *Times* aside and picked up the *Daily Mirror*. After a few minutes of review, I said: "According to this editorial, German nationalist parties, including the Nazis, have proposed the so-called Liberty Law, which assigns penalties to any German government official who supports war reparations."

I continued reading for a few minutes and then added: "The article goes on to say that the law also calls for the renouncement of 'war guilt' and the removal of French occupation forces from German territories."

"Humm," responded Hannibal. "Even if the Liberty Law fails in the Reichstag, it gives Hitler an issue for his continued campaign for the election of Nazis to political offices."

I flipped through the *Times* again and found another article. "Here it is," I said. "The Nazis have a substantial presence in Bavaria, and Herman Göring, a Nazi, represents Bavaria in the National Reichstag. However, the Nazis have only 12 out of a total of 491 seats."

Hannibal was silent for a moment. He then responded: "Hitler is an effective campaigner, and he espouses very popular issues. I think his star is rising."

The wind rose outside and began to moan softly. I shivered, even though the parlor was warm. My thoughts explored future possibilities.

Hannibal broke the silence with: "I read about events in Rome in the Italian newspapers."

"Oh?" I replied, as my mind returned to the present.

Hannibal smiled in response, and he picked up an Italian newspaper. As he read, his smile turned to a frown. Finally, he said: "The Italian government now requires all teachers and school children to take an oath of loyalty to Fascism."

He paused and added: "Mussolini has decreed that children owe the same allegiance to Fascism as they do to God."

"Scary and sad," I replied. "However, I read somewhere that Mussolini made peace with the Catholic Church."

"Yes," said Hannibal. "The Lateran Treaty, which was signed last February, makes Vatican City a sovereign state."

"I'm sure that was a popular diplomatic coup for Mussolini," I replied.

"Mussolini is an opportunist, and according to the newspapers, he wants to re-establish the Roman Empire," mused Hannibal. "Still, he remains popular in Italy." The wind continued to moan outside, and we watched the snow for a while.

Finally, I asked: "What about France? You know I have trouble reading the Paris newspapers."

Hannibal smiled sympathetically and said: "Well, the French government has turned over twice this year, socialists, communists and right-wing nationalists fight for power, and there are riots in the streets."

"Anything else?" I responded. "So far, the ladies fashion salons seem unaffected."

Hannibal laughed. "I read somewhere that the French military has begun work on a defensive line, proposed by André Maginot, along the border between France and Germany and between France and Luxembourg. It will extend all the way south to Switzerland, but not north to Belgium and beyond to the English Channel."

We were silent again, and both of us became absorbed in private thoughts. Finally, I asked: "Do you think Europe will experience another war soon?"

"Perhaps," replied Hannibal. "The French and British empires hold overwhelming power for now. Mussolini may be a wild card. Who knows what will happen in Germany?"

I shivered again. I began to better understand Soucet's desire for intelligence about Hitler and Mussolini. Hannibal and I will be more than just adventurers.

# 2

## TRAINING TO DIE

*Thursday evening, January 2, 1930*

Espionage training started today. Soucet had given us driving directions to the training facility. After breakfast at our plush townhome, we used our Duesenberg to travel a few kilometers north of Paris.

After 20 minutes, we arrived at a quaint chateau hidden in the forest near Enghien-les-Bains. The quiet, ornate buildings exuded secret purpose. Soucet met us as we parked the car.

"We need your help before you begin training, I'm afraid," said Soucet. "A most unfortunate death has occurred. Will you investigate?"

"Yes," I responded tentatively.

I looked at Hannibal, who raised his eyebrows. "What happened?" Hannibal asked.

"Herman Strasser, an agent in training, died on the running trail," replied Soucet. "Was it an accident or murder?"

As we accompanied Soucet toward the main chateau building, I asked: "Any witnesses?"

"Four other trainees found Strasser's body on the trail at about 9:30 this morning," replied Soucet. "According to Louis Du Bellay, the director of this facility, the trainees did not see anyone at the scene. After verifying that Strasser was dead, they returned immediately back to the chateau and reported what they had found."

The front door of the chateau opened as we walked up the steps. A tall, aristocratic, impeccably dressed man stood in the doorway.

As we approached, Soucet conducted the introductions. "Major Jones, Madame Jones, please meet my friend Director Louis Du Bellay. Director Du Bellay, please welcome your two newest trainees."

"Welcome," responded Du Bellay with a slight smile. "Pierre has told me so much about you." He extended his hand to Hannibal.

Du Bellay's voice was a deep baritone, and his English had only a slight accent. He and Hannibal shook hands.

Du Bellay then turned to me. "Ah, Madame Jones," he said. His smile warmed a little. He extended his hand formally, yet in a friendly manner.

My first impressions were good. I smiled in return. "Monsieur Director," I responded correctly, as we shook hands. "We look forward to training at your facility."

"You are most welcome," responded Du Bellay. "However, you have arrived at an unfortunate moment. I'm sure Pierre has told you about Herman Strasser's death."

"Just briefly," I replied. I waited for Du Bellay to continue.

Du Bellay stepped aside and motioned for us to enter. "Shall we go to my office?" As we passed the doorway, he added: "Albert Montague, one of the trainees who found the body, will tell you more."

The entry was beautifully paneled in creamy-white painted wood with gold trim. Tasteful Louis XIV style furnishings lined the vestibule. Several paintings of 17 Century aristocrats hung on the walls. "Nice," I thought to myself.

Du Bellay led the way down a hallway and into a spacious office that continued with the Louis XIV décor. The office held bookcases, a neatly arranged desk, a conference table with chairs and several more comfortable-looking chairs around a large coffee table.

A young man dressed in exercise clothing stood up from one of the chairs as we entered. Du Bellay introduced us to Albert. Soon we were all seated.

"Albert," said Du Bellay; "Please tell Major and Madame Jones what you experienced this morning as you prepared for your run and what you discovered this morning on the trail."

Albert took a deep breath, exhaled slowly and began. "I saw Herman leave the chateau area on his daily run at about 8:45 this morning, just after sunrise." He paused, and then continued: "Laurent, Jean, Michael and I followed about 15 minutes later."

"Did Herman leave alone?" Hannibal asked.

"Yes," replied Albert. "Herman was much faster than the rest of us. He always started and finished early."

"What happened on the trail?" I queried.

Albert's gaze shifted from Hannibal to me. His eyes were steady as he responded: "The four of us jogged along the slightly muddy trail. We saw Herman's footprints. Later on, I noticed the tire tracks of a bicycle."

Albert paused, as if recalling events. "Yesterday we had rain, so the prints and tracks were new."

"Good attention to detail," I thought to myself. To Albert, I said: "Oh? Did the tire tracks start at the chateau?"

"No," replied Albert. "About half a kilometer into the forest, a cross-trail intersects our running trail. The cross-trail comes from Enghien-les-Bains to the southwest. I don't know where it ends to the east. The tire tracks came from the direction of town and turned left onto our running trail."

"What happened next?" Soucet asked.

Albert looked over to Soucet. His gaze remained steady. "We jogged on for about another half-kilometer. We saw Herman lying on the right side of the trail. His eyes were open, and we saw a gash on his right temple."

The room was quiet as we waited for Albert to continue. After a few moments, he said: "We all stopped. I walked up to Herman and verified that he was dead. I noted the time on my wristwatch as 9:30. After a minute or so of discussion, we decided to return to the chateau to report what we had discovered."

"You did the right thing," said Du Bellay, and he smiled at Albert. "Did you see anything else as you returned?"

Albert was quiet as he collected his thoughts. "No," he finally replied. "We came back to the chateau and immediately reported our experiences to you."

Du Bellay looked around at Hannibal, Soucet and me and said: "After Albert's report, I called the local gendarme." He took out his pocket watch and looked at the time. "Inspecteur Cadieux should arrive soon. Any further questions for Albert?"

After a few moments of silence, I saw movement outside the window. A car drove into the parking area, and a man got out. An ambulance pulled up next to the car. Two men got out. Car and ambulance doors slammed shut. At the sound, everyone else around the coffee table looked out the window.

"I see Inspecteur Cadieux and two men with an ambulance," said Du Bellay. "Albert, perhaps you can lead Major and Madame Jones, along with Inspecteur Cadieux, to Herman's body."

"Oui, Monsieur Director," replied Albert, as he rose from his seat.

Du Bellay led everyone outside, made the introductions and then returned to the chateau. Soucet accompanied him; the pair were already in deep discussion as they disappeared through the doorway.

Hannibal retrieved our camera from our car. Fortunately, we had left it in the glove compartment. The film still had space for more photos.

After a brief discussion, Cadieux instructed the two men from the ambulance to wait in the parking area until he returned. He then retrieved a small case from the back seat of his car. "My tools," he said with a smile.

Hannibal and I both smiled in return. Inspecteur Cadieux seemed pleasant enough, and he showed no indication that he objected to Hannibal and me helping on the case. "Must have been briefed by Du Bellay," I surmised to myself. "Fortunately, he speaks excellent English."

Albert, Cadieux, Hannibal and I arrived near the death scene at about 11:00 AM. From a distance, we could see Strasser's body. It lay on the right side of the trail. He had fallen forward, and his head was turned to the right. I could see blood on his right temple.

The trail was clear of snow and slightly muddy from rain the previous day. The weather was unseasonably warm, and Strasser wore light cotton pants, running shoes, a thin shirt and a light cotton sweater.

"Strasser was last seen at the chateau at about 8:45 this morning, and his body was discovered at 9:30," mused Hannibal. "The distance to this point on the trail is about a kilometer from the chateau."

"Yes," I responded. I did a quick mental calculation. "Given that he was a fast runner, the time of death was after about 8:50 and before 9:30." Cadieux looked first at Hannibal and then me, with a slightly surprised expression. He took a notebook and pencil out of his case and scribbled a few notes.

"I agree," Cadieux finally said, as he put his pencil in his notebook and closed it.

At a distance of several meters from the body, we stopped and looked at the footprints and tire tracks on the trail, then at Albert's running shoes and then back to the trail.

After a moment's study, I said: "Albert, I see your footprints up to the body and then back toward us in the direction of the chateau. I also see the bicycle tire tracks."

Hannibal walked slowly down the side of the trail toward the chateau and back. He then peered up the trail toward the body. Everyone waited for him to speak.

After a few minutes of study, he said: "The victim staggered along the trail from back about fifty meters. I see his footprints on both sides and on the trail, ending where he fell."

Hannibal then looked to Cadieux. "Shall we walk toward the body well off to the left side of the trail? I will take photos of the footprints and tire tracks later."

Cadieux opened his mouth, closed it, and then replied: "Yes, of course." He then looked at Albert. "Wait here," he instructed. He then motioned to Hannibal and me. The three of us walked slowly, off on the left side of the trail, up to the body.

There was no sign of a struggle. A fist-sized, smooth stone lay along the right side of the path near Strasser's head.

Strasser's right temple had a nasty bruise and a bloody cut. The stone had blood on its surface and blood spots lay in the dirt next to it. However, the stone did not seem to belong in its current location. The amount of blood seemed small for the nature of the head wound.

A workman's leather glove lay on the trail just past Strasser's body. It was for the right hand. Cadieux made more notes.

Bicycle tire tracks passed along the left side of the body. The tracks showed that the rider had stopped and dismounted; the kickstand left a mark in the dirt on the trail. Footprints showed that the rider walked around the body. They were large, almost certainly male. The rider re-mounted the bicycle and continued along the trail away from the chateau.

Hannibal took photos of the death scene. Cadieux then bagged the glove and stone for evidence. I decided to concentrate on the tire tracks, which continued off into the distance past the body.

Albert was standing back a few meters. I turned to him and asked: "Where does the trail lead?"

Albert, who seemed to appreciate not being ignored, answered: "It runs north for another half-kilometer, then loops back around east and then south toward the chateau. The entire trail is about four kilometers from start to finish."

"Do other trails or roads intersect the trail ahead?" I asked and pointed north.

"The trail runs along a gravel road as it loops around east and before it turns south," responded Albert.

I looked over at Cadieux, who was just finishing with the glove, and said: "With your permission, Albert and I will follow the bicycle tire tracks on the trail north."

"Yes, please do," replied Cadieux. "Major Jones and I will finish up here."

Albert and I headed north along the trail. The tire tracks continued until we reached the gravel road. At that point, they left the trail and headed toward the road a few meters away.

Albert and I followed the tracks to the road, where they were no longer visible on the packed gravel. However, the angle of the tracks as they approached the road indicated that the bicycle rider had headed west.

I turned to Albert and asked: "Where does the road lead?"

"To Enghien-les-Bains," he replied. "It turns southwest after half a kilometer or so."

"The bicycle rider headed back toward the village," I stated. Albert nodded. After a moment, I added: "Other than the footprints of the bicycle rider by the body, I didn't see any other footprints on the trail past the body."

"Yes," responded Albert.

We walked back to the trail and returned to the death scene. Hannibal had finished with his photos and Cadieux had finished collecting the evidence that we had found next to the body. At about 12:30, the four of us returned along the trail back to the chateau.

When we reached the parking area, Cadieux allowed Albert to return to his training activities. Hannibal and I walked with Cadieux toward his car. As we passed the ambulance, he instructed the two attendants to retrieve the body and take it to the local morgue.

Hannibal loaned Cadieux our camera, which had photos that would be useful for the autopsy and police reports.

"I will visit Dr. Remy, the part-time medical examiner, at his office," said Cadieux as he put our camera in his case and got into his car. "I will let you know when he completes the autopsy." He then smiled in a genuine way and said: "I am glad you are working with me on this case."

"Glad to be of help," I replied. Hannibal smiled. Cadieux drove away, and Hannibal and I walked back into the chateau and to Du Bellay's office. Du Bellay and Soucet were waiting.

## Friday evening, January 3

After our return to the chateau on Thursday, Du Bellay introduced Hannibal and me to the teaching staff. We had a quick lunch, and then we began a class in French, along with several other students. "Du Bellay doesn't waste time," I thought to myself as Hannibal and I settled in the classroom.

Fortunately, we didn't have to participate in physical exercise classes. According to Du Bellay, that would come later. "Train the mind first," he had said.

I had a hard time concentrating on the lesson; the death scene kept appearing in my mind. Conjugating French verbs took second place to images of a dead body. However, I took volumes of notes, all in French.

Class started again Friday morning at 8:00 AM, which meant that I had to get out of bed at 5:30 AM. Hannibal was unrelenting in getting me out the door by 7:30. Such cruelty!

Class was unbelievably boring; we concentrated on French vocabulary. At noon, we had a sandwich and coffee in the classroom.

The torture ended at about 5:00 PM, and we prepared to drive home. I was totally exhausted.

Just as Hannibal and I were about to leave the chateau at about 5:15, Du Bellay met us in the hallway. He had two file folders in his hand.

"In addition to your homework, I think you will find these reports of interest for your night table reading," he said, with a twinkle in his eyes. "It's Dr. Remy's initial autopsy report and Inspecteur Cadieux's death scene report." He looked at Hannibal but handed the reports to me.

"Thanks," I blurted, as my mind shifted gears from French nouns and verbs to the death of Herman Strasser. I glanced at Hannibal. His face acquired a slight smile. I gave him a look that said: "Wipe that grin off your face." He didn't.

We arrived at our townhouse just after six. Lynette and Susanne had prepared a nice dinner. Hannibal opened a chilled bottle of chardonnay, and we each had a glass. I don't remember what I ate, but it tasted good. I relaxed a little.

After quick showers, Hannibal and I dressed in comfy robes and settled in the library. We had our homework, Remy's autopsy report and Cadieux's police report. Hannibal made me do the homework first. I grumbled a lot, but finished by 8:30.

The reports were next, and they were written in French. Hannibal was sympathetic; he helped as I laboriously read the text, there were lots of scientific words and phrases.

"The autopsy confirms that Strasser had a cut and a bruise on his right temple, but the skull was not fractured," I said, as we both finished reading.

"Dr. Remy concluded that the victim likely died as a result of a blow to the head," responded Hannibal.

He thought a moment and then added: "Cadieux speculated that either the victim fell and hit his head on the stone that lay next to his head, which would make the victim's death an accident, or someone, possibly the bicycle rider, used the stone to strike the victim, which would make his death murder."

I scanned the autopsy report again, and pointed to a short paragraph. "Remy also made a brief entry concerning a toxicology analysis," I responded. I smiled; I was proud of my slowly improving abilities with French technical words.

Hannibal looked closely. After a moment, he said: "The analysis revealed a slightly elevated level of potassium ions in the victim's blood."

He continued reading. After a minute or so, he added: "Following standard procedure, Remy took the blood sample from a femoral artery in the victim's groin." Hannibal leaned back in his chair and stared at the ceiling.

I could tell that the wheels were turning in his mind. Given Hannibal's concentration, I also thought back to what we had observed at the death scene. After about a minute, I said: "The head wound was all wrong." Hannibal looked at me and raised his eyebrows.

"The wound was on the right temple, yet the bicycle tracks were on the left of Strasser's footprints, even back on the trail where he started staggering," I continued. "If the bicycle rider struck Strasser with the stone, the wound would have been on the back of his head or on the left temple."

"Yes," replied Hannibal. "And the stone seemed out of place where we found it; so Strasser most likely didn't fall and hit his head on a stone that was already there."

I continued to follow the logic. "The blow didn't produce a fractured skull," I said. "Also, the wound didn't bleed much."

"Unlikely that the wound was fatal," replied Hannibal.

"Not much blood at the scene," I responded. The light came on in my mind, and I added: "The blow to Strasser's temple was post-mortem."

Hannibal thought a moment and then replied: "Agree." He then said: "The glove at the scene seemed odd."

"The bicycle rider left enough evidence to lead investigators to conclude exactly what was in Cadieux's report," responded Hannibal.

We both were silent for a while. Finally, I said: "Given that the blow with the stone didn't kill Strasser, what did kill him?"

"I will ask Dr. Remy to follow up on the potassium," responded Hannibal. "I remember from my lab days back in Chicago that potassium can cause cardiac arrest if sufficient amounts enter the heart."

"Humm," I responded. "How about asking Remy to take a blood sample from the victim's heart?"

"Good idea," said Hannibal. "However, we still have the problem of how potassium got into Strasser's blood."

"Shall we ask Remy if we can assist with a second autopsy?" I said with a grin, and added: "Another new experience!"

"Tomorrow is Saturday, so we don't have class. Are you caught up on your homework?" Hannibal responded with a chuckle.

After Hannibal saw my expression, he quickly added: "I'll call Du Bellay first thing in the morning. I'm sure he can arrange for us to meet with Remy."

"Yes, smarty," I replied. "However, I promise to double up on conjugating French verbs before Monday. Can we go to bed now?"

Hannibal just laughed. While in bed, I made these entries in my diary. I finished at about 11:00 PM. Hannibal was still in the library. How does he do it?

# 3

## STONES AND NEEDLES

*Saturday evening, January 4, 1930*

As promised, Hannibal called Du Bellay this morning right after breakfast. More phone calls followed. As I was finishing my third cup of coffee, Hannibal joined me in the parlor, where I had curled up on the couch, coffee cup in hand. The clock on the fireplace mantle had just chimed nine o'clock.

I was awake, more or less, but still in my robe and nightgown. As usual, Hannibal was already in his business suit and tie.

"Better get dressed," said Hannibal. "We have to be at the morgue in Enghien-les-Bains at 10 o'clock."

"Good heavens!" I exclaimed. "You couldn't get a later time?" I took a last slurp of hot coffee, set down the cup, got up from my comfy couch and headed for the bathroom.

As I turned the corner, I heard Hannibal add: "We also have a two o'clock appointment with Cadieux at the Hôtel de la Paix."

After frantic preparation in the bathroom and bedroom, I was showered, primped and dressed by 9:30, a new record time. My hair wasn't quite right, but my fashionable business attire was on straight, I think. Anyway, we were on the road in our Duesenberg by 9:40.

After a whirlwind trip, Hannibal drove up to the morgue entrance at precisely 10:00 AM. We joined Dr. Remy in the examination room a few minutes later.

Remy was a pleasant-enough man, and he spoke better English than my still amateur efforts at French. He confirmed that the victim's organs were still in place.

Following up on our conversation the previous evening, Hannibal suggested to Remy that he take a blood sample from the victim's heart. He also suggested that the sample be sent by courier to a Gendarmerie laboratory in Paris for a detailed analysis. Remy complied.

Hannibal made phone calls from Remy's office and determined that a blood analysis report would be sent to Remy within a week.

When the blood draw was done, Remy began a second examination of Strasser's body. Initially, Hannibal and I observed carefully. I found the process fascinating.

We didn't spot anything unexpected until Remy turned the body over and we examined the back. I couldn't help myself; I found a magnifying glass on a nearby bench and started a detailed exam.

Hannibal stepped back and watched me. He had a slight smile on his face. I doubt that he was surprised at my intense concentration. However, Remy stood by with his mouth open in complete surprise.

After several minutes, I spotted something unusual. "What's this?" I said, as I pointed to a tiny spot on the victim's back, about eight centimeters below the left shoulder blade. I handed Remy the magnifying glass.

Remy took the magnifying glass and peered intently at the spot. "Puncture wound," he said. He then looked at me and then Hannibal with a humble expression and added: "I did not see this earlier." He handed Hannibal the magnifying glass.

After a moment's study, Hannibal said: "Looks like a needle puncture. I suggest that you follow its internal path."

"Yes, of course," replied Remy. Exploration showed that the puncture was six centimeters deep. It entered between the eighth and ninth ribs and pierced the left lung.

Remy had a reasonably good lab in the morgue for simple tests. Tissue samples from the inside end of the wound tested positive for massive amounts of potassium cyanide in a water solution.

"What type of device did the assailant use to inject the potassium solution?" I asked.

Remy's face had a blank look.

After a few moments, Hannibal responded: "During my lab days in Chicago, we did work for the Illinois Department of Agriculture." He paused and added: "Veterinarians use large syringes with long needles for cattle and horses."

I thought for a minute and then asked: "Could the bicycle rider have approached Strasser from behind and injected the potassium solution with a syringe?"

Hannibal's brow furrowed a little, and he replied: "I think so. The assailant most likely used a common large syringe with an eight-centimeter needle and a full hand grip to easily operate the plunger. After inserting the needle with a body blow, the assailant simply squeezed the grip."

"Ah," I responded. "Given that the assailant was on a bicycle and approached the victim on the left side, he most likely used his or her right hand to deliver a hard blow with the syringe to the victim's back."

"The victim probably didn't know what hit him," Hannibal replied with a shake of his head.

Remy said: "I know of such syringes." He looked at Hannibal and then me. "I visited Georg Henke's firm in Tuttlingen, Germany, last year, looking for syringes and other equipment for autopsies. Henke manufactures syringes and needles just as you described."

"Much depends on the analysis of the heart blood sample, but I think potassium entered the heart shortly after the injection," said Hannibal.

"I agree," replied Remy. If the heart blood shows a lethal concentration of potassium ions, we have a new cause of death."

We finished at the morgue at 12:30. To my surprise, the autopsy procedure had not affected my appetite. As Hannibal and I walked out the door toward our car, I said: "Can we get something to eat before we meet with Cadieux?"

I could tell that my statement surprised even Hannibal. However, he recovered quickly, and replied: "Of course. When we passed through Enghien-les-Bains on Friday, I noticed that the Hôtel de la Paix has a brasserie right next door."

Hannibal and I arrived at the Brasserie de la Paix at just before one o'clock. I practiced my French and gave the waiter the order of soupe d'oignon, salade, pain, fromage, et un verre de chardonnay. "Si vous s'il vous plaît, Monsieur." I gave Hannibal a look of triumph.

Hannibal laughed and said: "Not bad, onion soup, salad, bread, cheese, and a glass of chardonnay. You even addressed the waiter politely and correctly."

We finished lunch and entered the hotel side of the establishment at precisely 1:55 PM. Cadieux met us in the lobby.

After the usual greetings, Cadieux said: "I have set up an interview with Brunelle Lavigne, the manager and maître d of this establishment."

He paused and smiled: "Lavigne and I are old acquaintances. He knows everyone of importance in the village. He is also a keen observer of his staff and patrons." Cadieux added: "I told him that Strasser was found dead, but nothing more."

Hannibal smiled and said: "Good approach."

Before our meeting, Hannibal and I agreed not to tell Cadieux about the second autopsy. Cadieux had local knowledge, and his unbiased, independent work might result in new information. Besides, we both wanted to wait until we had the heart blood analysis report from the lab.

Cadieux led the way to an office behind the hotel front desk. Lavigne was waiting. He knew a great deal about Strasser, who was a frequent patron of the brasserie and the adjacent taverné.

In response to Cadieux's questions, Lavigne said: "Strasser had a relationship with Anne De Rosé, one of my barmaids. Anne also has a suitor named Jean-Paul Gagne, who owns a nearby vineyard."

"Did Strasser have any other acquaintances in the village?" I asked.

Lavigne thought a moment and then said: "Marie Pereire, Strasser's fiancé from Strasbourg, checked into the hotel on New Year's Day. She visited Strasser on several other occasions over the past year."

Lavigne added: "As far as I know, Marie had not seen Strasser since she arrived this time, but she certainly knew from local gossip that her fiancé had a liaison with Anne De Rosé."

"Can you think of anyone who might wish harm to Strasser?" Hannibal asked.

Lavigne turned to Hannibal and said: "Gagne had an altercation with Strasser in the taverné side of the brasserie on New Year's Eve. A new man, a recent patron of the taverné and a guest at the adjacent hotel, held Strasser's coat. I remember because the pair had been drinking together several nights in a row."

"Do you have a name?" I asked.

"I can get it from the hotel register," replied Lavigne. "Just a minute."

Lavigne stepped out of his office. A few minutes later, he returned with the hotel register. He sat down at the desk, and Hannibal and I peered over his shoulder as he turned the pages.

"Ah, here it is," said Lavigne. "Marcel Villian. I remember because I checked him in myself." He paused and then added: "Strange man. Quiet, well-dressed, had a white scar here." He traced his finger on his left cheek.

"How did the fight between Gagne and Strasser end?" Hannibal asked.

Lavigne smiled a little and added: "Several patrons and I broke up the fight. We threw Strasser and Gagne out of the taverné. Villian handed Strasser his coat as he was being forced out the door."

"What did Villian do after the fight?" Cadieux asked.

Lavigne thought a moment and then answered: "I watched as he sat in the taverné for a while. After about 30 minutes, he left quietly, alone, as far as I could tell."

After we finished with Lavigne, Hannibal and I sat with Cadieux in the taverné. Cadieux spoke at length about other villagers who may or may not have known Strasser.

I became restless. After Cadieux's particularly long dissertation about barmaids, I said: "I will leave you two to the details of possible interviews; I will look around the hotel and the village for a while."

"Hannibal smiled and nodded. He would continue to politely listen to Cadieux.

"As you wish, Madame," responded Cadieux. He looked slightly crestfallen.

I quietly left. Outside, I walked slowly around the village square, and then in the alley behind the hotel and brasserie.

I spotted a bicycle leaning against a back wall, next to several trash cans, in the alley. After a brief inspection, I concluded that the tire treads matched the unique tracks on the trail and the death scene. I returned to the taverné and reported my findings to Cadieux.

Cadieux's eyes widened. Hannibal just smiled. The three of us exited the building. Cadieux retrieved his tool case from his car. I led Hannibal and Cadieux to the bicycle.

Cadieux was efficient in dusting the bicycle for fingerprints. Unfortunately, the bicycle had been wiped clean. However, both Cadieux and Hannibal agreed that the tire treads matched the tracks on the trail.

Cadieux went inside the hotel while Hannibal and I waited next to the bicycle. Within minutes, a police car arrived. A constable got out, loaded up the bicycle, and drove away.

A few minutes later, Cadieux returned. "I made a phone call," he said. "Evidence."

Cadieux, Hannibal and I met with De Rosé, who was working in the back room of the taverné. Cadieux asked good questions; Hannibal and I observed. De Rosé confirmed the nature of the love triangle between herself, Strasser and Gagne. However, she had an alibi; she was working at the taverné all morning on January 2. Lavigne confirmed her story.

We found Marie Pereire in her room at the hotel. Again, Cadieux asked the questions; Hannibal and I listened and observed.

Pereire seemed heartbroken at the death of her fiancé. She admitted knowing about Strasser's affair with De Rosé, but that knowledge seemed to cause deep sorrow rather than anger. She cried a lot, and asked when she might arrange to take her fiancé back to Strasbourg for a funeral.

She also had an alibi for the morning of January 2; she had been in the brasserie eating breakfast from 8:30 until 9:45 AM. Cadieux confirmed the alibi by checking with the brasserie staff and verifying the charge for the breakfast on Pereire's room bill.

After the two interviews, Cadieux asked us to accompany him to Gagne's nearby home and vineyard. Of course, we agreed. In our Duesenberg, we followed Cadieux's car and another police car with two constables.

Gagne answered the door when we arrived. After introductions, we went inside. Cadieux asked a series of intense questions, followed by a search of Gagne's farmhouse. Hannibal and I listened, but kept silent.

One of the constables found the mate to the right-hand glove that was found at the crime scene. The left-hand glove was in Strasser's jacket pocket.

When questioned further, Gagne claimed that he was home alone on the morning of January 2, but he had no witnesses to confirm his story. He said that he had no idea that the right glove was missing, but he last wore the jacket to the taverné in the Brasserie de la Paix on New Year's Eve.

Cadieux, Hannibal and I compared impressions as the two constables watched Gagne in the next room.

"Based on the interviews, we know that Jean-Paul Gagne had motive as a jealous suitor of Anne De Rosé," Cadieux stated matter-of-factly.

"Yes," Hannibal replied tentatively. "He also had a very public fight with Strasser at the Brasserie de la Paix, and his right glove was found at the crime scene. "

Cadieux nodded and added: "Also, the victim had been hit on the head with a stone found at the scene."

Hannibal and I looked at each other. By unspoken agreement, we would reserve judgment pending the expected lab report on the potassium.

Inspecteur Cadieux arrested Gagne on suspicion of murder. As Cadieux and his constables hauled Gagne off to jail, I noticed that Gagne's shoe size did not match the footprints at the crime scene.

## Monday evening, January 6

The heart blood sample test results arrived at the chateau this morning. Du Bellay gave us Remy's updated report with the results while Hannibal and I were sitting in French class.

As Du Bellay handed us the report, he whispered: "Remy made two copies. He sent one to Inspecteur Cadieux. This one is for you." He smiled and left the classroom. I could hardly wait until lunchtime.

Hannibal and I read the report as we ate our luncheon sandwiches. It revealed that a lethal concentration of potassium ions had entered the blood in the victim's heart. The laboratory technician estimated that death occurred in less than three minutes, which was consistent with the victim's staggering footprints over a distance of about fifty meters along the trail.

Herman Strasser was murdered by a massive injection of potassium cyanide into his lung and heart. The questions are: Who and why? How did Gagne's glove arrive at the crime scene, and why was Strasser hit on the head with a stone?

## Tuesday evening, January 7, 1930

Hannibal and I briefed Du Bellay on our findings to date after French class today. He seemed pleased. We left the chateau at about 5:30 PM and got home shortly afterwards.

After dinner, we finished our homework. Hannibal said my French has improved, and I recalled that the instructor even smiled at me in class. I feel much better. It is 9:00 PM; Hannibal is still in the library, and I am in bed. Time to concentrate on our murder case and write these notes in my diary.

In addition to Gagne, we have two remaining suspects with a possible love triangle motive. Marie Pereire, the offended fiancé, had motive. Anne De Rosé was the subject of amorous attention from both Strasser and Gagne. However, the footprints at the crime scene did not match either female's shoe size, and both had alibis.

Did Gagne or one of the females involved hire an assassin? "We need more information about Strasser and the shadowy person identified only as Marcel Villian," I thought to myself. "Also, I'll ask Hannibal to call Cadieux and ask him to check on the finances and bank transactions of Gagne, Pereire and De Rosé."

## Wednesday evening, January 8

Du Bellay anticipated our need for more information. This morning before French class, he met us just inside the chateau entryway.

"Good morning, Madame Jones," he greeted me formally, but with a twinkle in his eyes. He had two file folders in his hands. "I believe these files will be of interest to you and Major Jones." He looked over at Hannibal, who had entered the door just behind me, and smiled. He then handed the files to me.

I glanced at the labels on the folders. One read 'Marcel Villian' and the other read 'Herman Strasser.' My mouth opened in surprise. I quickly recovered and replied: "Oh? Does Villian have a history associated with espionage?"

Du Bellay observed me for a moment and then said: "Yes. Villian has been a person of interest to the Deuxième Bureau for some time." He paused a moment and then added: "Of course, you also need background information on Strasser."

I looked at Hannibal, who nodded. I then looked back to Du Bellay.

Du Bellay's expression evolved into a smile again, and he said: "By the way, your instructor told me that your French vocabulary has much improved." He concluded with: "Enjoy your class today." With that, he stepped aside.

I recovered my poise a little and responded: "Merci, Monsieur Director." I then swept by Du Bellay and headed for the classroom. I could hear a suppressed chuckle from Hannibal as he followed. I sniffed and maintained a snooty expression as I entered the classroom and found my seat.

All day long, I fidgeted and tried to concentrate on the French lesson. I could hardly wait to read the two files!

Hannibal and I got home about 6:00 PM. Lynette and Susanne had dinner waiting for us, and I finished homework in record time. Hannibal and I started on the two files at about 8:00 PM, beginning with Herman Strasser. I read slowly; both files were written in French. What fascinating reading!

## Saturday evening, January 11

Last Thursday, Hannibal called Inspecteur Cadieux and convinced him to follow up on Villian. Hannibal arranged for the three of us to meet at the Hôtel de la Paix this morning.

In the meantime, Cadieux verified that Villian had checked out of the hotel on January 2 at about noon. No one had occupied the room since. Cadieux told Hannibal that he would immediately have the room sealed, pending our investigation.

Hannibal and I met Cadieux at the hotel at 8:30 this morning. We immediately went to Villian's former room. The hotel staff had cleaned the room shortly after Villian had checked out.

However, during a thorough examination of the room, I spotted a tiny amount of a crystalline substance on the dresser near a wash basin. I carefully pushed the substance off the dresser with a piece of paper and into an envelope that I obtained from Cadieux. I gave the envelope to Cadieux.

We found nothing else of interest. After completing our search, Cadieux called Dr. Remy.

Cadieux arranged for Remy to analyze the substance taken from Villian's room. The three of us then drove to Remy's office with the evidence. The analysis was done by noon. The substance was potassium cyanide.

# 4

## ASSASSIN'S SHADOW

*Monday evening, January 13, 1930*

When we arrived at the chateau this morning, Hannibal and I stopped by Du Bellay's office. The door was open, and I could see Du Bellay at his desk. Hannibal tapped gently on the door frame. Du Bellay looked up from his work and smiled.

"Good morning," said Du Bellay, as he rose from his chair. "I trust you had a successful weekend?"

"Yes," responded Hannibal. "After reading your files on Villian and Strasser, we followed up with Cadieux in town. Suggest that we brief you, Capitaine Inspecteur Soucet, Inspecteur Cadieux and Dr. Remy at a meeting this week at your convenience."

Du Bellay nodded and replied: "Of course. Each attendee knows different parts of the investigation, but none of us knows everything. I will make appropriate phone calls. Would Wednesday after class work for you?" His steady gaze shifted from Hannibal to me.

Since he was looking at me, I responded: "Yes, I believe so." I looked over at Hannibal, who nodded.

After our conversation with Du Bellay, class passed slowly. I kept thinking about how to prepare and present our briefing on Wednesday.

I did learn a few new French words in class, and we practiced speaking conversationally. I am beginning to think in French rather than English. As a result, my French conversations are much smoother.

## Wednesday evening, January 15

Hannibal and I worked until midnight Tuesday. By this morning, we had finished our report and prepared a tabletop briefing for Hannibal's portable easel.

Mercifully, French class ended early today at about 4:00 PM. We had about an hour before our meeting with Du Bellay and his colleagues. Hannibal and I sat in an empty classroom, sipped coffee and reviewed our briefing notes.

At a few minutes past 5:00, I heard a tap-tap at the classroom door. Du Bellay was standing in the doorway. I could see several others, including Soucet, walking past behind him.

Du Bellay smiled and said: "Let's gather at the conference table in the library. We are all looking forward to your presentation." Du Bellay turned and disappeared down the hallway. Hannibal and I put down our coffee cups, rose from our seats and followed.

Soon, Du Bellay, Soucet, Cadieux and Remy were seated around the conference table. Hannibal stood at one end and set up his easel with flip charts. I sat next to Hannibal, ready to do my part.

Du Bellay looked around the table. He stared intently at both Remy and Cadieux. After a moment, he said: "This meeting is most secret. Do I have your word that you will not say or write anything in the future that involves this case without clearing everything with me?"

Remy and Cadieux stirred a little in their seats, as they considered Du Bellay's request. Both responded, almost in unison, with: "Oui, Monsieur Director."

Du Bellay then turned to Hannibal and gave a nod.

Hannibal slipped into his military briefing mode and said: "Herman Strasser died of acute potassium poisoning. The poison, in the form of potassium cyanide in a water solution, was delivered by a device that left a puncture wound in his back between the eighth and ninth ribs, about eight centimeters below his left shoulder blade."

Hannibal paused, looked around the table and continued: "The solution entered the victim's heart almost immediately. Given the size of the dose, death occurred within minutes."

I glanced around at each person in turn and then added: "Dr. Remy, Hannibal and I agree that the device was most likely a large syringe and needle. However, the device, syringe or otherwise, has not been found."

Remy nodded in agreement and said: "Large syringes and needles are readily available from medical supply companies."

Hannibal continued: "The killer had to have knowledge of how potassium cyanide poisoning works and how to deliver a lethal amount to the heart."

"Yes," responded Remy. "Based on a recommendation from Major and Madame Jones, tests were conducted on a blood sample taken from the victim's heart." He sighed and added: "The concentration of potassium ions in the sample was 160 millimoles per liter, which is over one and one-half times the lethal dose."

"How did the killer approach the victim?" asked Soucet. "Strasser was running along a trail in a heavily wooded area."

Hannibal nodded and replied: "Tire tracks at the crime scene showed that the killer approached the victim on a bicycle from behind on the left. He then delivered a blow to the victim's back with the murder device, which was most likely a large syringe and needle with a full-hand operated plunger," responded Hannibal. "The blow was efficient, and the victim had no opportunity to defend himself."

"Evidence at the scene showed that the killer attempted to throw investigators off by striking the victim with a stone after the victim was already dead, leaving the stone at the scene as a plausible cause of death," I added.

Hannibal continued: "Details are in our report, but in essence, further investigation by Inspecteur Cadieux, Madame Jones and myself gave us three persons with motive: Jean-Paul Gagne, who owns a local vineyard, Marie Pereire, the victim's fiancé, and Anne De Rosé, a local barmaid."

I picked up the narrative and said: "Strasser, De Rosé, Gagne and Pereire were involved in lover's relationships that resulted in jealousy and a bar fight between Strasser and Gagne on New Year's Eve."

"What about Gagne's glove at the crime scene?" Cadieux asked.

"Marcel Villian, a third person present at the bar fight, had access to Gagne's coat and gloves on New Year's Eve," replied Hannibal.

"His glove could have been planted, plausibly by Villian," I added. "Also, Gagne's shoe size does not match the footprints at the crime scene."

Hannibal continued: "The two remaining suspects with a possible love triangle motive, Marie Pereire, the offended fiancé, and Anne De Rosé, the subject of amorous attention from both Strasser and Gagne, had solid alibis for their whereabouts during the time of the murder."

"The footprints of the unknown person at the crime scene were almost certainly male, not female," I added. "Both females have much smaller shoe sizes."

Cadieux and Remy fidgeted a little; both were probably recalling their initial erroneous reports.

After a full minute of silence, Due Bellay responded. "Based on your comments to me on January 7, I gave you files on both Strasser and Villian. What did you discover?"

"Your file shows that Villian was suspected of being an assassin for hire," said Hannibal. Du Bellay nodded.

Hannibal continued: "Villian's presence in Enghien-les-Bains at the time of Strasser's murder and his sudden disappearance immediately afterwards make him a likely suspect."

I added: "Tests of a crystalline substance found in Villian's hotel room turned out to be potassium cyanide. Villian is almost certainly our murderer."

"The only remaining question is: Who motivated Villian to kill Strasser?" Soucet responded. "So far, persons with motive include Gagne, Pereire and De Rosé."

"Did Villian receive money from one of the suspects?" I asked.

"Not from Gagne, Pereire or De Rosé," said Cadieux. He had recovered from his earlier fidgeting and spoke with confidence.

"At Major Jones' suggestion, I checked their accounts through my local bank contacts. None of the three has the resources to hire an assassin, and their meager accounts show no unusual activity."

"The files that I gave Major and Madame Jones on January 7 has information that complicates the list of suspects," mused Du Bellay. He looked intently at me and then Hannibal.

"Yes," responded Hannibal. "Marcel Villian's file shows that he is a fascist sympathizer. He is also a known associate of Jacque Doriot, a current Parisian politician."

"Strasser was well-known for his anti-fascist views before we recruited him for espionage training," said Du Bellay. "He certainly had political enemies,"

Hannibal flipped the briefing page on his easel. The new page had a concise outline about Strasser.

Hannibal continued his presentation. "Strasser was born in Strasbourg, Alsace-Lorraine, of German parents. After the war, the French annexed Alsace-Lorraine and began mass deportations of ethnic Germans. In 1921, his parents relocated to Stuttgart, Germany."

Hannibal paused and looked at me. I said: "As an alternative to being deported with his parents, Strasser, then age 18, chose to stay with French friends and enroll as a law and journalism student at the University of Strasbourg."

Hannibal looked around the room. Du Bellay nodded, but our narrative was news to the others, even Soucet.

Du Bellay said: "Strasser graduated in 1926 with a law degree. Afterwards, he was openly pro-French and pro-Weimar Republic. He vehemently opposed fascism and national socialism."

Du Bellay then looked to Hannibal, who continued: "After graduation, Strasser wrote articles critical of German national socialists and French fascist sympathizers, including two prominent French political figures, Jacques Doriot and Jean Chiappe. His articles appeared in *Vossische Zeitung*, a liberal newspaper published in Berlin, and *La Renaissance Juive*, a Jewish-owned newspaper published in Paris."

Du Bellay added: "He was recruited by the Sûreté Deuxiéme Bureau in 1929 because of his German affiliations, political views, investigative skills and fluency in both German and French. He had been in training at the chateau for less than a year before he was murdered."

Silence reigned for a minute or so as the others digested this information. Hannibal flipped to the next page on his easel. The page had an outline about Villian.

Hannibal began again in his clipped, military manner: "Villian was born in Reims in 1890, the second son of French parents. He was a cousin and close associate of fascist Raoul Villian, who was also born in Reims."

Hannibal looked to me, and I added: "Raoul was tried for the assassination of French socialist leader Jean Jaurés in 1919. He was acquitted due to lack of evidence, which had conveniently disappeared from police files."

Soucet stirred uncomfortably at this. After a moment, he said: "I remember." The room was silent for a full minute.

Hannibal continued: "Marcel is well-educated, with degrees in mathematics, science and medicine. However, his university record showed that he let it be known that he was an admirer of German national socialist leader Adolf Hitler."

Soucet stirred again, and Hannibal paused.

Soucet said: "After graduation, Marcel Villian had a successful medical practice in Reims for a few years. Later, he moved to Paris, with no permanent address. His political views and association with his cousin Raoul brought him to the attention of the French police."

Soucet continued: "Villian was suspected of being involved in several political murders in Paris. He was questioned, but was never arrested due to lack of evidence. His passport record shows numerous visits to Spain."

Hannibal then said: "According to the file, Villian was often seen in the company of Jacques Doriot. The file included several photos of both men, including a photo of the pair together on a Paris street." He paused and then added: "Our research shows that from December 27, 1929 until January 2, 1930, Villian had a room at the Hôtel de la Paix in Enghien-les-Bains."

Du Bellay and Soucet exchanged long looks.

Du Bellay looked at Hannibal, then me and smiled. He then turned to Cadieux and his smile disappeared. He said: "I believe, Inspector Cadieux, that you should release Gagne from jail. Although the evidence is circumstantial, Villian was almost certainly the murderer."

"Oui, Monsieur Director," replied Cadieux. He scribbled another note.

Du Bellay turned to Soucet and asked: "Can you follow up on the financial activities of Villian and perhaps Doriot?"

Soucet was quiet for several moments. Finally, in a soft voice, he replied: "Yes, but care must be taken." He looked at Du Bellay intently. Du Bellay nodded.

Both men turned and looked at Hannibal. After a few moments, Soucet said: "Major Jones, you have international banking contacts." He paused, then asked: "Could you follow up?"

Hannibal was silent for a full minute. He turned to me, and his gaze said more than words. After a moment of contemplation, I gave him an affirmative nod and then held my breath.

Hannibal turned to Soucet and said: "I'll see what I can do." He paused and then added: "Inquiries may take some time."

"Understood," replied Soucet. I let my breath out. My gut told me that Hannibal and I would encounter Villian again. I looked at Du Bellay and asked: "May Hannibal and I keep a photo of Villian from the file?"

Du Bellay and Soucet exchanged glances. Soucet nodded. Du Bellay turned to me and said: "Yes. We have other photos." He then smiled and added: "A reasonable precaution. You may have need of it in the future."

I gulped a little, nodded and replied: "Thank you." I looked at Hannibal. His face had a grim expression.

Du Bellay looked at Hannibal and then me. He smiled and said: "Excellent work. You have given us the evidence that we have long needed to go after Villian." He looked at Soucet, who also smiled and nodded in agreement.

Du Bellay then turned to Cadieux and said: "Based on today's revelations, I suggest that you issue a warrant for the arrest of Marcel Villian through the Gendarmerie Nationale."

"Oui, Monsieur Director," replied Cadieux. He wrote furiously in his notebook.

Soucet added: "Also, I think you can allow Madame Pereire to claim Strasser's body." His demeanor softened as he continued: "She has been through enough heartbreak."

Cadieux nodded; no words were needed.

Du Bellay turned to Remy, and then to Cadieux, and finally, to Hannibal and me. His voice had a hard edge as he said: "Again, nothing that has been said at this meeting leaves this room. Each of you has skills that may be useful as this investigation continues."

He paused for effect and added: "I will have my staff review and sanitize all reports and notes on this case. Nothing written will leave this facility without my approval, including autopsy and police reports. Please deliver your reports to me, and leave your notes from today on the table. Understood?"

Everyone nodded affirmatively. Cadieux quickly put down his pencil and closed his notebook.

"Du Bellay is not a man to be crossed," I thought to myself. The meeting was over, and everyone filed out of the library.

"Watch your backs," warned Soucet softly, as we walked down the hallway. "Others in government have noted your part in all of this."

"What have we gotten ourselves into?" I thought to myself as we left Soucet and exited the door to the chateau.

Hannibal's expression became grave as Soucet made his comments. Later, as we approached our car in the parking lot, Hannibal said softly: "Soucet is right. This reminds me of 1918."

"Are we in danger?" I asked. I touched Hannibal's hand as he opened the car door for me.

Hannibal gave me a long, steady look. After a moment, he smiled and replied: "No more than usual."

## Friday evening, January 17

Hannibal and I have completed our part of the murder investigation, at least for now. Hannibal also made discreet inquiries about Villian and Doriot through his banker contacts, and the Gendarmerie Nationale issued an international warrant for Villian.

As I write these words, my thoughts return to the files on Strasser and Villian. "There is something odd about the career of Strasser, but I can't put my finger on it," I thought to myself. "Something will turn up," I concluded. "Also, I wonder if Villian has more than one employer?"

Back to training: we are two weeks into French class, and all conversations and written work are in French. "Total immersion," our instructor said.

Hannibal helps by speaking slowly and distinctly in French during our conversations. He also corrects my written assignments before I turn them in.

I am determined to keep writing English in my diary, except for emphasis in French, German or Italian, and where the English translation would be awkward. When Hannibal noticed, I said: "English helps remind me who I am." Hannibal laughed.

## Friday evening, February 28

Two months have passed, with no word on Villian or Doriot. Hannibal has continued his inquiries through his contacts in French, Swiss and German banks.

Today, I studied the photo of Villian. "Neatly dressed in a tailored suit, medium height, dark hair, handsome yet somehow sinister face and a penetrating gaze," I thought to myself. I noticed the scar on his left cheek of course, but the most striking feature was his eyes; they scared me. "A formidable opponent," I concluded. I shuddered a little and put the photo away.

On a brighter note, we have finished French class, and we start German next Monday. This weekend, Hannibal and I are free. I am going shopping!

## Sunday evening, March 2

Paris will never be the same. I shopped at Coco Chanel's, Elsa Schiaparelli's and Princeps. I have a new summer wardrobe. Hannibal was very patient. He bought a new tie and socks. He is always well-dressed, but I never see him shop. How does he do it?

### Friday evening, May 2

I have not had time to write in my diary for two months. German is hard!

### Friday evening, July 4

German classes are over: Independence Day! Ich kann ein Gespräch auf Deutsch mithalten und deutsche Zeitungen lessen. Not bad for a small-town Indiana girl. On Monday, Hannibal and I begin weapons training.

### Friday evening, July 11

I didn't know weapons training involved running four kilometers every morning. I'm sore all over. However, our instructor was pleased with my marksmanship with a new, prototype Walther pistol. I told him that Indiana girls know about guns. Hannibal laughed.

### Friday evening, August 8

We have just two weeks left of hand-to-hand combat training. I added new 'dirty tricks' to my repertoire of Wabash River rat street-fighting techniques, including several ways of delivering eye-gouges, elbow, foot and knee strikes, throat punches, stomps, kicks and choke holds.

We practiced with partners in the chateau gym every day for four weeks. Yesterday, my partner was an overconfident and slightly arrogant young male. Hannibal and the instructor had already left for the male dressing room.

After Hannibal had left, the young man pushed the boundaries with unnecessary holds and inappropriate groping.

Infuriated, I hit him full in the nose with the heel of my right hand. As he fell back, I spun him around with a stomp with my left foot to the side of his right knee. He hit the floor on his hands and knees.

I then dropped to his back with my knees and full body weight. He sprawled on his face, doing more damage to his already bloody nose.

I was about to finish him off by grasping his hair with my left hand and under his chin with my right and pulling his head back and to the side, when I heard a soft voice. "Easy, Caroline." Hannibal had returned.

Slowly, the fury left me, and I got up. Hannibal led me away toward the ladies' locker room door. As we walked away, the entire gym was as quiet as a church on Saturday night. I assume someone took care of my recent opponent.

After the incident, the instructor seemed to think that I had achieved adequate hand-to-hand combat training. The other students, mostly male, treated me with deference for the remaining two weeks.

## Friday evening, September 5

Hannibal and I have nearly completed our espionage training. Both Du Bellay and Soucet seemed pleased. Soucet mentioned Berlin as a possible first assignment. How exciting!

## Friday evening, October 3

It's official, Hannibal and I will travel to Berlin in December. Burrr! We will spend the next month or so preparing for departure and studying European art for our cover. I will miss Paris.

# 5

## DESTINATION BERLIN

*Saturday evening, October 11, 1930*

Hannibal and I spent the past week visiting Paris art auctions and galleries. We bought a Pissarro painting of a street scene in Paris and a Monet painting of a view within his Giverny water garden. I just love Pissarro's sense of human activity in the context of a Paris street. Monet's contrasting colors and play of light upon simple flowers captures the essence of manicured nature, tamed, yet independent.

Hannibal has an extensive background in traditional old masters' paintings. He is especially fond of Dutch and Flemish landscapes.

Tradition is OK, but I love modern works by Monet, Renoir, Gauguin, Pissarro, Liebermann, Lyongrün and other impressionists. I also want to learn more about surrealism and cubism.

Hannibal moved smoothly through the galleries, with me in tow. I am learning by observing his practiced manners, smiles and casual conversation. What a change from Chicago!

During our visits, we encountered several well-known and powerful politicians who were often indiscreet in their conversations. Art, politicians and scandalous revelations: what a fascinating combination!

When we move to Berlin, we will be connoisseurs of fine art as a cover for our espionage activities. Like Paris, the art social swirl will provide opportunities. We intend to eavesdrop on rich and influential Nazis and their Weimar government opponents.

*Friday evening, October 17*

Hannibal and I attended another Paris auction today. We didn't buy anything, but as we viewed paintings in the auction catalogs, we met Samuel von Fischer and his wife Hedwig. They graciously introduced themselves. Both spoke French, but with a German accent.

My training had prepared me for such encounters. We had a casual conversation in French, and I discovered that the Fischers love impressionist art.

Hedwig saw that I had been looking intently at a catalog photo of a Pissarro painting of a Rue Saint Honoré street scene. "I just love Pissarro," she said. "Our holdings include his Le Quai Malaquais Printemps."

I smiled and described our recent acquisition of a similar Pissarro painting. I also told Hedwig that Hannibal and I were moving to Berlin.

"Ah," she replied. "We are also Berliners. Perhaps you would like to visit us at our home in Grunewald, once you have settled."

"Why thank you," I responded. "We will be new in Berlin. Your invitation is most gracious."

Hedwig smiled and said: "We can talk about all of the impressionist artists." She then gave me a gold-engraved card with her name and address.

As she handed me the card, she added: "You can take the Berlin Stadtbahn train from several Bahnhof stations in Berlin to Grünewald Bahnhof in the eastern suburbs. Taxicabs are readily available at the Bahnhof or from the nearby commercial goods Platform 17 for the short drive to our home."

While Hedwig and I were in conversation, I overheard snippets of conversation between Samuel and Hannibal. They were discussing political events in Germany.

Samuel expressed concern over the increasingly virulent anti-Jewish rhetoric of the Nazi press. "Articles in *Der Angriff* by Josef Goebbels are particularly vehement," said Samuel. "Several of our friends from our synagogue in Berlin are divesting their holdings and moving either to Paris or to Vienna. "

Later, on our way home, Hannibal told me that Herr Fischer founded the Berlin publishing house S. Fischer Verlag. In addition to publishing, he is a well-known philanthropist and promoter of theater and other arts.

## Saturday afternoon, October 25

Hannibal received a coded telegram today from a contact at the Reichsbank in Berlin.

When we were alone after dinner, Hannibal said: "My contact works directly for Hans Luther, the Reichsbank President. The telegram stated that the name Marcel Villian has surfaced on payments made from a Nazi Party bank account."

Hannibal paused for a moment and then added: "Herman Göring authorized the payments."

"You should notify Soucet," I responded.

Hannibal was quiet for a full minute. Finally, he said: "Yes. I will send him a coded note by mail."

"I agree," I replied. "From now on, the less personal contact the better."

Hannibal nodded and said: "We have a connection between the Nazi Party and Villian. Who knows where it will lead?"

## Wednesday, evening, October 29

As we finished dinner earlier this evening, the phone rang. Hannibal got up and answered. It was Soucet. I could hear Soucet's voice as he simply said: "Thank you. Keep digging."

Hannibal returned to the table. As we sipped our wine, he looked at me for quite a while. Finally, he said: "Hans Luther is a liberal and not a Nazi, but according to my contact, Nazi elements have infiltrated the Reichsbank staff."

The wind howled outside our windows. I shivered, even though the dining room was warm.

## Friday evening, November 7

Hannibal made arrangements to close the lease on our Paris townhome. I found positions for Lynette and Susanne, and Hannibal arranged for the storage of our furniture and art. We will vacate our townhome on the day after Christmas and spend four days at the Ritz.

The distance between Paris and Berlin is over 1100 kilometers. This time of year, the roads will have snow and ice. Hannibal wisely arranged for transport of our Duesenberg and most of our luggage by rail from Paris to Berlin.

The car, along with luggage, will leave Paris on December 1 and arrive at the Hotel Adlon, our new residence in Berlin, in a few weeks. Starting on December 29, we will travel first class on a comfortable passenger train, destination Berlin.

## Friday evening, December 26

Hannibal and I spent both Thanksgiving and Christmas in our Paris townhome. Thanksgiving was rainy, but new snow covered everything on Christmas. We had a beautiful view out our window.

We exchanged gifts Christmas morning. Hannibal bought me a lovely set of pearls, and gave him a pair of fur-lined gloves. Both gifts are perfect for traveling.

Hannibal turned in our keys today, and we moved to the Ritz. I will miss our townhome.

## Monday afternoon, December 29

We boarded the train in Paris this morning. We will arrive in Cologne this evening and spend the night in the Excelsior Hotel Ernst am Dom, Trankgasse 1-5 Domplatz, near the train station and the Cologne Cathedral.

Our train accommodations are luxurious and comfortable, but the view outside the window is dreary rain mixed with snow. The train makes a steady clickity-click sound as it races over the rails.

After breakfast in the dining car, Hannibal and I sipped coffee. My thoughts turned to our assignment.

"Tell me about Hitler," I began. "I read the newspapers, but what about the man behind the propaganda mask?"

Hannibal set his cup down and looked out the window. After a moment, he turned to me and said: "Remember the Fischers?" I nodded, and Hannibal continued: "Samuel Fischer is a publisher based in Berlin. He told me about the book that Hitler wrote while in prison in 1925."

"Oh?" I responded. I was intrigued. "Should I read it?"

"Probably," Hannibal replied. "Me too." He picked up his cup, took another sip and continued: "According to Fischer, Hitler's book, which is only available in Germany, provides a blueprint for action, if he ever gains political power."

"Has Fischer read it?" I asked.

"He said that he did, and it scared him," replied Hannibal. "I could see it in his face as we talked." Hannibal paused, leaned back in his seat and looked at me for a long moment. "According to Fischer, Hitler's views as expressed in the book are very anti-Semitic."

"Humm," I responded. "The Fischers are Jews, so Hitler is a threat."

"Yes," said Hannibal. "You heard him say that some of his friends are leaving Germany. I expect their concerns are connected to Hitler and the Nazis."

"Did Fischer give you a book title?" I asked.

"*Mein Kampf*," replied Hannibal.

The clickity-click sound of the train continued as Germany passed by our window.

## Tuesday afternoon, December 30

Hannibal and I both felt the wind chill as we walked the short distance between the Bahnhof and our Cologne hotel. The wind blew snow all around.

We each carried only a small overnight bag; Hannibal had put the rest of our traveling luggage in a locker in the Bahnhof. We hurried inside out of the wind. The room was warm and comfortable, but I slept fitfully all night. Germany seemed oppressive.

We boarded the train again at 7:00 AM this morning. After breakfast in the dining car, we both perused German newspapers. Hitler was on the front page everywhere.

Hannibal began the conversation. "The Nazis did well in the September elections. They increased their seats in the Reichstag from 12 to 107."

"From this article in the *Berliner Tageblatt*, Hitler was the driving force during the campaign," I responded.

I leafed through the newspaper, found another article and added: "According to this article, Hitler traveled across Germany using an airplane. At every stop, he gave a speech, signed autographs and posed for photos with ordinary Germans."

Hannibal nodded and replied: "According to this Frankfurt newspaper, he's a very effective speaker." Hannibal paused and then added: "This article also mentions Josef Goebbels. Apparently, Goebbels introduces Hitler and sets the stage for most speeches."

"Humm," I said as I continued to read. "Hitler offers something to everyone: Work to the unemployed, profits to industry, expansion to the army, an end to class distinctions and restoration of German greatness on the world stage."

"This article gives excerpts from his speeches," responded Hannibal. He was quiet for a few minutes as he continued to read. "It says that Hitler plans to deal harshly with the Jews. Fischer was right to be concerned."

"Hitler's campaign was very well organized," I replied. I thought a moment, then added: "We should find a way to get inside Hitler's social circle."

"Good idea, but how?" mused Hannibal.

"Let's work on it," I responded. "Maybe one or more of the Nazi bigwigs likes art."

Hannibal chuckled and then said: "Berlin has several galleries."

Our conversation ended, and I spent most of the day reading and writing. I thought a lot about Hitler. I understood nationalism, but why this hatred of the Jews?

Late this afternoon, we will arrive at the Potsdam Bahnhof. From Potsdam, we will use the Stadtbahn train to travel to the Bahnhof Unter den Linden in downtown Berlin. From there, we will take a taxi for the short drive to the luxurious Hotel Adlon, Unter den Linden 1, Pariser Platz.

I hope the rest of our luggage and our Duesenberg have already arrived. Despite first class accommodations on the entire trip, I am exhausted.

## Thursday, New Year's Day, 1931

Hannibal and I spent a quiet New Year's Eve in our suite at the hotel. Nazi officials, most in ostentatious uniforms, had taken over the main ballroom downstairs. We have been sent here to gather intelligence, but we are not yet ready for Nazi social functions.

Hannibal ordered room service for dinner. We must adapt to German foods, so we had a beef roulade with braised red cabbage and potato dumplings for the main meal, and apple cake with vanilla ice cream for dessert.

Our wine was a light, semi-sweet Riesling kabinett, Qualitäts mit Prädikat. I had tried the sweeter and fruitier spätlese in Cologne, but somehow it didn't seem right with a meal.

I suppose that I must transition from elegant, French cuisine to the heavier, hearty, more sugary German food and wine. Oh well.

After dinner, we made ourselves comfortable on the couch by the windows overlooking Pariser Platz. We each sipped our second glass of wine.

Sunset had occurred at about 4:00 PM, so all we could see were street lights and the shadowy outlines of buildings. A few revelers hurried here and there across the Platz, but mostly people wisely stayed inside. Cold!

Hannibal began our conversation. "Samuel Fischer told us about *Mein Kampf.* I will look for a copy at a bookstore tomorrow."

I nodded and said: "I'm sure it's written in German. I don't suppose an English translation is available."

Hannibal smiled and replied: "Interesting that you should mention it. Samuel said that he has a draft of an English translation from E.T. Dugdale." He paused and then added: "Samuel also said that there are copyright issues, so he can't publish it. However, I bet that we could get a copy of the draft."

"Great!" I responded. "Reading German is still a slow process for me." I thought a moment, then said: "I want to visit the Fischers, but we should be careful, for their safety and also for our own public profiles."

"Jews are not popular with the Nazis, and we want to get inside the Nazi inner circle," Hannibal agreed. He leaned back on the couch and was quiet for a full minute. Finally, he said: "I will call Samuel tomorrow."

"I will buy a small gift to take on our visit," I replied.

## Sunday evening, January 11

Our visit to the Fischer's home yesterday was a pleasant affair. Hedwig played the piano, and Samuel proudly showed us their art collection. Their paintings include works by Corinth, El Greco, Gauguin and Pissarro. Toward the end of the evening, Samuel gave us a copy of Dugdale's draft.

I now have both German and English versions of *Mein Kampf.* What a revelation! I understand the Fischer's concerns.

## Tuesday evening, January 13

Yesterday, Hannibal met a representative from the French Embassy in the quiet, snowy Tiergarten Park, just down the Unter den Linden on the other side of the Brandenburg Gate. The pair arranged a clandestine method of passing reports through the embassy to Capitaine Inspecteur Soucet in Paris.

We will place our reports in unmarked, sealed envelopes and leave the envelopes on the desk in our hotel suite. The maid, who is a French embassy operative, will pick up the envelopes when she cleans the room. She will then secretly take the envelopes home after work.

The maid will pass the envelopes to her next-door neighbor, who is a janitor in the French Embassy. The janitor, also an embassy operative, will deliver the envelopes to the embassy when he goes to work.

The reports will be transported from the embassy to Paris in a diplomatic pouch. Pierre de Margerie, the French Ambassador in Berlin, is fully aware of and supports our efforts.

## Sunday evening, January 18

Hannibal and I attended a display of paintings at the newly completed Pergamon Museum yesterday. Featured works included landscapes by Heinrich Böhmer, farm animals by Anton Braith, expressionist paintings by Max Beckmann and Lovis Corinth, and farm family scenes by Adolf Wissel. We also saw works by Adolf Zeigler, Emil Nolde, Ernst Barlach and Erich Heckel.

The display was well attended by Nazis. I recognized Josef Goebbels from photos in Berlin newspapers. He was dressed in a business suit, very different from his uniformed companions. He nodded politely as he walked by Hannibal and me in the gallery.

However, he was having a heated discussion with his uniformed companion.

They spoke in German, but I'm translating to English for this diary. As closely as I can translate, their conversation was as follows.

"Ah, Herr Rosenberg, we must embrace some of the modern artists; their works are popular with the people," said Goebbels.

"Degenerate, degenerate," replied his companion, who apparently was named Rosenberg. "The Führer would never approve."

"We National Socialists are not un-modern; we are the carrier of a new modernity, not only in politics and in social matters, but also in art and intellectual matters," replied Goebbels.

The debate continued as the pair walked away from us. "Interesting," I thought to myself. "Will the Nazis control the art world too?"

As Goebbels and Rosenberg walked away, I saw a heavy-set man in an imposing Nazi uniform, standing before a large painting of a nude. He was surrounded by others in uniform, all of whom appeared to hang on his every word.

"Herman Göring," whispered Hannibal. "According to the *Der Angriff*, Goebbels' newspaper, Göring advocates building a new German Luftwaffe in defiance of the Treaty of Versailles."

Hannibal paused and then added: "According to an article in *Die Weltbühne* by Carl von Ossietzky, the Luftwaffe build-up has already started, and Göring is the key figure."

"Apparently, he likes paintings of female nudes," I whispered back. Hannibal chuckled. Göring was pointing to and commenting about the painting, which was titled: Die Frau und Rücken, by Adolf Ziegler.

"We may have our ticket into the Nazi inner circle," replied Hannibal. "Goebbels, Rosenberg and Göring appreciate art, and so far, their tastes are rather eclectic."

I stifled a giggle.

## Friday evening, February 6

Hannibal is well-known to several bankers and businessmen in the rather small American community in Berlin. As a result, we have been invited to a party at the temporary American Embassy at Bendlerstrasse 39 on Saturday, February 21.

The party was set up to welcome Frederick Sackett, the new American Ambassador, to Weimar Germany. In addition to observing the interactions of German government officials, I want to size up Sackett.

## Sunday morning, February 22

The American Embassy party went well last evening.

Hannibal wore a perfectly tailored white tie outfit with formal black tailcoat, trousers and cummerbund. What a handsome escort!

I wore a shimmering silver evening gown by Madeleine Vionnet, with matching wrap, shoes and purse. My jewelry sparkled with diamonds. Not bad for a small-town Indiana girl.

We blended nicely with the embassy crowd. Hans Luther, the Reichsbank President, was there, and he knew Hannibal from previous encounters. Hannibal knew several others from the business and banking communities.

We moved easily through the social swirl, nodding, smiling, meeting and greeting. Finally, an embassy secretary introduced us to Ambassador Sackett.

Sackett was a large, stolid-looking man. As the introductions were made, his gray eyes had a steady gaze.

"Good evening, Major and Mrs. Jones," said Sackett. "I understand that you have recently arrived in Berlin." His eyes shifted from Hannibal to me and back to Hannibal. The two men shook hands.

"Yes sir," responded Hannibal in a precise, military manner. We came from Paris, and we have an interest in German paintings."

"Humm," responded Sackett. He smiled, but his eyes somehow seemed calculating, as if he were evaluating us.

He then turned to me and said: "Welcome to Berlin, Mrs. Jones." His smile warmed, and his eyes twinkled a little. "I have heard about your exploits in France. The French Ambassador speaks highly of you and your husband."

"That's better," I thought to myself. "Thank you, Mr. Ambassador," I responded with a nod of my head and a slight smile. "Ambassador de Margerie is most kind."

I was curious, and I thought a little more: "de Margerie knows our espionage mission. What did he tell Sackett?" Hannibal's eyes squinted a little, I could tell he had thoughts similar to mine.

Sackett glanced around. No one was nearby. He turned to Hannibal and said in a low voice: "Tell me, Major Jones, what do you think of Hitler and the National Socialists?"

I took a sharp breath. Sackett was blunt and typically American. After the diplomatic and impeccably polite conversations that we had grown used to in Europe, his approach was somehow refreshing. "No nonsense and to the point," my thoughts continued.

Hannibal glanced at me and then back to Sackett. He then said: "We have recently obtained a copy of Hitler's book titled: *Mein Kampf.*" He paused and then added: "We found it interesting reading."

Sackett smiled and nodded. I could tell that he liked Hannibal's answer. He then replied: "I will obtain a copy and read it."

He then turned to me and said: "Ambassador de Margerie and I share many insights."

At that moment, another couple approached. Sackett had to attend to his other guests. However, before he turned away, he looked at Hannibal, then me, and back to Hannibal. He then said: "Best wishes with regard to your interest in art."

Hannibal and I both noted Sackett's emphasis on the word 'art.'

The evening passed, and we continued with our smiles, polite conversations and social mixing.

As we ended our evening and caught a taxi back to the Adlon, I turned to Hannibal and said: "I think you should send a message to de Margerie and Soucet. Tell them that we have no objections to their sharing our reports with Sackett."

Hannibal nodded and replied: "Agree. Our message should let Soucet know that we know about the French-American sharing of information." He paused and then added: "I also like the idea that America may benefit from our work."

"Yes," I responded. I tucked my hand under Hannibal's arm and snuggled a little.

# 6

## FIVE BY ONE

*Thursday evening, February 26, 1931*

Late this afternoon, Hannibal and I returned to the Adlon from a shopping trip to the Wertheim Department Store on Leipziger Platz. I bought several warm cashmere sweaters and a scarf. Berlin is so cold!

As we passed through the main door of the hotel, I noticed a well-dressed older gentleman sitting in a comfortable chair, away from the draft of the door. He was watching us as we crossed the lobby.

As we approached, he rose from his seat. "Verzeihung, sind Sie Major und Mrs. Jones? Ich bin Helmut Reischl, von der Berliner Poliezi."

"Ja, ich bin Hannibal Jones," replied Hannibal cautiously. "Das ist mein Frau Caroline."

Our conversation continued in German. As before, I have translated the German to English for the purposes of my diary.

Reischl smiled, bowed slightly to me, offered his hand to Hannibal and said: "Capitaine Inspecteur Soucet told me about your crime-solving expertise."

As Reischl and Hannibal shook hands, he continued: "We have five related murders in Berlin." His face acquired a serious, slightly pleading look. "We in the Berlin Criminal Police Department would very much appreciate your help."

My mind raced. What did Soucet tell Reischl? How can we use this to further our research on the Nazis? Is Reischl a Nazi?

Reischl smiled; I'm sure he surmised my questions from my facial expressions. He said: "Pierre Soucet and I are old colleagues; we have worked together on several international criminal investigations."

His smile broadened and he added: "Please give Pierre a call through the French Embassy."

"Good heavens!" I thought to myself. Should we trust this man?" To Reischl, I blurted: "We will."

Reischl's eyes twinkled. He turned to Hannibal and said: "If you decide to help, here is my card."

He then handed Hannibal a business card with the symbol of the Berlin police department and the title 'Berlin Kriminal Polizei, Außerplanmäßigen Kriminal Kommissar Helmut Reischl.' The titles and name were followed by a phone number.

I quickly translated in my mind. "Reischl is the Chief Inspector for the Berlin Police Criminal Investigation Bureau," my thoughts continued. "He knows Soucet, and he doesn't mind that we will check him out."

I looked over at Hannibal, who saw my glance, nodded and smiled.

Hannibal turned to Reischl and said: "Mrs. Jones and I will discuss your request tonight. May I call you in the morning?"

"Of course," replied Reischl. "My phone number is on the card." With that, he turned to me, bowed slightly, turned again, walked across the lobby and disappeared through the door.

That evening, Hannibal called the French Embassy. To our surprise, a message was waiting. It simply said: 'Trust Reischl: Soucet.'

## Friday evening, February 27

Hannibal and I accepted Reischl's request for our help on his murder investigation. He offered a lucrative fee. We accepted the fee; I am always the entrepreneur. Besides, it would seem odd if we worked for free.

Reischl invited us to his office in the Polizei Präsidium on Alexander Platz on Monday morning. Our car arrived a week ago, and Hannibal cleared our French driver's licenses with the German authorities. We can drive in Germany, so we will use our Duesenberg to visit Reischl.

## Monday evening, March 2

The Polizei Präsidium was easy to find, it's called the 'Red Castle' due to the reddish hue of the stone façade. We parked in the lot at rear of the building.

Reischl's austere office was on the second level, next to an open squad room. Several detectives moved about the squad room, performing various tasks. After we finished the social pleasantries, we sat in Reischl's office, and he briefed us on the case.

"Five women have been brutally murdered in Berlin over the past six months," he began. "The wounds on all five are nearly identical, suggesting ritual murders by a single, deeply disturbed person."

"Place and time?" I asked.

Reischl nodded and replied: "All five murders took place on streets in the upscale Mitte neighborhood of Berlin, northwest of Alexander Platz."

He paused and added: "The circumstances of the murders are the same: a woman alone on a dark street at night, in the same upscale neighborhood, no robbery and no sexual assault. Otherwise, the women were different in employment and lifestyle. "

Hannibal asked: "Any leads?"

"No," responded Reischl. "We have no suspects and we have not made any arrests." He paused and added: "We in the department are getting pressure from the National Socialists." He sighed and added: "One of the women was the niece of a prominent party member."

I looked at Hannibal. I'm sure we had similar thoughts. Solving this case might result in goodwill in the right places. My gaze returned to Reischl. His face had showed obvious distaste as he spoke about the Nazi Party. "Reischl doesn't like Nazis," my thoughts concluded.

"May we review the case files?" I asked.

"Of course," replied Reischl. "We have set up a vacant office for you next to mine." He nodded toward a small room nearby.

I looked in the door and saw a table with a stack of files, several chairs and a desk. "Thank you, this will do nicely," I responded. "Do you have coffee?"

Reischl chuckled and said: "Yes, of course." So, our work began.

## Tuesday evening, March 3

Hannibal and I spent Tuesday morning reviewing the files on the five victims. I decided to build a psychological profile of the killer.

"So, what motivates our killer?" I mused.

From the photos, I noticed that all five women were slim, well-dressed, attractive and had very similar hair styles.

I looked at the photos of the bodies taken at the scenes of the murders. All of the victims had been killed in alleys just off streets lined with well-appointed townhomes.

From the postures of the bodies, the women had been pinned to the cobblestones. Bruises around the mouth and cheeks indicated that their mouths had been covered, probably by a heavy hand.

Their torn clothing and exposed bodies had been brutally cut in many places, yet the autopsies showed that no sexual assault had occurred. Death came slowly. I shuddered and set aside the photos.

Hannibal looked up, saw my shudder and watched me closely.

I then said: "The killer is probably male."

"Yes," responded Hannibal. "The killings required brute strength to overpower a relatively young female fighting for her life."

After a moment, I said: "The killer may strike again."

"Agree, but when?" said Hannibal, as he put down a file that he had been reviewing.

"The killer has a need to show that he is still out there," I stated. Hannibal waited.

I thought for a few moments and then said: "Let's use his probable need for recognition to our advantage."

I thought for a full minute. Finally, I said: "I bet the killer would react quickly if someone else received credit for his exploits." Hannibal raised his eyebrows.

We spent the next two hours devising a plan. By lunchtime, we had enough notes to explain our plan to Reischl.

Reischl returned just before noon. Thoughtfully, he brought bratworst sandwiches with stone-ground mustard. He also had cardboard containers of sauerkraut and applesauce. Hannibal and I explained our plan as the three of us consumed the very German lunch. We washed the food down with coffee instead of beer.

"Let's begin with a faked but very public arrest," Hannibal began. "The German press can be allowed to observe." He paused and then continued: "The person arrested can be a policeman in disguise."

"The police spokesman will make no statement, except to say the arrest concerns the recent serial killings of five women," I added. "Let the press assume that you have a suspect in custody."

"The press will most likely publish sensational stories in the newspapers that the police have arrested the alleged killer," Hannibal continued.

"We should keep the plan secret, with only trusted police participants," I said.

Reischl perked up at this, and muttered: "We should not tell the Nazis who have infiltrated our department."

I looked at Hannibal. Both of us were surprised. Without commenting, we both filed away Reischl's statement in our minds for future reference. "Soucet will have an interest," I thought to myself.

"The true killer will see the newspaper stories," Hannibal continued. "If we profiled him correctly, he will be incensed that someone is getting credit for his actions. He will be motivated to strike again."

"If we are wrong about his motivations, nothing is lost," mused Reischl. "Go on."

"I will become bait," I said. "I will arrange my hair in the same style as the victims and dress in a similar manner. I will walk a residential street in the Mitte neighborhood at night, following their previous pattern with regard to time and place."

"Your detectives can follow at discreet distances," Hannibal added.

"Still, you will be in danger," responded Reischl.

Both Hannibal and I smiled. Hannibal spoke first. "Caroline can take care of herself."

I reached over for my purse and took out my new Walther automatic. Reischl's eyes widened.

"She also carries a long, thin sheath knife," Hannibal said with a broad smile.

Reischl's mouth opened wide. After a moment, he simply said: "You are full of surprises."

"Are we agreed?" I asked.

Reischl thought a moment, smiled and replied: "Pierre said you had innovative ideas." He took a deep breath and continued. "Let's try it."

## Friday evening, March 6

Our faked arrest went well. Through contacts in the press, Reischl surreptitiously let it be known that an arrest had been made in a Berlin suburb in connection with the serial killer murders. On Thursday afternoon, the suspect would be transported from the suburb station to the main jail at the Polizei Präsidium.

By Thursday noon, the parking lot at the Präsidium was buzzing with reporters. Right on cue, a police van drove up to the side door jail entrance.

Uniformed policemen led a disheveled man in non-descript clothing and handcuffs out of the back of the van. His head was covered with a hood, so reporters couldn't see his face.

Hannibal and I watched from a nearby alcove as the 'suspect' disappeared through the jail door. Reischl stood on the steps of the doorway as reporters shouted questions.

Reischl's only response was: "Yes, we have a man in custody with regard to the serial killings of five women." After a few moments, he turned and went inside, leaving the clamoring reporters in the parking lot.

Stories, full of wild speculation, appeared as headlines in almost every Berlin evening newspaper. Only a handful of Reischl's closest associates, including the police van driver and the attendant uniformed policemen, knew about the fake. Even the Nazi agents assigned to monitor the case were deceived.

## Tuesday evening, March 10

Beginning last Saturday night, I became bait. I walked residential streets in the Mitte neighborhood northwest of Alexander Platz. Each evening, I wore a different outfit, similar to those of the victims. Very few women were on the street; I was essentially alone.

I was ready for action. My purse contained my Walther, and my sheath knife was strapped to my right thigh. The knife was under my clothes, but it was easily accessible through false pockets in my coat and dress. My shoes were stylish but very suitable for fighting and running. As backup, Hannibal and other detectives followed at discreet distances.

Saturday evening just after the Tietz Department Store had closed, I walked northwest on Koenig Strasse. I turned right on a dark side street and right again on Georgen Kirch Strasse back towards Alexander Platz. Nothing.

Sunday evening, my route began at the Tietz Department store on Alexander Platz. I walked along Alexander Strasse to Keibet and turned left. After a couple of blocks, I turned left on Linien, left on Grenadier, left again on Münz and back toward Alexander Platz. Again, nothing.

The attack came on Monday evening. My route started on the northwest corner of Alexander Platz, along Alexander Strasse, towards its junction with Münz.

I had just turned right on Prenzlauer Strasse toward the Prenzlauer Kirchhoff. A street light on the corner provided dim illumination.

A sudden movement from a narrow alley between townhomes on my right caught my peripheral vision. A shadowy male figure loomed out of the darkness.

I spun around to meet my attacker head on. His right fist swung toward my head. I ducked, flexed my knees, then raised up, swinging my left arm in an uppercut at the same time. My fist hit under my opponent's ribs. I felt hardened muscle, and the man hardly flinched.

"Oh boy," I thought, as the man's forward momentum crashed his body into mine. I went down on my back, hitting my butt and elbows on the hard cobblestones. "This guy is tough!" My purse with its Walther went flying off into the darkness.

The man continued past me for a few steps, spun around, and headed back toward me. I had just enough time to spin around on my back, flex my knees and strike up with both feet. My feet caught him on his right thigh and groin. He lost his balance and fell backward.

I scrambled up, slid my right hand through my false pockets and grabbed the hilt of my sheath knife. I swung my knife hand wide, held my left hand forward and flexed my knees in a knife-fighter's stance.

My opponent saw the knife. He stopped a few meters away, stared at me for a couple of seconds and then turned and ran back toward the alley. He stumbled briefly as his body brushed a metal sign that was fastened to a post at the alley entryway. I heard the sound of tearing fabric.

The man disappeared into the darkness. I looked wildly around, spotted my purse, retrieved my Walther and gave chase. As I ran, I switched my knife to my left hand and held my Walther in my right.

The chase lasted for only half a minute; my opponent had a head start in the darkness. After about hundred meters, I stopped. Narrow paths between townhouses branched in a dozen locations off the alley. "He could be anywhere," I muttered.

I carefully re-traced the chase route. "He ran into a sign at the alley entrance," I thought to myself. I soon found the sign. A torn piece of fabric hung on the ragged edge of the metal. I tucked my knife back in its sheath and gently retrieved the piece of fabric.

As I was doing so, Hannibal, Reischl and a couple of uniformed policemen arrived on the scene. "Are you OK?" Hannibal said, as he looked me over.

"I'm fine," I replied, even though my elbows and butt hurt. "He got away." My Walther was still in my hand.

After I caught my breath, I outlined what happened and described my opponent: "Male, slim, athletic, well-dressed with a fedora hat over dark hair." I paused and then added: "It was too dark to make out facial features, but he was young, perhaps twenty to thirty."

I showed Hannibal and Reischl the torn fabric. "From my attacker," I explained. "We might be able to trace this. The fabric looks like worsted wool."

Reischl looked closely at the fabric. "Good quality," he said. "We can check tailor shops."

Reischl's gaze returned to me. He stared, grinned and said: "I suspect that your opponent is a little worse for wear."

Hannibal looked me over again. After a moment, he seemed satisfied. He then smiled and said: "Let's go back to the station. A couple of police cars are waiting for us on Alexander Platz."

## Thursday evening, March 12

Inspector Reischl had one of his detectives compile a list of Berlin tailor shops. Using our piece of fabric and the list, Hannibal and I began our hunt for a killer.

Our list included several shops on and near Alexander Platz. We had no luck with the first two shops; the fabric was not in their inventory.

The third shop was the right place. It was located just around the corner from the Tietz Department Store on Keibet Strasse. One of the suits on display in the store front window was made from the same fabric as the piece obtained from my attacker's clothing.

The proprietor was an elderly gentleman named Josef Weitzel. After proper introductions, we explained our association with the police and briefly discussed the purpose of our visit.

Herr Weitzel led us to his office at the back of the shop. A stack of ledgers lay on a table next to rolls of fabric.

"Ich habe nur vier Anzüge aus deinem Stoff gemacht," said Weitzel. "Sehr wenige Berliner können sich einem solchen Anzug leisten."

Weitzel opened one of his ledgers, peered over his spectacles and searched the entries. "Ja, Ja," he finally said: "Hier sind die Namen und Adressen: Myer, Ritter, Middendorf und von Kleist."

"Humm," I thought to myself. "Weitzel's comment that few Berliners can afford suits made from the fabric helps with our killer's profile." I leaned over the ledger and copied the names and addresses into my notebook. After a minute or so, I raised up and said: "Danke, Herr Weitzel. Du warst sehr hilfreich."

Our conversation continued. Weitzel described Myer, Ritter and Middendorf as older men. His measurement notes showed that Myer and Ritter were portly. Middendorf was smaller, but elderly. According to Weitzel, von Kleist was young, and his measurements showed that he was slim and trim.

"Our prime suspect," mused Hannibal.

"He's certainly worth a visit," I agreed.

# 7

## CLOSING ON A KILLER

*Friday evening, March 13, 1931*

This morning, Hannibal and I returned to the Polizei Präsidium and briefed Reischl on our findings. Reischl called the von Kleist residence and made an appointment; after all, the family was old aristocracy.

Reischl, Hannibal and I visited the von Kleist townhouse on Thursday morning. A butler answered the door.

Reischl provided introductions and explained the purpose of our visit. He told the butler that we were investigating serious crimes in the neighborhood, and we wanted to know if anyone in the home had seen suspicious persons lurking about.

Reischl ended with: "As I stated on the phone, we would like to speak to everyone in the household."

The butler escorted us to the library, where we were imperiously greeted by Frau Helga von Kleist, an older but still slim and beautiful matron.

She introduced her son Erich and daughter Maria, who remained seated in soft, elegant chairs by a window.

The window provided a view of a well-tended garden and courtyard. Hundreds of books in bookcases lined the walls on either side of the window and the wall at the left end of the room.

The right wall had a fireplace and a portrait of a man in a German officer's uniform. Several soft, expensive-looking chairs, lamps and coffee tables on both sides of the doorway completed the room's luxurious furnishings.

As we entered the library, I noticed some intricate wood and ivory carvings on a coffee table. The carvings were quite good.

Reischl, Hannibal and I were soon seated. In the small talk before getting down to business, I mentioned the carvings.

"Erich made them," stated Frau von Kleist. "He is very talented when he applies himself."

Erich gave his mother a venomous look. After a moment, he said softly: "One of my hobbies. I use special carving tools."

I looked at the portrait of the German officer. Frau von Kleist saw my glance. "My husband," she said. "He was killed during the war."

"I'm sorry for your loss," I responded.

Frau von Kleist sniffed a little and replied coldly: "Thank you."

Reischl began the questioning. For the most part, Hannibal and I listened and observed reactions. Reischl started with questions about possible strangers in the neighborhood.

Frau von Kleist responded that she had seen several tramps, that was all. "Mostly old derelict soldiers," she said, with obvious distaste. "Not of our class," she added, with a glance at the portrait on the wall above the fireplace.

After several additional questions about strangers and meaningless responses, Reischl got to the point. "A piece of worsted wool fabric was found near a crime scene, and we traced it to suits made by Weitzel's tailor shop."

Erich shifted a little in his chair, and Reischl continued: "One such suit was sold to Erich von Kleist," said Reischl. He looked at Erich intently. "Do you have such a suit?"

Frau von Kleist looked at her son and raised her eyebrows. "That look said be careful," I thought to myself.

Erich glanced at his mother, thought a moment, returned his gaze to Reischl and responded: "I did own such a suit, but I disposed of it."

He paused, sniffed a little and added: "The suit was ruined when I accidentally burned a hole in the sleeve with a cigar that was left on a side table at our country club."

"Humm," I thought to myself. "He knows that we have seen Weitzel's records, and he's smart enough to not deny owning the suit." I glanced over at Hannibal, who nodded slightly. "Our suspect is no fool," my thoughts concluded.

Reischl then asked: "How and when did you dispose of the suit?"

"Let's see," replied Erich. "I tossed it in the trash can in our alley last Sunday morning."

"How convenient," I thought. "That's the day before I was attacked."

"Were there any tears in the fabric?" Reischl asked. I could tell that Reischl had also noted the importance of the date of disposal.

Erich thought a moment, then answered: "No, just the burn of the cigar."

I looked at Frau von Kleist. She let out a sigh but maintained her imperious demeanor.

I glanced over at Maria, whose eyes remained downcast. "She knows something," I surmised to myself.

Reischl then asked Erich about his whereabouts on the nights of the five murders.

"I was at home with my mother and sister," Erich replied. Frau von Kleist and Maria both said: "Yes, he was," almost in unison.

After a few more questions, the interview with the von Kleist family ended.

Reischl then questioned the servants. All were nervous; they clearly were afraid of Frau von Kleist. They confirmed that Erich had a suit made from the fabric in question, but they denied any knowledge of the suit's current whereabouts.

None of the servants would confirm Erich's story that he was at home on the night of the murders and the assault on me on March 9. Finally, when specifically asked, the cook told us that the trash cans in the alley were emptied by the city service every Wednesday.

After the visit to the von Kleist home ended, Reischl returned to the Polizei Präsidium. Hannibal and I returned to our suite at the Adlon. Hannibal called down to the dining room and made dinner reservations for 7:00 PM.

We had all afternoon to discuss the case, so we sat in our parlor and looked out our window with a view of Pariser Platz. The afternoon was cloudy, but no rain. People moved about on the Platz.

After people watching for a while, I began the conversation: "Frau von Kleist is a piece of work."

"She and the sister are both attractive ladies," responded Hannibal with a slight chuckle.

"Hummf," I responded with a sniff and toss of my head. I thought a moment then added: "Did you notice that they both look a lot like our five murder victims?"

Hannibal looked out the window again. I could tell he was planning something. Finally, he said: "I think we should set up a surveillance of the von Kleist townhome."

I thought a moment, then responded: "Agree. If Erich did dispose of the suit like he said, maybe we can spot its current owner." I paused, thinking, and then added: "Someone wore the suit during the attack on Monday."

"Let's talk it over with Reischl. I'm sure he will agree to surveillance," replied Hannibal. "We can meet with him Friday morning."

Hannibal looked at me with a twinkle in his eyes. "Our dinner reservations are at seven o'clock, and it's only two o'clock. Do you have any plans for the next few hours?"

"Just you," I responded with a giggle. I got up from my chair, walked over to Hannibal and sat on his lap. The afternoon passed, and we had a lovely dinner that evening.

## Saturday evening, March 14

With Reischl's concurrence, Hannibal and I set up a surveillance post this morning in a carriage house across the alley and at an angle from the von Kleist townhouse. Reischl made the arrangements. We could see the townhouse doors, front, side and back from the second-floor loft window.

From our perch in the loft, we saw several people come and go, mostly servants taking trash from several townhouses to the row of cans in the alley. However, nothing of interest happened, except that it rained. Surveillance can be so boring.

## Sunday evening, March 15

We had better luck today. Mid-morning, we spotted an old man rummaging in the trash cans. The man wore an ill-fitting suit that appeared to be made from the same fabric as the torn fabric in our possession.

As the man finished his rummaging, we surreptitiously climbed down from the loft of the carriage house and followed him to his hovel in another seedy alley.

We questioned the man, who turned out to be an old soldier, fallen on hard times. The suit he was wearing had a burn mark on the sleeve. It also had a missing piece of fabric from the same sleeve.

After intense but kindly questioning, the old soldier remembered seeing a young man dispose of a suit in a trash can. When the young man left, the old soldier said that he walked over to the can and took out the suit, which lay on top of other trash and foodstuffs.

More importantly, the date that he saw the suit being tossed was the Tuesday after the day of the attack. He remembered the date because it was the same day that he visited the once per week soup kitchen at a local Catholic Church, wearing his new suit from the trash can.

Hannibal and I escorted the old man to the church, which was only a couple of blocks away. We were greeted by a priest, who confirmed that the old soldier was a regular each Tuesday at the soup kitchen.

The priest also confirmed that the old soldier wore the new suit for the first time on Tuesday, March 10. The priest and his attendants fed the man, cleaned him up and found him fresh clothes. We took his suit as evidence.

During our conversation with the priest, I revealed the location of the trash can in the alley behind the suspect's townhouse.

The priest recognized the location. "I know the von Kleist family," he said. "Irwin von Kleist, the father, was a distinguished Prussian officer in the German army." The priest paused and shook his head sadly. "Colonel von Kleist was killed during the war. He is buried in the church cemetery."

In response to my questions, the priest stated that the suspect and his sister visit their father's grave often. "Maria also attends mass every Sunday." He paused and then added with a sigh: "Erich and his mother seldom attend mass."

## Monday evening, March 16

We took the suit to the police station this morning. A quick forensic analysis showed residual food stains on the suit, in addition to ash and damage from a cigar burn. The lab identified the food stains as orange juice and coffee grounds, as well as other kitchen foodstuffs.

Reischl, Hannibal and I returned to the von Kleist townhouse this afternoon and questioned the servants again.

The cook confirmed that orange peels and coffee grounds, along with other kitchen refuse, were placed in the trash can that week on Tuesday, the day after the attack. In spite of fear of Frau von Kleist, the cook also revealed that she did not see a suit in the trash can when she emptied her kitchen leftovers.

After we returned to the Präsidium, Reischl, Hannibal and I compared impressions.

I began the conversation. "Erich clearly lied about when the suit was tossed in the trash can," I said. "It had to be after the cook emptied her kitchen trash and same day that the suit was picked up by the old soldier."

"Humm," responded Hannibal; "He could have put the cigar burn on the suit any time after his attack on you."

Reischl took a deep breath, let it out and said: "I have enough evidence to arrest Erich von Kleist and search the townhouse." He called in one of his subordinate detectives and two uniformed policemen. He gave them instructions.

Within an hour, Erich was in the Präsidium jail. After the booking and fingerprinting process, the detective reported back to Reischl.

"Did you find a murder weapon?" Reischl asked.

"No," responded the detective. "We searched the townhouse and the surrounding property thoroughly. We found nothing." He paused and then added: "However, Frau von Kleist protested loudly. 'You will be hearing from my attorney,' she said."

"Without a murder weapon, conviction of Erich is unlikely," Reischl responded.

"Where is it?" I mused.

Hannibal heard me. "Let's continue our surveillance," he said. "The mother and daughter know more than they are telling."

## Thursday evening, March 19

Wednesday evening, I was on watch, alone, in the surveillance post in the carriage house. Hannibal was with Reischl at the Präsidium.

A steady, cold rain chilled the air. As darkness approached, the back door of the von Kleist townhouse opened, and a slim woman stepped out.

The woman wore a raincoat and a bandana. I couldn't see her face. She walked down the alley to a side street and continued toward the Catholic church. I slipped down from the carriage house loft and followed.

The woman walked around the church into the cemetery. I hid in a nearby grove of trees and watched. A lamppost at the cemetery entrance provided dim illumination.

The woman glanced around. No one, including me, was in sight. Apparently satisfied, she walked to a large tombstone, knelt down and worked her hands around a stone urn used to hold flowers. I could see the name 'Kleist' on the tombstone.

After a minute or so, the woman stood up. She held a small box. She then tidied up around the urn, took the box and walked out of the cemetery. Again, I followed.

The woman entered an alley some distance from the von Kleist townhouse. I watched while she placed the box in a trash can.

The woman glanced around again, then headed out of the alley and back towards the von Kleist townhouse. After she left, I put on gloves and retrieved the box from the trash can. The box contained artist cutting tools.

On Thursday morning, Hannibal and I took the box to Reischl at the Präsidium. Reischl immediately ordered a forensic analysis of the box and its contents. The lab matched the cutting tools to the wounds on all five victims.

"Good work," said Reischl with a smile. "We have the murder weapons."

Hannibal nodded and said: "I suggest that you bring Erich, who is already in a cell downstairs, and Frau von Kleist and Maria to your office for a confrontation." Hannibal then explained his plan.

Reischl agreed, and sent a team to bring in Frau von Kleist and Maria. Within an hour, the team delivered the pair to the Präsidium.

Reischl, Hannibal and I watched as Frau von Kleist and Maria were fingerprinted. Frau von Kleist protested vehemently at the indignity of being treated as a common criminal. Maria acted surprised, but submitted meekly.

Reischl, Hannibal and I waited in Reischl's office while the fingerprints of Erich and the two women were compared to the fingerprints on the retrieved box and its contents.

The von Kleists, in the company of two uniformed policemen, were allowed to stew in an interrogation room.

In less than thirty minutes, a detective returned to Reischl's office with a report on the analysis of the fingerprints. He gave the report to Reischl, who shared it with Hannibal and me.

The three of us then entered the interrogation room and started asking questions. We needed a motive.

In response to intense questioning, Erich revealed that his father died when he was only five years old. He also said that he and his sister were raised by his mother.

Erich's bearing and attitude showed that he deeply resented his overbearing mother, who constantly berated and humiliated him as he tried to respond to questions.

After about an hour, we took a break from interrogation. The von Kleists were left in the interrogation room, and Reischl, Hannibal and I returned to Reischl's office.

I began the conversation. "Erich von Kleist murdered and mutilated the five women. They were all similar in appearance to his mother. His acts were his way of revenge for his mistreatment," I hypothesized. "Still, we need more than circumstantial evidence."

Reischl and Hannibal nodded. We returned to the interrogation room.

As soon as we arrived, Frau von Kleist stood up and stated: "I killed all five women." She then sat down. Erich smiled, and Maria seemed aghast.

I looked first at Hannibal and then Reischl. Words were not needed; the three of us knew that the confession did not fit the facts.

Reischl pressed Frau von Kleist for details about the murders. He quickly tripped her on her own words. Her detailed answers did not match the evidence at the crime scenes and the forensic analysis of the victims' wounds. Most important, the fingerprints on the box and the murder weapons were not hers.

Reischl, Hannibal and I stepped outside the interrogation room again and closed the door.

"A good defense attorney can be counted upon to refute the confession, ostensibly obtained under duress, during a trial," I whispered to Reischl and Hannibal. Both men nodded.

Reischl said: "In the meantime, her confession will require us to release her son, who will then disappear." He paused, smiled and added: "Nice gambit."

The three of us returned to the interrogation room. Reischl stated: "Frau von Kleist, your answers show that you were never at the crime scenes and the fingerprints on the cutting tool box reveal that Maria handled the box, not you. Your confession is false."

Reischl's gaze shifted to Erich. "Only Erich's fingerprints are on the cutting tools inside the box."

I looked intently at Erich and said: "Erich von Kleist, you murdered five women as a way of getting back at your mother, whom you dared not attack directly." Erich squirmed in his seat.

Hannibal added: "We have evidence in the form of fabric from your suit jacket that places you at the scene of an assault on Mrs. Jones on the night of Monday, March 9."

I then said: "Other than your mother and sister, you have no witnesses to confirm that you were at home on the nights of the five murders and on the night of the assault on me. Not even your servants back up your claim."

Reischl then completed the indictment: "Your cutting tools match the wounds on the five victims, and your fingerprints are on the tools." He paused and watched for a moment as Erich continued to squirm.

Reischl then added: "Motive, method and probable opportunity: Erich von Kleist, you will remain under arrest for five murders and the assault on Mrs. Jones." Reischl signaled to a uniformed policeman, who led Erich out of the interrogation room.

I then turned to Maria and said: "Why did you retrieve the box from the cemetery?"

Maria started crying. Between sniffles, she said: "I wanted to put the police off the track with regard to Erich." She paused and added: "I knew that Erich hid the box with the cutting tools in the urn next to our father's grave."

Further questions revealed that Maria was naïve and unaware that the police could use fingerprint analysis to determine who handled the box and the cutting tools inside.

Reischl then stated: "Maria von Kleist, you will be held as an accomplice after the fact to the murders."

Maria cried softly. A police matron entered the room and led Maria away.

Reischl then called in two uniformed policemen and a matron to escort Frau von Kleist to her townhouse. In a complete reversal of her personality, she seemed totally crushed. She was led away by the matron without another word.

In a discussion after the interrogation, Reischl said: "Erich will most likely be convicted of five murders and the assault on you. He probably will be executed." He paused, sighed and added: "The sister will serve time in prison."

"Sad," I responded: "It is unclear whether or not Maria collaborated with her brother on the murders, but she knew where he had hidden the box with the murder weapons."

After a moment, Hannibal said: "The mother may or may not have known about her son and daughter's involvement in the murders and the cover-up attempt by her daughter."

He looked first at me and then Reischl. "Her defense attorney will most likely get her declared not guilty of any crime due to lack of evidence."

"Yes," responded Reischl. "However, in spite of her wealth, she will fall from her high place in society and will spend the rest of her life in misery over her disgraced son and daughter."

# 8

## SOCIETY SWIRL

*Sunday evening, March 22, 1931*

Hannibal and I gained entry into Berlin society as a result of our solution to the Mitte neighborhood serial murders. In addition to the trust of Chief Inspector Reischl, we earned the heartfelt thanks of Konrad Goebbels, the uncle of one of the slain young women.

Konrad introduced us to his brother Josef, a member of the Reichstag and the Propaganda Chief of the Nazi Party. Josef invited us to a banquet held to celebrate his engagement to Magda Quandt, a beautiful, well-to-do divorcée and patron of the arts in Berlin.

Of course, we accepted. The event was held last evening in the banquet room of the Adlon, just downstairs from our suite.

I found Magda to be an engaging conversationalist. We talked about artists, paintings and trends in art.

"I just love the landscapes of Heinrich Böhmer and the flowers of Emil Nolde," Magda said in a bubbly voice.

"The works of both artists are beautiful," I agreed. "Nolde's expressionist style puts him at the forefront of modern art."

"Yes," responded Magda. "His brushwork and choice of colors are exquisite." She paused and then added in a whisper: "I don't think the Führer would approve." She then giggled.

In a voice that others could hear, she then said: "Of course, Böhmer's realism appeals to all right-thinking Germans."

I glanced around. Several eavesdroppers nodded in approval. I glanced back at Magda, and her eyes twinkled.

In another whisper, she said: "Max Liebermann's portraits are so detailed and accurate. The Führer especially liked the portrait of Field Marshal von Hindenburg, until he found out that Lieberman is a Jew." She giggled again.

Our conversation continued for a while, before her attention was taken by her fiancé. As Josef Goebbels and Magda slipped away, I thought to myself: "Magda is a good person to cultivate; who knows what she might reveal?"

As Hannibal and I moved through the party swirl in our now practiced manner, I overheard senior Nazis in resplendent uniforms discussing cooperation with the communists to undermine the Social Democrats in the Reichstag.

Interesting party! When Hannibal and I returned to our suite, we compared impressions. We also composed and sent a secret report to Soucet in Paris.

## Tuesday evening, March 24

Heinrich Brüning is Germany's current chancellor. Newspapers report that he is unable to command a majority in the Reichstag. For the most part, he governs with the support of President von Hindenburg, a conservative monarchist, and the Army.

Newspaper editorials claim that the Reichstag is a shambles. A middle-class liberal party strong enough to block the right-wing Nazis does not exist. Several centrist parties, including the Catholic Center Party and the Social Democrats, represent narrow self-interests.

The Nazis and communists both have seats in the Reichstag. This afternoon, we witnessed violent clashes between the opposing parties on downtown streets. The police seemed unwilling or unable to control the riots.

## Friday evening, March 27

Reischl asked Hannibal and me to review his unsolved case load and provide advice to his detectives. We visit our little office in the Präsidium several times each week. Reischl's detectives seem to especially appreciate our little seminars on crime scene processing and follow-up investigation.

Many of the unsolved murders in Berlin involve Nazis and communists. The write-ups simply show 'killed during a riot,' with a given date. The murder victims included Horst Wessel, a Nazi Sturmführer, murdered on February 23, 1930. His file includes clippings from Nazi affiliated newspapers. They have made him a martyr.

Reischl introduced us to Polizeikapitän Paul Anlauf, the Commander of Berlin's Seventh Precinct. The Headquarters of the German Communist Party is located in his precinct. Reischl told us that Anlauf is a prominent member of the Social Democratic Party and a well-known anti-communist.

I noticed that Reischl observes our rise in the esteem of prominent Nazis with bemused yet attentive interest. Although he had expressed private disapproval of Nazis and their methods on several occasions, he seems astute enough about politics to avoid attention and entanglements.

## Sunday morning, April 5

The weather has improved considerably, so Hannibal and I began exploring city nightclubs. Berlin makes Al Capone's Chicago appear tame. Decadent and provocative cabaret shows, excessive alcohol and drug use and hedonistic parties are pervasive throughout the city.

Newsstands display guidebooks that feature Berlin nightlife. For example, Curt Moreck's *Guide through Depraved Berlin*, published in German, French and English, seems wildly popular.

Newspapers, especially *Der Angriff,* show that this freedom of thought and social interaction has drawn the ire of the Nazis, who, perhaps surprisingly, are very conservative in their publicly professed social mores. If Nazis eventually take power, Berlin's lifestyle will undoubtedly change.

Yesterday, Hannibal and I sent a slightly titillating coded report to Soucet. I'm sure he was amused.

## Saturday morning, May 2

Hannibal spent Friday afternoon at the Reichbank. His banker contact provided more information on Nazi financial transactions. Money was sent from Berlin to Nazi supporters. Two transfers were of particular interest.

Substantial sums were sent to an account in Geneva, Switzerland under the name Jacques Doriot. I followed up on the transfer to Doriot by reading Paris newspapers. On February 1, Doriot was elected mayor of Saint-Denis, just outside Paris.

According to a Paris newspaper editorial, Doriot is an avowed communist. However, he is currently at odds with other party members over the potential for an alliance between communists and socialists. The flow of money from the Nazis suggests that his allegiance may change.

Another transfer went to a small bank in the town of Sant Joan de Labritja on the island of Ibiza, Spain. Marcel Villian owns the account.

Hannibal followed up on the transfer of money to Villian. Our contact at the French Embassy confirmed that Villian had recently passed the French-Spanish border into Spain at Col du Pourtalet. The arrest warrant arrived at the border the day afterwards.

Raoul Villian, Marcel's older cousin, had fled France to Ibiza in the 1920s, after his acquittal of the assassination of socialist Jean Jaurés. Marcel may be hiding with his cousin Raoul on Ibiza. The money transfer could be a payment for a future activity.

Hannibal and I reported our findings on both transfers and the implications to Soucet in Paris.

## Sunday morning, June 7

In addition to providing advice on unsolved cases, Hannibal and I use our time in the Präsidium to observe the politics of the Berlin Kriminal Polizei.

The Berlin police are currently led by Albert Carl Grzesinski, a prominent member of the Social Democratic Party and the current Police President. Grzesinski is an ardent foe of both the German Communist Party and the Nazis.

In 1929, Grzesinski banned the Rotfrontkämpferbund, the armed militia of the Communist Party, and brutally supressed communist led rallies in Berlin. Acting under orders from Grzesinski, police shot 33 communist rioters during the first three days of May, 1929.

Earlier this year, he also tried to gag Hitler, who is an Austrian citizen, from public speeches in Germany. He ordered him deported as an undesirable alien. However, Chancellor Brüning did not sign the order. Grzesinski's future does not look bright if Hitler comes to power.

The Berlin Kriminal Polizei continues to be infiltrated by Nazis, either by political appointments or by recruitment of current policemen. One such convert is Detective Inspector Konrad Raeder, one of Chief Inspector Reischl's subordinates. Reischl and Raeder have an icy relationship.

## Saturday morning, July 11

Are Jews really a threat as Nazi newspapers assert? Hannibal and I decided to do some research. We spent Thursday and Friday at the Prussian State Library just off Unter den Linden. The huge octagonal reading room has statistics on population, ethnic groups, culture, income by class and political parties. It also has copies of Jewish newspapers, pamphlets and advertisements.

According to census records, Jews represent less than one percent of the total German population of about 67 million. Half of all Jews live in the ten largest German cities, including Berlin. However, Jews have played a significant part in German culture, far above what census numbers suggest.

Jews hold important positions in the Weimar government and teach in Germany's great universities. Of the 38 Nobel Prizes won by German writers and scientists between 1905 and 1930, fourteen went to Jews. Plays by Max Reinhardt are popular in Berlin and other German cities. Arnold Schoenberg and Kurt Weill compose music, artists Max Liebermann and Lesser Ury create beautiful paintings and Otto Klemperer and Bruno Walter conduct concerts to huge audiences.

Jewish communal institutions thrive. Berlin has sixteen synagogues. There are numerous Jewish newspapers. Organizations such as B'nai B'rith, Poalei Zion, and Hibbat Zion have attracted many new members.

In spite of Hitler's open antisemitism, editorials in Jewish newspapers show that under the Weimar government, most Jews seem confident of their future as Germans. For example, the Jewish German newspaper *Jüdische Rundschau* had a recent editorial that said: "… that also within the German nation, still the forces are active that would turn against a barbarian anti-Jewish policy."

However, my thoughts return to my conversations with Samuel and Hedwig von Fischer. They are sophisticated and well-informed. If Hitler and the Nazis eventually control the government, the von Fischers are convinced that the impact on the Jewish community will be catastrophic.

We informed Soucet about our research and reiterated the concerns of the von Fischers.

## Tuesday evening, August 11

The past three days passed in a bewildering, searing flash. Hannibal and I witnessed the killing of three people during a riot, and we put the finger on the bad guys.

It all began on August 9, a balmy Sunday afternoon. We attended a movie at the Babylon Theater near the corner of Bülowplatz and Kaiser Wilhelm Strasse. We saw the matinee showing of *People on Sunday*, a pleasant avant-garde film about daily life in Berlin. The screen play was written by Billy Wilder and Curt Siodmak.

As we left the theater at about 7:00 PM, we were greeted by the sound of gunfire, just a few blocks away. Hannibal pushed me gently but firmly into a doorway.

"Not good," I muttered. "What's going on?" I peered around Hannibal's shielding body.

Hannibal slipped his right hand inside his jacket, where he kept his service forty-five in a shoulder holster. "Another riot," he responded.

Both of us watched from the shelter of the doorway. We saw dozens of people, mostly in work clothes, running away from the source of the gunfire in the distance. Most continued down Kaiser Wilhelm Strasse in the general direction of Alexander Platz.

I saw a few men in uniforms. Some were dressed in Nazi Sturmabteilung SA brownshirts, others were in banned communist Rotfrontkämpferbund uniforms.

I also spotted a couple of policemen with rifles. One stopped at a corner just across the Bülowplatz. He raised his rifle and fired at a fleeing man in a Rotfrontkämpferbund uniform. The targeted man screamed, fell and thrashed around on the pavement. Two other men ran out from a storefront, grabbed the wounded man and half-dragged, half-carried him to a sheltering alley.

The policeman paid no attention to the fleeing trio. He turned and ran back on Linien Strasse, turned left on Prenzlauer and headed away from us. More gunfire erupted in the distance.

I heard the chatter of automobiles. Suddenly, four police cars and a van whipped around the corner of Prenzlauer from the north and turned right on Linien. They stopped just before they reached Kaiser Wilhelm Strasse, about half a block away. A dozen policemen got out of the vehicles.

I recognized Polizeikapitän Paul Anlauf. I could hear him giving orders to his attentive squad. After a few moments, two pairs of policemen headed across the Bülowplatz in the direction of sporadic gunfire. Three other pairs headed down Linien in the opposite direction. I could see them turn right at the corner of Kleine Alexander Strasse.

"Riot control," said Hannibal in a soft voice. "The three pairs are probably headed toward the Karl Leibknecht Haus. It's on Kleine Alexander Strasse." He paused a moment and added: "That's the headquarters of the Communist Party."

"Communists, Nazis and police," I replied. I was surprised at the calmness of my voice. "Let's stay and watch for a while."

Hannibal looked down at me, smiled and responded: "OK, but let's stay in this doorway."

I nodded and smiled back. In spite of the gunfire, I felt safe with Hannibal.

Not much happened for about thirty minutes. Even the gunfire stopped. We watched as Polizeikapitän Anlauf received runners from various directions and sent them off with new orders.

At just before 8:00 PM, Anlauf saw Hannibal and me in the doorway on the other side of the Babylon Theater. He waved in recognition. After a few minutes and more orders, he and two other policemen started walking in our direction. Hannibal and I stepped out on the sidewalk.

The trio had just reached the front of the theater when I spotted movement in the alley just behind them. I stepped out in front of Hannibal and yelled: "Achtung! Hinter dir!"

The next sequence of events took seconds, but to me, everything seemed to happen in slow motion.

Anlauf started to turn. I then heard "Wangen des Schweins!" The voice came from the alley. Anlauf drew his pistol. Three men stepped out of the alley. The two policemen with Anlauf also drew their weapons.

"Pig cheeks is an interesting bit of name-calling," my thoughts raced.

Before I could react, Hannibal shoved me back in the doorway and sprinted toward Anlauf. He drew his forty-five as he ran.

Pop! Pop! Pop! Pistol shots echoed between the buildings. More gunfire followed. I could tell Hannibal's forty-five from the others; it had a heavier sound. I lost count of the shots.

Anlauf and the two other policemen went down. One of the assailants also fell; Hannibal's forty-five had found its mark. The man screamed.

One of the policemen, wounded and on the ground, emptied his pistol as two of the assailants dragged their wounded companion back into the alley. I couldn't tell if the policeman's fusillade hit anything.

Hannibal ran toward the alley. He dropped to one knee as he reached the corner of the building at the alley entrance. He swung around with his forty-five in both hands and peered down the alley. After a few moments, he raised his weapon and stood up. The assailants were gone.

In the meantime, I drew my Walther from my purse and ran toward the trio of fallen policemen. One was crawling toward Anlauf. I arrived just as the wounded man sat up and cradled Anlauf's head in his lap. I heard Anlauf as he uttered: "Wiedersehen, Willig." His eyes then glazed.

I looked over at Hannibal. He had arrived at the other downed policeman. He put his forty-five back in its holster and knelt beside the man. After a moment, Hannibal stood up. He saw me and said: "Dead."

Hannibal used his pocket knife and cut strips from the dead man's shirt. He then walked over to Willig, who was bleeding from wounds to his left arm and abdomen. Hannibal applied his makeshift bandages and pads of shirt as best that he could. The external bleeding stopped, but the wounded man needed immediate medical attention.

In the meantime, I looked around. Other policemen were running towards us.

Hannibal took charge. As he began giving orders, I walked over quietly and said: "I'm going down the alley."

Hannibal nodded, turned to two breathless policemen and said: "Gehen Sie mit Frau Jones. Sie weiß, was getan werden muss!" The pair looked at me with uncertain expressions. Hannibal turned to another policeman, ordered an ambulance for Willig. He sent others to provide a cordon against other possible attacks.

I knew what to do. I looked at my two dedicated policemen and said in a steely voice: "Folgen Sie mir!" The look in my eyes must have convinced them to obey, and the pair followed me to the alley. Both had rifles, and I had my Walther.

Light was beginning to fade, but I found a blood trail. My two companions and I followed cautiously.

The beginning of the alley had trash cans and refuse outside the back doors of businesses that fronted on Kleine Alexander on one side and Bartel Strasse on the other. We crossed Hirien Strasse.

A narrow alley continued between buildings across Hirien and past the end of Bartel. From Hannibal's description earlier, I knew we were headed in the general direction of Alexander Platz and the rear of Karl Leibknecht Haus.

The blood trail stopped by a set of trash cans at the beginning of the narrow alley. I saw a pair of legs. They moved spasmodically.

With hand signals, I directed one of my companions to watch our backs and the other to a spot a few meters into the narrow alley. Walther at the ready, I approached.

A disheveled man in workman's clothes lay with his back propped against the wall of the building behind the trash cans. His eyes were closed. The front of his shirt and jacket were soaked in blood. A Lugar lay by his right hand. I kicked it away with my right foot.

At the sound of the Lugar skittering across the cobblestones, the man muttered: "Comreade Mielke, Ziemer, du bist zurückgekehrt. Hilf mir."

"Mielke and Ziemer must have been his companions," I concluded. I filed the names in memory as I continued to observe; the man's life was ebbing away.

The man stirred and opened his eyes. When he saw me, his eyes widened. He tried to speak again, but words wouldn't come. His breath left his body in a long sigh.

I left my two policemen with the body and returned to Hannibal at the murder scene. Uniformed men were everywhere. Most were police, but quite a few wore brownshirts.

"SA Brownshirts," I muttered to Hannibal, as I approached.

Hannibal nodded and smiled with a wry expression. "Inspector Raeder has also arrived," he replied. "Raeder and the SA seem to have an understanding." He pointed to a man in front of the theater, giving orders.

Raeder saw me and walked over. I explained what I had found in the alley. I also gave him the names Mielke and Ziemer.

"Good, good," said Raeder. His lips curled into a smile, but his eyes had a cold look. "I know them. Mielke and Ziemer are communists."

He called to several policemen who were waiting in front of the theater. I overheard his directions. He turned back to me and added: "I have just issued orders for their arrest."

I looked around. Anlauf and the other two policemen were gone. I then asked Hannibal: "What about Anlauf, Willig and the other policeman?"

"Anlauf died before the ambulance arrived," replied Hannibal. "Willig was taken to hospital." He paused and added: "The other policeman was named Lenck. He died immediately."

The rest of the evening passed in a swirl.

On Monday morning, Hannibal and I arrived at the Präsidium at about nine o'clock. As we entered the squad room, Reischl approached.

He smiled warmly and said: "Your courage and resourcefulness are greatly appreciated." He shook hands first with Hannibal and then me. "Our investigation has attention at the highest levels."

Reischl filled us in on the details. "Anlaug and Lenck were assassinated by Mielke, Ziemer and Klaus, the man you found in the alley." All three are known members of the Rotfrontkämpferbund, the paramilitary force of the German Communist Party."

He added: "Walter Ulbricht, head of the communists in Berlin, probably ordered the assassination. My notes are on the table in your office." He pointed, and I saw a stack of papers.

Reischl smiled mysteriously and continued: "I'm sure you have an interest in the details."

Raeder entered the squad room. Soon he and Reischl were in deep conversation.

Hannibal and I spent the rest of Monday morning reading Reischl's papers.

Later Monday evening in our hotel suite, we prepared a report for Soucet in Paris. In our report, Hannibal asked André François Poncet, the new French Ambassador in Berlin, to send a copy to Sackett, the American Ambassador.

# 9

## BAUMER WAS MURDERED

*Wednesday evening, November 18, 1931*

Hannibal and I arrived at the Präsidium early this morning. We spent most of the day reviewing files on the aftermath of the murder of Polizeikapitän Anlauf and Officer Lenck.

Late in the afternoon, our review was interrupted by a breathless young detective, who entered the squad room just outside our door. The young man had note papers in his hand, and he exclaimed: "We have another murder!"

Hannibal and I both got up from our seats and entered the squad room. We watched as Reischl appeared at his office door, looked at the young detective and calmly said: "In my office, please."

The young man took a deep breath, exhaled slowly and followed Reischl into his office. He closed the door after he entered, but we could hear a muffled conversation.

After about five minutes, Reischl opened the door and beckoned to Hannibal and me. As we stepped into the office, Reischl returned to his seat behind his desk. He motioned us to a couple of nicely padded chairs, and we made ourselves comfortable. The young detective remained standing to one side, fidgeting.

Reischl looked at us. His eyes twinkled, and he said: "Detective Reisinger has brought us a most interesting case."

He glanced over to Reisinger, smiled in a paternal way and added: "Please sit down, Reisinger." He motioned to an uncomfortable-looking wooden chair across the room. Reisinger sat down and continued to fidget.

Reischl said: "Tell Major and Mrs. Jones the facts, please."

Reisinger took a deep breath, exhaled and began: "We just received a report from Schmidt, a uniformed sergeant, who responded to a phone call from Georg Klein, a private secretary to Josef Baumer. At Klein's urgent request, Schmidt drove to the Baumer mansion. He found Josef Baumer in his home office, at his desk, with a dagger in his back."

Reisinger looked at his papers for a moment and added: "The home has several servants, one guest and three residents other than Josef. No one admits to seeing the murder take place." Reisinger stopped his narrative and looked at Reischl.

Reischl smiled and said: "Very good, Reisinger." He turned to Hannibal and me and continued: "Josef Baumer is a prominent industrialist. This case will have interest at the highest level. Will you investigate?"

Within a few minutes, we were in our Duesenberg, following Reischl and Reisinger in their police car. Days earlier, Hannibal had prudently stashed a briefcase in our back seat. The briefcase contained a low-light camera and our crime scene processing equipment.

We sped down Kaiser Wilhelm Strasse, across the Spree and towards the western suburbs. Soon we were on Charlottenburger Road, passing through the west end of the Tiergarten.

We headed in the general direction of the Grünewald Bahnhof, which was near the von Fischer home. "Wealthy neighborhoods," I mused.

Hannibal heard me. "Yes," he responded. "Reischl said that we will continue on Heer Strasse to the Westend, a suburb just north of the Grünewald Bahnhof." He paused and then added: "Reisinger said that the Baumer home is just off Linden Alle in the Westend."

After another 15 minutes, we arrived at a substantial mansion on a quiet, tree-lined street just off Linden Alle. We got out of our Duesenberg and followed Reischl and Reisinger toward a covered portico and the front entrance.

The sidewalk had been swept, but the small lawn was covered with a few centimeters of slushy snow. Coal soot dotted the snow. Smoke rose from several chimneys of the mansion.

As we walked under the portico and approached the door, I saw a pair of rubber overshoes just outside the door. One of the pair lay bottoms up. The sole had a distinctive tread. A little bench rested next to the overshoes for a person to sit while removing footwear.

A uniformed police sergeant met us at the door. I looked at my wristwatch; the time was 5:30 PM.

"Report, Sergeant Schmidt," said Reischl, as we approached the front step.

"Yes, Herr Chief Inspector," replied Schmidt. He opened a notebook and continued: "Josef Baumer's body is in his office, just down the hallway to the right. I sealed the crime scene. No one has entered the office since I arrived."

Schmidt continued: "Colonel Ewin Meier, a former soldier and current industrialist, is a houseguest. Frau Franz Baumer, the widow of Josef's brother, her daughter Greta, and Alfred, Josef Baumer's adopted son, are residents."

He paused a moment and added: "Frau Josef Baumer died earlier this year. Josef was a widower."

He flipped a note page and added: "Servants include Johann Hofmann, Baumer's butler, Bertha Becker, the cook, and Maria Lehman, the housekeeper."

Schmidt looked at Reischl, who nodded. Schmidt continued: "Georg Klein, Josef Baumer's private secretary, phoned the local police station shortly after the body was discovered. The police operator's log shows that Klein called at 3:05 PM. "

Schmidt flipped more pages and said: "Klein lives in an apartment just over the carriage house in back. The servants live in quarters in the main house."

"Who discovered the body?" I asked.

Schmidt looked at Reischl with a questioning glance.

Reischl said: "Major and Mrs. Jones are private investigators on this case." He paused and then added: "They have my complete trust."

That was enough for Schmidt. "The body was discovered by Klaus Rosen, Josef Baumer's business partner, whose home is a block away on Rüsten Alle."

Schmidt flipped another page and continued: "Rosen said he had a meeting with the victim in his office from 10:00 until 11:00 AM. He left for his home at eleven and returned at just before three. He discovered Baumer's body at about 3:00 PM."

"Humm," I responded. "Were all of the people that you mentioned in the house when the body was discovered?"

"No," replied Schmidt. "Alfred, the adopted son, returned to the front door at 4:00 PM. I was here when he arrived. Alfred said that he had left at about 1:30 PM for a walk."

"In this weather?" Reisinger exclaimed. There was an awkward silence. Reischl gave his protégé a quick glance.

After a moment, Hannibal asked: "Anyone else?"

Schmidt replied: "One other person was present. Dr. Hans Fuchs, a prominent local physician, arrived at noon and left at 12:30 PM. He treated Frau Josef Baumer with pain-easing medications before her death, and he currently treats Frau Franz Baumer for similar ailments. He returned again at 2:18 PM. He's still here."

My instincts perked up when I heard the exact times. "Was Fuchs latest arrival time confirmed by others?" I asked.

Schmidt replied: "Yes. Meier and Klein confirmed all of Fuchs' times, which they said they had read from the large grandfather clock in the hallway."

"Excellent work, Sergeant," said Reischl. Schmidt beamed. Reisinger frowned.

"Bucking for a promotion," I thought to myself. "Good for him." I smiled at Schmidt. He returned the smile.

Reisinger said: "We would like to ask more questions. Are the people that you mentioned available?"

"Yes, Herr Detective," responded Schmidt. He gave Reisinger a slightly condescending look. "Everyone is waiting in the library. It's down the hall to the left." He turned and led the way.

As we continued down the hallway, I saw a tall man standing by a doorway to the left. He was wearing a formal black coat, trousers and tie with an old-fashioned white shirt and starched collar. "Butler," I surmised to myself.

Schmidt handled the introductions. Hofmann, the butler, clicked his heels together and responded with typical German reserve. His eyes gave me an up and down look as I approached. I smiled sweetly.

After Hofmann's quick appraisal, he said: "Follow me, please. Household members are waiting in the library." Reischl, Reisinger, Hannibal and I followed Hofmann, who introduced us to the guest, residents and servants. Reisinger began to ask questions.

I caught Reischl's eye and whispered: "Suggest that Hannibal and I inspect the murder scene."

"Yes," replied Reischl, with a quick smile. He returned his attention to Reisinger, who continued with questions.

As Hannibal and I discreetly stepped back into the hallway, Inspector Raeder entered the front door. He nodded curtly to Hannibal and walked past us into the library without a word.

"Arrogant," I thought to myself. I glanced at Hannibal. I could tell he agreed.

Hannibal and I listened for a moment. We heard Raeder say: "Herman Göring, a leader in the Reichstag, sent me a message by courier. He directed me to represent him during this investigation."

"I see," responded Reischl in an icy voice.

I glanced at Hannibal, who whispered: "Interesting." He then motioned toward Baumer's office across the hall. I walked over and opened the door.

My eyes were immediately drawn to the body, which was sitting in a chair behind the desk. "Baumer," I muttered. The desk was centered in the room and faced the doorway.

The body slumped across papers on the desk. The hilt of a dagger protruded from the middle of Baumer's back. A dark stain surrounded his suit coat around the dagger hilt. The desk was a mess; drawers were open and papers scattered.

"Someone was looking for something," I thought to myself.

Hannibal and I took a couple of minutes to survey the whole room. French doors at the back led out to a patio. The wall on the right side of the French doors had a tall bookcase filled with books and various objects of art. A display of medieval daggers and swords decorated the wall on the left.

A gap in the display showed that one of the items was missing. I glanced back at the body. "Source of the murder weapon," I mused.

The side wall to the left had a credenza. A new-fangled Dictaphone rested on top. The Dictaphone mount did not have a cylinder. However, I could see three cylinders with blue end caps on an open shelf in the credenza. An easy chair, end table and lamp rested in a nearby little nook. "Comfortable spot for using the Dictaphone," I concluded.

I turned around. To the right, I saw a small table next to the hallway door. A Gramophone rested on top. A shelf underneath had four cylinders with orange end caps. However, the Gramophone mount had a cylinder with blue end caps.

To the left, I saw another easy chair and a standing lamp. Lovely landscape paintings hung on the walls on both sides of the hallway door.

"A comfortable and functional office befitting a wealthy executive," I said aloud.

Hannibal nodded. He set his briefcase on the floor, took out his low-light camera and began taking photos.

I watched for a moment, then walked over to the French doors. A few centimeters of snow covered the patio. Footprints, coming and going, led between the doors and a swept sidewalk about ten meters away.

The swept sidewalk led from a carriage house adjacent to an alley along the back of the property. The sidewalk made a ninety-degree turn and led around to the front of the main house. "Klein goes from his carriage house apartment along the sidewalk to the front door of the mansion," I thought to myself.

I turned to Hannibal and said: "Footprints outside on the patio." Hannibal nodded. I walked over to the briefcase and fished out a measuring tape.

I stepped outside and laid the measuring tape alongside one of the footprints. The tread marks matched the tread on the overshoes at the front entrance to the mansion. Hannibal took photos. We repeated the process for several more footprints.

After Hannibal finished with the photos, we cooperated and dusted the hilt of the knife, the desk and various items of furniture for fingerprints. The knife hilt was clean, but we obtained fingerprints from other surfaces.

We also collected Baumer's fingerprints from his dead hands. I kept a clinical attitude, even as I held the dead man's hand.

After collecting fingerprints, we made notes. The whole process in the office took less than an hour.

As we finished, I said: "Did you notice the tread of the footprints on the patio? Let's take photos and measurements of the overshoes next to the bench outside the main entry."

"Humm," Hannibal responded. "You have a good eye, will do."

He frowned and added: "The overshoes are rubber and are unlikely to retain fingerprints. He paused a moment, smiled and said: "I will check for fingerprints on the bench."

Hannibal finished photos and fingerprints in the office and on the portico while I waited. We then returned to the library. Reisinger and Raeder were still asking questions.

Reischl looked over to Hannibal and me as we quietly entered the room.

"We have finished in the office across the hall and outside on the portico for now," I whispered. "Your technicians can do their work and also remove the body for autopsy."

Hannibal added: "Please ask them to leave everything else in place. We would like to return tomorrow for more detailed work."

Reischl nodded, turned to Sergeant Schmidt and softly gave the necessary orders. Reisinger and Raeder continued with questions of the household members. Both took voluminous notes. Finally, at about 7:00 PM, they ran out of questions.

Reischl breathed a deep sigh and then looked at the seated members of the household. "Sergeant Schmidt will take fingerprints from everyone. Afterwards, those of you who live elsewhere may return to your homes."

Reischl looked at Rosen and Fuchs, in turn. He added: "You will give the sergeant your address and phone number before you leave this house." He paused for emphasis and added: "No one may leave town."

He turned to Reisinger, Raeder and then Hannibal and me. "We will meet in the squad conference room tomorrow at 9:00 AM."

*Thursday evening, November 19*

Reisinger, Raeder, Hannibal and I assembled in the conference room by 9:00 AM this morning.

At precisely on time, Reischl walked in and sat at the head of the table. In a soft voice, he said: "I have written reports from Major and Mrs. Jones and Sergeant Schmidt. Do you have a report, Detective Reisinger?"

Reisinger looked a little crestfallen. After an uncomfortable pause, he replied. "Just my notes, Herr Chief Inspector."

Reischl sighed and said: "What can you add to the information already provided by Sergeant Schmidt?"

Reisinger flipped open his notes and began to speak. "Josef Baumer was a wealthy industrialist. His wife Anna was recently deceased. At the instigation of the government, Baumer was involved in the secret manufacture of military weapons and munitions."

Reischl and Raeder both stirred a little at this, everyone knew that such activity was in defiance of the Treaty of Versailles. "Continue," said Reischl.

"Baumer was murdered in his office at his mansion during the late afternoon of Tuesday, November 17. The preliminary autopsy report estimates his time of death as between 2:00 and 3:00 PM."

"House residents?" I asked.

Reisinger looked over at me and replied: "In addition to Josef, the mansion has three permanent residents: Alfred Baumer, Frau Franz Baumer and Greta Baumer, Josef's niece," Reisinger responded. "Colonel Ewin Meier is a guest."

Reischl nodded, and Reisinger continued: "Alfred Baumer is Josef's legally adopted son. He admitted that Josef made him the heir to the bulk of the family fortune." Reisinger looked to Reischl. His face expressed a look of satisfaction.

Reischl merely nodded.

Reisinger looked down at his notes and continued: "Mrs. Franz Baumer and her daughter are financially dependent on Josef. They admit to being provided for in Josef's will." Reisinger looked closely at Reischl and waited. Reischl gave no sign.

"Colonel Meier?" Hannibal asked.

Reisinger sighed and replied: "Colonel Meier is an expert in the development of tanks and other innovative weapons. He served as a consultant to Baumer."

"What was his involvement on the day of the murder?" I asked.

Reisinger looked at me and responded: "He said that he spent the afternoon of the murder in the library. He entered Baumer's office just after Klaus Rosen found Baumer's body."

Reischl asked: "Tell me about Rosen."

Raeder interrupted and stated: "Rosen is Josef Baumer's business partner and a frequent visitor at the Baumer mansion. With obvious distaste, Raeder added: "He is a Jew, and lives a few blocks away on Ebereshen Alle."

Reischl looked at Raeder intently and said in a mild voice: "Of course, you and Herr Göring also know that Rosen is a well-known collector of art."

Raeder reacted by squirming a little. After a moment, he said: "Yes, Yes."

"That was interesting," I thought to myself. I glanced at Hannibal. I could tell that he also noted Reischl's statement.

After a few moments of silence, Reischl turned to Reisinger and said: "Tell me about Dr. Fuchs."

Reisinger replied: "Dr. Hans Fuchs is a prominent physician. His home and adjacent office are a block from the Baumer mansion on Ahorn Alle."

He paused in an uncertain manner and added: "According to Sergeant Schmidt, Fuchs met with Baumer in his office on the day of the murder."

"Yes," replied Reischl. His eyebrows raised a little. "Anything else on Fuchs?"

Reisinger fidgeted. "No, Herr Chief Inspector," he finally responded.

Reischl sighed and said: "Tell me about the servants." He added: "Again, I have already read Sergeant Schmidt's written report."

Reisinger hurriedly flipped through his notes. Finally, he said: "Georg Klein, Baumer's private secretary, told me that he is an expert in transcribing dictation from a machine called a Dictaphone."

Reisinger looked at Reischl. Reischl gave no sign.

Reisinger then said: "Klein said he spent the afternoon of the murder in the library, along with Mrs. Franz Baumer and Colonel Meier. He entered Baumer's office with Meier and Fuchs just after Rosen found Baumer's body."

Reischl nodded.

Reisinger continued: "Bertha Becker is Josef Baumer's cook. She said she last saw Baumer at 12:30 PM, when she took a sandwich and tea to his office."

Reisinger paused and said: "Maria Lehmann, the housekeeper, saw Bertha enter and leave Baumer's office and confirmed the time. Both women said that Fuchs was in the office with Baumer between noon and 12:30 PM."

"Anything on Hofmann, the butler?" I asked.

"Hofmann said that he spent the afternoon of the murder in and out of the kitchen and library. He also said that he did not enter Baumer's office until after the body was discovered. His activities were confirmed by Becker and Lehmann," Reisinger replied.

"Humm," responded Reischl. He put his hands behind his head, leaned back in his chair and mused: "We need to establish motive and opportunity."

He turned to Hannibal and said: "You said earlier that you planned to return to the mansion and continue your investigation."

Hannibal replied: "Yes. With your permission, we will report back to you tomorrow, perhaps at 9:00 AM?"

Reischl nodded and his eyes twinkled. He turned to Reisinger and said: "Work with Inspector Raeder. I expect a joint written report by tomorrow morning."

Both Reisinger and Raeder squirmed. "Yes, Herr Chief Inspector," Reisinger finally replied.

"Very well," said Reischl. "This meeting is adjourned until tomorrow at 9:00 AM."

Hannibal smiled at me as we walked out of the conference room. "I'm glad Reischl gave Reisinger and Raeder something to do here at the Präsidium."

I chuckled a little and replied: "Reischl is a shrewd operator." Hannibal laughed.

# 10

## HE KNEW TOO MUCH

*Thursday midnight, November 19, 1931*

After a quick lunch of bratwurst on a bun washed down with coffee at the Präsidium cafeteria, Hannibal and I drove across town. We spent Thursday afternoon and evening at and near the Baumer mansion.

As we arrived on Linden Alle in our Duesenberg, I saw an elderly gentleman walking his dog on the sidewalk. The man waved politely as we got out of our car. I waved back. "Humm," I muttered. "It's worth a try."

Hannibal heard and gave me a quizzical look. I nodded toward the man with a dog and said: "Walking a dog is a daily routine. Perhaps that man can tell us about comings and goings from the Baumer mansion and the neighborhood. Can I meet you inside later?"

"Good idea," Hannibal replied. "In the meantime, I want to find out more about Dictaphones and Gramophones. Did you notice the location of the cylinders by the two machines yesterday?"

"Yes," I responded. "After we have finished with these two tasks, perhaps we can do individual interviews with Baumer mansion residents, guest and servants."

Hannibal smiled and said: "We can also visit Fuchs' office and Rosen's home."

He paused and added: "I'll have the on-duty policeman in the Baumer mansion set up interviews. I will also call ahead to Fuchs and Rosen."

"Let's return to the Baumer mansion after we visit Fuchs and Rosen," I responded. I thought a moment and added: "I hope Schmidt is on duty; he seems to be a good detail man."

Our interviews, including the man with a dog, went well. So did our visits to Fuchs' office and Rosen's home.

Schmidt was on duty when we returned to the Baumer mansion. He said: "The police lab will compare the fingerprints that I obtained from everyone who had been at the house on the day of the murder to the fingerprints that you collected at and near the crime scene."

"A full report will be sent to Reischl before your meeting tomorrow," Schmidt promised.

Hannibal phoned the Aldon concierge before we left the mansion. He arranged to have a nice room service dinner, including a fine, dry Riesling wine, arrive when we returned to the hotel. After the phone call, Hannibal and I drove back across town.

Dinner arrived a few minutes after we walked into our suite. "Hannibal is so efficient," I thought to myself. To Hannibal, I said: "I hope you ordered a good wine."

Hannibal grinned; He knew that I was teasing. "Yes, Madam," he responded. "Would you taste it to be sure?"

I made a big production of tasting the wine. After just a sip, I said: "It will do."

Hannibal just laughed. We put aside the case for a moment and enjoyed dinner and each other's company.

As we finished dinner, Hannibal and I discussed our findings. "Let's begin with our interview of Meier," I said.

"OK," responded Hannibal. "Meier said that Josef Baumer hosted a dinner at the mansion on the evening of November 16, the day before the murder."

Hannibal read his notes for a moment and then continued: "In addition to Meier, dinner guests included Fuchs, Rosen, Alfred Baumer, Mrs. Franz Baumer and Greta. Secretary Klein and servants Hofmann, Lehman and Becker were also present."

"Humm," I responded. "According to Meier, Josef Baumer made a little speech after dinner. He told everyone that the body of Kurt Hartmann, a high Nazi official involved in the rearmament program, had been found in the Tiergarten by the police. A pistol was in Hartmann's hand. The police had told Baumer that Hartmann had committed suicide."

"Yes," replied Hannibal. "Apparently, Baumer and Hartmann were friends. Josef revealed to his dinner guests that he had received a suicide letter from Hartmann in the mail that morning. He had written that his life was a despondent mess, and he was addicted to heroin and other drugs."

Hannibal paused and then said: "Both Meier and Klein recalled that Baumer then expressed anger over drugs administered by Fuchs to his wife before she died and also currently to Frau Franz Baumer."

I added: "According to Meier and confirmed by Klein, Baumer also said that Hartmann's letter confided disturbing details on the supplier of the heroin. Baumer's killer may have been searching for the letter. Fortunately for us, he didn't find it."

"Thanks to Bertha Becker," responded Hannibal with a smile. "Interesting relationship."

"Klein's comment about Alfred Baumer's demeanor at dinner was also interesting," I said. "Alfred was polite, but he didn't say a word to the elder Baumer, even when the elder Baumer tried to engage him in conversation."

"Yes," replied Hannibal. "Klein also said Alfred had a whispered conversation with Greta, the elder Baumer's niece. Both seemed very upset."

After another sip of wine, I said: "I'm not surprised. Our interview with Maria Lehmann provided details on Baumer family relationships."

"What a tangled web," agreed Hannibal. "Alfred is Josef Baumer's legally adopted son and heir to the family fortune. However, Alfred is secretly the elder Baumer's illegitimate son by the family's longtime cook, Bertha."

Hannibal continued: "According to Maria, Anna found out about Alfred years ago, but she forgave her husband and had no apparent ill will toward Bertha. Maria also said that the Baumer's had a satisfactory marriage, but no children of their own. Anna treated Alfred as her own son."

"Yes," I responded. "Also, according to Maria, until Anna's death, Alfred did not know that Josef Baumer was his biological father. He was always told that he was abandoned and taken in by Josef and Anna."

"Alfred admitted that Anna told him about his true relationship to Josef and Bertha on her deathbed," said Hannibal.

"Maria said that Alfred became estranged from his father after Anna's death," I added.

"Sad," responded Hannibal. "When we interviewed Bertha, she broke down, cried but confirmed the story about Alfred, along with giving us the Hartmann letter."

"I feel so sorry for Greta, Josef's niece," I continued. "She admitted that she and Alfred had a secret love affair. Until the day of the murder of her uncle, she did not know Alfred's true relationship to Josef."

"Humm," responded Hannibal. "Alfred and Greta are first cousins. I think both knew that their love affair could not continue, which explains the whispered conversation at dinner and Alfred's resentment of his father."

I had a lump in my throat, so I merely nodded after Hannibal's last comment.

Hannibal watched me carefully for a moment, as I recovered my composure. He then continued: "Klein and Meier witnessed Rosen rush out of Josef's office at just after 11:00 AM. From overheard words, the pair had a heated argument. Rosen insisted that he did not return until 3:00 PM, just before finding Josef's body."

"And the tread on the overshoes at the mansion entry match the tracks in the snow on the patio," I responded. "When we interviewed Rosen, he admitted that the overshoes that we found at the Baumer front door are his. However, he insisted that he had forgotten them when he left the mansion at 11:00 AM."

"Unfortunately for Rosen, no one at the mansion would confirm his story about the overshoes," I added.

"In addition, Rosen would not give us an explanation on his activities between 11:00 AM and 3:00 PM," said Hannibal. "He simply said that he was at his home, but offered no witnesses. He seemed very frightened."

"Yet we know the answer on his activities from other sources," I said. "My interview with Rabbi Aaron Feldmann, the man walking his dog, was most interesting."

Hannibal raised his eyebrows and waited.

"Rabbi Feldmann regularly walks his dog in the neighborhood near the Baumer mansion," I began. "He walked by the Rosen house just before 2:00 PM on the 17th."

"Did he see Rosen?" Hannibal asked.

"Yes," I replied. "Feldman said he saw a plainclothes man leading a team of Brownshirts to the Rosen house on November 17 at about 1:45 PM. Klaus Rosen answered the door. The Nazis went inside."

"Anything else?" Hannibal asked.

"According to Feldmann, he heard commotion and loud voices emanate from the house. He hid by some trees and watched. The Nazis left after about an hour."

Hannibal responded: "That's about 2:45. Did Rosen leave the house during that time?"

"No," I replied. "But Feldmann also said that he overheard some of the conversation as the Nazis left, including a name."

I paused and then added: "The plainclothes man called one of the Brownshirts Sturmführer Heinemann."

"How interesting," responded Hannibal. "Anything else?"

"Yes," I replied. "Feldmann said that he saw Alfred Baumer on the street near the Rosen home at about the same time as the commotion with the Nazis."

After a moment, I added: "Feldmann also said that has known Alfred since he was a child playing on the street. On November 17, Alfred seemed preoccupied and didn't notice him or the commotion at the Rosen house."

"Very interesting," responded Hannibal. "Did Feldmann provide a time?"

"Yes," I replied. "He saw Alfred continuously from 2:00 until about 2:45 PM. He also said that Alfred leisurely walked down the street, away from the Baumer mansion."

"Will Feldmann agree to provide a written statement?" Hannibal asked.

"Already done," I replied. "He promised me that he would deliver a written statement to the policeman on duty at the Baumer house by tomorrow morning."

"Good," responded Hannibal. "I will call our friend Sergeant Schmidt tonight; I have his home phone number. I'm sure he will see to it that Feldman's statement gets to Reischl."

"Also ask him to follow up on Sturmführer Heinemann," I said.

"Will do," replied Hannibal. He then leaned back in his chair and closed his eyes. Finally, he said: "Let's move on to Fuchs' activities on the day of the murder."

Hannibal leaned forward and looked at his notes for a moment. He then said: "According to Meier and Klein, Fuchs met with Josef Baumer in his office between noon and 12:30 PM. Although they couldn't hear the words, they said Baumer and Fuchs argued."

"Hummm," I replied. "Hofmann, who saw Fuchs in the hall, said that Fuchs looked very frustrated when he exited the front door of the mansion."

"Fuchs said that he returned to his office about a block away," mused Hannibal. "He said he received a phone call at his office from Hofmann about his meeting with Baumer at about 2:00 PM. Hofmann confirmed the phone call, but he said he made it on November 16, not the 17."

"Either man could be mistaken about the date," I responded. "Fortunately for Fuchs, Margarete Koch, his nurse, confirmed Fuchs version of the date, which places Fuchs in his office at 2:00 PM. She also said that Fuchs was in the office from 1:30 until 2:10 PM."

"How convenient," responded Hannibal. Fuchs arrived at the Baumer mansion at 2:18 PM." He paused and added: "Still, Koch works for Fuchs," replied Hannibal. "She could be covering for him."

"While you were talking to Koch in her office, I did a little snooping," I said, with my best mischievous expression.

"Oh?" responded Hannibal with a grin. "As I recall, you had excused yourself to go to the restroom. OK, what did you find?'

I chuckled and replied: "I searched Fuchs office instead. Nurse Koch had left her phone log on Fuchs' desk. The entries for November 17 are most interesting." Hannibal raised his eyebrows and waited patiently.

After a moment for suspense, I said: "One patient called at 2:00 PM on November 17. Koch had recorded the patient's name, address, phone number and future appointment date."

"Do you remember who it was and the phone number?" Hannibal asked.

"Of course," I replied. I gave Hannibal the name and number. "Would you please make a phone call?"

Hannibal immediately got up and walked into the hall to our phone.

Hannibal returned after a few minutes with a big grin on his face. "Most interesting," he said. "Herman Schwarz, the patient, said that when he called at 2:00 PM, Nurse Koch told him that the doctor was not in, and the next available appointment would be on November 19."

"Did Mr. Schwarz agree to make a statement in writing?" I asked.

"The duty policeman at the Baumer home will have it by tomorrow morning," replied Hannibal.

Hannibal and I paused as we digested food, wine and our facts. Finally, I broke the silence. "Tell me about Dictaphones and Gramophones," I said.

Hannibal smiled and replied: "Both machines are made by the Columbia Graphophone Company. They are very similar in design."

I nodded and waited. Hannibal continued. "The user of a Dictaphone presses a button, which starts the turning of a mounted cylinder. The user then speaks into a mouthpiece. The sound vibrates a membrane attached to a needle that cuts a groove in the wax surface of the cylinder. The needle inscribes a record of the sound vibrations on the cylinder."

"How does the secretary get the recorded message?" I asked.

Hannibal responded: "To replay and listen, the mouthpiece is detached and replaced with a pair of stethoscope-type earphones. The cylinder is turned on and the needle picks up the recorded sound from the cylinder. In turn, the needle vibrates the membrane, and the user listens through the stethoscope."

"OK, sounds straightforward," I replied. "What about Gramophones?"

"The Gramophone has a horn that amplifies recorded sound from a wax cylinder rather than a mouthpiece for recording and stethoscope earphones for listening. Otherwise, the two machines are essentially the same," replied Hannibal.

"Baumer had eight wax cylinders," I mused. "I suppose that the four cylinders for the Dictaphone are blank until the user records his or her voice."

"Yes," replied Hannibal. "I checked all of the cylinders. Baumer's collection of four cylinders for the Gramophone have recorded music of Bach, Wagner, Beethoven and Strauss. These cylinders have orange endcaps."

Hannibal paused and then said: "Baumer's Dictaphone cylinders have blue endcaps. They can be shaved by a special machine and reused. Only one had been used; the others were clean. The used cylinder was mounted on the Gramophone."

I thought a moment. Finally, I asked: "How long are the recordings?"

"All of the cylinders have a recording capacity of slightly over six minutes," Hannibal replied.

"Very good," I responded. "I think we are ready to lay out a timeline for the murder."

"Agree," replied Hannibal. We spent the next two hours writing our report and preparing briefing charts for Friday morning. We know the name of the killer.

## Friday evening, November 20

The meeting in the Präsidium conference room began precisely at 9:00 AM this morning. Attendees included Reischl, Reisinger, Raeder, Schmidt, Hannibal and me.

Raeder sat next to Reisinger, who was nervous. Raeder's face expressed confidence, bordering on cockiness.

After everyone had taken a seat, Reisinger handed Reischl a typed report. Reischl leafed through the report in silence for a couple of minutes.

Finally, Reischl laid the report on the table. He took a stack of additional reports from a briefcase by his chair and laid them on the table next to the Reisinger and Raeder report.

Reischl looked at Reisinger and said: "Detective Reisinger, please tell us about your findings." He then gave Raeder a bland look and added: "Feel free to add to the presentation as appropriate."

Reischl glanced over at me, and his eyes twinkled. He then leaned back in his chair, folded his hands in his lap, looked at the nervous Reisinger with a frown and waited.

Reisinger stood and began his narrative. "Based on the autopsy and other evidence, Josef Baumer was murdered in his office with a dagger between 2:00 and 3:00 PM on November 17. The dagger was taken from Baumer's collection, which was on display in his office."

Reisinger glanced around the table, ending with a glance at Reischl. Reischl nodded.

"Two people at the mansion do not have an alibi confirmed by witnesses for their whereabouts between 2:00 and 3:00 PM." Reisinger paused for effect and added: "These two are Alfred Baumer and Klaus Rosen."

Everyone remained silent for a moment; then Reischl said: "Proceed, Detective."

Reisinger gulped a little and continued: "Laboratory technicians took fingerprints at the crime scene, but none were found on the murder weapon. Fingerprints of everyone in the household were found at various locations in the office, but none provided evidence that linked a particular person to the murder."

Raeder stirred and interjected: "Alfred Baumer and Klaus Rosen both had motive for murder."

"Continue, Detective Reisinger," said Reischl.

Reisinger said: "Alfred was heir to the family fortune. According to several witnesses among the servants, Alfred recently found out that Josef was his biological father."

Reader added: "This relationship interfered with a love affair between Alfred and Greta, Josef's niece. The pair found out that they were first cousins. As a result, the romance ended, and father and son became estranged."

"And Rosen?" Asked Reischl.

Reisinger's confidence visibly improved as he glanced at Raeder and then back to Reischl. "Several members of the household overheard Rosen and Josef Baumer having a heated argument in Baumer's office between 10:00 and 11:00 AM on the day of the murder."

Raeder added: "Klein, Hofmann and Meier all agreed that Rosen stormed out of Baumer's office at 11:00 AM and left the mansion."

"What did Rosen say about the argument?" Reischl asked.

"He didn't say anything at all," Reisinger stated. "We asked several times." Reisinger paused, frowned and added: "He seemed frightened."

Raeder then said: "Laboratory technicians found footprints in the snow leading to and from the French doors to Baumer's office. The footprints matched a pair of overshoes found near the front door of the mansion."

Reisinger added: "Rosen admitted that the overshoes were his." He paused for effect and then said: "While Alfred Baumer and Klaus Rosen both had motive, Rosen had the best opportunity. Detective Raeder and I believe Rosen murdered Josef Baumer sometime between 2:18 and before 3:00 PM." Reisinger looked at Raeder, who smiled and nodded.

Reischl also smiled and said: "Why after 2:18 PM?"

"Dr. Fuchs arrived at the mansion at 2:18 PM," responded Reisinger. "Fuchs, Hofmann, Meier and Frau Franz Baumer all heard Baumer's voice, coming from Baumer's closed office, for several minutes during and after Fuchs' arrival."

Raeder added: "Fuchs, Hofmann, Meier and Frau Baumer all agree that Rosen returned to the mansion just before 3:00 PM, went directly to the office, opened the door and went inside. A few seconds later, he exited the office, loudly declaring the Baumer had been murdered."

Reisinger continued with a look of triumph. "Rosen entered the French doors to Baumer's office a few minutes past 2:18 PM, took a dagger from a display and stabbed Baumer in the back. He then rummaged through the desk, probably looking for some business papers."

Raeder added: "Rosen left the office through the French doors and walked around to the front of the mansion. Hofmann let him in the front door. Rosen went directly to Baumer's office and pretended to discover Josef Baumer's body."

Silence reigned for several minutes. Reisinger sat down. Finally, Reischl turned to Hannibal and then to me. He asked: "Do you have anything to add to Detective Reisinger's presentation?"

"Yes," Hannibal responded: "Klaus Rosen did not murder Josef Baumer. Neither did Alfred Baumer."

Reisinger's face had a blank look. Raeder sputtered and said: "But the evidence!"

Reischl looked intently at Raeder and said: "I believe you are acquainted with Sturmführer Heinemann." Raeder's mouth dropped open. He quickly closed it, but his face acquired an expression of surprise tinged with fear.

Reischl calmly turned to Sergeant Schmidt and said: "I read your report. Would you please summarize for us?"

Schmidt stood and said: "At the request of Major Jones, I located Heinemann. He talked proudly and freely about his visit to the Rosen residence between 1:45 and 2:45 PM on November 17." Schmidt paused and added: "The purpose of the visit was to frighten Rosen into selling his art collection at bargain prices. Rosen is a Jew."

Schmidt looked directly at Raeder, and added: "Rosen was at home during the entire time. Further, Heinemann said you led the team that entered Rosen's house." He paused and then said: "Heinemann signed an affidavit."

Raeder stood up, sputtered, started to say something, thought better of it and sat back down. Reisinger's blank look continued.

Schmidt said: "At a fast walk, it takes 10 minutes to walk from the Rosen house to the Baumer mansion." He looked at me, smiled and finished with: "I walked the distance myself to check."

Reischl smiled grimly. I could also detect a look of satisfaction. After a moment, he turned to me and asked: "If not Rosen, who murdered Josef Baumer?"

I glanced around the table and then said: "Major Jones and I verified that Alfred was nowhere near the mansion between 2:00 and 3:00 PM. Dr. Hans Fuchs is the murderer, not Rosen or Alfred. Major Jones and I are prepared to explain why and how Fuchs did it."

"Please do," replied Reischl.

Hannibal began. "Bertha Becker gave us a letter written by Hartmann that was addressed to Baumer. She stated that Josef Baumer had given it to her for safekeeping."

I added: "The letter reveals that for several years, Fuchs supplied Hartmann with heroin. Fuchs was blackmailing Hartmann over his addiction."

"Based on the testimony of Meier, Klein and Hofmann, Fuchs found out at the Baumer dinner on November 16 that Baumer had Hartmann's letter. Baumer therefore knew about Fuchs' relationship with Hartmann," said Hannibal.

I added: "Based on his anger and comments at dinner on the 16th, Josef most likely made the connection between Hartmann's addiction and the medications that Fuchs had provided to his wife and sister-in-law."

Hannibal continued the logic. "Almost certainly, that connection was the cause of Josef's argument with Fuchs on the 17th."

Reischl took a deep breath and nodded. Reisinger's face expressed dawning consternation. Raeder's glared, first at Hannibal, then me and then back to Hannibal.

Hannibal's steady gaze never wavered, and he said: "Fuchs met with Baumer in his office between noon and 12:30 PM on November 17. Since Becker already had the letter, he was unable to get the letter from Baumer."

Hannibal paused and added: "We don't know for sure, but it seems likely that Fuchs learned that Baumer intended to expose his activities with drugs and blackmail. Fuchs therefore had motive to kill Baumer."

I then said: "Fuchs left the mansion at 12:30 PM. Hofmann let him out the front door."

Hannibal picked up the narrative. "Since the overshoes are rubber, fingerprints do not show up. However, I found Fuchs fingerprints on the bench next to Rosen's overshoes. Although the evidence is circumstantial, Fuchs almost certainly picked up the overshoes."

"But what about the voice coming from Baumer's office at 2:18 PM?" Reisinger asked. Baumer was alive when Fuchs arrived at the front door of the mansion."

"No," replied Hannibal. "Fuchs had already murdered Baumer. At about 2:00 PM, Fuchs walked across the patio and through the French doors wearing Rosen's overshoes. He purposely left tracks in the snow on the patio."

"We don't know exactly what happened in the office," I said. "But Fuchs probably saw Baumer at his desk, reading documents.

He retrieved a dagger from the collection mounted on the wall and stabbed Baumer in the back, killing him instantly and without a sound."

Hannibal continued: "Fuchs then searched Baumer's desk and files to find the Hartmann letter, to no avail. He probably was in a panic, because someone might walk in the office at any moment."

"But what about the voice that Meier, Klein and the others heard at 2:18?' Reisinger asked again.

"The Dictaphone and Gramophone in the office provide the answer," I replied. "We found Fuchs' fingerprints on both machines and on one of the blue-capped cylinders normally used on the Dictaphone."

"The blue-capped cylinder with Fuchs' fingerprints was mounted on the Gramophone," Hannibal said. "It had been labeled, and it had a recording of Josef Baumer's voice."

I glanced at Reischl. His eyes had a knowing look. "Please continue," he said.

Hannibal nodded and responded: "Fuchs set up the Gramophone so it played the recording loud enough for the people in the library to hear Baumer's muffled voice. He turned on the Gramophone and departed through the French doors."

I picked up the narrative. "Fuchs took off Rosen's overshoes when he reached the bench near the front door of the mansion at just before 2:18 PM. He placed the overshoes where he found them and then knocked on the door."

Hannibal added: "Hofmann let him in. The Gramophone was still playing; Baumer's muffled voice was heard as Fuchs walked into the library and joined Klein and Meier."

I then said: "Fortuitously, Rosen arrived at the front door just before 3:00 PM. Hofmann let him in. Rosen then walked to the office, opened the door and discovered Baumer's body."

Reischl and Schmidt nodded affirmatively. Reisinger looked stunned. Raeder looked like a scared rabbit.

After a full minute of silence, Reischl said: "Clearly, Rosen did not murder Josef Baumer." He paused and added: "The evidence is sufficient to arrest Fuchs. Whether or not the evidence is enough to convict is for a court to decide."

Reischl looked at Schmidt, Hannibal and then me. He smiled openly. "Excellent work. Your reports, including photos, fingerprints and narrative, are logical and thorough."

He turned back to Schmidt and added: "I believe a promotion to Detective Sergeant is in order."

Schmidt grinned from ear to ear. Reisinger had a look of surprise and then consternation.

Reischl looked at Reisinger and said: "After this meeting, please see me in my office."

Reisinger gulped and replied: "Yes, Herr Chief Detective." Reischl glanced at me. I could see a twinkle in his eyes.

He then turned to Raeder, frowned and said: "You knew that Rosen could not have murdered Baumer." Raeder's mouth opened and closed several times, but nothing came out.

Reischl paused and added: "You will have an opportunity to explain your behavior to Poliezi President Albert Grzesinski. In the meantime, you are relieved of all duties in my department."

Raeder stood, started to say something, thought better of it, turned and left the conference room without another word. So ended a very satisfying meeting.

# 11

## THE FINE ART OF ESPIONAGE

*Saturday evening, November 28, 1931*

Friday evening was party time for the Nazis. They were beginning to dominate the Reichstag. I read in the Berlin newspapers that the celebration was in recognition of the recent founding of the Harzburg Front, which united the Nazis and other right-wing groups in opposition to the government of Chancellor Heinrich Brüning.

Hannibal and I were invited. Our host was Herman Göring, and we had received an engraved invitation. The party was set up in the Adlon ballroom, downstairs from our suite. Of course, we accepted; espionage requires association with the bad guys.

I spent all Friday afternoon preparing my clothes and primping in the bathroom. As I made myself beautiful, my mind tried to piece together the 'why?' of the invitation.

"Göring probably knows about our high-profile involvement in solving the serial killings in Mitte, the clash with communists during the murder of Polizeikapitän Anlauf and the arrest of Dr. Fuchs for the Baumer murder," I thought to myself.

"The solution to the serial killings and the clash with the communists probably made positive impressions with the Nazis; one of the serial victims was related to Josef Goebbels, and the Nazis and communists are mortal enemies," I mused.

"Our solution to the Baumer case is a mixed bag," my thoughts continued. "On the positive side, Fuchs, the murderer, was a blackmailer of Kurt Hartmann, a high-ranking Nazi. On the negative side, Detective Inspector Raeder was foiled in his attempt to frame Klaus Rosen, a Jew, for the murder."

My thoughts followed this thread: "Raeder procures valuable art for Göring, and he was unable to confiscate Rosen's art collection. So again, why did Göring invite us to the party?"

To this thought, there were alternative answers, and most were not good. "Oh, well," I concluded. "Wait and see."

I decided to wear my new Elsa Schiaparelli form-fitting gold silk gown with a slightly daring neckline. I had a pale gold floral Chantilly lace Mantilla wrap for pretend modesty. My gold-colored shoes, pale gold pearls and handbag, minus my Walther automatic, matched my dress perfectly.

"In my considered opinion, I am the epitome of high fashion," I decided.

Hannibal peeked in the bathroom as I was finishing up. "Ummm," he said. "You are beautiful."

I pirouetted and replied: "Thank you sir, you clean up pretty good yourself."

In his typical way, Hannibal blushed a little. He wore a formal black evening coat with tails, black trousers with a black satin stripe, a white tie and a silver cummerbund. In keeping with the style of the occasion, he also pinned on his rows of military medals over his right breast pocket.

Six o'clock arrived; we were fully primped and prepped; it was time to party.

Hannibal and I walked down the stairs into the ballroom a fashionable five minutes late. An orchestra played soft music by Strauss in the background. A footman greeted us and accepted our engraved invitation.

The footman gave the invitation to the Maître d'hôtel. In turn, the Maître d' announced the arrival of 'Major and Frau Jones from the United States.'

Nods, smiles and 'Willkommen' greeted us from nearby guests. Several men in the crowd stared and gave me a thorough up and down look. I smiled and gave them an aristocratic sniff.

Several ladies gave Hannibal a 'come-hither' look. I tossed my head a little and sniffed again. I glanced suspiciously at Hannibal, who smiled, but he remained the model of circumspect behavior. Hummf!

I spotted Göring across the room. He was wearing a resplendent black evening coat with SA Lieutenant General insignia, black trousers and white tie. His Pour le Mérite centered on his white shirt, and his two Iron Crosses and other medals were prominently displayed on his evening coat.

Göring looked the part of a classic Prussian warrior, dressed for attendance at some imperial court, which, from his proud bearing, was probably the impression he wanted to give.

I watched, as his icy-blue eyes strayed from his immediate companions and turned in my direction. At first, his eyes had an intense gaze, cold and calculating. After a few seconds, his face expressed a smile, and he walked over towards Hannibal and me.

As he started toward us, Hannibal whispered: "I read in the newspapers that Göring's wife Carin passed away last month."

"OK, Hannibal will use that," I surmised. "Follow his lead."

"Ah, Major Jones," said Göring as he approached and glanced at Hannibal's medals. "It is a pleasure to meet a fellow soldier with such a distinguished record." He extended his hand.

"The honor is mine," responded Hannibal. "Your exploits in aerial combat are well-known in America." The two men shook hands.

Göring's expression softened, and his smile broadened.

"Hannibal always knows exactly what to say," I thought to myself. "I hope I can match his performance."

Hannibal gave me a look that implied: "Göring has done his homework."

Hannibal then said: "Caroline, please meet Gruppenführer Göring of the Sturmabteilung." He paused, turned to Göring and said: "Herr Gruppenführer, please meet mein Frau, Caroline Case Jones."

Göring turned to me and his eyes glittered. I offered my hand. Göring took my hand gently, bent slightly at the waist and kissed it in a formal manner. He straightened and replied: "Ah, Frau Jones, I have heard so much about you." His smile broadened.

"It's an honor to meet a distinguished soldier and member of the Reichstag," I responded. My thoughts raced. "OK, what does he know?" To Göring, I smiled with a slightly condescending expression.

Göring turned to Hannibal and said: "You are so fortunate to have a beautiful and talented wife." His eyes misted a little as he paid the compliment; his emotion seemed genuine.

Hannibal caught Göring's expression and replied: "We are so sorry to hear about your recent loss of Frau Carin. She was a lovely and talented lady. We wish you and your family the best in this difficult time."

It was precisely the right thing to say, and Göring seemed touched. He choked a little, recovered and replied. "Yes, thank you for your concern."

He took a deep breath, turned to me, smiled again and said: "Your work with our Kriminal Polizei has been noticed by Dr. Goebbels and myself." He paused and then added: "Perhaps your abilities could be applied to a higher purpose." His eyes watched my face intently.

"Hannibal and I are collectors of European art," I replied. "Our travels will take us to many centers of culture in Germany and beyond."

Göring considered my careful but suggestive response for several moments. Finally, he said: "We have interests in common with art and perhaps other endeavors." His eyes glittered again.

"Oh, boy," I thought to myself. I glanced at Hannibal, and his eyebrows raised a little.

I decided to put the Raeder issue to rest, one way or another. "Detective Inspector Raeder said that you intend to expand your art collection," I said. "What genre excites your passion?" My memory of Göring's intense interest in Ziegler's nude at the Pergamon Gallery flashed in my mind.

Göring was caught off guard; my comment gave him two things to consider. His eyes flickered a little. "Ah yes," he finally responded. "Raeder is a good man, but lacks finesse. He will be reassigned to tasks more consistent with his talents."

I nodded, smiled and waited.

After a moment of silence, Göring continued in a voice that others could hear: "My art interests are entirely consistent with those of the Führer, who has said that art should glorify the German people and the Aryan race."

Göring's eyes twinkled and he added in a low voice meant only for Hannibal and me: "Of course, I sometimes take a broader view."

He glanced around the room and said: "Ah, there is Gurlitt." He pointed to a thin man with spectacles and added: "Gurlitt helps me with my art collections now." The thin man noticed Göring's pointing finger, smiled and bowed slightly.

"Whew!" My mind raced. "Göring has written off Raeder, and Hannibal and I still have the cover as art collectors." I looked Göring in the eyes and let my smile broaden a little.

Göring smiled, turned to Hannibal and said: "In your travels, perhaps you and your lovely wife will notice activities other than art exhibits that would be of interest to me in my official capacity."

There it was. We were being offered an opportunity to spy for the Nazis. My mind raced again. "Has Göring found out that we work for the French?" I looked at Hannibal, whose eyebrows had raised a little higher. "Does Göring want us to be double agents?"

Hannibal responded to Göring. "Perhaps," he replied carefully. "We will keep an open mind."

"Good, good," replied Göring. "Now I must attend to my other guests." He turned back to me, bowed slightly and added: "You look lovely tonight, Frau Jones. I hope to see you at other events."

Göring turned back to Hannibal. He continued to smile, but his eyes glittered again. He offered his hand and then said: "Until our next meeting."

Hannibal nodded and shook hands in a reserved and formal manner. Göring saw a nearby footman with a tray of champagne, motioned him over and said: "Champagne for my guests!"

The footman dutifully stepped up. Hannibal and I each took a glass. As we did so, Göring slipped away into the crowd.

I let out a long sigh. I hadn't realized that I had been holding my breath. I almost spilled my champagne.

Hannibal leaned over and whispered: "Well done." He gave me a quick hug.

I snuggled a little in response and then looked around the room. I spotted Göring, who was talking to a young man in a black uniform. I read his lips. I caught a name. My heart almost stopped, and I uttered: "Oh!"

Hannibal saw my reaction, leaned over, and whispered: "What's wrong?"

I nodded in Göring's direction. About the same time, Göring pointed discreetly in our direction for the benefit of his companion. The young man nodded.

I read Göring's lips again as he elaborated and repeated the name in the context of an instruction: "Kontaktieren Sie Marcel Villian. Lassen Sie ihn das Jones-Paar beobachten."

"Did you catch that?" I whispered to Hannibal.

"Um-hum," responded Hannibal. "Villian will be on our trail. Göring doesn't trust us."

"Oh, boy," I muttered again. Göring saw that I was looking in his direction. He smiled at me. I responded in kind and turned away. Fortunately, Magda Goebbels was walking in our direction.

"Ah, Caroline," said Magda, in her bubbly voice. "So nice to see you again! I hope you and your handsome husband have taken advantage of the wonderful art galleries in our capital city!" She gave Hannibal an appraising glance and then concentrated on me.

I chose to be cautious. "Good evening, Magda. Yes, we visited the Pergamon during an exhibit in January. We saw many lovely paintings by German artists."

Magda came close and whispered in my ear: "I hope you found a few paintings by more forward-looking artists." She smiled mischievously. "Not just the approved old masters, landscapes and stuffy old portraits."

"Hannibal and I do like impressionist and other modern works by Monet, Beckmann, Renoir, Pissarro, Liebermann, Nolde and others," I replied in a whisper. In a normal voice, I added: "Of course, we enjoy works by Böhmer, Wissel, Zeigler, Peiner, Kampf, Hommel and other traditional German artists." I watched for Magda's reaction.

Magda giggled and said: "I understand." She gave me a long look and her eyes twinkled.

I smiled in return, and waited.

"You attracted the attention of Herman Göring," whispered Magda. Her smile disappeared, and she added: "Be careful. Herr Göring is a collector of all types of art, usually stolen."

"Oh, my goodness," I whispered in return.

After watching me carefully for a moment, Magda continued: "I heard about the Baumer murder and Reader's failed attempt to confiscate Klaus Rosen's paintings for Göring." Magda paused for a moment and then added: "Göring does not forget."

As we were whispering, the thin, bespeckled man pointed out by Göring earlier approached Hannibal. Magda saw him and gave a grimace. She put her hand on my arm and whispered again: "That's Gurlitt. Be careful."

She then smiled and said for all to hear: "I am so glad you like paintings by Böhmer, Wissel, and Zeigler. So does the Führer."

With this last repartee, Magda nodded towards the approaching bespeckled man. She turned to me and said: Caroline, Hannibal, please meet Herr Hildebrand Gurlitt, the curator and managing director of the Kunstverein Gallery in Hamburg."

She then turned to Gurlitt and continued: "Herr Gurlitt, please meet my friends Major and Caroline Jones."

Gurlitt gave me a cold smile, bowed slightly and then turned and offered his limp hand to Hannibal. His stare at each of us was one of appraisal and slight suspicion. I didn't like him.

"Careful, Caroline," I thought to myself. Magda's warning echoed in my mind.

Hannibal shook hands and said: "Honored to meet you, Herr Gurlitt. Your reputation as a collector of fine paintings has impressed collectors throughout Europe."

"Hannibal should be a diplomat," I thought to myself. I then put on my best cocktail party smile and said: "We have heard so much about you, Herr Gurlitt. Perhaps you can tell us about your collection efforts."

Gurlitt's smile softened a little at the flattery. He sniffed, looked at Hannibal briefly and then turned to me. "Yes, well, the Führer's efforts to promote Aryan-inspired art consumes my time. Perhaps you can visit one of his sponsored events in the near future."

"Cold and arrogant," I concluded in my assessment. To Gurlitt, I smiled sweetly and replied: "Perhaps." Hannibal raised his eyebrows again.

Gurlitt puffed himself up and added: "Along with "Hauptsturmführer Bruno Lohse, I also help Gruppenführer Göring and others of the party enhance their private collections." He paused a moment, eyeing me carefully. I returned his stare.

He added: "Lohse is a member of the Schutzstaffel. They will become important in the future Reich. We are friends."

"Name dropping toad," I thought to myself. To Gurlitt, I smiled sweetly and said: "How nice!" I heard Hannibal as he suppressed a chuckle.

At that moment, a brief commotion at the far end of the ballroom caught my attention. Magda and Gurlitt both turned toward the raised voices and polite applause. Adolf Hitler had arrived. Gurlitt immediately forgot Hannibal and me and headed toward Hitler.

I muttered a couple of less than flattering words. Hannibal heard and chuckled again.

Hitler made the rounds to everyone in the room. I noticed that he did not shake hands. I glanced at Hannibal. He nodded; no words were needed.

Finally, our turn arrived. Magda made the introductions. "My Führer, please meet my friends Major and Frau Jones from the United States."

Hitler smiled briefly at me and bowed slightly. "Frau Jones, Magda told me about you. Welcome to Berlin." His voice was soft, very unlike the image I had from listening to his bombastic speeches on the Berlin radio. Mostly however, I saw his piercing, steady eyes. The look he gave me was almost hypnotic.

After a couple of seconds, he turned to Hannibal and gave him a sweeping look of appraisal. His eyes fixed on Hannibal's medals for a second or two, and then his gaze returned to Hannibal's face.

"I see that you served during the war," he said in a conversational, almost intimate voice. "It's always an honor to meet a fellow soldier from the trenches, even a former opponent."

"Indeed," responded Hannibal; his eyes met and held Hitler's gaze. "Your courage in battle is evident from your Iron Cross, both first and second class."

Hitler smiled, and Hannibal added: "Perhaps a better world will result from our efforts so long ago."

"Yes," replied Hitler. He turned his hypnotic stare back to me. "Frau Jones, I understand that you collect fine art. Enjoy your time in Berlin and in our many fine galleries."

With that, Hitler bowed slightly again and turned to other guests. Our meet and greet with Hitler had ended. I let out my breath slowly.

Shortly after meeting Hitler, Hannibal and I decided to say our formal goodbyes to Göring and of course, Magda.

We both wanted to leave the party without engaging with Gurlitt again. I caught a glimpse of him near Hitler, fawning over every word.

Göring wished us well in our art collection efforts and again, hinted about future contacts. Hannibal handled it in his usual non-committal way. Göring was left with a puzzled expression, which was precisely Hannibal's intent.

Our goodbye to Magda was last and the most enjoyable. She gave us warm smile and whispered: "Well! You have met the Führer. What do you think?"

I thought a moment and replied: "He has an intense, compelling personality; I can see why so many Germans follow him."

Magda's eyes twinkled and she replied: "Well-said." She touched my arm and for the third time, added: "Be careful!" In spite of her Nazi connections, I like her.

### Sunday morning, November 29

After leaving the party, Hannibal and I returned to our suite, took off our party clothes, freshened up, put on nightwear and soft luxurious robes and sat by our window overlooking Pariser Platz.

The street lights around the Platz glowed in the cold winter night. Snow drifted down from the blackness above and began to accumulate. For quite a while, we enjoyed the silence and each other's company.

I broke the silence. "Hitler's entourage, especially Göring and men like Gurlitt, will take advantage of their position if Hitler comes to power."

"Uh hum," agreed Hannibal. "Göring is a dangerous, very intelligent man." He paused, leaned back on the sofa, looked at me with a steady gaze and added: "He killed over twenty men in personal aerial combat, was wounded twice and has demonstrated utter ruthlessness in his rise to the top in the Nazi Party."

"If I read Hitler's book '*Mein Kampf* and interpret his speeches correctly, he won't mind if Göring, Gurlitt and others expand their art collections at the expense of wealthy Jews like the Fischers and Rosen," I replied.

"I fear for all Jews in Germany," responded Hannibal. "We should emphasize our suspicions in our next report to Soucet."

I shivered in spite of the warm room. After a moment, I responded: "Göring mentioned Villian to his aide, and he looked in our direction."

"I overheard Magda's warning to you," replied Hannibal. "And she is right."

Silence reigned for several minutes. Finally, I said: "I want you near me." I shivered again and then snuggled. Hannibal wrapped a protective arm around my shoulders.

We went to bed soon afterwards. I had fitful dreams; I kept seeing a sinister figure in the distance. He had a penetrating gaze, and he was waiting.

# 12

## FROZEN SHOPPERS

*Friday evening December 4, 1931*

More political turmoil. Hannibal and I discussed the situation after dinner this evening, as we sat by the window and sipped our second glasses of Kabinett.

"According to the newspapers and rumors in the detective squad room at the Präsidium, the Nazis are pushing to take over the government of the Free State of Prussia," I said.

"Flexing their muscles," replied Hannibal. "Brüning's days as German Chancellor are numbered."

"Reischl looked worried," I responded. "According to Reisinger, Raeder has been reinstated on the detective squad."

"Um Humm," mused Hannibal. "I would guess that Grzesinski's days as Poliezi President are also numbered; he was probably pressured into Raeder's reinstatement."

He paused and then added: "I expect the Nazis will see to it that one of their own takes over as Poliezi President."

"I heard the name 'Kurt Melcher,' the current head of the police in Essen, mentioned," I replied.

Hannibal nodded and said: "Berlin is a step up on the career ladder, but Melcher, or whoever, will be expected to support the Nazi party line."

"Soucet will be interested," I responded. "We need to tell him about the Nazi takeover of the police."

Hannibal nodded and replied: "Our report should provide names, dates and implications."

We were silent for a while as we watched out the window. Falling snow began to obscure the street lights around Pariser Platz. The Platz was deserted.

I put down my wine glass and said: "Gurlitt mentioned the Schutzstaffel at the party last week. Do you know about them?"

"A little," replied Hannibal. "From what I have read in Nazi newspapers, the Schutzstaffel, or SS, was originally a small guard unit that provided security for Nazi Party meetings and events."

Hannibal leaned back on the sofa and continued: "Goebbels newspaper *Der Angriff* said that since Heinrich Himmler took over in 1925, the SS has grown to over 200,000 men."

He paused and added: "I overheard gossip in the detective squad room that the SS will overshadow the SA soon."

"Sounds like intrigue," I mused. "Perhaps we should do more research on Heinrich Himmler."

"Yes," responded Hannibal. "Along with Göring and Goebbels, Himmler seems to be a rising star in the party."

We finished our wine; I wrote this entry in my diary, and soon we snuggled in bed. Hannibal's warmth was comforting.

## Sunday morning, December 6

Saturday was a shopping blitz. Berlin is so cold! We intended to buy more woolens at the big department stores around Leipziger Platz, but the blitz turned out quite different.

As Hannibal and I got out of our taxi in front of the big Wertheim store at the corner of Leipzigerstrasse and Volstrasse, the first thing we saw was a large contingent of SA Brownshirts.

Several carried signs that read: "Deutsche, verteidigen Sie sich gegen jüdische Propaganda - nur in deutschen Geschäften kaufen!" Others were accosting shoppers as they approached the Wertheim entryway. I heard one say: "Juden besitzen diesen Kaufhaus!"

"Oh my," I uttered. "The Nazis are pressuring shoppers to boycott Jewish-owned stores!" Some shoppers turned away, but others went inside the doors, in spite of Brownshirt curses.

"Um-Humm," Hannibal said in a low voice. "Let's go inside." Several of the Brownshirts glared at us as we slipped around them and through the doors.

Inside, Brownshirts harassed clerks and patrons. I spotted a familiar face. It was Raeder. He was in civilian clothes, but he was directing the activities of several Brownshirts.

"Hannibal, look!" I said in a low voice and pointed. I then added: "Turn, so he can't see us!"

Hannibal quickly spotted Raeder, and we slipped around a corner by a staircase. I glanced over my shoulder; Raeder gave no indication that he saw us.

Relieved, I watched surreptitiously with Hannibal as Raeder and his Brownshirts continued their harassment of bewildered clerks and shoppers.

"Raeder has been given duties consistent with his talents," I whispered to Hannibal. "I wonder what Reischl knows."

After a while, we moved off and left the store at one of the other entrances. We could see that the harassment continued outside as we caught a taxi.

As we drove off, I nudged Hannibal and said: "Look; entrances are being blocked by those beefy and belligerent Brownshirts. Shoppers who are trying to get inside are being forced to stand out in the cold."

"I wonder about the other department stores," replied Hannibal. Wertheim, Tietz and Kaufhaus des Westens are all owned by Jews."

"The three biggest stores in Germany," I mused. "Where is this going?"

"Not good," responded Hannibal. "The Nazis may try other ways to pressure the Jewish owners." We were silent, each absorbed in thought, as the taxi headed back toward the Adlon.

## Monday evening, December 7

Hannibal and I drove over to the Präsidium this morning. Soon we were in Reischl's office. In a low voice, Hannibal explained what we had witnessed on Saturday.

Reischl listened attentively. When Hannibal finished, he got up from his chair and paced back and forth for a minute or so.

Finally, he stopped, looked at me and then Hannibal. His face was ashen. He took a deep breath and let it out slowly. He then said: "I know. My hands are tied."

Silence reigned, and I stared at Reischl. After a moment, he added: "Do what you have to do. In the meantime, I hope you will continue to help me on criminal cases."

I was astounded. "Reischl knows about our relationship with Soucet, and he has put two and two together," my thoughts raced.

"You will not betray us?" I blurted.

Reischl smiled at me and replied: "No." He then looked at Hannibal and said in a low voice: "I will shield you as long as I can."

## Christmas Eve, December 24, 1931

The Nazis are having a party downstairs in the hotel ballroom. Magda invited us, but we declined. I had said that I had a cold, which was true. However, the real reason was that both Hannibal and I thought of Christmas Eve as something special, and the Nazis didn't fit with the occasion.

We stayed in our room, dressed in casual holiday sweaters and slacks and ordered a light dinner from room service. We chose a crisp French chardonnay instead of a heavier, sweeter Riesling.

After dinner, we settled on the sofa and exchanged gifts. Hannibal gave me a lovely set of ruby earrings and a matching pendant on a platinum chain. I gave him a pair of woolen socks.

Hannibal carried off the exchange with his usual aplomb and thanked me for my 'very practical gift.'

I burst out laughing between sniffles; I still had a cold. Finally, I said: "Look inside the socks."

Hannibal gave me a quizzical look and then put his hand inside one of the socks. A look of surprise appeared on his face as he drew out a small box.

He looked at me, grinned and opened the box. His face lit up like a Christmas tree. "Oh!" he exclaimed. He took out a set of gold cufflinks with his engraved initials.

"You sneaky, loveable Santa's elf," he finally said. "They are beautiful."

I leaned over and kissed him on the cheek, amid a couple of sniffles. It was so nice to forget our duties for a while.

## Christmas afternoon, December 25

What a beautiful morning! My sniffles have subsided. We got up early and had coffee by the window. The scene outside was brilliant, with new snow and a clear blue sky. Merry Christmas!

"After breakfast, let's walk around the Platz," I said, as we both sipped hot coffee.

"Room service is on the way," responded Hannibal. "Think you can get dressed before we go out?"

Hannibal gave me a quick up and down look. I was still in my robe, which was open, and I wore a very skimpy negligée underneath.

"Yes, Smarty," I replied, as I gave him a snooty look and closed my robe. Hannibal just laughed.

After breakfast, I fulfilled my promise and dressed in warm wool and fur. Hannibal did the same. We went downstairs and outside into the sunshine.

Hannibal hurried down the steps from the hotel entrance ahead of me. He made a snowball. Not to be outdone, I did the same. We heard giggles from down the sidewalk to the right. A well-dressed couple with two small, bundled up children were watching us.

Hannibal and I exchanged shots. My snowball found its mark; I ducked and Hannibal missed. The children burst out laughing.

I sauntered down the steps toward Hannibal, laughing as I approached.

"Oh!" I exclaimed. My heart nearly stopped. Hannibal gave me a puzzled look. The cause of my exclamation was a man, standing by the corner of the building to the left, behind Hannibal. Hannibal saw my stare and turned.

I recognized the man just before he slipped behind the corner of the building. "Neatly dressed, medium height, handsome yet sinister face, penetrating gaze and a white scar on his left cheek," my thoughts raced. "Just like the photo."

Hannibal and I hurried to the corner. We reached the spot and looked around. Villian was gone.

# 13

## CREATE A MARTYR

*Monday evening,* December 28, 1931

Hannibal and I drove to the Präsidium this morning. The squad room was deserted, but Reischl was in his office. He looked up from his work as Hannibal tapped gently on the door frame.

Reischl smiled and said: "Good morning. Come in. I trust you had a good Christmas?"

"Yes and no," responded Hannibal. "The holiday was enjoyable, but we are being watched by an old nemesis." He then briefly explained about Villian.

Reischl rose from his chair, walked to the window and stared outside for a while. He then turned and looked first at Hannibal and then me. His eyes were steady. "Villian is one of Göring's assassins."

I was astounded. Reischl was a policeman, yet he knew that a political leader, ostensibly subject to the law, used assassins.

Reischl smiled grimly; I'm sure he read my expression of surprise correctly. "I have no evidence," he responded. "Further, even if I did and pursued the matter, the result would be my own demise."

He paused, and his eyes expressed a slightly pleading look. "I do what I can; you two are one of my few avenues of obtaining justice."

Reischl then looked back to Hannibal and said: "I think Villian has a watching assignment. Otherwise, you would be dead already."

I gasped a little, I couldn't help it. Reischl continued: "I have a source close to Göring." His expression remained steady. "I will check out my suspicions and give you an update."

Hannibal looked at me for a moment. I nodded; I knew what he was going to say.

Hannibal turned to Reischl and responded: "Thank you. In the meantime, Caroline and I will do our best to avoid arousing more suspicions among the Nazis."

Reischl replied: "Yes. Your seminars for my detectives are safe enough. Also, your presence at Nazi social functions will continue to allay suspicions." He looked at me, smiled and added: "You both make good impressions at parties."

My mouth dropped open, but I quickly closed it. "Reischl's knows and observes," I thought to myself. "Who is his spy in the inner circle?" I looked closely at Reischl's eyes. They twinkled a little.

"I'm sure Reischl knows that Hannibal will update Soucet on Villian," I thought to myself.

We were silent for a few moments. "Time to break the somber spell," my thoughts continued. I looked first at Hannibal and then Reischl and said: "Can I still go shopping?"

Both men laughed, and I'm sure they understood my intent.

## Monday evening, January 25, 1932

I saw the headline in *Der Angriff* this morning. Herbert Norkus, a member of the Nazi Youth, was brutally murdered yesterday. He died at the Moabiter Hospital. I read the article out loud to Hannibal as he drove us to the Präsidium.

As soon as we arrived, Reischl called us into his office. "I want you to lead an investigation into the Norkus affair," he said. Of course, Hannibal and I agreed.

The three of us understood the implications. In addition to solving the case, the outcome could improve our reputation among the Nazis, especially with Göring.

In a paternalistic way, Reischl added: "Detective Inspector Reisinger and Detective Sergeant Schmidt will assist."

"Reischl wants both men to learn from us and remain true policemen rather than minions for the Nazis," I thought to myself. "Good," I concluded.

Reischl called a meeting in his office at 9:00 AM. In addition to Reischl, Hannibal and me, Reisinger and Schmidt attended.

After the usual preliminaries and visits to a pot of coffee on the side table, we all found seats. Reischl began: "Detective Sergeant Schmidt, you visited the Moabiter Hospital last evening. Will you please state the facts of the case to date?"

As usual, Schmidt was ahead of the game. He stood, leafed through his notes and began. "I interviewed Albert Klein, the investigating constable, and two of the companions of Herbert Norkus, the victim."

He looked around the table. Reischl nodded and said: "Proceed."

Schmidt cleared his throat and continued: "At 6:00 PM on January 24, the Moabit Police Station received a telephone call from the Moabiter Hospital. Constable Klein responded to the call. Upon arrival and initial assessment, Klein called the station and requested support from the Präsidium. I answered the call, and arrived at the hospital at 6:45 PM."

Schmidt paused and looked at Reischl. Reischl nodded, and Schmidt continued. "When I arrived, the waiting area next to the emergency room was crowded with members of the Hitler Jugend, Bund deutscher Arbeiteringend."

"Ah, Hitler Youth," I translated to myself. "Hitler's teen-aged street fighters." I returned my attention to Schmidt.

"I recognized Hauptgefolgschaftsführer Klingemann, a Jugend unit leader from Mitte, who seemed to be in charge," Schmidt added.

Schmidt paused, looked around the table and continued. "Klingemann stated that one of the Jugend members from the Tiergarten neighborhood named Herbert Norkus had been killed by members of the Rote Jungfront, the youth organization of Roter Frontkämpferbund, the paramilitary arm of the German Communist Party."

"Circumstances of the killing?" Reischl asked.

"Klingemann introduced me to fourteen-year-old Johannes Kirsch, who was with Norkus when they were attacked," replied Schmidt. "I have his written statement and his address in Tiergarten." Schmidt took out a sheaf of papers from his stack of notes and glanced through them.

"According to Kirsch, during the evening of January 24, he and Herbert Norkus were distributing leaflets that advertised a forthcoming Nazi rally. At about 4:00 PM, he and Norkus were working alone on Zwingli Strasse, when they were confronted by a gang of about forty young street toughs."

Schmidt scanned his papers again and continued: "Kirsch recognized some of the gang as members of the Rote Jungfront. One shouted: Still stehen!"

Schmidt paused. He had everyone's rapt attention. "Kirsch went on to say that he defiantly put one of his leaflets into the doorway mail drop of a nearby apartment house. As he turned to flee, one of the threatening gang members leaped upon him, striking him in the back."

Schmidt looked at Reischl, who nodded. Schmidt continued: "Kirsch said he went down, but he managed to regain his footing. He fled into a dark alley and hid behind a garbage can. He saw Norkus fleeing down Zwingli Strasse with a large group of the gang chasing him."

Schmidt flipped through several pages and added: "From a distance, Kirsch said that he saw several gang members knock Norkus down next to an apartment building and begin kicking him."

The room was silent as everyone visualized the brutality of the attack.

Schmidt continued: "After several minutes, Norkus broke loose and ran up the steps of the apartment building. Kirsch said he saw a man open the door. When the man saw the gang, he slammed the door. The gang knocked Norkus down again and viciously beat and kicked him."

Schmidt flipped another page and said: "Kirsch said he then ran back out on the street away from the fight yelling for help. No one came, and he did not see any more of the fight between Norkus and the gang. In his statement, he said the address of the apartment building where he last saw Norkus was Zwingli Strasse Number 3."

The room was silent as everyone digested Schmidt's vivid narrative. After a moment, I asked: "Did you meet anyone else at the hospital? I read the *Der Angriff* editorial this morning."

"Yes," replied Schmidt, and he smiled ruefully. "While I was talking to Kirsch, Dr. Goebbels arrived. Both Klingemann and Kirsch immediately scurried over to Goebbels. I was not able to get anything else out of them."

"That explains this morning's editorial," I responded. "Goebbels has all of the details."

"Did you visit the crime scene on Zwingli Strasse?" Reischl asked.

"Only briefly," replied Schmidt. "At about 7:30 PM, Constable Klein and I drove over to Zwingli Strasse and stopped in front of Number 3. A dim streetlight provided illumination. We saw bloody handprints on the building façade and blood smears on the cobblestones."

Schmidt stopped his narrative. "And?" I asked.

"A large gang of street toughs showed up. I lost count after thirty. I recognized several members of the Rote Jungfront." Schmidt paused, collecting his thoughts. "I saw Herbert Klingbeil, Werner Simon and Harry Tack from Mitte, Herman Lessing from Neukölln,

Alfred Scherlinski and Otto Singer from Fischerkietz and Alfred Richte from Wedding."

I marveled at Schmidt's attention to detail and recall. "His recent promotion was well-deserved," I thought to myself.

Anticipating my next question, Schmidt said: "Klein and I were unarmed and outnumbered. We drove away, back to the Mitte station. I dropped off Klein and returned to the Präsidium."

We were all silent for several moments. Finally, Reischl said: "Very good, Detective Schmidt. Excellent report." I glanced over at Reisinger, who sat with his mouth open. He saw my glance and closed his mouth.

Hannibal ended the silence by saying: "I suggest that we visit the neighborhood of the killing during daylight." He paused for a moment and added: "We need evidence and independent witnesses before we can conclude whether or not the assailants were communists. We also need names."

I added: "Hospital staff can confirm the time and probable cause of death. To build our case, we will need the official autopsy."

"We have files and photos on known communist agitators and common street delinquents in Mitte and surrounding districts," said Reisinger. He had recovered from his awe of Schmidt's performance.

He added: "I can review the files and photos. We can show relevant photos to the persons we interview."

Reischl smiled at Reisinger and said: "Good." He turned to Hannibal and added: "Major Jones, please make assignments and continue."

Hannibal nodded and then looked at Reisinger. "Detective Reisinger, please obtain the photos that you described. Summarize the contents of the files. Each of our new files should contain a photo and a brief description of the person, including affiliations." Hannibal added: "Also, please build a file on Norkus, the victim."

Reisinger nodded in agreement.

He turned to Schmidt. "Detective Schmidt, would you follow up with the hospital? We need the autopsy report."

Schmidt smiled and nodded. I could tell he was determined to prove himself. Good for him.

Hannibal then looked at me. His eyes twinkled. He said: "Ms. Jones and I will walk the neighborhood of the killing. Later, we will lay out detailed interview assignments."

He paused and added: "Shall we meet in the conference room at 2:00 PM tomorrow?"

Everyone rose. Reischl smiled at Hannibal and said: "This meeting is adjourned. Major Jones, please keep me posted on your progress."

## Tuesday evening, January 26

Our meeting at the Präsidium went well today. Reisinger provided summary files with photos and Schmidt had the autopsy report. Hannibal and I had a written report and notes on our visit to the crime scene. Reischl attended, but let Hannibal run the meeting.

Hannibal asked Reisinger to brief us on his files.

Reisinger began by summarizing the file on Norkus. "Herbert Norkus was a member of the Hitler Jugend. According to Kirsch, his comrades nicknamed him 'Quex' because he carried out orders faster than quicksilver. He was born to a working-class family in the Tiergarten District."

Reisinger flipped through the file and continued: "Herbert's father identified his son's body at the Moabiter Hospital. The father is a semi-invalid; he had been wounded during the World War. After the war, he initially had communist sympathies, but later became a member of the SA Brownshirts. The elder Norkus opposed his son's Nazi activities because of the danger." Reisinger stopped and looked at Hannibal.

"Very good, Detective Reisinger," said Hannibal. "The other files?"

Reisinger summarized files on Rote Jungfront members Herbert Klingbeil, Werner Simon, Harry Tack, Herman Lessing, Alfred Scherlinski, Otto Singer and Alfred Richte. Reisinger beamed when he saw Reischl smile.

Hannibal then asked Schmidt to present the autopsy report.

"There are no surprises," said Schmidt. "Norkus died of massive internal bleeding caused by a severe beating and four stab wounds in his lungs and abdomen."

After Schmidt finished, he looked over at Reisinger. Both men smiled. Good! I looked over at Reischl. His eyes twinkled.

Hannibal then looked at me and said: "Caroline, would you please begin the narrative on our findings at Zwingli Strasse Numbers 3 and 4?"

I smiled at Hannibal. I just loved the way he handled a set-piece meeting. His eyes twinkled, just like Reischl.

I cleared my throat and began. "We visited Zwingli Strasse Number 3. No one was home. We then went next door to Zwingli Strasse Number 4. A young lady named Marie Jobs answered the door."

I paused and glanced at Reisinger and then Schmidt. I could tell that having a woman detective speak with confidence and authority was novel experience for them. However, they listened attentively.

I continued. "Marie said that on the evening of January 24, she was awakened from a nap by the sound of yelling and pounding outside the building. She hurried through her apartment door and found her mother bending over the crumpled body of a boy in the corridor leading from the building doorway."

I glanced at Reischl. He was paying rapt attention. I smiled, returned his gaze and said: "Marie said she heard the boy gasp: 'Help me, I've been attacked.' Marie said she then went to the building doorway. Outside, she saw a gang of many youths. One yelled: 'He's done for, let's go!' The gang then ran down the street into the darkness."

I looked over at Hannibal, who picked up the narrative: "In the meantime, Marie's mother called a friend who operated a taxi service. When the taxi arrived, the driver helped the two women load the bleeding and battered boy inside."

I continued by saying: "I showed the two women a photo of Herbert Norkus. Both women identified the image as the boy in the corridor."

Hannibal added: "They also gave us the phone number and name of the taxi driver." He paused and then said: "We contacted and interviewed the driver. His name is Reinholf Schuber, and he said that he drove the boy, who he identified as Norkus from the photo, to the emergency entrance of Moabiter Municipal Hospital."

"After we finished with the taxi driver, we drove to the hospital, I said. "The hospital staff confirmed that Norkus died shortly after 5:30 PM."

Silence. Finally, Reischl looked at Reisinger and then Schmidt. "Good police work. Such details, presented in a written report, are necessary to build a case for prosecution." Both men nodded. Reischl turned to Hannibal and waited.

"We need follow-up interviews, said Hannibal. "Detectives Reisinger and Schmidt, would you please take the files on gang members and re-visit Marie Jobs and her mother?"

Both men nodded; they seemed aware that they were being tested on proper police procedure.

Hannibal continued: "Also, please re-visit the taxi driver and Johannes Kirsch." He paused and looked at Reischl, who smiled. Hannibal then said: "Let's meet back here tomorrow at 2:00 PM."

The meeting ended. The two young detectives hurried off on their joint assignment.

## Thursday evening, January 28

The team met again on Wednesday at 2:00 PM, as scheduled. Reisinger and Schmidt had completed their assignment. We know the names of the killers.

Again, Reischl let Hannibal run the meeting. Reisinger and Schmidt worked as a team to present their written report, which, based on Reischl's smiles, was exactly what he had in mind.

Reisinger began the discussion. "Detective Schmidt and I visited Marie Jobs and her mother yesterday evening. They picked out three of the photos from our collection."

He paused, looked at each of us in turn and continued: "The two women said that Herbert Klingbeil, Werner Simon and Harry Tack were very close to the apartment door when they looked out at the gang. Klingbeil had a knife in his hand and blood on his shirt. The other two had blood spatters on their uniforms."

Schmidt continued the narrative: "Next, we interviewed Schuber, the taxi driver. He also picked out Klingbeil, Simon and Tack. They were lurking in the alley near Zwingli Strasse Number 4 as he drove off toward the hospital with Norkus. The trio stepped out in the street and made threatening gestures. Schuber stated that he saw blood on their hands and uniforms."

"Did Schuber and the Job women have contact after the evening of January 24?" I asked.

Reisinger smiled with a slight look of triumph. "No," he replied. "We asked similar questions at both interviews, but their recollections are independent."

"Did the Job women or Schuber identify anyone else from your photos?" Hannibal asked.

"No," replied Schmidt; "both said the larger group hung back across the street, out of the illumination of the streetlight. However, the two women estimated the gang as having thirty to forty members."

"How about your interview with Johannes Kirsch?" I asked.

"I interviewed Kirsch at his parent's home in Tiergarten," replied Reisinger. "He identified Alfred Richte as the youth who initially threatened him and hit him in the back. However, he did not identify anyone else."

Everyone was silent for a while. Finally, Hannibal said: "We have motive; the Hitler Jugend and the Rote Jungfront are well-documented mortal enemies. Klingbeil, Simon, Tack and Richte are known members of the Rote Jungfront. We also have opportunity; the four were identified at the scene of the murder."

"We do not have a knife or other weapon, and the culprits will undoubtedly wash out or dispose of their bloody clothing," I added. "Still, I think we have enough for arrests."

Everyone looked at Reischl. After a moment of consideration, he said: "I agree. I will obtain warrants." He looked around the table and added: "Good job, everyone." Reisinger and Schmidt grinned from ear to ear.

Reischl looked at Hannibal and then me. He said: "Major and Mrs. Jones, will you join me in my office?"

He then looked at Reisinger and Schmidt. "Please finish up with written reports and summaries suitable for presentation in court. I expect your work on my desk by Monday morning."

Both young men still grinned from ear to ear. They got up from the conference table, collected their files and notes. I could hear them talking as they passed out into the squad room.

"Mission accomplished," I stated matter-of-factly. Both Hannibal and Reischl laughed.

The three of us adjourned to Reischl's office. Reischl had fresh coffee already available on a side table. After we each got a re-fill, we made ourselves comfortable in soft chairs close together.

Hannibal and I waited for Reischl to speak. After several sips of coffee, he said: "I have good news. My contact in Göring's inner circle told me that Villian has a watching brief only. Göring is not sure about you two, but I think, as you Americans say, you will be OK, at least for now."

I thought a moment and said: "Villian wanted us to see him. Göring was sending a warning."

Hannibal looked at me and raised his eyebrows. Reischl smiled and said: "You may be right."

Both Hannibal and I let out sighs of relief. After a moment, Hannibal said: "Our work on the Norkus case should help alleviate Göring's suspicions."

"Definitely," responded Reischl with a smile. His expression clouded a little, and he added: "However, I doubt that the killers will ever come to trial. They will either disappear into hiding as a result of Communist Party efforts or be killed in continued street fighting."

I sipped my coffee again and mused: "The Nazis have another martyr."

We were silent for several minutes. Finally, Hannibal looked at Reischl and asked: "Have things gone that far?"

Reischl sighed and replied: "Yes, and I fear for my country."

I wanted to change the mood. After all, we just had a successful investigation. I asked: "Who is your contact with regard to Göring?"

Both Hannibal and Reischl burst into laughter. After gaining control, Hannibal said: "Nosy!" Reischl's laughter finally subsided, and he leaned over and whispered in my ear.

I leaned back and replied: "Just as I thought." I then looked at Hannibal and gave him my best snooty expression. Reischl laughed again.

# 14

## LOW STREETS AND HIGH CRIMES

*Saturday evening, January 30, 1932*

Herbert Norkus was buried in the Sankt Johannes Friedhoff II Cemetery in Berlin's Wedding District yesterday. Hannibal and I watched the street violence from various points at safe distances.

What a spectacle! Thousands of Hitler Youth and SA Brownshirts marched through Berlin's communist districts in Wedding and Moabit. They dared communists to step into the streets. Here and there, we observed scuffles between rival gangs. We did not see any uniformed police.

Goebbels made the most of his newly created martyr in *Der Angriff*. According to Goebbels' editorials, Nazis participated in 'spontaneous' demonstrations and speeches about the heroic youth in cities throughout Germany.

Klingbeil, Simon and Tack have not been found and arrested for the Norkus murder, despite a nationwide manhunt. Reischl said they will likely be tried in absentia in the Landgericht court in Moabit.

*Friday evening, February 26*

Alfred Richte, the gang member who led the attack on Norkus and Kirsch, was arrested two weeks ago. Within a week, he was convicted by the Landgericht court of accessory to murder and crimes against the state. He was given a twenty-year sentence. According to Reischl, Richte probably won't survive in prison.

Reischl wisely keeps his detectives out of the line of fire on the streets. Investigations of murders have dropped off significantly. Violence between Nazi and communist gangs are not reported to the police by either side.

Reisinger and Schmidt do a good job as a team on routine street crimes. Hannibal and I continue to consult on cases and provide seminars on crime scene investigation and processing.

## Friday evening, March 18

Two weeks ago, Samuel von Fischer, our Jewish publisher friend, called us at our hotel suite. Hannibal answered the phone. I listened on the extension in the bedroom. Fischer was frightened.

In a shaky voice, he said: "The Nazis are about to confiscate the art collections of my friends Alfred and Betty Flechtheim, Karl and Amelia Rosen and Aaron and Rosa Samuelson."

"My friends desperately want to leave Germany," Fischer continued. "They need cash for bribes and immigration permits. I am under surveillance and can't help them."

The next day, Hannibal sent a secret message to Soucet. With Soucet's connivence, Hannibal paid all three families more than fair prices for several paintings each. He deposited payments in newly opened accounts in Geneva. He notified the families through Fischer.

Through the French Embassy, Soucet contacted a small delivery company. Our new paintings were quietly picked up at night and secretly delivered to the embassy. The next day, they were shipped off to Paris through diplomatic channels.

Soucet sent a message back that he stored the paintings in a bank vault for safekeeping. I don't think the Nazis spotted the activity.

Yesterday, Fischer called us again. Hannibal answered, and I picked up the extension in the bedroom.

In a grateful voice, Fischer said: "The Flechtheim and Rosen families have made it to Switzerland. Thanks to you, they were able to draw on their new accounts in Geneva, finance their immigration and set up living arrangements in Switzerland."

There was a pause. I could hear Fischer's labored breathing through the phone. After a full minute, Fischer continued: "Aaron and Rosa Samuelson have disappeared. Their house is empty of people, furniture and possessions."

After another pause, he added: "I talked to their frightened servants at the synagogue today. The Nazis took the remainder of the Samuelson art collection."

Hannibal asked: "Do you know the names of the Nazis who pressured your friends?"

"Yes," replied Fischer. "The servants said that Hildebrand Gurlitt and Bruno Lohse led a group of SA Brownshirts."

"Surprise!" I thought to myself. "We met both men at Göring's party."

Fischer continued: "Lohse was particularly threatening. He wore an SA Hauptsturmführer uniform."

There was a pause on the phone. After a moment, Fischer added: "Gurlitt and Lohse were accompanied by a shadowy character named Günther Kellerman. He was in civilian clothes."

This morning, Hannibal sent the three names to Soucet through the usual channels. This evening, Soucet sent a message that French operatives will watch the three men.

So far, our undercover Jewish contacts and art purchases don't seem to have attracted Nazi attention. However, we are playing a dangerous game. I constantly look around as we move about Berlin, but I have not seen Villian since Christmas Day.

Reischl is probably aware of what we did with regard to the three Jewish families. I think he secretly approves, but he has not said anything.

## Friday evening, April 8

We attended another Nazi-sponsored party last Saturday. Magda was her usual bubbly self, and husband Josef complimented us on our work on the Norkus case.

Göring was enthusiastic about Hitler's showing in the presidential election on March 13; he will compete with von Hindenburg in a run-off on April 10.

No hint of suspicion about our activities. I think the Nazis are too busy campaigning for the next election to bother with us.

## Tuesday evening, May 31

Newspaper headlines! Hitler was defeated in the second-round Presidential election in April by von Hindenburg, who won by a narrow margin.

Goebbels published an editorial in *Der Angriff* today that von Hindenburg dismissed Brüning as Chancellor. According to Goebbels, Franz von Papen will replace Brüning. Von Papen is a renegade from the Centre Party. He will head a non-partisan 'Cabinet of Barons.'

Hannibal's contact at the Reichbank phoned last week. A transfer of 50 thousand marks from a Nazi account was sent to Villian's account in the Sant Joan de Labritja Bank on the island of Ibiza.

Hannibal notified Soucet about the transfer. Soucet sent word today that 25 thousand was withdrawn from the account just after it was deposited. Is Villian back in Spain?

## Friday evening, June 3

According to Goebbels' editorial today, von Papen's cabinet has almost no political support. Only three days after his appointment, he had von Hindenburg dissolve the Reichstag and call for new elections on July 31. As a result, the Reichstag cannot dismiss him immediately.

## Friday evening, July 1

More headlines. Following a policy of appeasing the Nazis, von Papen's government lifted a ban on the SA and SS, which had been in place since April.

*Der Angriff* reported riots and open street fighting between Nazis and communists in Berlin again. Goebbels was ecstatic in his editorial praise of the Nazi prowess in street fighting.

## Friday evening, July 22

Last week, Berlin newspapers reported that an SA and SS demonstration in the city of Altona was approved by Prussian police president Otto Eggerstedt. Despite threats by the communists, the Nazis scheduled the demonstration for July 18.

On July 18, *Der Angriff* headlines reported a massacre in Altona. The demonstration had triggered a major confrontation between Nazis and Altona's communist residents. According to the article, 18 people, including two SA members, were killed.

Two days after the massacre, Berlin newspapers reported that von Papen had stripped Prussia of its status as a German province. He appointed himself Reichskommissar and dismissed all Prussian government ministers on the grounds that they had failed to prevent fresh street violence.

*Der Angriff* was reserved in its praise of von Papen's action. Goebbels' editorial hinted that von Papen does not fully support the Nazi political agenda. I think that without full Nazi support, von Papen's days as chancellor are numbered.

## Friday evening, August 5

Newspapers were full of election reports. With 230 seats, the Nazis have become the largest party in the Reichstag. However, neither the Nazis nor von Hindenburg's coalition of conservative parties could muster a governing majority.

Other parties refuse to co-operate with the Nazis, which means that no coalition government can be formed. Von Papen's minority government continues in office.

## Friday evening, September 16

Berlin newspapers reported that von Papen asked von Hindenburg to dissolve the Reichstag in order to pre-empt a motion of no confidence introduced by the Communist Party. Hindenburg agreed. Elections are scheduled for November 6.

## Friday evening, November 11

Federal elections were held in Germany last week. Most Berlin newspapers pointed out that the Nazis lost 34 seats and failed to form a coalition government in the Reichstag.

*Der Angriff* took a different tack, emphasizing that the Nazis took 33 percent of the vote, and they remain the largest party. Goebbels also reported that von Hindenburg is considering General Kurt von Schleicher as a replacement for von Papen.

As we prepared for bed this evening, Hannibal said: "The chancellorship is a game of musical chairs. The only question is: How long will it be before Hitler grabs the seat?"

Hannibal reported the detailed election results and our projections to Soucet through the usual channels.

## Monday evening, December 5

Big news! Von Papen is out and Kurt von Schleicher is in as chancellor. *Der Angriff* confirmed that talks are underway between von Schleicher and the Nazi Party.

According to a talkative Nazi aide that we encountered in the Adlon lobby, Schleicher had praised the Nazis as "the only party that could attract voters away from the radical left."

## Sunday morning, December 11

The Christmas season seems cold and bleak this year. Berlin is in turmoil, Nazi thugs rule the streets, and shoppers are afraid to visit the big department stores.

Reischl continues to keep his detectives out of the fray between the Nazis and the communists. Reisinger and Schmidt occupy their time with relatively straightforward cases. All three avoid Nazi entanglements. Good for them!

Raeder seldom shows up at the Präsidium. With a cynical smile, Reischl told us that Göring has picked Raeder for 'special duties.'

Reischl has not requested our help on a major case since the Norkus affair. Given his knowledge about our clandestine activities, I think he is concerned about our safety.

Hannibal and I declined an invitation to a gala Nazi Christmas Day party in the Adlon ballroom downstairs. We cited prior personal commitments. I assured Magda that we will attend future parties. She seemed to understand.

## Sunday morning, December 18

Last Friday evening, we invited Reischl, Reisinger and Schmidt to our suite at 5:00 PM for a quiet celebration. All three men are bachelors, and they seemed grateful for the invitation.

I suggested casual dress; Hannibal and I will wear sweaters and slacks.

I spent Friday afternoon working with room service. We set up wine, hors d'oeuvres and seasonal decorations. The living room area of our suite looked very festive, if I do say so myself.

At precisely 5:00 PM, I heard a knock at the door. I opened it, and Reischl, Reisinger and Schmidt stood there, wearing traditional German holiday sweaters, slacks and smiles.

"Willkommen!" I said, as I returned the smiles. "Bitte komm herein!" All three men had small gifts for the host and hostess.

Hannibal walked into the entryway from the living room. In a hearty voice, he said: "Merry Christmas gentlemen! Caroline worked all afternoon, preparing for your arrival."

"Hummf!" I responded. I gave Hannibal my best snooty look. Our three guests laughed.

We had a merry time for over an hour, with wine, snacks and pleasant, non-controversial conversation. All of us temporarily forgot the dire situation outside of our little enclave.

We finished the snacks and settled on the sofa and soft chairs near our glowing fireplace. To one side, the window provided a view of lights from around Pariser Platz. Light snow twinkled in the glow.

Silence settled over the room as we all enjoyed the moment. Everyone seemed to know that the conversation would change to more serious matters.

Reischl turned from looking out the window and gazed at me with steady eyes. He said: "We have been observing your activities."

My heart skipped a beat. After a moment, I responded: "Oh?"

Reisinger turned to me, smiled and said: "We approve."

Hannibal stood and looked out the window for a full minute. Along with our guests, I waited for him to speak.

Finally, Hannibal turned back to the group and said: "Your understanding is appreciated. However, your views are not shared by the Nazis."

"Yes," responded Schmidt. "We three will have to eventually make adjustments." His eyes said more than his words.

"The danger is greatest for you and Mrs. Jones," said Reischl. "Our ability to shield you will diminish as more and more Nazis move into the police hierarchy."

"We also know about your contacts at the Reichbank," said Reisinger. He gave a wry smile and added: "We also have contacts."

Reischl then stood. He looked first at Hannibal and then faced me. His eyes showed concern. He said: "Villian is still in Berlin."

"Oh!" I exclaimed. I couldn't help it.

As if by unspoken agreement, Reisinger and Schmidt stood next to Reischl. Reischl offered his hand to Hannibal. The two stared at each other as they shook hands. The process was repeated with Reisinger and Schmidt.

All three men turned to me. Reischl said: "Mrs. Jones, thank you for a lovely evening."

I stood and offered my hand. Reischl took it, bent slightly and kissed it in a formal manner. He then said: "May the spirit of Christmas follow you in all of your activities."

Without another word, our three guests quietly headed for the entryway and door. Hannibal followed. I could hear their courteous goodbyes as I stared out the window.

# 15

## THE ADELMAN MURDER

*Wednesday evening, December 21, 1932*

Hannibal and I drove to the Präsidium at about 9:00 AM this morning. Dawn was beginning to add a lighter grey to the dark, snow-filled clouds that obscured Berlin from the rising sun. Lights glowed along the streets, accenting rather than alleviating the gloom. A few pedestrians hurried from shelter to shelter along the sidewalks, and a couple of cars passed us on the icy, snow-covered streets. Cold!

Over the sound of our chattering Duesenberg engine and the crunch of crusted snow under the wheels, I said: "I think we will have the office mostly to ourselves today." I paused and added: "We can review bulletins and incident reports."

"Humm," responded Hannibal with a nod. "Soucet will be interested in the level of Nazi activity." He paused for a moment and then added: "He will also be interested in the continued harassment at the big department stores."

"Yes," I replied. "I read *Der Angriff* last night. The Tietz, Wertheim, Jandorf and other prominent Jewish store owners were vilified as usual."

We were silent as Hannibal navigated and dodged piles of dirty snow and drifts. Soot from coal heating fires speckled the snow everywhere.

Finally, we pulled into the lot behind the Präsidium and parked. I looked up at Hannibal as he helped me out of the car, and I said: "The harassment extends to rich Jews in general."

"Uh Humm," responded Hannibal. "The Fischer, Flechtheim, Rosen and Samuelson families are probably the tip of the iceberg." He shook his head sadly and added: "Who will be next?"

We soon found out.

As expected, most of Reischl's detectives were out on cases. "Not many are off for the holidays," I mused as we entered the squad room.

As we shed our coats. I saw Reischl and Reisinger standing by the conference table, looking at scattered pages on the table. Other than their low voices and the hissing of the steam radiators along the windows, no sounds greeted us.

Reischl looked up. His eyes stared intently. I felt a sense of being evaluated.

Reisinger looked first at Hannibal and then me. After a moment, he said: "Friedrich Adelman, a Jewish financier, was found dead in his bedroom last evening by his wife Rachel. She called Dr. Albert Schäfer, the family physician. At 11:30 PM, Dr. Schäfer called the local police station and reported the death as suspicious."

I noticed that Reisinger spoke in a confident, matter-of-fact tone. "Very different than our first encounter," I thought to myself. "Reischl's patience and our training have paid off." I glanced at Reischl and smiled.

Reischl smiled at me in return, as if he had read my thoughts. He then said: "We need your expertise." He turned to Reisinger and said: "Please continue."

Reisinger focused his attention on Hannibal and said: "Schmidt is on the scene now. The Adelman home is in Westend, not far from the Baumer mansion, the scene of our previous case. Would you two care to follow me to the Adelman home?"

I looked at Reischl, who nodded. "Interesting," I thought to myself. "Reischl trusts Reisinger and Schmidt to handle the case." Reischl smiled again.

The drive to Westend took almost an hour on the icy, snow-covered streets. The Adelman home was on Nussbaum Alle, about six blocks from the Baumer mansion. "Dangerous neighborhood," I muttered as Hannibal and I got out of the car. Hannibal just nodded.

We joined Reisinger as he walked up the swept sidewalk to the main entrance. Schmidt met us at the door. An elderly man in butler's attire stood behind him.

As the butler took our coats, Schmidt gave us an update. "Rachel Adelman found her husband on the floor of his bedroom at about 10:30 last night. She immediately had Werner Krüger, the butler, call Dr. Schäfer, who arrived at about 11:00 PM."

As we stood in the spacious entry hall, Schmidt continued: "A constable from the local station arrived about midnight. After checking the body, he closed off the bedroom. He allowed Dr. Schäfer to return home, with a promise to return this morning. Servants were allowed to retire to their bedrooms for the night. Mrs. Adelman retired to a spare bedroom away from the master suite."

Schmidt glanced at Reisinger, Hannibal and then me. He added: "I had the on-call duty, so I responded to a phone call from the station to my home. I arrived here at about 6:00 AM. The responding constable had remained all night, and he briefed me upon arrival. His replacement arrived at about 6:30."

Schmidt paused as he pulled out a notebook. He then continued: "I interviewed Schäfer when he returned to this house this morning at about 8:00 AM. He said that when he inspected Adelman's body last night, it showed signs of convulsions. The lips were blue. Schäfer also found vomit on the floor. The symptoms and vomit suggested poison, so he called the police station."

"Members of the household?" I asked.

Schmidt replied: "You have already met Krüger, the butler. Other servants include Heidi Schultz, a maid, Teresia Weber, the cook, and Walter Huber, the groundskeeper."

"Anyone else?" I asked.

"No," Schmidt replied. "Friedrich and Rachel Adelman have one son, Herbert, who attends Leipzig University Medical School. Although he visits frequently, he doesn't live at the Adelman home."

"Have you questioned members of the household about events prior to Friedrich's death?" I asked.

"Not yet," replied Schmidt. "However, I had the on-duty constable keep everyone in the library this morning, including Dr. Schäfer. Based on Schäfer's initial assessment of poisoning, I have treated the entire house, except the bedrooms where people slept, as a crime scene."

"Good," responded Reisinger. "I will contact a forensic team and arrange processing of the body in situ and then the rest of the house." He took a deep breath and added: "I will also follow up with Herbert, the son."

"Tough duty," Schmidt responded. "According to his mother Rachel, he lives in Leipzig, but may be visiting friends in Berlin. He has not yet been contacted. He paused and then added: I'll get an address and phone number."

"With your permission, Hannibal and I will begin our inspection before the forensic team arrives," I stated. I looked first at Reisinger and then Schmidt. Both men nodded.

Reisinger then turned to Schmidt. He said: "Suggestions for a private room for interviews?"

"There is an alcove off the library," replied Schmidt. "We can begin the interviews as soon as you are ready."

Reisinger turned to Hannibal and me. "Major and Mrs. Jones, we can compare notes when you are finished with your inspection. The four of us can do follow-up interviews if necessary."

Reisinger looked at Schmidt, Hannibal and me in turn. We all nodded. "Good," he replied. "Let's get to it."

"Reisinger and Schmidt work as a team; they have learned their lessons well," I thought to myself. I looked at Hannibal, who smiled.

Hannibal and I began our inspection tour in Friedrich Adelman's bedroom. As we entered from the hallway, my eyes were immediately drawn to the body on the floor. "Knees drawn up, fists clenched, face contorted and blue lips," I muttered.

"Humm," responded Hannibal. "Dressed in pajamas, robe across the foot of the bed, covers turned back, but the bed not rumpled."

I looked around the room. "Silver tray and teapot on a small table by an easy chair, nearby standing lamp turned on, newspaper on the floor by the chair," I mused. I walked around the body and bed and over to the table.

"Remains of an evening snack," I continued. I bent over the tray and peered closely at the remains of a muffin and sniffed. "Almonds," I stated.

Hannibal walked over. After a moment, he said: "Teapot, half-empty cup, half-eaten muffin." He then sniffed. "I smell almonds too."

I looked closely at the remains of the muffin, which lay on a plate and paper doily. "Two circular stains on the doily," I said. "Two muffins were on the plate. Adelman ate about one and one-half."

"Good eye," responded Hannibal. He then returned to the other side of the bed and stood by the body. "Small vomit on the rug near Adelman's head."

I walked over and stood next to Hannibal. We both looked around the room.

"Adelman sat in the easy chair, had tea and muffins, read the newspaper, got up, took off his robe and prepared to get into bed," I stated.

"Yes," responded Hannibal. "But he never made it. He was suddenly seized by convulsions, vomited, collapsed to the floor and died."

"Poisoned by either the tea or by the muffins," I stated matter-of-factly.

"Agree," said Hannibal. "Forensics will provide the details."

We both looked around the room. "Beautifully decorated bedroom, with original paintings on the walls," I mused.

"Two doors," responded Hannibal. "We came in the door that opens to the hallway." Hannibal then walked over to the second door, which was open. He disappeared through the doorway for a minute and then returned.

"Short hallway, adjoining bathroom and another bedroom on the other side," he said. "The Adelmans have separate, adjoining bedrooms." He paused and then added: "Typical master suite for wealthy couples."

"Did you notice the paintings here and in the hallway?" I asked.

"Yes," replied Hannibal. "All originals. I recognized landscapes by Pieter Bruegel and Joachim Patenier."

"And I saw several impressionist paintings in the hallway," I responded. "I wonder how many more objects of art decorate this house."

"Quite a few," said a voice from the hallway door. "The Adelman home is filled with expensive art."

Hannibal and I both turned. Reisinger stood in the doorway.

"The forensics team is here," Reisinger continued as he looked at Hannibal. "Would you please supervise?"

"Yes," Hannibal responded. After a brief discussion, he agreed to spend the next hour working with the forensics team in the bedroom, gathering fingerprints and samples, taking photos and gathering other evidence.

He went to our car outside and returned with our case of forensic equipment. He looked at me and said: "We have two cameras if you need one."

I took one camera and a measuring tape. "I'll tour the kitchen and then go outside," I responded. Hannibal nodded and turned to the forensics team assembled by the bedroom door.

With camera in hand, I left the bedroom and entered the hallway. The door to the library was to the left, across the hall from the bedroom, near the entryway. I looked in. I could see three women and three men sitting on chairs and sofas. A uniformed constable stood at the far end of the room; arms folded.

"Dr. Schäfer, butler, groundskeeper, maid, cook and Rachel Adelman," I surmised. I turned and looked toward the entryway. Reisinger was talking quietly to another uniformed constable. As I watched, I heard a knock. The constable opened the front door. A young man stood just outside.

"Well-dressed, tall and thin, pleasant but sad features," I thought to myself. After a brief discussion, Reisinger escorted the young man towards me.

"Mrs. Jones, meet Herbert Adelman," said Reisinger. "I have told him about his father."

"My condolences on your loss," I responded sympathetically.

Herbert Adelman choked a little, swallowed convulsively, took a deep breath and replied: "Thank you." He turned back to Reisinger and asked: "Where is my mother?"

"In the library," responded Reisinger.

Without another word, young Adelman stepped around me and disappeared into the library. I heard sobs.

Reisinger and I exchanged glances. I said: "We can follow up on the initial interviews later this afternoon."

Reisinger took out a pocket watch, glanced at it and replied: "It's now one o'clock. Shall we meet in the library at two?"

I thought a moment, then said: "Sounds good. Hannibal should be done in the bedroom by then." I paused and added: "In the meantime, I will tour the kitchen and the grounds. Can you ask the groundskeeper to escort me when I go outside?"

"Good idea," responded Reisinger. "Let me know when you are ready."

"Fifteen minutes," I replied. I turned and headed down the hallway toward the back of the house.

The hallway ended in a spacious kitchen. "Pantries, stove, ovens, sinks, cooler and preparation counters," I thought to myself. "Standard stuff for a wealthy home."

A used muffin pan lay in the sink. It was designed for a dozen muffins. My thoughts continued: "Adelman had two, so where are the remaining ten?" I opened the cooler. A plate with ten muffins rested on a shelf. "I'll have the forensics team check for poisons," I concluded.

Windows and a door lined the back wall of the kitchen. I walked over to a window. "Two-story carriage house, gardens and an alley," I mused. "Old snow on the yard and gardens, but the brick pathway to the carriage house has been cleared."

The wind had blown thin snowdrifts into the pathway in several places. I could see footprints. I could also see tire tracks in the snow of the alley. "Time for a tour of the outside," I decided.

I returned to the library. Members of the household looked up as I entered. Herbert and his mother sat close and held hands. Dr. Schäfer, the cook and the maid sat nearby. All three women had tears in their eyes. I spotted Krüger the butler and the grizzled old man that I had seen earlier.

I noticed that unlike the others, the grizzled old man had calloused hands. "Walter Huber the groundskeeper," I surmised.

I entered and addressed the on-duty constable. Reisinger had already briefed him.

Within a couple of minutes, Huber and I left the library and put on coats, hats and gloves. Huber put on overshoes; I still wore my leather boots. With camera and measuring tape in hand, I followed Huber through the kitchen door.

Huber helped as I put my measuring tape next to one of the clearest footprints in a pathway snowdrift. I took several photos. We found more of the same footprints in the alley, next to the tire tracks. We took more photos. Huber seemed fascinated as I worked.

As we finished in the alley, I said: "What's in the carriage house?"

"Herr Adelman's automobile, my workroom and a kind of laboratory above," replied Huber. "Young Herbert set up the laboratory years ago. He has a most interesting hobby."

"Would you show me?" I asked.

"Of course," replied Huber. "I have a key." He took a ring of keys from his coat pocket and led the way to a side door.

Huber turned a light switch just inside the door. As soon as we entered, I could tell that the carriage house was heated. I saw the automobile on the far side and a neat work area on the near side. Steam radiators under a row of windows hissed. A set of inside stairs led up to a landing and another door.

"I take care of my tools and do repairs in here," explained Huber. "Herr Adelman set up the heating system several years ago. A small, coal fired boiler at the back of the main house heats water. Steam pipes go to both buildings."

He paused and smiled wanly. "Herr Adelman was very thoughtful and innovative."

I glanced around at the neat workbenches and tools. I could see nothing that related to the death of Friedrich Adelman. "Can we go upstairs?" I asked.

Huber nodded and led the way up the stairs. He unlocked the door to Herbert's laboratory, reached inside and turned a light switch.

The 'laboratory,' as Huber called it, was neat, clean and filled with worktables, cabinets and bookcases. Display cases of butterflies, moths and a variety of other insects rested on several of the tables. I looked closely at one of the cases. Each specimen had a label written in Latin. "Scientific names," I thought. Out loud I said: "Beautiful."

"Yes," replied Huber. "Young Herbert won many prizes." He pointed to a bulletin board next to one of the cabinets. Several ribbons and certificates were arranged in a display.

I glanced around the room. The worktables had tools for mounting tiny creatures. Three closed glass jars rested on a counter under shelves of reference books. I looked at the titles on the spines of the books. Several titles had the word 'Entomologie.'

I turned to Huber with a questioning look. "The study of insects," he responded with a smile. "Herbert published in scientific journals."

I walked over to the glass jars on the counter. I could see a crystalline substance in the bottom of each, covered by a layer of a cream-colored substance. I reached out to the lid on one of the jars.

"Careful," admonished Huber. "Those are killing jars."

I drew my hand back quickly and turned to Huber.

"The jars contain potassium cyanide on the bottom, covered by a layer of hardened plaster of Paris," he said with a smile. "Herbert uses the jars to kill insects before he mounts them in a display case."

"Poison," I replied. "You seem to know a lot about Herbert's activities in here."

"I have helped young Master Herbert with his hobby since he was a boy," replied Huber.

"The forensics team will have a field day in here," I muttered. Huber did not respond.

After a few more minutes of looking around the room, I took a dozen photos. Afterwards, we turned out the light, left the laboratory, locked the door and descended the stairs. Huber also switched off the light and locked the ground-level door as we left the building. We then headed back to the main house.

As we took off our coats inside the hallway, Hannibal stepped out of the master bedroom suite. "Finished," he said. "The body is on its way to the morgue for autopsy. We'll have a report in the morning." He looked at me with a quizzical expression. "How about you?"

I explained what I had found, including the muffins in the kitchen, the footprints and tire tracks outside and the potassium cyanide in the jars in the carriage house. Hannibal turned to the forensic team as they came out of the master bedroom. He gave instructions. Huber led the team back toward the kitchen.

Hannibal turned to me, took out his pocket watch and glanced at the time. He looked up and smiled. "Five minutes until two," he said. "Right on schedule." He then walked into the library.

I was about to follow when I heard a loud knock on the main entryway door. The nearby constable started to open the door, but he didn't have time. It flew open. Detective Inspector Konrad Raeder stood in the doorway.

# 16

## LEADS AND MISLEADS

*Thursday morning, December 22, 1932*

It's 5:00 AM, and I'm wide awake. I can't sleep, so I may as well write. I keep thinking about Raeder's visit to the Adelman home yesterday.

When Raeder stepped through the doorway, he saw me and immediately strode in my direction. "Sinister, devious and dangerous," the thoughts flashed through my mind.

"I'm investigating the financial transactions of Friedrich Adelman," Raeder said as he stepped up and snarled right in my face. "What are you doing here?"

Raeder's attempt at intimidation triggered a primal urge to strike. My body tensed. Raeder seemed to sense my temper; I'm sure my face flushed. He stepped back a little.

I forced my rising fury back down and replied in an even, controlled voice: "Friedrich Adelman is dead. He was most likely poisoned last night." I stared intently into Raeder's eyes. "At Chief Inspector Reischl's request, my husband and I are assisting in the investigation."

As I finished my sentence, Hannibal slipped out of the library and silently walked up behind Raeder. "Is there a problem, Caroline?" He said softly.

Raeder jumped a little; he had not heard Hannibal's approach. He turned and looked up. Hannibal towered at least a foot above.

"No," I replied. Raeder was facing Hannibal, so he couldn't see my face. I smiled and continued: "I think Inspector Raeder was about to offer his help with our investigation."

Raeder stepped back a little more, looked at me and then at Hannibal. Reisinger emerged from the library and stood by Hannibal. He stared intently at Raeder's face.

Raeder gulped a little. "Yes," he finally responded. "I will help in any way I can." His voice quivered. "I'm sure Gruppenführer Göring would approve."

As Raeder mentioned Göring's name, he seemed to regain a little confidence. I smiled sweetly and said: "I'm sure we can accommodate Herr Göring's interest in this case."

Reisinger caught the meaning behind my reply, turned to Raeder and said: "You are welcome to participate in our investigation, Inspector Raeder." He paused and smiled grimly. His eyes glittered. "I will inform Chief Inspector Reischl about your cooperation."

Raeder lost his bluster again. His eyes shifted between Reisinger, the towering Hannibal and me. "Yes, of course," he finally replied. "Well, I'm sure you have matters in hand." He paused again and added: "I have other pressing duties elsewhere."

He backed up, turned and walked quickly past the library and out the front door. The constable at the door grinned openly as Raeder closed the heavy front door with a loud 'thump.'

As Raeder passed the open library door, I heard a couple of exclamations followed by a murmur of voices. I looked in. I saw fear in the faces of the female servants and especially in the expression of Rachel Adelman. Herbert looked surprised, but I couldn't detect any other emotion. Krüger and Huber had expressions of anger.

My instinct tells me that Raeder has played a role in all this, as yet undiscovered. Why did he come to the Adelman home right after the murder?' I will find out. My resolve hardened. Red thoughts swirled in my mind. "I despise that man."

## Thursday evening, December 22

After Raeder left, Reisinger, Schmidt, Hannibal and I met in the library alcove. After we were all seated, Hannibal summarized our findings.

"We will know more about our future direction when we get the autopsy report," Hannibal concluded. He looked first at Reisinger and then Schmidt. "Any luck with your interviews?"

"We have a timeline for the day of Adelman's death," replied Schmidt. "Friedrich had several meetings in his study. He met with his son from 10:00 until about 10:30 AM, Inspector Raeder from 11:00 until about 11:15, a man named Siegfried von Braun from noon until about 12:45 and a man named Günther Kellerman from 2:00 until 3:15 PM."

"The names and times were confirmed by Friedrich's wife Rachel, Krüger the butler, and Schultz the maid," added Reisinger. "Except for Raeder, the men all arrived shortly before and left shortly after their respective meetings."

Schmidt then added: "The meetings with son Herbert, von Braun and Kellerman involved heated arguments behind closed doors. Bits of conversation were overheard by Rachel, Krüger and Schulz."

Schmidt continued: "The arguments were muffled, but the one between Friedrich and Herbert involved a gentile girl named Greta Beck. The argument with von Braun was about money for paintings, and the argument with Kellerman was about the sale of paintings to cover unpaid back taxes."

"Kellerman is an associate of SA Hauptsturmführer Bruno Lohse and Hildebrandt Gurlitt, an art collector," I stated. I paused, digging back in my memory. "Hannibal and I met Lohse and Gurlitt at a Nazi party last year."

I looked at Hannibal and added: "Kellerman accompanied the other two at the homes of Flechtheim, Rosen and Samuelson in March."

"Humm," Hannibal responded. "Given that Lohse and Gurlitt collect art for Göring, Kellerman probably does the same."

Schmidt made a few notes. "I'll check it out," he replied.

"What about von Braun?" I asked.

Schmidt flipped through his notes and replied: "According to Rachel, Siegfried von Braun is a Berlin aristocrat who lost his family fortune in the stock market crash of 1929. He is deeply in debt to Adelman."

Reisinger added: "According to Krüger and Rachel, von Braun sold some of his family's old masters paintings to the Adelmans at bargain prices to service his debt. He visited the Adelman home several times over the past year to deliver paintings."

We pondered this information for a few moments. I then looked at Reisinger and said: "You indicated that Raeder didn't leave right away after his meeting with Friedrich. What happened?"

"According to Krüger and Schultz, Friedrich's meeting with Raeder did not involve arguments that could be overheard," replied Reisinger. "In fact, Krüger and Schultz both said that the meeting was strangely quiet."

Schmidt added: "Krüger and Schultz also said that after the meeting, Raeder walked leisurely through the entire house and looked intently at paintings and other objects of art. He took notes and left about 11:45 AM."

"Interesting," I mused. "Kellerman showed up at 2:00 PM and had a lengthy, stormy meeting with Friedrich over the sale of paintings to cover back taxes."

"Raeder is required to keep police records of his investigations, including his investigation of Adelman finances," said Hannibal. He looked at Reisinger, who immediately caught the drift.

"I'll call the Chief Inspector," Reisinger replied. "I'm sure we can review the files."

"The argument between Friedrich and his son over Greta Beck is also of interest," I mused. "I can follow up with Rachel and the servants."

Everyone was silent as we thought about implications. After a couple of minutes, I asked: "How did Friedrich get his tea and muffins?"

Schmidt grinned and responded: "According to Teresia Weber, the cook, she takes a snack and hot tea to Herr Adelman's bedroom almost every night. On the night of his death, she said that she delivered two muffins and a pot of hot tea."

"Time?" I asked.

Schmidt flipped through his notes and replied: "According to Weber, about 8:00 PM. The time was confirmed by Krüger, who was in the kitchen when Weber prepared the tray."

Schmidt read for a moment and then said: "Krüger also said that he saw the two muffins on a plate on a kitchen counter before 8:00 PM, as he periodically entered and left the kitchen."

Schmidt looked up at me and added: "I asked Weber about it, and she said that she left the two muffins on the counter at about 11:00 AM when she finished baking. She put the remaining ten in the cooler at the same time."

Hannibal and I leaned back in our chairs. Reisinger and Schmidt waited politely. After a couple of minutes, I said: "Tomorrow we get the autopsy report. Hopefully, the Chief Inspector will also obtain the files on Raeder's investigation."

"Afterwards, we will have more questions," added Hannibal. "I am also interested in Herbert's lab, the footprints and tire tracks in the snow."

"I will follow up on the mysterious von Braun and Kellerman," stated Schmidt.

Hannibal reached in his case and pulled out his camera. I walked over to the table where I had laid mine and brought it back to the group. Hannibal looked at Reisinger and said: "Caroline and I have taken many photos."

Reisinger nodded and said: "I'll have them developed. "

Hannibal looked at his watch. "Four o'clock," he said. I think Dr. Schäfer can go home. Please ask Herbert to stay; I think he will want to be with his mother in any case."

"I'll take care of it," responded Reisinger. "I'll also leave one constable on duty here at the house until we solve the case." He paused and then added: "Let's all meet in the squad conference room tomorrow at 9:00 AM."

My tummy suddenly growled audibly. I blushed a little. Suddenly, I realized that I hadn't eaten since breakfast.

Schmidt looked at Reisinger, Hannibal and then me. He grinned and said: "How about dinner? I know a good Italian-style restaurant near the Präsidium."

"Sounds great," I said a little too quickly. My three companions chuckled.

After nearly an hour's drive, the four of us spent a quiet dinner at Schmidt's choice of restaurant. No one mentioned the case during the entire evening.

## Friday evening, December 23

Busy day. Hannibal and I drove to the Präsidium in time for the nine o'clock meeting. After our first cups of coffee, we assembled with Reischl, Reisinger and Schmidt in the conference room. We all had re-filled our cups.

Reischl lay the autopsy report, a forensic report for the Adelman home and a stack of photos on the table. "I think we are approaching the end game," said Reischl. "Good work everyone." Confident smiles touched the faces of Reisinger and Schmidt.

Reischl sat down, leaned back and waited. The rest of us found seats. Reisinger picked up and read the autopsy report. Hannibal and I scanned the photos. Schmidt read the forensics report. Everyone sipped coffee.

After about ten minutes, Reisinger said: "Fredrich Adelman died of acute potassium cyanide poisoning."

Schmidt looked up an added: "The forensics report from the scene shows that potassium cyanide was present in the remains of the muffin from the bedroom, but not in the tea or in the ten muffins in the kitchen cooler."

Hannibal said: "Based on the photos of the footprints, someone walked from the alley into the back door of the kitchen and out again." He paused and then added: "The tracks didn't stop at the carriage house door."

"What about the killing jars in the carriage house?" I asked. "Did the team find any other potassium cyanide in the laboratory?"

Schmidt carefully examined the forensic report. After a moment, he replied: "In total, the three killing jars contained precisely 28 grams of crystalline potassium cyanide. In each jar, the cyanide was covered by a solid, porous covering of plaster of Paris."

"Humm," responded Hannibal. He paused for a moment. I could see that he was performing mental calculations. Finally, he said: "That's slightly less than half a liter."

Everyone waited as Hannibal paused again. After about a minute, he asked: "Did the team find a container as the source of the cyanide?"

Schmidt leafed through the report. After a minute or so he replied: "The team found an empty half-liter jar with a hand-written label that stated: 'Stein Apotheke Kaliumcyanid.' The jar had been washed clean; there was a residue of soap."

After a moment of thought, I said: "Potassium cyanide is a controlled substance. We need to follow up with the Stein Pharmacy." The four men nodded. "I'll take care of it," responded Reisinger.

"What about von Braun?" I asked.

Schmidt flipped through his notes. "I checked von Braun's bank account and then visited him at his home in Westend." He paused and added: "Von Braun said that he went to his bank on Reich Strasse after his meeting with Friedrich Adelman and to his club shortly afterwards."

"Humm," mused Hannibal. "We need to verify his bank and club visits." He smiled and added: "I have friends who can help."

"What about the tire tracks?" Reischl asked. He leaned forward and took another sip of coffee. "Berlin has very few private automobiles."

"Ah," responded Hannibal. "I looked at the tread marks. They were made by tires designed for snow and ice."

"Not many of those in Berlin," responded Reischl. "Taxicabs and police cars, but very few others. Most private owners put their cars away for the winter."

My mind made a connection. "Can we check the cars in the police fleet?" I asked.

For a moment, the faces of my companions had blank expressions. Hannibal was the first to smile.

"Good idea," he replied. He turned to Schmidt and said: "I think we should also compare the photos of the footprints to the footwear of everyone who has recently been in the Adelman house."

Schmidt nodded slowly, grinned and replied: "I'll get right on it."

"What about fingerprints?" I asked.

"The forensics team found useful fingerprints on teacups on a tray in the Adelman study," replied Schmidt. "Schultz, the maid, had served tea to Raeder, von Braun and Kellerman during their respective meetings with Friedrich. The tray had been forgotten and remained on a side table."

Schmidt paused and grinned. "Schultz poured the tea, and she remembered that Raeder took his tea straight, von Braun had cream, and Kellerman had two teaspoons of sugar. The team was able to identify the cups used by each man from the residue in the cups."

"Ah," I responded. "So, we have fingerprints of Raeder, von Braun and Kellerman." I smiled at Schmidt and asked: "Did the team obtain prints from members of the household?"

"Yes," replied Schmidt. "The team was very thorough." He skimmed through the report to refresh his memory. After a moment, he added: "Nothing unusual was noted with regard to their fingerprints in the study."

The room was silent for a few minutes. Only the steam radiators hissed in the background. Finally, I said: "Suggest that Hannibal and I check alibis for the period 11:00 AM until 8:00 PM on the day of the murder. We can go over to the Adelman home today."

Reischl nodded and said: "Good. I have yet to obtain Raeder's investigation files, but I will have them later today. Shall we meet in the Adelman library at nine o'clock on Monday, December 26?"

He looked closely at me, smiled and added: "I'll bring the files, and Reisinger will make sure that Inspector Raeder is present." He stood up. So ended a very satisfying meeting.

Hannibal and I made plans as we prepared to leave for the Adelman home. We had many questions. We also agreed to follow up later concerning von Braun.

Reisinger and Schmidt conferred for a few minutes and then followed us out the door of the Präsidium. Hannibal and I got in our car. I saw Schmidt and Reisinger head for the police garage on the far side of the parking lot.

As Hannibal and I drove away, I mused: "Four persons had motive. We know the method. Who had opportunity?"

# 17

## PROCESS OF ELIMINATION

### Saturday evening, December 24, 1932

Christmas Eve: a time for gifts, reflection and murder resolution. Hannibal and I know who killed Friedrich Adelman. Along with our police detective colleagues, we will reveal our findings on Monday.

Tonight, Hannibal and I will spend a quiet evening in our suite. Only the very noisy Nazis are celebrating in the streets. Sadly, their antics are about achieving political power; the spirit of Christmas is not in them. Hannibal predicts that Hitler will be Chancellor soon.

### Monday evening December 26

Chief Inspector Reischl presided over the assembly in the Adelman library this morning. All of the players, except one, were there.

Reisinger stood next to a seated Raeder. I sensed that Raeder was nervous, in spite of his attempts to appear blustery and confident. He kept glancing at Reisinger, who, I'm certain, had made sure that he was present.

Schmidt stood by the door, along with a rather beefy uniformed constable. Siegfried von Braun sat in a chair within easy reach of the constable and chewed on his fingernails.

Herbert and his mother Rachel sat together on a sofa. Herbert occasionally whispered in his mother's ear, but I couldn't detect what he was saying.

The four servants, Krüger, Huber, Weber and Schultz, sat on straight-backed chairs brought into the library for the occasion. The two women fidgeted and the two men sat in stony silence.

Reischl began the meeting at precisely nine o'clock. "German efficiency," I thought to myself. I looked at Reischl and smiled. Everything was ready.

Reischl's smiled, and he said: "As you know, Major and Mrs. Jones conducted follow-up interviews on Friday. Detectives Reisinger and Schmidt collected additional evidence over the past two days."

Reischl looked around the room. Several attendees squirmed in their seats. "Major Jones, would you begin?"

Hannibal stepped forward. He spoke in his practiced, military briefing manner. "Friedrich Adelman was poisoned with two muffins laced with potassium cyanide during the evening of December 21. Three people in this room had motive. One is the murderer."

Hannibal looked around the room. His glance paused on von Braun, Herbert Adelman and Raeder. He then continued: "The two poisoned muffins were placed on a plate in the kitchen at 11:00 AM on the day of the murder. They were periodically unattended from that time until about 8:00 PM, when Frau Weber took them, along with a pot of tea, to Friedrich Adelman's bedroom."

Hannibal paused again. The room was deadly quiet. He looked directly at von Braun. "Herr von Braun, you are deeply in debt to the Adelmans. You have been servicing your debt by selling them your family heirloom paintings at bargain prices. Further, you argued with Friedrich in his study between noon and 12:45 PM on the day of the murder."

Von Braun half-rose from his seat. The beefy constable put a hand on von Braun's shoulder. He sat back down. The constable took his hand away.

Von Braun responded in a quavering voice: "I, I didn't kill Friedrich." His voice rose in pitch. "As I told you, I arrived here at noon, left at 12:45 and walked directly to my bank on Reich Strasse about three blocks away. Afterwards, I spent the rest of the evening at my club, also on Reich Strasse."

"Herr Krüger and Frau Weber verified your arrival and departure times through the front door," Hannibal responded in a soft voice. He then looked over at Schmidt.

Schmidt stepped forward, looked directly at von Braun and said: "The account manager at the bank verified that you were at the bank from about 1:15 until about 5:00 PM, trying to secure a loan." Schmidt smiled grimly and added: "You were not successful."

Von Braun's face turned red, and he hung his head.

Schmidt continued: "I checked with the bartender at your club. He verified that you were at the bar from shortly after five until after 8:00 PM." Schmidt paused and then added: "He also said that you became quite drunk. He called a taxi to take you home at about 8:30." Schmidt looked at Hannibal.

Hannibal responded: "Your situation is sad, Herr von Braun, but your story checks out. You didn't kill Friedrich Adelman."

Von Braun let out a heavy sigh. There were murmurs among the members of the Adelman household. Herbert whispered to his mother. She nodded.

Hannibal then looked intently at Herbert, and said: "Herbert Adleman, you had an argument with your father the day he was murdered. You also had access to potassium cyanide, which was the poison infused into the muffins that killed him."

Herbert stared back at Hannibal and took a sharp breath. He turned to his mother as she drew back a little.

"I didn't kill father," Herbert protested. "We argued about Greta, but I, we...," he stuttered. "We wanted to marry."

Raeder rose from his seat. "I know about Greta Beck," he said in an accusing tone. "She is the niece of Generalleutnant Ludwig Beck, a prominent Army staff officer."

Raeder scowled at Herbert and said: "The General is a devout Christian and sympathetic to the National Socialist vision. He would never approve of Greta's relationship with you!"

Everyone in the room was shocked into stunned silence. Raeder continued: "True Germans do not marry Jews." Raeder sat back down.

After another moment of silence, Rachel wiped away a tear, took a deep breath and softly said: "My husband and I knew about Greta." She paused and looked at her son. More tears formed and trickled down her cheeks.

"Inspector Raeder is right," she continued. She wiped away her tears again. She looked at Raeder, and her eyes gained a steely look. "It is also forbidden for us to marry outside our faith."

Rachel then turned to her son and said softly: "Your father loved you dearly. Greta is a nice girl, but your father would never have given permission."

The room was silent again. Finally, Raeder looked at Herbert and said: "I know about the potassium cyanide in your laboratory." He triumphantly looked back at Hannibal. "You have your murderer."

"Humm," responded Hannibal. "Inspector Reisinger, please tell us about the findings with regard to the potassium cyanide in Herbert's laboratory."

Reisinger glanced at Raeder first and then focused his attention on Herbert. "Our forensics team found a total of precisely 28 grams of crystalline potassium cyanide in three insect killing jars in the laboratory." He paused and looked around the room. "Potassium cyanide is a controlled substance, and we traced it to Stein Apotheke."

Herbert nodded and replied: "I bought it at Stein's about two years ago."

"Yes," replied Reisinger. "I checked. The pharmacist kept records. On November 3, 1930, you purchased precisely 28 grams of crystalline potassium cyanide at Stein's."

Reisinger then stated: "I also checked on your whereabouts after you left your parent's home at 10:30 AM on December 21."

"I visited Greta," Herbert replied. "She was staying at her uncle's house." He paused and then added: "She had an argument with her parents over me and had left home a few days earlier."

"Yes," replied Reisinger. "She was staying at her uncle's home in Lichterfelde, a suburb on the south side of town. According to General Beck, you arrived by taxi at about 11:15 AM."

I looked at Raeder as his mouth dropped open. "He's beginning to see where this is going," I thought to myself. I did my best not to smile.

"General Beck was nice, but he said the same thing as my father and Greta's parents," replied Herbert. "Marriage with Greta was out of the question."

"Humm," Hannibal responded. "How long did you stay at General Beck's home?"

Herbert sighed and said: "General Beck allowed me to talk with Greta until evening. The General's chauffeur drove Greta to her parent's home near Grunewald Bahnhof at about 7:00 PM. I left shortly afterwards."

"What did you do then?" Hannibal asked.

"I took a taxi to my friend Alfred's house on Ahorn Alle, not far from here," replied Herbert.

Hannibal turned to Reisinger, who said: "Verified. Alfred Feldstein lives with his parents on Ahorn Alle. According to Alfred and his father, Herbert arrived at about 8:00 PM."

The room was silent for several minutes. Raeder squirmed, and his eyes darted around the room. Reisinger put a restraining hand on his shoulder. Raeder looked up, saw the no-nonsense look in Reisinger's eyes and wilted. Reisinger removed his hand and smiled.

Finally, Reischl stood, looked intently at Raeder and said: "Inspector Raeder, you murdered Friedrich Adelman." He paused and glanced at Reisinger, Schmidt, Hannibal and me, in turn.

He looked back at Raeder, and his expression turned grim. He added: "Mrs. Jones will now explain why and how you did it."

I rose from my chair, looked directly at Raeder and said: "Based your visits to this house on several occasions, including December 21, you were well aware of the value of the Adelman art collection." Raeder sat in stunned silence.

"According to my interview with Frau Adelman and Krüger last Friday, you had pressured Friedrich to sell his paintings to Günther Kellerman at bargain prices. In return, you would end your investigation of Adelman finances and alleged back taxes."

"During my interviews with Weber and Schultz, also on Friday, they said that you entered the kitchen at about noon during your tour of the house on December 21." I paused, looked over at Weber and then Schultz. Both nodded.

I continued: "Weber said that you reached for one of the muffins on the plate on the counter. She also said she told you that the muffins were for the master and not to touch them." I smiled at Raeder, and added: "According to Weber, you looked long at the muffins, smiled, turned and left the kitchen."

No one spoke for nearly a minute. I then looked over to Reischl, who nodded and said: "Detective Raeder, I have your files on your investigation of Adelman finances. Major Jones followed up with the banks that hold Adelman accounts."

Reischl paused, looked at Raeder intently and continued: "After a thorough review of the files and the Adelman accounts by bank auditors, the threat of back taxes is fiction, made up by you." Reischl turned to me and smiled.

"Friedrich Adelman knew your threat was false," I said. "Based on overheard elements of conversations during his meeting with Kellerman on December 21, Friedrich vehemently refused to sell." I looked at Rachel, Krüger and Schultz, in turn. All three nodded.

I turned my attention back to Raeder and said: "Police dispatch records show that you checked out an unmarked police car at 4:00

PM on December 21 and back the same evening at 7:30 PM. Detective Schmidt and a forensic team found your fingerprints on the wheel and Kellerman's fingerprints on passenger side of the dash."

I looked over at Schmidt, who nodded and said: "The car remained in the police garage, untouched, from the time you turned it in until Friday afternoon, when I found the fingerprints."

Schmidt looked at me and added: "We also found other evidence. Fragments on the floor of the car match the rubber and glass used in poison cyanide capsules known to be readily available to members of the SA Brownshirts. Some of the larger fragments had traces of cyanide. Cyanide capsules were therefore broken open in the car. The liquid was most likely placed in a syringe. The SA uses such syringes in common practice."

Schmidt looked over at Reisinger, who took up the narrative. "The footprints in the light snow leading to and from the Adelman kitchen back door and the alley match the rubber overshoes owned by you and found at the police station."

Raeder started to speak, thought better of it and limited his response to venomous looks at Schmidt and back at Reisinger. If looks could kill, both men would have been dead on the spot.

"I compared the photos taken by Mrs. Jones of the tire tracks in the alley to the tires on your police car," said Schmidt. The tread was a perfect match."

"The footprints clearly show that you entered the Adelman home through the kitchen," I continued. "According to Krüger, Weber and Schultz, the kitchen was periodically occupied all day, from morning until about 6:45 PM the day of the murder. Afterwards, it was vacant until about 8:00 PM."

Reisinger added: "You picked up the police car at 4:00 PM. You had to have entered and left the kitchen after 4:00 PM, most likely after 6:45, and before 7:30 PM, when you turned in the car."

Reischl then said: "The evidence strongly indicates that you and Kellerman arrived by car in the back alley. Based on your visit earlier that day, you knew about the muffins and who would eat them. You slipped in the back door to the kitchen, found the muffins, inserted liquid potassium cyanide, probably with a syringe, and left the way you came."

I looked at Raeder with an expression of distaste and said: "With Friedrich out of the way, I'm sure that you expected his wife Rachel to be an easier mark."

Although I kept my voice controlled and even, memories of my encounter with Raeder on December 21 boiled inside, and I added: "You have demonstrated a tendency to bully females."

Raeder jumped up from his chair and exclaimed: "Kellerman!"

Your footprints say otherwise," I responded coolly. "Guilt is for a court to decide."

Reisinger pulled a set of handcuffs out of his pocket, firmly pulled Raeder's arms back, and slipped on the cuffs. The meeting was over. Where is Kellerman?

# 18

## RED ROAD FROM BERLIN

*Tuesday evening, December 27, 1932*

Magda Goebbels called me early this morning. Her warning was short, almost whispered. "Göring is livid about the arrest of Raeder," she said. "You upset his plans to confiscate the Adelman art collection. For political reasons, my husband supports Göring."

Before I could respond, Magda said: "Best wishes, my good friend." I heard a click as she hung up the phone.

I told Hannibal, and he made a phone call. His call was also short; only a few words were spoken. After he hung up, he turned to me, smiled and said: "Let's have breakfast here in the room. I'm expecting a return phone call."

As we were finishing breakfast, the phone rang. Hannibal answered. All I heard was Hannibal as he said: "Will do."

With some trepidation, Hannibal and I drove to the Präsidium at about nine o'clock. He briefly explained his phone calls as we bumped along the frozen lumps of snow and ice in the street.

We arrived at the Präsidium at about ten o'clock. Except for Reischl, the squad room was empty. Reischl looked at us as we entered; he had been pacing the floor next to the windows. His face was drawn and haggard. He smiled, but I could tell it was forced.

He had a cup of coffee in his hand, and he motioned with it toward the coffee pot. "Please get your coffee, and join me in my

191

office," he said. With that, he turned and disappeared though the office door.

Hannibal and I took off our coats, got our coffee and followed Reischl. He stood by the window, looking out at the grey sky. Without turning around, he said: "I have been offered a chance to retire. I plan to take it."

I opened my mouth to speak, but before I could formulate words, Reischl turned, looked intently at me and then at Hannibal. He added: "I will be fine, but you two are in grave danger."

We were silent for a full minute. Finally, Hannibal asked: "What about Reisinger and Schmidt?"

Reischl raised his eyebrows a little and smiled warmly. "You think of others; I have always appreciated that quality in you." His smile faded and he added: "I will not be around to shield them."

"Perhaps I can help," Hannibal responded. "I have friends in Switzerland."

I looked at Hannibal in surprise. "How?" I then remembered his phone call. My thoughts explored possibilities.

Hannibal continued: "Reisinger and Schmidt are both bachelors. Do they have close ties?"

Reischl's eyebrows raised again and he replied: "No, they were emersed in their work." He paused, and a slow smile touched his face. "What do you have in mind?"

"I think I can arrange well-paid security positions for them in Switzerland," responded Hannibal. "Swiss banks need men with skills like those of Reisinger and Schmidt."

"Hannibal, you are a kind and wonderful man," I thought to myself. I stepped over and put my arm through his. He responded by taking my hand and squeezing it softly.

Reischl let out a deep sigh, smiled again and said: "I can make arrangements on this end." He looked at me, then back to Hannibal and continued: "What about you and Mrs. Jones?"

Hannibal glanced at me, then looked to Reischl and said: "We have been told that Vienna is beautiful in the spring." He smiled and added: "We plan to leave Berlin within a few days, disappear for a while and show up in Vienna when the snow melts."

Reischl smiled broadly and replied: "Good. I also plan to leave Berlin. I have a small family estate near Heidelberg." He looked at me, and his eyes had their old twinkle. He added: "I know some people in Vienna."

The day had turned to a more promising outlook.

## Monday evening, January 2

The phone rang at eight o'clock this morning. I was still in bed. As usual, Hannibal had already gotten up, bathed, dressed and had ordered room service breakfast. I heard him answer the phone in the living room of our suite. I picked up the bedroom extension. It was Reischl.

I heard Reischl say: "I have cleaned out my desk. My superiors took our files on the Adelman case. I have my retirement papers and pension documents. Reisinger and Schmidt have taken holiday leave, pending our arrangements."

"OK so far," I thought to myself. However, Reischl's voice appeared hurried.

"Raeder is out of jail," Reischl continued. "A Nazi judge had him released on a technicality. Be careful!" Reischl hung up the phone.

## Tuesday evening, January 3

Hannibal and I agree, it's time to get out of town. As he told Reischl, we plan to disappear for a few months. But where?

Over breakfast this morning, Hannibal asked: "Have you ever thought about skiing?"

I put down my coffee cup. My mouth opened as if I were going to say something, but nothing came out. My mind drew a blank. In hindsight, I'm sure my expression was very comical.

Finally, I gave Hannibal my best snooty expression and replied: "No, but I'm sure I could do it."

Hannibal laughed heartily, but reached over and patted my hand. "I know of a little town in Switzerland with a great view of the Matterhorn," he said. "The town is called Zermatt. It's a ski resort."

His face grew serious, and he added: "Years ago, I stayed at a hotel there. It's called the Mont Cervin Palace. It's a great place to hide for a while."

I thought for half a minute. I put the real reason for leaving Berlin at the back of my mind and concentrated on the fun part. "Why not?" I thought to myself. "Learning to ski might be fun."

Images of travel posters danced in my mind. Beautiful people, snow-covered mountains and me, gliding effortlessly down a snowy slope. "How romantic!" I concluded.

I looked at Hannibal again, tossed my head, sniffed and said: "Only if I can go shopping first. I'll need the proper wardrobe."

Hannibal leaned back, laughed again and replied: "Of course!"

"He always knows what I'm thinking," my thoughts continued. "How does he do it?"

Hannibal spent the day making arrangements to ship our car and most of our baggage by rail to Vienna. Our things will be stored at the Grand Hotel Wien, Kaerntner Ring 9.

We, on the other hand, will travel light to the little town of Zermatt, with several stops along the way. What should I wear?

## Wednesday evening, January 4

Things are moving so fast! After breakfast, Hannibal made phone calls about hotels, trains and planes. Airplanes? Wow! I had dreamed of flying, but it was always a fantasy.

By this afternoon, Hannibal had settled our bill with the Aldon through Thursday night, prepared a set of schedules for getting out of Berlin and made reservations at the Schweizerhof hotels in Zurich and Bern and the Mont Cervin Palace in Zermatt. He also made the proper arrangements with regard to our passports and modes of travel.

We have reserved tomorrow afternoon for shopping.

## Thursday noon, January 5

Thursday started in a pleasant manner. After breakfast, Hannibal and I packed our steamer trunks with most of our stuff for Vienna and our travel suitcases for our 'vacation' in Zermatt.

I left room in our suitcases for several new skiing outfits. Bellmen helped us pack the car. We made a gay production of it; we both wanted to set aside thoughts about our real reason for leaving Berlin.

After these hurried notes and lunch, we plan to shop all afternoon for skiing clothes. We will return to our 'bare bones' Adlon suite for the night.

On Friday morning, we will turn in the keys to our suite and drive to the Schöneberg freight train platform, where we will process our car and steamer trunks for shipment to Vienna.

Afterwards, porters will help us with our suitcases and we will take a taxi from the freight platform to the S-Bahn passenger side, where we will board the underground train to the airline terminals on Tempelhof Field.

From Tempelhof, we will fly on a Deutsche Luft Hansa Airlines Junkers G31 tri-motor to Zurich, with refueling stops at Leipzig and Stuttgart. The airplane carries 15 passengers, a flight attendant and three crew members. How modern! Our airplane takes off at 3:00 PM Friday, so we have plenty of time.

After an overnight stay in the Zurich Schweizerhof, we will take a train from Zurich to Bern, stay at the Bern Schweizerhof and then travel to Zermatt.

## Thursday evening, January 5

Shopping was so much fun! I was reminded of our times in Paris. The after-Christmas sales had started, and for a change, there were no SA Brownshirts in the Wertheim Department Store. I felt almost normal, even though Hannibal and I carried our usual weapons.

We were both dressed casually; I wore wool slacks, a turtleneck sweater and a warm leather coat. Even Hannibal had opted for slacks, a sweater and a heavy wool coat.

Hannibal was very patient with me. I picked out matching Dale of Norway sweaters, scarves and stocking hats for Hannibal and me. I chose ivory with black decoration, perfect for the ski resort. I also bought a lined white wool coat and a jaunty, matching beret for myself.

We also each bought black wool slacks; mine were form-fitting and accented my slim figure. Hannibal, always the practical one, suggested long cotton underwear and thick cotton socks. Oh, well.

We also bought fur-lined leather gloves and hiking footwear. How are we going to get all of this in our suitcases?

Events worked out as planned until we finished shopping at about 3:00 PM. My nightmare began when Hannibal and I left the Wertheim Department Store. It seems like a dream now, but I know it was real.

We had just walked out the Wertheim doors on Voss Strasse. We were both loaded with packages.

Hannibal said: "Wait here; I'll get the car and pick you up."

"OK," I replied. The wind was whipping around the corner of the building, and I didn't relish the prospect of walking to our car, which was in a lot nearly a block away.

"I'll be waiting over there, out of the wind." I motioned with one of my bags toward a nearby alcove that bordered on a narrow alley.

"Back in a couple of minutes," responded Hannibal, as he hurried east, into the wind, on the Voss Strasse sidewalk. He carried most of the packages.

As I stepped into the alcove, I glanced down the alley. I saw a familiar face. Raeder! Four burly men in SA Brownshirt uniforms stepped up behind him.

Raeder glared and yelled: "Angriff diese Frau!" The four men rushed forward.

I dropped my packages. I realized that I wouldn't have time to take out my Walther, so I also dropped my purse. In two smooth motions, I pulled off my right glove with my left hand and slipped my right into the false pocket of my pants. I had just enough time to grasp the hilt of my sheath knife that was strapped to my thigh.

In seconds, three men confronted me, close up. Two passed to my sides and one approached directly in front. The fourth was a little behind the others.

I flexed my knees and brought my knife up. The point caught the man in front under his chin, slid up in his mouth and deep into his upper palate. I pushed the knife forward and then pulled it down and out. He let out a gurgling scream; red blood sprayed everywhere.

Hands grasped at my shoulders and arms. I dropped to the sidewalk and rolled to the right. The grasping hands didn't get a grip.

I slashed with my knife in a sweeping stroke. I felt it cut muscle and tendons as it passed behind the knee of my opponent on the right. Another scream.

A red filter passed over my sight as I scrambled to my feet. My fury rose to a fever pitch. I no longer thought; my body heaved and twisted. I was aware that two men were down.

I focused on the man who had trailed behind. I saw terror in his eyes as my knife slashed across his face. Blood sprayed as he fell back.

I dropped into a knife fighter's stance and spun toward my remaining opponent on the left. He started to turn and run. I didn't let him. As I stepped forward, my knife hit him in the right side. I felt raging satisfaction as the knife slid in up to the hilt. More screams as the man fell to the pavement.

Only Raeder remained. I saw him as he stood back a few meters from the fray. His face was twisted into a hideous mask. I gave out a primal, animal scream and sprinted forward.

Raeder's right hand held a Luger. He pointed and fired. Bang! I heard a whizzing sound by my right ear.

I closed the gap between us. I held my knife forward and focused all of my energy, my being, into its point. My mind had already stabbed the point into that hideous face.

Boom! The sound came from behind. Raeder's Luger flew from his hand. He twisted and fell. More blood, this time from Raeder's mangled right hand.

My momentum carried my body over Raeder as he lay face down on the pavement, screaming. I spun around to face the source of the last gunshot.

Through my mind's red haze, I saw a calm face, yet with glittering, icy eyes. Hannibal stood there, with his forty-five. Our car rested along the curb, engine running.

"Get in the car, Caroline;" Hannibal said softly, yet clearly. His voice had a calming effect. Slowly, the red faded.

I looked around. Several bystanders stood near the entryway of Wertheim's. All had expressions of amazement.

I looked down. My packages and purse lay scattered on the sidewalk. Hannibal opened the passenger door of our car. He then walked over where he could see all five men who writhed in agony on the pavement at the edge of the alley.

I took a deep breath and let it out. I bent over my nearest fallen opponent, wiped the blood from my knife on the leg of his pants and slipped the knife through my false pocket into its sheath.

I then picked up my purse and packages and tossed them through the open door of the car. I calmly got in on the passenger side and shut the door.

After a few seconds, Hannibal got in on the driver's side. He looked closely at me for several moments. "OK?" he finally asked.

I looked at him and tried to smile. "Yes," I finally uttered. "Let's get out of here."

"We'll turn in the car and head for the airfield," Hannibal replied. "There is a street map in the glove compartment. You navigate."

I could tell that Hannibal was giving me something constructive to do so I wouldn't dwell on recent events.

Yet I felt something; someone was watching. I looked out the car window. Across the street, I saw a figure. It was Villian.

Hannibal revved the engine and sped away. I reflected for several moments as we careened between piles of crusted, dirty snow on Voss Strasse. "What have I become?" I thought to myself.

My thoughts continued: "Those five men were alive when we left." This thought, though comforting, was not enough. "When the red rage boiled to the surface, I tried my best to kill," I concluded.

I put my dark thoughts into a deep recess of my mind and fumbled for the map in the glove compartment.

I unfolded and concentrated on the map. Finally, I said: "Turn left on Königgrätzer." I looked ahead through the windshield. "It's a block away."

We sped to our turn, made it, and headed east-southeast. I gave directions. We turned right on Belle Alliance Strasse, and right again on Dreibund Strasse. Fifteen minutes later, we passed the Tempelhof Military Bahnhof on the left and pulled up by the Schöneberg Bahnhof civilian freight platform.

Hannibal arranged to turn in the car and our trunks. I scrambled and packed our new purchases in our suitcases. I had to concentrate;

the suitcases were stuffed. Concentration was a good thing. The dark thoughts were temporarily forgotten.

We took a taxi from the freight platform to the S-Bahn passenger terminal and boarded the underground train to Tempelhof Terminals 1-2.

"Will we be stopped by the Nazis?" I asked, as the train sped toward the terminal.

Hannibal was quiet for a moment. Finally, he answered: "I think we'll be OK. The old customs bureaucracy is still in place, and we have American passports." He reached over and held my hand. "However, we need to leave now."

Hannibal checked in at the ticket counter. Fortunately, Deutsche Luft Hansa Airlines had a late Thursday evening flight to our destination; we wouldn't have to wait until Friday afternoon. Grateful for our good fortune, we took the evening's flight.

We are now above the clouds, with roaring engines on either side and one in front. While events are clear in my mind, I have chosen to write these pages.

I put my hand into my coat pocket and pulled out my Aldon room key. "A souvenir of two years in Berlin," I mused wryly. I looked out the window. Clouds obscured Germany below.

# 19

## INTERLUDE

*Wednesday afternoon, January 11, 1933*

Hannibal and I arrived at the Zermatt Mont Cervin Palace Hotel late last night. We were both exhausted. I remember lights glowing along streets, snow and crisp cold.

We checked in at an ornate front desk and took a lift to the floor with our suite. Inside, I undressed, slipped into my nightwear and fell into bed. No nightmares, I was so tired.

I slept until almost noon. I finally rolled out of bed and, after a detour to the bathroom, I padded, barefoot and rumpled, into the living room. My hair was tousled and down across my eyes. I'm sure I was a sight to behold.

Hannibal was waiting, fully dressed as usual. He stood by the fireplace, sipping a cup of coffee. How does he do it? "Hummf," I muttered. "Morning."

Hannibal chuckled a little and responded: "Good morning."

I looked around. The drapes were closed; the lamps by the sofa gave out a golden glow, and embers crackled in the fireplace. "Nice," I mumbled.

Hannibal chuckled again and set his cup on the fireplace mantle. He walked over to a side table that held a silver tray with a coffee pot and cups and poured a second cup.

I padded a few steps, stumbled and semi-fell onto the sofa. After regaining my composure, I stretched, yawned, blinked my eyes and focused on Hannibal, who held a steaming cup of coffee out to me.

"Thank you," I responded. This time, my words were little more distinct. I took a couple of sips. "Humm," I added. I realized that my conversation had not been at a very high level.

Hannibal leaned over and kissed me on the cheek. I smiled and kissed him back.

"I want to show you something," Hannibal said softly. He walked over to the closed drapes and opened them slowly; the whiteness was blinding.

My eyes adjusted and I stared. Snow-covered pine trees, lovely houses and a soaring mountain peak glistened in the bright sunlight. Wow!

"The Matterhorn," Hannibal said softly. Welcome to Zermatt."

I put down my cup, got up, walked over to Hannibal and slipped into his arms. Memories of our last day in Berlin were firmly under control.

## Saturday evening, January 14

Hannibal and I rented skis and rode the Gornergrat Bahn from the Zermatt station up the mountain to a ski stop well below the Gornergrat Glacier. We wore our new ski outfits. I felt very chic.

Hannibal called the ski run a 'bunny slope.' What does that mean? He wouldn't tell me.

Skiing is hard! I spent more time on my butt than on my feet. Hannibal glided by, smoothly, effortlessly, with practiced twists and turns. When I fell, he courteously came back and helped me up. It was infuriating.

## Sunday evening, January 15

My skiing was better today. I was only on my behind half the time.

We spent a wonderful evening in the hotel bar, looking out the window at lights, snow and beautiful people.

I tried Kafi Luz. It was delicious. Hannibal explained that it is coffee with a splash of Träsch, a fruit brandy made from pear and apple pomace. I had a third round before Hannibal cut me off.

## Saturday evening, January 21

The days have passed in wonderful succession: skiing, fine dining, glowing fireplaces and snow, snow and more snow. I am completely relaxed. I know that Hannibal has spent time writing reports for Soucet and sending telegrams, but I have not participated. Hannibal understands.

## Tuesday evening, January 31

I read the newspaper this morning as I sipped coffee. Adolf Hitler is now Chancellor of Germany.

Thoughts about the rest of the world intruded into my images of our cozy Swiss vacation. After reading the newspaper, I reviewed my memories of our last day in Berlin.

I distinctly remember seeing Villian during my fight with Raeder and his stormtroopers. He was watching but didn't interfere. Why?

## Friday evening, February 3

Hannibal received two telegrams today. One was from Soucet. It was short and to the point. It read: 'Good work. Substantial deposit in your bank account. Vienna confirmed.' The other was from Reischl, and it read: 'Safe in Heidelberg. Reisinger and Schmidt in Zurich. See Chief Inspector Georg Richter in Vienna. He knows you are coming.'

Our idyllic Swiss sojourn will end too soon.

## Friday evening, February 10

My skiing has much improved. I didn't fall down once today. I am so proud of myself!

Late this morning, we rode the Gornergrat Bahn to ski run number six. We made our way to the Chez Vrony Restaurant for lunch. The chef, who seemed to know Hannibal, introduced us to Sprüngel and Lindt chocolate truffles for dessert. Exquisite!

I topped it off with Kafi Luz. Hannibal stopped me after three glasses. I don't remember how we got off the mountain; I think we took the Gornergrat Bahn. I do remember having the hiccups.

## Tuesday evening, February 28

I read several Berlin newspapers this morning. Yesterday evening, the Reichstag building was set on fire. In a *Der Angriff* editorial, Göring blamed the communists.

In another editorial, Hitler has urged von Hindenburg to sign a decree that would suspend citizen civil rights and allow detention without trial. The round-up of communists has begun. More violence in the streets.

I'm glad we are going to Vienna. Hannibal is already making plans and schedules. We will travel by train. I am now ready to help.

## Friday evening, March 3

Hannibal and I studied train routes today. For obvious reasons, we chose a route that avoids Germany. From Zurich, we will travel to the Swiss-Austrian border at Feldkirch. Hannibal said that the Austrian customs process will be tedious, but for us, safer than Germany.

At Feldkirch, we'll change trains after customs and continue on to Innsbruck, where we will rest for a couple of days. We will then travel to Salzburg, spend the night, and then on to Vienna.

## Sunday evening, March 5

We will leave Zermatt on Saturday, March 11 and arrive in Vienna on Saturday, March 18. Our Duesenberg and trunks should be waiting for us at the Grand Hotel Wien, Vienna.

We have hotel reservations at the Schweizerhof hotels in Bern and Zurich, the Schwarzen Adler in Innsbruck and the Hotel Sacher in Salzburg. Feldkirch will be a customs stop only.

The Schwarzen Adler is located at the corner of Universität Strasse and Kaiserjager Strasse, just a few blocks from our train stop at the Hauptbahnhof. Hannibal said we can take a taxi.

The Hotel Sacher is at Schwarz Strasse 5-7, which is a couple of kilometers by taxi from the Salzburg Hauptbahnhof. Hannibal said we will have a great view of the Hohensalzburg Fortress, one of the largest castles in Europe. Sounds romantic!

I plan to make the most of our five remaining days in Zermatt. Shopping is at the top of the list.

## Thursday afternoon, March 9

A couple of days after Hannibal and I arrived in Zermatt, I spotted a quaint jewelry store on the south side of Bahnhof Strasse, just west of the Gornergrat Bahn. I saw a beautiful wrist watch in the window. I made a mental note to return. Today was the day.

This morning just after breakfast, I dressed stylishly and warmly in my winter resort ensemble. After I donned my white wool coat, spun on my cashmere scarf, perched my beret at a cocky angle on my hairdo and slipped on my fur-lined gloves, I sauntered into the living room of our suite.

Hannibal was at a small desk, writing a report for Soucet. I slipped over and kissed him on the cheek. "I'm going shopping," I whispered in his ear. "You know, a woman's day out."

Hannibal, smiled, leaned back and replied: "So I see. Will you be back for dinner?"

"Of course," I replied. "I'll have a light lunch while shopping, but I expect fine dining tonight." I grinned mischievously. "What do you have in mind?"

"We can eat downstairs in the Mont Cervin Palace dining room," Hannibal responded. "How about six this evening?"

"Sounds good," I replied. "I'll be back this afternoon." I kissed him again, turned and slipped quietly out the door.

The street outside the hotel was a winter wonderland. Blue sky, deep snow everywhere and the Matterhorn gleaming in the bright sun. I put on my dark glasses.

The doorman hailed a taxi for me, and I was on my way to Bahnhof Strasse.

The taxi driver dropped me off right in front of the jewelry store. A sign above the door read: 'Uhrmacher Schoenberg.'

A little bell jingled above the door as I walked inside. Glass cases of lovely necklaces, rings, watches and other women's items lined the walls on both sides and in front.

A little old gentleman stepped out from a back room, looked at me, smiled and said: "Guten Morgen, schöne Dame. Was kann ich dir zeigen?"

"Guten Morgen. Ich bin Caroline Jones. Ich sah eine reizende Rolex-Uhr im Fenster. Kann ich es sehen?"

"Ah," responded the old man. "I am Adolf Schoenberg. You have excellent taste." He paused and then gave his sales pitch. "Rolex watches are the finest in the world." His eyes twinkled and he added: "A gift?"

I liked Herr Schoenberg instantly. I smiled and replied: "For my husband."

Schoenberg slipped out from behind the counter and toddled over to the window. Half a minute later, the Rolex lay on a green felt cloth on the counter. It was beautiful.

"It's the newest model 2323 Rolex Oyster," said Schoenberg in a soft voice. "Self-winding, stainless-steel case and waterproof. The front is plated in 18-karat gold."

As I reached down and picked up the watch, Schoenberg added: "With proper care, it should last a lifetime."

Twenty minutes later, I walked out of Schoenberg's with the Rolex. Herr Schoenberg had kindly placed it in a gift box and wrapped it in lovely gold paper.

"I'll give it to Hannibal tonight over dinner," I thought to myself. I had a light lunch at a nearby café and thought endlessly on how I would make the presentation. "Dinner first, and presentation over wine and dessert," I decided. "I will hide the gift box in my purse."

## Saturday morning, March 11

I gave Hannibal his new watch at dinner on Thursday evening. He was so surprised! The moment was wonderful. I'm now ready to go to Vienna.

# 20

## ISAAC ROSENFELD HAS DISAPPEARED

*Saturday evening, March 18, 1933*

Hannibal and I arrived at the Vienna West Bahnhof early this afternoon. We had lots of luggage, so we took a taxi to the Grand Hotel Wien. What an experience!

At breakneck speed, the driver made the trip in less than 15 minutes. Street signs whizzed by as we zipped along Ziegler Gasse and Neubau Gasse to the Burgring. We whipped a right turn on the Burgring and somehow ended on the Kärntnering.

The hotel was on the left on the other side of a tree-lined median, so the driver passed the hotel, did a daring U-turn and dropped us off right in front. Whew!

As I caught my breath; the doorman opened our taxi door, tipped his hat and then led a squad of bellmen to our luggage. Like a swarm of bees, they loaded carts and whisked everything away. Hannibal took care of tips and checked us in at the front desk. I tried, with only moderate success, to stay out of the way.

I looked around outside the hotel entrance. "Too early for spring flowers," I mused. However, budding trees lined the street median and tulips were just peeking through the soil in planters by the hotel door. "Lovely," I remarked to one of the bellmen, as he loaded suitcases on a cart.

"Yes, Madame," he replied with a grin. "We had rain Thursday; the snow has melted, and everything is fresh and clean." He looked up at the clear blue sky and added: "Cool and sunny yesterday and today. The weather should be nice for the next few days. Enjoy our city." He then trundled the loaded cart inside.

After finishing in the lobby, Hannibal and I took the lift to the fourth level above the ground floor, walked down a long, brightly lit hallway and ended at a corner suite. Inside, the drapes were open, and I could see a busy square just a block away down the Ringstrasse. People, autos, streetcars and lorries were everywhere.

Hannibal slipped up behind me, pointed out the window and said: "The Opera House is on that square. Welcome to the heart of old Vienna."

I didn't have time to answer, the luggage arrived. Hannibal took care of everything. Finally, the door closed, and our suite was quiet.

I slipped off my coat and shoes and collapsed on my back across the bed. I could hear Hannibal's chuckles as I faded away. My final thought was: "Zermatt was a sleepy little town. Not so, Vienna."

Hannibal woke me up with a soft kiss at about five o'clock. "Nice," I whispered, as I opened my eyes and focused on Hannibal. He was fully dressed. "Hummf," I muttered.

Hannibal's smiled and said: "I made some phone calls while you slept. Our car and steamer trunks will be delivered to the hotel on Monday morning."

"I also called Capitaine François Coulondre, who, according to Soucet, is our trusted French Embassy contact," Hannibal continued. "The embassy is on Schwarzenberg Platz, a few blocks south of our hotel. We arranged to exchange information in Stadt Park, which is a convenient walking distance from this hotel and the embassy."

"Hummf," I responded again. I listened, but my mind was just beginning emerge from pleasant contemplation.

Hannibal chuckled again and said: "We have dinner reservations downstairs at seven. Chief Inspector Georg Richter will join us." He paused and added: "Richter said our meeting was urgent."

"Humm," I responded. My voice came out in a hoarse whisper. I cleared my throat and my brain at about the same time. "Business first, I suppose," I added more distinctly, with a seductive smile.

Hannibal chuckled again and said: "We'll keep the meeting short." He gave me another kiss and a quick hug.

"Very nice," I whispered again, as I reached up and pulled him down for another kiss.

Hannibal kissed my cheek, smiled knowingly and said: "Now get out of bed."

"OK, OK," I responded with a deep sigh. I got up, slowly shed my clothes on the way to the bathroom and closed the door with a soft click.

"That will give him something to think about," I muttered and then giggled. I showered, dressed and fixed my hair just in time for dinner.

We took the lift down and entered the main dining room just before seven. When we arrived at the hotel earlier, I had noticed that people in Vienna dress much more formally compared to vacationers in Zermatt, so we both wore suitable business attire.

As Hannibal checked us in for dinner, I spotted a well-dressed gentleman, with white hair and luxuriant mustachios, sitting on a sofa in an alcove just inside the dining room. The gentleman saw my glance, got up and walked over. He carried a small briefcase.

"Guten Abend. Habe ich die Ehre des adressenden Major und Madame Jones?" He said with a slow smile.

"Guten Abend," answered Hannibal. "Ja, ich bin Hannibal Jones und das ist meine Frau Caroline. Bist du Chief Inspector Richter?

"Yes," replied Richter. "Welcome to Vienna." The two men shook hands. Richter turned to me, smiled again, clicked his heels and bowed formally. "Ah, the lovely Mrs. Jones," he said.

I offered my hand and Richter kissed it gently. I liked Richter immediately.

Soon we were seated. The head waiter came over, offered us menus and a wine list and poured water. I looked at the menu and drew a blank.

I could tell that Richter noticed my expression. He turned to Hannibal and said: "May I offer some suggestions?"

Hannibal glanced at me, then turned back to Richter and said: "Please. We would appreciate your assistance."

"Ah, then you must try kürbiscremesuppe for starters," responded Richter. "The pumpkins are grown locally." He paused and then added: "Our salads are made with vogerlsalat lettuce, tomatoes and black beans. For a main course, you must try our Wiener schnitzel, white asparagus and boiled potatoes."

Hannibal looked at me, and I nodded. Hannibal turned to Richter and said: "We appreciate your recommendations." He paused and added: "I bet Caroline would also like this hotel's version of a Sachertorte with Viennese coffee for dessert."

Richter smiled politely, signaled the waiter, and ordered for the three of us.

The dinner, including a local semi-dry Riesling wine, was wonderful. By the time I had my second cup of coffee, I was stuffed.

As we sipped our coffee, I could tell that it was time for business.

Richter looked long at Hannibal and then me. He set down his cup and said: "My friend Chief Inspector Reischl sent a letter about your exploits in Berlin." He paused and added: "I have a case that would benefit from your unique skills."

Hannibal and I waited. I took another sip of coffee, fiddled with my teaspoon and listened intently.

After a long moment, Richter said: "Isaac Rosenfeldt, a prominent Jewish businessman and banker, has disappeared."

My expression asked the obvious question, so I waited for Richter to continue. My thoughts raced through possibilities.

After a moment, Richter added: "Frau Rosenfeldt reported Isaac missing this morning, March 18. Based on our initial investigation, we don't know what happened to him."

"Background?" I asked.

Richter nodded and replied: "On Tuesday, March 14, Isaac Rosenfeldt filed a complaint with my department. He said that Ludwig Schweiger, a Viennese art dealer, and Günther Kellerman, his associate, had visited his home on March 13, along with two other men."

I looked up, and I'm sure my eyes widened.

Richter noticed my expression. After a pause, he continued: "Schweiger and Kellerman made veiled threats and offered to buy the Rosenfeldt art collection at ridiculously low prices. The four men left with twelve paintings. Rosenfeldt's complaint lists the paintings, and they are quite valuable."

"Kellerman!" I blurted.

Richter smiled. "Chief Inspector Reischl told me about your previous encounter with Kellerman in Berlin." He paused and then continued: "I checked, and Schweiger has a gallery near the corner of Schottenring and Borsegasse, not far from this headquarters. He, and apparently Kellerman, operate from that location."

After a pause, Richter continued: "Isaac and Frau Rosenfeldt follow family tradition and collect art, including many old masters. They own medieval religious works by Giotto di Bondone, Piero della Francesca and later paintings by Van Eyck, Vermeer and Rubens, among many others."

"I have seen some of the Rosenfeldt collection," responded Hannibal. "When I was young, my parents and I visited Vienna. Many of the paintings owned by the family were loaned to the Akademie der Bidenden Kunste on Schillerplatz for display. I visited the gallery several times. The collection is worth a fortune."

I looked at Hannibal. "You are full of surprises," I thought to myself. I'm sure my expression belied my thoughts. Hannibal saw my expression and just smiled.

"Ah," responded Richter. "I see that you are well-versed in our Viennese art culture. Rosenfeldt family members have been patrons of the arts for generations."

"Where do the Rosenfeldts live?" I asked.

"Isaac and Frau Rosenfeldt have a mansion on Rohr Warthestrasse in Döbling, which is northeast of the Vienna city center," replied Richter. Their home is about a 40-minute drive from here."

Mentally, I had already accepted the case. I gave a nod to Hannibal, and he understood. He turned to Richter and said: "Caroline and I will do our best to help."

"Shall we meet again at my office?" Richter responded. "It is on the second level in the Police Headquarters building at Schottenring 11." He reached into his briefcase, which he had placed by his chair. He pulled out a file and gave it to Hannibal. "Some light reading before our meeting," he added. His eyes twinkled a little.

"Directions?" I asked. "We will soon have a car."

"Follow the Ringstrasse along the Operaring, Burgring and Rennering, and you will arrive at Schottenring," replied Richter. "The headquarters is on the left at the corner of Schottenring and Hohenstaufengasse. You can park in the police lot at the rear of the building. It's about a 20-minute drive from this hotel."

Hannibal nodded and said: "Would nine o'clock Tuesday morning be OK? Our car will be delivered Monday morning, and we have some research to complete before our meeting." He held up Richter's file.

"Yes," replied Richter. He frowned a little and added: "Be careful who you speak with and what you say at the headquarters and elsewhere; the Nazis have spies everywhere." He paused and added: "As you may have guessed, I am not a member of the Nazi Party."

After a final sip of coffee, Richter leaned back in his chair and said: "I am relieved that you are in Vienna. My friend Reischl said that you are the best in the business." He paused and added: "This has been a most pleasant evening."

He then signaled the waiter and insisted on paying the bill. After the usual pleasantries, Richter left and Hannibal and I returned to our suite.

As expected, Hannibal followed up on my seductive teasing earlier. I had pleasant dreams afterwards.

## Monday evening, March 20

Hannibal and I decided to expand our homework before our meeting with Richter on Tuesday. In addition to reading Richter's file on the Rosenfeldt case on Sunday, we spent today at the Österreichische Nationabibliothek, the main library in Vienna.

The Richter file included Isaac Rosenfeldt's written complaint of March 14, an undated carbon copy of a bill of sale for twelve paintings and a missing person report signed by Frau Rosenfeldt on March 18.

Rosenfeldt stated in his complaint that Schweiger and Kellerman threatened both himself and his wife and coerced him to sign the bill of sale for the paintings at bargain prices. Hannibal and I agree, the prices amount to confiscation.

The missing person report was signed by Frau Rosenfeldt at 10:00 AM, Saturday, March 18. It stated that Isaac had disappeared at 9:00 AM on Friday, March 17.

At the library, Hannibal and I reviewed books on Austrian government, Viennese ethnic groups, foreign and local newspapers and current Austrian political flyers and pamphlets. It was heavy reading, but we wanted to know how the Rosenfeldt case fits into the big picture of Austrian events.

Current publications show political and social turmoil. After the outbreak of the World War and the first Austrian defeats on the eastern front, an exodus of 350,000 refugees began in the eastern regions of the empire, especially Galicia.

According to the *Arbeiter Zeitung* newspaper, the refugees included some 70,000 desperately poor Jews, all of whom arrived at Vienna's Northern Railway Station. The article went on to say that these 'Ostjuden,' for the most part, remain unassimilated into Vienna society.

Last year in May, a new cabinet was formed under the leadership of Chancellor Engelbert Dollfuss of the Christian Social Party (CSP). Dollfuss's coalition, composed of the CSP, the Landbund, and the Heimatbloc, had a one-vote majority in the Nationalrat parliament.

Just last month, the Social Democratic Worker's Party (SDAP) and the Nazi Party pressed Dollfuss for new elections, but he refused. Instead, he sought support from the Heimwehr, a right-wing fascist militia.

Last week, urged on by Benito Mussolini, Dollfuss completely ended parliamentary government. Austria is now an Italian-style fascist state.

Among his first acts as dictator, Dollfuss outlawed the Nazi Party, the politically insignificant Austrian Communist Party and the SDAP, including its well-armed, well-trained, 80,000 strong Republikanischer Schutzbund militia.

Rather than disband, the Schutzbund went underground. Street battles between opposing Heimwehr and Schutzbund militias occur frequently in Vienna, Linz and other cities.

According to articles in the *Kronen Zeitung*, an Austrian newspaper with strong Nazi ties, old files of the *Arbeiter Zeitung* and SDAP publications sympathetic to the Jews, the Nazis also remain active. The Ostjuden refugees are the victims of many prejudices because of their poverty and non-conventional appearance, and they are frequently the targets of violent anti-Semitic attacks.

A few older, assimilated Vienna Jewish families have wealth. Several SDAP flyers allege that greedy Nazis see an opportunity.

With popular anti-Semitic support, the Nazis have made threats and have begun the illegal confiscation of Jewish property.

After our somber readings, Hannibal and I agree. The Austrian government is in the process of collapse. Anti-Semitism, fueled largely by the Nazis and other right-wing groups, is rampant in Vienna. The Rosenfeldts are among its many victims.

Even before we begin the Rosenfeldt case, Hannibal and I will compose a report for Soucet on the political and social situation and pass it through secret contacts to the French Embassy.

## Tuesday evening, March 21

Hannibal and I arrived at police headquarters just before 9:00 AM this morning. The parking lot had several older, rather battered police cars. After a quick look around, we entered the headquarters building.

As the bellman had predicted when we arrived, the weather was cool but sunny. We wore light coats over our business attire.

Inside the headquarters, we shed our coats and found a directory. Richter's suite was in a quiet corner on the second level of the building. We walked up the broad stairs and found the suite with no problem.

A young lady rose from her desk just inside the suite main door and greeted us politely. Her name was Rachel, and she took our coats and escorted us to Richter's office.

After the usual pleasantries, Richter gave us a quick tour of his oak-paneled office, an austere adjacent squad room with furniture for a dozen junior detectives, a conference room and of course, a coffee bar. He also showed us a smaller but very nice office for visiting investigators, which was just across the squad room from his office.

"Please make yourselves at home," said Richter as we entered the visitor's office. "Rachel can provide you with any supplies that you may need."

I looked around. Our oak-paneled office contained a desk, a table and four chairs. I looked out the large window and saw the Schottenring below. "Very nice," I said. "We appreciate your hospitality."

Richter smiled and responded: "Reischl told me that you two are well worth your fee." His smile turned to a frown and he added: "Given the current turmoil in Vienna, you will earn it."

He lowered his voice and continued: "When he returns, I will introduce you to Eric Lackner, my key investigator. His voice dropped to a whisper. "Several of my other detectives are members of the Nazi Party."

After a long pause, Hannibal asked: "Have there been any new developments in our current case?"

"Yes, responded Richter in a normal voice. "After you get your coffee and settle in, please come into my office." With that, he turned, walked quietly out of our office, across the squad room and into his own.

I looked around, spotted a couple of coffee cups and gave one to Hannibal. We then stepped out into the squad room. Only two detectives were there at the far end, reading files scattered on a table. "The rest must be out on cases," I whispered to Hannibal.

"Humm," responded Hannibal. "Let's get coffee and introduce ourselves."

After we got our coffee, we stopped by the two young men. Both looked up as we approached. They smiled, but with a look of curiosity.

Hannibal introduced us. "I am Major Jones and this is Mrs. Jones. We have been asked to help with one of Chief Inspector Richter's cases."

The pair introduced themselves as Detectives Hans Ritter and Johann Altman. I saw immediately that each man had a silver pin in the lapel of his jacket. The pins had an eagle above a swastika within a wreath. I had seen them before, in Germany, worn by SA Brownshirts.

A warning thought echoed in my mind: "Careful, Caroline."

The men were cordial enough. They seemed curious about American detectives working in Vienna, but they only asked polite questions.

Hannibal soon excused us, and we headed to Richter's office with our coffee. The pair watched us quietly as Hannibal closed the door behind us.

Richter rose from his seat behind a desk and said: "I saw that you met Ritter and Altman."

"Yes" I responded. "And I saw the pins in their lapels."

Richter smiled, nodded and replied: "Let's discuss the Rosenfeldt case." He then picked up a file from his desk and motioned use to seats around a table by the window.

After we were seated, Richter said: "We have had several new developments since we met on Saturday. I received this report on Monday morning." He held up a file folder.

Hannibal and I waited as Richter leafed through the file. After a moment, he said: "According to this report, a citizen found a crushed and bloody Homburg hat on the bank of the Danube Canal on Saturday, March 18. Local constables investigated."

He paused and then added: "The inside leather hatband had the name Isaac Rosenfeldt."

"Did the constables find a body?" Hannibal asked.

"No," responded Richter. "If there was a body, it is probably in the Danube."

Richter smiled grimly and added: "The hat was found on the canal side of the Franz-Joseph Kai, only four blocks from the Schweiger Gallery."

# 21

## SHADOW NAZIS

*Early Wednesday morning, March 22, 1933*

Last evening passed quickly, and I was exhausted from a long day. These entries document our continued work on Tuesday, following our discussion in Richter's office.

"Nazis in the shadows," my instincts tell me. "It's just a matter of time before Austria follows Germany."

As our meeting in his office ended, Richter introduced us to Eric Lackner, who had just arrived in the squad room.

After the preliminaries, Richter said: "Detective von Lackner, would you please escort Major and Mrs. Jones to the Rosenfeldt residence? I'm sure they have many questions for Frau Rosenfeldt and her household staff."

"Of course, Herr Chief Detective," responded young Lackner. He stood at attention, seemingly in awe of his superior. "I have notes on my initial interviews. I can explain my findings to date on our drive."

Richter nodded, looked at Hannibal and said: "I'll leave you in good company." He smiled at Lackner and then turned to me. "I will call the Rosenfeldt home and let them know you are on the way." He then bowed slightly and returned to his office.

I noted Richter's use of 'von' with regard to Lackner's name, even though noble titles were no longer legal in Austria. "Sign of respect, or perhaps Richter has old-fashioned ideas," I thought to myself. I tucked away this thought for future reference.

Hannibal turned to Lackner and said: "If you don't mind, I will drive so you can refer to your notes. Our Duesenberg has plenty of room for three."

Lackner's eyes widened a little; I'm sure our Duesenberg was a step up from the rather austere and battered police cars that he normally used. "Thank you, Herr Major," Lackner responded.

Soon we were on our way to Döbling and the Rosenfeldt residence on Rohr Warthestrasse. To put the somewhat nervous Lackner at ease and to assess his political views, I initially made polite conversation as Hannibal navigated Vienna's streets.

"Von Lackner is a distinguished name," I said over the chatter of the Duesenberg engine. "Is Vienna your family's home?"

Lackner smiled slightly; he seemed pleased that I had taken an interest in his background. However, his smile turned to a sad expression.

"No, my family had an estate in Galicia before the war. It was lost during the fighting, and my family was killed." He paused, and his expression turned wistful. "I'm the only survivor."

"I'm so sorry for your loss," I responded. I didn't know what else to say.

Lackner smiled again slightly and said: "As a boy, I was taken to Vienna by Jewish refugees. One of the prominent families in Döbling took me in and gave me a home and education."

He paused and then added: "After schooling, Chief Inspector Richter gave me a position in his department, for which I'm most grateful."

My instincts told me that Lackner's story was genuine. "We can trust him," my thoughts concluded.

To Lackner, I asked: "What can you tell us about your interviews at the Rosenfeldt home?"

Lackner took out a notebook, flipped a few pages and replied: "I visited the Rosenfeldt mansion on the afternoon of March 18. Since her husband disappeared, Frau Rosenfeldt, Klein the butler, Werner Krause the gardener, Anna Neuman the cook and Greta Schulz, a maid are the only occupants of the home."

"Recent guests or visitors, other than Schweiger and Kellerman?" I asked.

"No guests," responded Lackner. "However, according to Klein the butler, Reinhardt Steiner, Isaac's business partner, is a frequent visitor."

He glanced at a page in the notebook. "In fact, Klein said that Steiner arrived at the mansion on March 13, just as Schweiger, Kellerman and two burly men in militia uniforms were leaving."

"Militia?" I asked. I remembered Richter's mention of two other men with Schweiger and Kellerman.

With an expression of distaste, Lackner replied: "According to Frau Rosenfeldt and Klein, the two men wore Nazi badges, but they didn't know their names."

"Facts while Schweiger, Kellerman and the two militia men were at the home?" Hannibal asked, as he navigated traffic.

"According to Frau Rosenfeldt and her household staff, Isaac had a stormy meeting with Schweiger and Kellerman. They made threats."

Lackner flipped another page of his notes and continued: "After the meeting, the four men loaded twelve paintings into two automobiles waiting at the front of the house. Just before they drove away, Schweiger gave Isaac a carbon copy of the bill of sale that Rosenfeldt had been forced to sign earlier."

"Yes," I responded. "The copy was in the file that Richter gave us on Friday." I thought a moment and then asked: "Was payment made?"

"Not according to Frau Rosenfeldt and Klein," replied Lackner. "Frau Rosenfeldt said that Schweiger, in a sinister voice, told Isaac that if he wanted the money, he would have to visit his gallery. He gave Isaac a business card with an address."

"Did Isaac go to the gallery?" Hannibal asked.

"According to Frau Rosenfeldt, early on Friday morning, March 17, her husband stated that he was going to the gallery. She didn't see her husband again after he left the mansion at 9:00 AM."

Lackner paused and then added: "She reported him missing the next day at 10:00 AM, as you saw in her report."

"Have you interviewed Steiner or visited the Schweiger Gallery?" I asked.

"I have not interviewed Steiner, but I did visit the gallery at about 4:00 PM on Wednesday, March 16, in response to Isaac Rosenfeldt's complaint dated March 14," replied Lackner. He smiled grimly and added: "I took two uniformed constables with me."

"Wise," I responded. "Results?"

"The gallery was closed, the doors were locked and no one answered our repeated knocks," replied Lackner.

He paused a moment, smiled and then added: "There was one odd event while we were there."

"Oh?" I responded and then waited for Lackner to continue.

Lackner's eyes twinkled, and he said: "The constables and I saw a rather seedy-looking man in the alley behind the gallery. The man was loud and disorderly, so we approached him. We could smell whiskey, he put up a rather ineffective fight, so the constables cuffed him and loaded him in our car."

Both Hannibal and I looked at Lackner and waited. After a moment, he grinned and continued. "We took the drunk to this headquarters, since it has the nearest jail from our location at the gallery. We had him tossed in the drunk tank. The next day, the magistrate gave him 10 days for public drunkenness."

"He's still there?" I asked.

"I believe so," replied Lackner. "He won't be released until March 25."

"Interesting," I thought to myself. To Lackner, I said: "Perhaps I can question him before he is released. He may have seen something related to the confiscation of the Rosenfeldt paintings."

Lackner nodded and said: "Good idea. I'll arrange it."

"Do you have his name?" I asked. "And a description?"

Lackner leafed through his notebook and then said: "Herman Strader." He paused as he continued to read.

After a moment, he added: "He was an older man, perhaps mid-fifties. His workman's style clothes were tattered and dirty, and he had a cut on his left hand." I remember the cut because it was treated at the headquarters when we took his fingerprints. A clerk cleaned and bandaged his hand before he was sent to the drunk tank."

Except for the Duesenberg engine and traffic noise, silence reigned for the rest of the trip. I thought about Lackner's narrative and our upcoming interviews.

After another ten minutes or so, we arrived in Döbling. The neighborhood streets were lined with expensive homes. "Lots of wealth here," I said.

"Yes," responded Lackner. "The Rosenfeldt mansion is over there." He pointed.

## Wednesday evening, March 22

Lackner, Hannibal and I arrived at the Rosenfeldt mansion at about 1:00 PM. Hannibal parked our Duesenberg in the circular driveway, and we walked up to the mansion entrance.

A tall, distinguished-looking man in butler's attire opened the door and stood aside as we approached. I also saw a grey-haired but attractive lady watching us from a large bay window to the right of the entrance.

"I am Klein," said the butler, as we entered. "Frau Rosenfeldt and Herr Steiner are waiting for you in the library. Greta will take your coats."

"Steiner," I whispered to Hannibal. "How fortuitous." Hannibal nodded.

I looked behind Klein and spotted Greta, as she gave a brief curtesy. She was also in uniform. "Mid-twenties, attractive, well-trained," I thought to myself. I smiled to Klein and then to Greta.

Lackner, Hannibal and I shed our coats. As Klein helped me with mine, I noticed his hands. "Scratches, cuts and a broken fingernail," I thought to myself. "Unusual for a house servant."

Klein noticed my stare and quickly lowered his hands as he handed our coats to Greta. After we finished with the coats, Klein led the way to the library.

Lackner made the introductions, and Klein moved quietly to an attentive stance by the library door. Frau Rosenfeldt, in a gracious manner, said: "Please, have a seat." She motioned to comfortable-looking chairs near the window.

As we took our seats, I looked carefully, first at Frau Rosenfeldt and then at Steiner. Small and slender, Frau Rosenfeldt was dressed in the latest conservative fashion. Steiner was grey-haired, thin and impeccably dressed. I saw his hands; they had cuts and scratches like Klein's. Steiner didn't seem to notice my quick stare.

From both, I sensed old-fashioned, aristocratic manners. "Wealth and education, but not arrogance," I thought to myself. "Good first impression, except for Steiner's hands."

"Do you have any news concerning my husband?" Frau Rosenfeldt asked as Lackner, Hannibal and I made ourselves comfortable.

Lackner explained about the hat that had been found on the 18th. "We have nothing else to report, Madame," he concluded. He then turned to me and said: "Do you have questions?"

"Yes, thank you," I responded. I turned to Frau Rosenfeldt and asked: "What can you tell us about the visit of Schweiger and Kellerman on March 13?"

Frau Rosenfeldt looked at me for a moment and said: "Herr Schweiger and Herr Kellerman took twelve of our paintings. Details are in my husband's complaint to the police."

"Did they threaten anyone?" I asked.

"Yes," replied Frau Rosenfeldt. The two uniformed men with Schweiger and Kellerman held my husband and twisted his left arm behind his back while Klein and I were in Isaac's office."

Frau Rosenfeldt blinked her eyes several times. I could see tears. "Reliving the moment," I thought to myself. She took a deep breath, sighed and closed her eyes. After a moment, she opened them, and they had a hard expression. I detected controlled anger.

"They forced my husband to sign a bill of sale," she continued. "They also threatened Klein, who tried to intervene."

She looked at Klein, who stepped forward and said in a soft voice: "After the bill of sale was signed, the two uniformed men also threatened Greta, Anna Neuman, our cook and Werner Krause, our gardener."

He paused as he looked at Lackner, Hannibal and then me. He continued: "We were told that Aryans should not work for Jews, and we should leave this household."

"Yet you have not," said Lackner. "Do you want to sign a complaint?"

Klein looked at Frau Rosenfeldt and Steiner, who had shifted slightly in his chair as Klein was talking. I sensed Steiner's anger, but he quickly masked his emotions.

"No," Klein finally responded. "Greta, Anna, Werner and I agree. We trust Frau Rosenfeldt and Herr Steiner to do the right thing."

I looked at Frau Rosenfeldt and said: "In your missing person report, you mentioned that your husband left this house about 9:00 AM on March 17. What method of transportation did he use?"

Frau Rosenfeldt glanced at Klein, who answered: "He took the Rosenfeldt automobile. It's a black Mercedes-Benz W21. I can get you the license plate number."

"Yes, please," I replied. Klein left the room and returned shortly. He gave me a slip of paper with the Vienna license number W–40949. I memorized the number and passed the slip of paper to Lackner.

The room was silent for a while. Finally, I asked: "Herr Steiner, can you add anything to Frau Rosenfeldt's description of events?"

Steiner glanced quickly at Frau Rosenfeldt and Klein. He turned to me and said: "I arrived just as Schweiger, Kellerman and their two uniformed henchmen were loading the Rosenfeldt paintings in their two cars."

He paused and added: "All four saw me arrive, but they didn't say anything." He smiled grimly and continued: "They were too busy loading their loot."

Hannibal looked at Frau Rosenfeldt and asked: "Do you have other paintings and objects of art besides the paintings that were taken?"

"Good question," I thought to myself. I remembered Hannibal's statement on the 18th about the Rosenfeldt collection on display at the Akademie der Bidenden Kunste.

Frau Rosenfeldt's eyes flickered, and she glanced at Steiner. After a moment, she replied: "We had an extensive collection in our names. However, we have worked with Herr Steiner to protect it."

Steiner smiled grimly and said: "I am not Jewish."

"Ah," I thought to myself. "I wonder about all of the other Rosenfeldt assets in Vienna." I looked over at Hannibal and smiled.

He nodded. "Isaac Rosenfeldt and Reinhardt Steiner are bankers, but so is Hannibal," my thoughts continued. "Hannibal can check."

Hannibal looked at Frau Rosenfeldt and asked: "Other than your husband, do you have family members in Vienna?"

Frau Rosenfeldt returned Hannibal's steady gaze and replied: "No, but we have two married sons, Albert and Hans. They both have families. They work at our bank in Geneva."

She sighed and added: "All of our older relatives have passed." She paused, smiled wistfully and continued: "Isaac and I are the last in Vienna."

Lackner asked a few more questions to verify details in Isaac's written complaint and Frau Rosenfeldt's missing person report.

Lackner's questions reminded me; we didn't have a photo of Isaac in the file. During a pause between his questions, I turned to Frau Rosenfeldt and asked: "Do you have a photo of Isaac that we might use as we continue our search?"

Frau Rosenfeldt looked carefully at me for a moment and then said: "Yes, of course."

She got up from her chair, walked over to a table by the window, and picked up a beautifully framed photograph. She opened the back of the frame, took out the photo and brought it over to me.

"Please return it when you have finished," she said softly. "It's my favorite photo of Isaac."

"Yes, certainly," I responded. I will take good care of it." Frau Rosenfeldt returned to her seat.

Lackner continued his questions. I listened for a few minutes. "Nothing new," I thought to myself. "Time to question the cook, the maid and the gardener." I whispered in Hannibal's ear. He nodded.

I caught Lackner's attention and briefly explained my intentions. "Yes," he said. "Please do." I excused myself and headed to the door.

Klein opened the door and escorted me down the hall to the kitchen. Greta, Anna and Werner were waiting, drinking coffee.

They started to rise, but I motioned them to remain seated. Klein and I joined them at the table.

We talked for about thirty minutes. They added nothing to what we already knew, except that all four were devoted to the Rosenfeldts.

The interviews went well, but I sensed that Frau Rosenfeldt, Klein and Steiner have a hidden agenda. Was Isaac Rosenfeldt murdered? The bloody hat that was found on the bank of the Danube Canal suggests foul play, but we don't have a body.

We finished at the Rosenfeldt mansion at about 4:30 PM. "Do we have time to visit the Schweiger Gallery?" I asked as Lackner, Hannibal and I walked out the front door.

"Yes," replied Lackner. "We can stop on our way back toward the headquarters. However, it may be closed."

Lackner was right. Hannibal parked our car in front. Lackner walked up to the entrance while Hannibal and I waited in the car. Lackner knocked several times, but no one answered. He then looked at the lettering on the glass of the door and returned to the car. "They closed at five," he said. "It's now five-fifteen."

"Let's drive around the building toward the canal," Hannibal suggested. "Who knows what we might find?"

Lackner had a puzzled expression, but said: "Yes, of course."

Hannibal drove slowly to the end of the block toward the Danube Canal. He turned right on Neutor Gasse and left on Zelinka.

On the left, halfway down the block, I saw an empty lot next to the back of buildings that fronted on Schottenring. I spotted a black car behind some scrubby trees and bushes.

"There!" I exclaimed and pointed. Hannibal turned left on a dirt track that entered the lot. He stopped twenty meters from the black car.

The three of us got out of the Duesenberg. I could see the license plate. "Mercedes-Benz, license number W-40949," I stated.

"Good eye," responded Hannibal. "I'll take photos and lift fingerprints." He returned to our car to retrieve our forensics case.

To myself, I thought: "How very convenient." I walked around the car and looked behind the rear wheels. The dirt was smooth, no tire tracks.

I then recalled the bellman's statements about the weather when we arrived at the hotel on Saturday. "Rain on Thursday, which would be March 16, no rain since." The conclusion was clear: "This car was here before March 16!"

"Only a block from the gallery and three blocks from where the bloody hat was found," said Lackner. "We have probable cause. I will have a warrant for a search of the gallery tomorrow morning."

"Good," I said. "Shall we meet at headquarters about noon tomorrow?"

"Yes," replied Lackner. "I'll have the warrant by then. We can go to the gallery in the afternoon."

Hannibal walked up to me with the forensics case. Lackner was some distance away, looking in front of the Mercedes. I gave Hannibal a look and a grin and whispered: "The police search will be limited by the constraints of the warrant. Let's come back here tonight, alone."

Hannibal's eyes squinted as he looked at me. After a moment, he replied: "OK." No other words were needed.

# 22

## WHERE'S THE BODY?

*Thursday morning, March 23, 1933*

Hannibal and I have our meeting with Lackner at police headquarters in a few hours. I have time to write these notes about our adventure last night. I am still evaluating the implications with regard to our findings in the gallery.

At about midnight, we drove along deserted streets from the hotel to the dirt lot where we found the Rosenfeldt Mercedes. We were both dressed in black, and we wore gloves. Hannibal carried a backpack that contained a low-light camera, a flashlight, a fingerprint kit and my breaking and entering tools.

The Mercedes was still in the lot, waiting on the police to pick it up in the morning. We parked our car on the other side, behind some bushes.

We slipped silently along the backs of buildings to the rear of the gallery. The back door had an old-fashioned padlock with a hinged latch. "Piece of cake," I whispered to Hannibal. "Hold the flashlight while I pick the lock."

I took my lock picks out of the backpack and turned the lock up so I could see the keyhole. I saw scratches. "This lock was recently picked," I whispered to Hannibal.

Hannibal held the flashlight close and said: "Agree. Let's take fingerprints before you do your own picking. Hold the light."

We switched places. Hannibal found usable fingerprints on the latch. After he finished, we traded places again and I went to work. In just a few minutes, we opened the door.

We stepped into the pitch-black interior and closed the door silently behind us. Hannibal shined the light all around. We were in a warehouse. Shelves with tools and a variety of office supplies, picture frames and other odds and ends lined the room. We also saw a large wooden crate in a corner.

We walked over and looked carefully at the crate. On the side, I spotted a stenciled name and address. It read: 'Hildebrandt Gurlitt. Care of Pergamon Gallery, Berlin, Germany.'

"Gurlitt!" I whispered to Hannibal. "Remember the party? He's Göring's procurer of art. Kellerman is his associate."

"Humm," responded Hannibal. "Let's see what's inside." We both examined the edges of the crate. After a minute of detailed inspection, Hannibal said: "This crate was nailed shut, but it was pried open again. See the pry marks and the slightly bent nails?"

"Yes," I responded. I looked around at the tools on a nearby shelf and spotted a pry bar. "I bet this was the tool used to open the lid."

"Good guess," responded Hannibal. "I'll inspect for fingerprints before we use it ourselves."

Hannibal finished his fingerprint process in a few minutes. We then pried open the lid and looked in the crate. We saw packing materials and a dozen empty picture frames.

After a few minutes, Hannibal replaced the lid and gently tapped the nails down with the pry bar. We both stepped back and checked our work. Everything was back in place.

Hannibal looked at his wristwatch. "It's 1:30," he said softly. He grinned and added: "We have time. Want to explore?"

I giggled a little and replied: "Why not? We are already guilty of breaking and entering." I thought a moment and added: "I bet Schweiger has an office close to the front of the gallery. Let's look."

We slipped around the interior warehouse wall toward the gallery side and found a door. It opened into the main gallery building. Sure enough, we found an office down a short hallway. I could see the spacious gallery at the end of the hall.

Hannibal shined the flashlight in the office. We saw desks, chairs, tables, bookshelves and a filing cabinet. I thought a moment and then said: "Let's look at files."

"Good idea," replied Hannibal. "Any file with the name Rosenfeldt, Kellerman or Gurlitt would be of interest."

Soon I was leafing through files while Hannibal held the light. After a couple of minutes, I said softly: "Rosenfeldt!"

I pulled the file, and we walked over to a nearby table. I opened the file and turned pages while Hannibal held the light.

I found the original of the Rosenfeldt bill of sale. I peered closely. It matched the carbon copy in the police file except for one detail. "Look at the entry under Rosenfeldt's signature," I said.

Hannibal leaned over and looked. "An entry in the same hand writing as the signature," he mused. 'Paid in full, March 17, 1933.' He stepped back and added: "Hold the light while I take photos."

After a few minutes, we finished. I replaced the file in the cabinet, and we inspected all around to make sure everything was in place as we found it.

When we were done, Hannibal looked at his watch again and said: "It's 2:00 AM. Time to leave."

"Agree," I responded. We walked back down the hallway, through the warehouse and out the back door. After we locked up, we slipped back along the buildings to the lot with our car. We were back at the hotel by 3:00 AM.

## Thursday evening, March 23

I'm totally exhausted. In addition to our midnight adventure, Hannibal and I met with Richter and Lackner at police headquarters at noon and accompanied Lackner when he conducted an authorized search of the Schweiger Gallery. After this diary entry, I'm going to bed and sleep forever.

As expected, Lackner had the search warrant ready when we arrived at police headquarters. "Schweiger has friends in high places," cautioned Richter as we conferred in his office. "Be careful."

"Yes, Herr Chief Inspector," replied Lackner. "We'll also pick up Rosenfeldt's car and have it taken to the police impound lot."

Richter nodded and added: "The warrant allows you to search the gallery concerning Isaac Rosenfeldt's disappearance on March 17, but nothing else. Your evidence so far is a bloody hat and Rosenfeldt's car, both found nearby."

Richter turned to Hannibal and then to me and said: "Of course, if Schweiger and company volunteer any information, such disclosures can be used as evidence in court." He smiled.

Soon Lackner, Hannibal and I were on our way to the gallery. Lackner drove a police car, and he was accompanied by two constables. Hannibal and I followed in our Duesenberg.

We arrived at the gallery at about 1:00 PM. Schweiger and a couple of secretaries were there, but Kellerman was not.

When I asked about Kellerman, Schweiger had a puzzled look and replied: "I haven't seen him since last Wednesday evening."

"That would be March 15?" I asked.

"Yes," replied Schweiger. "He went out through the warehouse. I was in the gallery with customers. I assume that he walked to his nearby apartment on Neutor Gasse. It's only a short walk."

Address?" Lackner asked. Schweiger got it from a secretary and gave it to Lackner.

"We'll check his apartment," said Lackner. He turned to one of the constables and gave instructions. The constable left the gallery and headed down the street.

"According to Frau Rosenfeldt, Isaac said he planned to visit this gallery on the morning of March 17. We found his car in a vacant lot just a block away. Did Isaac Rosenfeldt visit this gallery on that date?"

"No," replied Schweiger. Again, his face had a puzzled expression. "I was here all day on the 17th. I have not seen Herr Rosenfeldt since our visit to buy paintings at his home on March 13."

"Do you have the paintings and a bill of sale?" Hannibal asked.

"Yes," responded Schweiger with confidence. "The paintings are in a crate in the warehouse out back." He paused, smiled and added: "We already have a buyer in Berlin. They'll be shipped within a week."

"May we see the paintings?" I asked.

"Of course," responded Schweiger. "Follow me."

Lackner, the remaining constable, Hannibal and I followed Schweiger down the hallway, past the office and into the warehouse. Schweiger walked up to the crate. "Boxed and ready to go," he announced. "I'll have the warehouse man open the crate if you want."

"Yes, please," I stated in a soft voice. Lackner gave me a puzzled look.

Schweiger found a warehouse worker and gave him haughty instructions. Soon the crate was open. Schweiger and Lackner looked inside.

"What?" exclaimed Schweiger. "The paintings! They're gone!"

Hannibal and I managed to keep bland expressions on our faces. Lackner's expression combined surprise with puzzlement.

"Of course, you have a bill of sale to show ownership," I stated softly. Hannibal suppressed a chuckle.

"Yes, yes," said Schweiger. His expression was priceless. I covered my smile with my hand. We followed Schweiger as he hurried back through the hallway to his office.

He pulled the Rosenfeldt file from the cabinet and laid it on the same table that Hannibal and I had used the night before. He then leafed through the pages and extracted the bill of sale.

"Here it is," he said, as he laid the bill of sale out where everyone could see.

I leaned over and pretended to discover the annotation under Rosenfeldt's signature. "It looks like Isaac Rosenfeldt acknowledged payment on March 17, I stated. "As I recall, you said you had not seen Rosenfeldt since March 13."

"What?" exclaimed Schweiger. "Let me see." He looked at the bill of sale closely. His expression changed from surprise to puzzlement and then to anger. "Kellerman!" he exclaimed.

Lackner gave Schweiger a hard look. "Herr Schweiger, you are under strong suspicion of being involved in the disappearance of Isaac Rosenfeldt. You will therefore accompany us to police headquarters." He turned to the nearby constable and said: "Do your duty."

Hannibal and I watched as Lackner and the constable loaded Schweiger into the police car. As we watched, the other constable returned from his errand.

"I checked Kellerman's apartment," he said. "No one was at home."

Schweiger overheard. "Kellerman!" he exclaimed again.

So ended our duty day. Hannibal and I made our excuses, and we drove back to our hotel. I ate something, I think, and then headed for bed. "Very satisfying," I thought as I dozed off. "Only one loose end to tie up."

## Friday evening, March 24

Hannibal and I visited police headquarters at about noon today. I brought the photo of Isaac Rosenfeldt with me. Hannibal brought the fingerprint file that he had accumulated during our investigation.

Lackner was out, but after touching base with Richter, I was escorted by a constable to Strader's jail cell. Hannibal worked with another constable to compare the fingerprints in his file to police files.

The constable let me in Strader's cell and closed the door behind me. Strader sat on the edge of the bunk on the other side of the cell. As soon as I saw him, my expectation was confirmed. The meeting was short and the conversation implied much more than the words spoken.

Strader smiled. I'm sure he knew that I knew. "Why jail?" I asked.

"Safest place," replied Strader. His smile broadened. "I'll be released tomorrow."

"Plans?" I continued.

"Geneva is nice this time of year," responded Strader. "I have friends and family there."

"Humm," I responded. "Do you have any ties in Vienna?"

"None," replied Strader. His smile faded. "Still, I will miss Vienna; my family has been here for generations." He leaned back on the bunk, looked at me with a cautious expression and said: "What are your plans?"

I took a deep breath and replied: "I wish you the best of luck in Geneva."

Strader smiled and said: "Thank you."

I nodded, turned, tapped on the door, and the constable let me out.

I returned to our office on the second level. Hannibal was waiting. He looked up from his writing when I entered. I told him about my meeting with Strader.

He smiled and said: "Strader's fingerprints were on the latch at the back door to the gallery, but nothing inside. We have no proof that he entered. He paused and then added: "I talked with Richter."

I felt a presence behind me. I turned and saw Richter standing in the doorway. "May I come in?" he asked.

"Of course," I replied. Soon the three of us were sitting around the table. Lackner appeared in the doorway. He carried a tray with four cups of coffee, some delicious-looking apple tarts and napkins. "Let's celebrate," he said with a broad smile.

I was taken aback a little. My thoughts raced. "How much do Richter and Lackner know?" I looked at Hannibal, and he smiled. My expression said: "You told them everything!" Hannibal's smile broadened a little.

Lackner served apple tarts on four of the napkins. As we all sipped coffee and munched on our treats, Richter said: "Detective Lackner, are things in order for Strader's release tomorrow?"

"Yes, Herr Chief Inspector," Lackner replied. "I also checked the Rosenfeldt residence this morning, and it is vacant. Everyone, including the servants, are gone."

"My banking friends tell me that all Rosenfeldt assets in Vienna have been transferred to Steiner," said Hannibal. "I don't know for sure, but I expect that the missing paintings are in Geneva."

Hannibal paused and then added: "The 'Paid in Full, March 17' annotation on the bill of sale was made on March 15, the night the paintings were taken." He smiled and his eyes twinkled. "Nice touch."

"Good, good," Richter responded. "Is Schweiger still in custody?"

"Yes," replied Lackner. "However, we will have to release him soon, his attorney has already petitioned the magistrate. We don't have enough evidence to charge him with a crime."

Richter smiled and said: "Make sure that his release is delayed until the day after tomorrow." Lackner nodded and took another bite of an apple tart.

I listened to the exchange between Richter, Lackner and Hannibal with rapt attention. After a moment of silence, I ventured: "We still have a missing person."

"Ah, yes," replied Richter. He sipped his coffee for a moment and then added: "If Kellerman is in the Danube, he will probably never be found. If not, I think his Nazi friends will seek him out."

"Either way," responded Lackner, "justice has been served." Everyone remained silent for a minute or so.

Finally, I said: "When I find out Frau Rosenfeldt's new address in Geneva, I will send her the photo of Isaac." My three companions laughed.

# 23

## BROKEN GLASS

*Saturday evening, June 3, 1933*

Hannibal met with Capitaine François Coulondre, our French Embassy contact, this morning. As usual, their clandestine meeting took place in the Stadt Park, just three blocks from our hotel.

I stayed in our parlor on the sofa, reading the *Kronen Zeitung*, the *Arbeiter Zeitung*, *Der Angriff* and various Austrian political party flyers. Headlines and editorials described street battles in lurid detail.

Most of the fighting is between the Republikanischer Schutzbund, which supports the out-of-power Social Democratic Worker's Party, and the Heimwehr, which, for now, supports the Dollfuss government and the Christian Social Party.

As best that I could tell, both parties are conservative, nationalist, sympathetic to fascism, but not necessarily pro-Nazi.

The *Arbeiter Zeitung*, the Jewish newspaper based in New York, has editorials that point out that German Nazis have various splinter groups in Austria.

In addition to the 'Hakenkreuzler,' who are mostly common street thugs who wear the swastika, the main Nazi militia group is the Austrian Legion, which is sponsored by the SA Sturmabteilung.

"For the most part, the Legion appears to be based in Bavaria," my thoughts continued as I perused the *Arbeiter Zeitung*. "Also, according to Christian Social Party flyers, the Legion makes periodic incursions into Austria to disrupt transportation hubs, assassinate government officials and harass shopkeepers."

Other than political chaos, the fighting has resulted in massive damage to Jewish-owned shops and department stores, mostly by Nazi-sponsored Hakenkreuzler thugs.

Glass from broken windows litter the sidewalks, even in fashionable shopping districts. It's all very violent and confusing.

When Hannibal returned at about noon, I heard him unlock the door, enter and say: "It's me."

After half a minute of shedding his jacket and hat, he walked into the parlor, gave me a kiss on the cheek and sat down in the easy chair across from the sofa. He had a large envelope in his hand. He watched me for a moment, and I could tell that something was bothering him.

I smiled reassuringly and asked: "How did it go?"

"Coulondre said that he and Ambassador Gabriel Puaux have been warned by Soucet that the French Embassy's third secretary Henri Taittinger may have fascist sympathies."

"Taittinger?" I responded. "Here in Vienna?" I thought a moment and then asked: "Evidence?"

"Soucet passed the word to Puaux that Henri's cousin, Pierre Taittinger, is now the head of the Jeunesses Patriotes in France. They are known for their far-right politics. Henri and Pierre had meetings in Paris recently, during one of Henri's regular trips back to France."

"Humm," I responded. "Far right does not necessarily mean fascist or Nazi."

"True," responded Hannibal. "However, Soucet also passed the word that Henri met with Jacques Doriot, who has just been expelled from the Communist Party."

Hannibal paused and then added: "From our earlier money trails, we know that Doriot received money from Göring in Berlin.

According to Soucet, Doriot has become a rabid anti-communist, and he has made public statements in support of a Nazi-style government."

"I can see why Henri Taittinger's contacts have aroused suspicion," I replied. "Will our reports to Soucet through the French Embassy in Vienna remain secret?"

"I think so," Hannibal responded. "Coulondre said he will continue to safeguard our reports. Soucet trusts him."

Hannibal paused and then said: "Soucet sent word that he wants us to observe Henri Taittinger's activities."

"So many tangled webs," I responded.

Hannibal opened the flap on the envelope, took out a photo with an attached note, handed it across to me and added: "Coulondre gave me this photo of Henri Taittinger. I also have his profile and his Vienna address. He rides the streetcar to the embassy every workday."

"Surveillance?" I asked.

"Yes," responded Hannibal. "Taittinger has an apartment at number six, near the corner of Königsklostergasse and Mariahilfer Strasse. For the moment, we have no cases with Richter, so I can accompany you while you shop and snoop."

"Moi?" I replied, with a grin.

Hannibal laughed and responded. "I understand that a number of upscale boutiques with the latest in ladies' fashions line Mariahilfer Strasse."

"That's better," I replied. "How about eateries?"

"Lots of coffee shops and restaurants within sight of Taittinger's apartment," Hannibal replied. "You and I can take turns, sit inside a coffee shop by a window and watch."

"Taittinger has to get to work at the embassy," I mused. "How?"

"Coulondre found a marked-up streetcar schedule on Taittinger's desk," replied Hannibal. "He made notes."

"Humm," I responded. "Results?"

Hannibal smiled and continued: "According to Coulondre, Taittinger catches a streetcar at the corner of Königsklostergasse and Mariahilfer Strasse. The streetcar travels Mariahilfer and Babenberg Strasse to the Burgring. He changes streetcars on the Burgring. The streetcar follows the Ringstrasse east to Schwarzenberg, turns right and continues past the French Embassy. Taittinger gets off at the corner of Schwarzenberg Platz and Bruckner Strasse and walks to the embassy."

"What's our objective?" I asked.

"Find out if Taittinger meets with anyone at or near his apartment or on his way to work," replied Hannibal. "Report on who, when and what happens." He paused and added: "Soucet also cautioned us about the increasing violence in the streets. We are to observe and report."

"Have you read the newspapers?" I asked.

Hannibal nodded and replied: "Staying safe may be difficult. That's what's bothering me."

## Saturday evening, June 23

Hannibal and I keep up appearances at police headquarters by visiting a couple of times each week. Richter has been preoccupied with street violence, and Lackner has been out on unspecified cases.

We discussed Richter's situation over dinner downstairs in the Hotel Wien dining room last evening.

"Richter seems increasingly isolated," I said, as we sipped our after-dinner wine.

"Humm," responded Hannibal. "Lackner remains loyal, but the other detectives, especially Ritter and Altman, are more open about their Nazi sympathies."

"I think Richter will have a crisis soon," I responded. "He may be forced out, especially if the Dollfuss government falls."

"Agree," said Hannibal, "In the meantime, we can read daily police incident reports and provide advice, but that's about it."

"We also have our marching orders from Soucet," I replied. "With the cover story of shopping, we should continue to shadow Taittinger."

"So many troubling cross-currents," I thought to myself as Hannibal and I finished dinner and took the lift up to our suite.

When we first started our surveillance last week, we found a couple of nice coffee shops near the streetcar stop at the corner of Königsklostergasse and Mariahilfer. One or both of us visit a coffee shop each morning and evening. We alternate between shops to remain inconspicuous.

Monday through Friday, Taittinger boards the streetcar at 7:30 AM and returns at 5:30 PM. As far as we can tell, he travels alone, and we have not seen any visitors to his apartment.

On several days, Hannibal boarded the streetcar, both near Taittinger's apartment and also at the Burgring transfer, and observed Taittinger during his trip to the embassy. Nothing.

Very boring. "Get a life," I muttered once to Hannibal, as we observed Taittinger disappear into his apartment house door at 5:35 PM. Hannibal laughed.

My shopping excursions during the day have provided welcome relief. The shops along Mariahilfer have wonderful selections of hats, gloves, purses and other accessories. Sadly, the dresses, slacks and tops do not compare well with my Paris purchases.

I have therefore limited myself to leather and wool accessories. At last count, I bought six new purses, three wool scarves and two leather jackets.

Once, as I returned to the coffee shop with packages, Hannibal sighed, shook his head and said: "Our surveillance keeps the local economy afloat." I gave him my best snooty look.

So far, the only excitement has been our observation of men wearing swastika badges as they patrol the streets. On several occasions, I was in a store when a couple of them stopped and stared in the window. In each case, the sales clerks cringed and remained silent until the men moved on.

## Friday evening, July 7

I had a break in my routine today. At about two in the afternoon, I was visiting a nice leather shop on Mariahilfer Strasse. I wore my Chanel form-fitting navy-blue slacks, matching jacket, jaunty hat and tall leather boots. I wanted to find an accent belt for my outfit.

"If Marlene Dietrich can wear slacks in Hollywood, I can do it in Vienna," I told myself with a toss of my head and a sniff.

Hannibal had followed Taittinger on the streetcar. We planned to meet at one of the coffee shops late this afternoon and compare notes.

A young lady sales clerk was showing me a selection of lovely belts that accented my slacks.

As we prattled on about which belts were best, the bell over the door jingled and two burly men walked into the store. Both wore swastika badges. "Hakenkreuzler," whispered the clerk. Her face expressed sheer terror.

One of the men looked at me and in a bullying voice, growled: "Dieser Laden ist im Besitz eines Juden. Du bist Aryan. Warum bist du hier? " The clerk recoiled, put her hand to her mouth and backed away.

I didn't reply. "OK," I thought to myself. "These thugs don't want Aryans to shop in stores owned by Jews."

One of the men stepped behind me, grabbed my left elbow in a tight grip and started pushing me toward the door. "Raus," he growled. The man in front put his hand on a pistol in a holster on his belt.

"Bad mistake," the thought seared into my consciousness.

I twisted counterclockwise toward the man holding my elbow, flexed my knees, braced, and brought my right fist up into his gut as hard as I could.

The air left the man's lungs in a 'whoosh!' His eyes widened in surprise; he lost his grip on my elbow, and he stumbled back against the counter.

I continued my counterclockwise spin and faced the other man. He had his pistol out of its holster, but before he could raise it, the heel of my right hand caught him under the chin, and he stumbled backward.

I grabbed the pistol with my left hand and pulled down and away as he stumbled backward. The pistol clattered to the floor. At the same time, my left foot landed with my full weight against the inside of his left knee. He spun and fell forward and down.

I know my body twisted and turned with lightning speed, but to my mind, everything seemed to move in slow motion. I slipped my right hand through the false pocket in my slacks and found the hilt of the knife strapped to my thigh.

I turned and saw the first man as he regained his balance and breath. His eyes blazed as he moved away from the counter toward me. His right hand held a Nazi dagger. I was faster. My knife caught him across the gut just above his belt buckle. Blood oozed through the cut across his shirt.

"Aheee!" screamed the man, as he stumbled back against the counter. He dropped his dagger and clutched his sliced abdomen with both hands. I swung my knife in a sweeping arc. Blood spurted from a gash on his face, and he tripped over his own feet. In half a second, he was on the floor and moaning in pain.

"He's done," my thoughts raced.

I spun around toward the other man, who was scrambling to his knees, trying to regain his pistol. I took a quick step, raised my left foot high, and stomped down and forward into the man's side. He sprawled and rolled onto his back. I dropped on both knees to his abdomen, and the air left his lungs in a combined cry and whoosh.

His neck was exposed, and I grabbed his throat with my left hand, pinned him so I could crush his Adam's apple and shoved the point of my knife in his left nostril. His wide-open eyes could see the knife and my face, which I'm sure held an expression of hate, fury and blood-rage mixed together.

"Sie werden Ihren Begleiter nehmen, verlassen und niemals in diesen Laden zurückkehren. Verstehen?" I snarled.

My thoughts filtered through the red tint in my mind. "Get out and don't come back should be clear enough." I twisted my knife in his nostril a little to emphasize my point.

"Ya," responded the man in an abjectly frightened voice.

I extracted the knife from his nose, wiped the blood from the blade across his shirt front, cut the Nazi badge from his breast pocket, stood up, slipped my knife back in its sheath and moved over beside the horror-struck sales lady.

My most recent opponent got slowly to his feet, walked unsteadily over to his moaning companion and helped him to his feet. The pair stumbled through the door. The little bell above the door jingled a fitting end to the encounter.

I sensed movement at the rear of the store. I turned, and my right hand slipped through my pocket to my knife hilt.

Two young men stepped out from a doorway. The first said: "Thank you for defending my sister and my father's store." He held up both hands in a gesture of peace. "We belong to the Jüdische Selbstwehr, the Jewish Self-Defense League."

The young man's companion stepped forward and said: "We can take it from here."

The red slowly cleared from my vision. I took my hand off my knife hilt, straightened my clothes, smiled at the sales clerk and said:

"I like the thin blue belt with a gold buckle; it accents my navy-blue slacks nicely, don't you think?"

The two young men chuckled. One walked back through the doorway and returned with a bucket of water and some rags. The other picked up the abandoned Nazi pistol and dagger and took them through the back doorway. He returned in a few moments and said, with a grin: "For the Danube."

After my purchase, I watched as the pair cleaned the blood from the floor. When I left a few minutes later, the shop was fresh and clean, as if nothing had happened. The street was deserted as I walked back toward the corner of Mariahilfer and Königsklostergasse. However, I sensed that eyes were watching me.

Hannibal was in the coffee shop nearest the corner; I could see him through the window. He rose politely from his seat as I arrived at the table. I laid my package with its belt on a spare chair, along with my purse. My sheath knife was twisted a little under my slacks, and I made a few adjustments as I sat down.

Hannibal noticed. He raised his eyebrows a little and said: "How was your shopping experience?"

"Oh, just a typical day in Vienna," I replied with a smile. "How about you?" I reached in my left pocket, extracted the Nazi badge and laid it on the table. "I'll explain later," I added.

Hannibal was silent as he observed me for a long moment. Finally, he said: "I saw Taittinger meet with Detectives Ritter and Altman on the streetcar today. We have a tentative Taittinger-Nazi connection."

# 24

## VIENNA INTRIGUE

### Saturday evening, July 15, 1933

Our surveillance bore fruit again on Thursday. Instead of catching the early morning streetcar, Henri Taittinger met with two unknown men in the restaurant where Hannibal and I were having coffee and apple tarts.

Hannibal moved from our table to an unobtrusive corner and surreptitiously snapped a couple of photos. Taittinger and his two companions gave no indication they noticed.

After about ten minutes, Taittinger got up and departed. The two others remained and continued talking in low voices. I continued to watch and read lips.

I caught a couple of phrases uttered by one man as he said: "Dollfuss muss gehen. Wir haben Pläne." The other man nodded and replied: "Ya. Himmler wird uns von Berlin unterstützen."

I was stunned. "Dollfuss must go implies a coup," I thought to myself. "Himmler is a top Nazi in Berlin."

I whispered what I had heard to Hannibal when he returned to our table. He nodded, and his expression was grim.

After about thirty minutes, the pair parted company. As they left the restaurant, they gave no indication they had noticed us.

On Thursday evening, Hannibal gave the film to Coulondre. On Friday evening, after we returned from dinner downstairs, we got a phone call. I got up from the sofa where Hannibal and I had been reading our notes and answered.

It was Coulondre. "The two men with Taittinger were Otto Planetta, a known Austrian Nazi, and Anton Rintelen, a politician with Nazi sympathies," he said. He then hung up the phone.

I turned to Hannibal, who had remained sitting on the sofa. "We have another Nazi connection with regard to Taittinger," I said. I then relayed Coulondre's message.

Hannibal leaned forward and leafed through more notes on the coffee table. After a couple of minutes, he replied: "I don't know Planetta, but Anton Rintelen is a member of the Christian Social Party and a vocal opponent of Engelbert Dollfuss, the chancellor."

I thought a moment, then asked: "Do you think Richter has a file on Planetta?"

Hannibal leaned back on the sofa and responded: "Probably. We can ask." He paused and added: "We have to be careful of Ritter and Altman. They may be aware of your encounter with the Hakenkreuzler thugs a week ago Friday."

I shuddered a little as I remembered the feeling of being watched when I left the leather shop. I then asked: "Will our questions about a file put Richter at risk?"

"Possibly," replied Hannibal. "However, Richter is anti-Nazi. I think he knows the risks."

## Tuesday evening, July 18

Hannibal and I arrived at Schottenring police headquarters on Monday morning. Richter was in his office, and several detectives were in the squad room, including Lackner, Ritter and Altman.

The detectives in the squad room were cooperating on the latest street violence between the Heimwehr and the Schutzbund. "We have been deluged with complaints from merchants, and we have to do something," said Lackner, as Hannibal and I looked over at his plots on a city map.

Ritter looked up and his brow furrowed a little. "Yes," he said. "Bad for business." Altman merely nodded, but his eyes gazed at me for an uncomfortable moment.

"He knows about my altercation with the Hakenkreuzler," I thought to myself. To Altman, I returned his gaze, smiled sweetly and said: "If you need help, please let me know."

My ploy seemed to work; Altman lowered his gaze and returned his attention to the map. I moved toward Hannibal, who was a few steps ahead of me at the doorway to Richter's office.

"Come in," I heard Richter say. "Close the door behind you."

Soon we three were sitting in soft chairs around the coffee table. We were all silent for a while. The sun gleamed through the window, but I could see thunderclouds gathering in the distance. I looked over at Richter. He was also looking out the window.

"Late summer is foreboding in Vienna," said Richter, almost to himself. "It's the pause before fall rains and the winter of our discontent."

He turned first to Hannibal and then to me, sighed and said: "Forgive the musings of an old man. I think you have questions for me."

Since Richter was looking at me, I said: "I had an encounter with a pair of Hakenkreuzler thugs last week. Based on our research, we think a person named Otto Planetta may be involved in Hakenkreuzler activities."

Richter's smiled and replied: "And I'm sure you are gathering information for your French friends."

My heart nearly stopped. I looked over at Hannibal. He took a deep breath, leaned back in his chair and waited.

I turned to Richter and also waited. After a moment, Richter smiled and said: "I have known about your French connection since you were recommended by our mutual friend Chief Inspector Reischl."

Richter stood up, walked over to the window and looked outside for a full minute. Finally, he turned and said: "I fear for the future of my country, and I will help you against the Nazis."

He walked back to his chair and gave me a long look. His smile returned. "Ritter and Altman told me about your encounter with the Hakenkreuzler last week."

My mouth dropped open, and it took a couple of seconds for me to recover. "And?" I finally responded.

Richter chuckled, and he said: "I told them that the two men probably tried to strong-arm you while you were shopping, and you reacted in a typical American fashion."

I squirmed a little in my chair. Richter added: "I also told them that I would talk with you about it." His smile broadened a little, and he continued: "They seemed satisfied."

Hannibal also smiled and said: "Caroline doesn't like it when someone interferes with her shopping."

"I'll keep that in mind," responded Richter. He and Hannibal looked at me, waiting for a response.

I felt my cheeks flush, so I tossed my head back, gave both men my best snooty look and uttered: "Hummf." Both men laughed openly.

After a moment of recovery, I asked: "What about Otto Planetta?"

"I'll check for a file," replied Richter.

## Friday evening, July 21

Hannibal and I arrived at police headquarters this morning at about 9:00 AM. Late summer thunderstorms have started, and we both wore raincoats and carried umbrellas.

After shaking off the water and shedding our raincoats in the empty squad room, we retrieved cups and poured hot coffee at the little coffee bar. Thus fortified, we entered our little office. A thick file lay on the desk.

"No markings on the outside," I mused as I picked up the file and opened it. A quick scan of the first page revealed the names Otto Planetta, Fridolin Glass, Paul Hudl and Franz Holzweber. I also saw SS Schutzstaffel, Berlin and the name Heinrich Himmler.

I looked over at Hannibal, who had finished opening and spreading our umbrellas to dry, and said: "Richter kept his promise."

Hannibal walked over to our office door, closed it, and returned to the desk. We spent the next hour reading.

At just after 10:00 AM, we heard a knock. "May I come in?" said a soft voice. It was Richter. I immediately walked over and opened the door.

Richter entered, looked first at Hannibal, then at me and said: "At the direction of Vice Chancellor Emil Fey and his predecessor Franz Winkler, the Vienna police have been tracking all militia groups operating in Austria for several years."

He pointed to the file on our desk and added: "The men and organizations identified in that file are considered by many, including me, as a threat to the Austrian government."

"Wow!" I thought to myself. I then looked intently at Richter and asked: "Why are you sharing this information with us?"

Richter smiled and replied: "You have sources of information that are not available to us." He paused and added: "Perhaps we should pool our information for mutual benefit."

I took a deep breath, and my mind raced. "What's the downside to sharing? Richter knows we are French operatives. He could betray us if he wanted. Although not pro-French, he is certainly anti-Nazi."

I looked over at Hannibal, and he returned my gaze. I could tell we were thinking the same thing. I nodded.

Hannibal turned to Richter and said: "Agreed. We are also anti-Nazi." He then told Richter about the meetings between Taittinger, Ritter and Altman and between Taittinger, Planetta and Rintelen. He emphasized the threat of a coup against Dollfuss.

When Hannibal finished, Richter walked over to the window and looked outside for several minutes. Finally, he turned, looked at Hannibal and then me and said: "The Nazi reach is long. I'm glad we are working together."

He offered his hand to Hannibal. The two men shook hands. Richter then turned to me, smiled and said: "From all accounts, the Nazis have found out that you are a formidable opponent."

Hannibal chuckled and said: "Caroline is a very talented lady." "Hummf," I uttered. Both men laughed.

## Friday evening, July 28

Hannibal and I finished dinner early this evening, and we returned to our suite. After we made ourselves comfortable in the parlor, I began the conversation.

"So, what do we know?" I asked rhetorically. "The Nazis have taken over Germany; they have a strong presence here in Austria, and they have established adherents among French politicians."

"According to Italian newspapers, Mussolini supports an independent Austria as a buffer against Germany," responded Hannibal.

"Planetta and his associates scare me," I responded. "In addition to what I overheard in the restaurant, Richter's file shows that the Austrians consider them a serious threat." Hannibal nodded.

After a minute or so of silence, Hannibal said: "Other than contacts between Henri Taittinger, his cousin Pierre and Jacques Doriot, the Nazi-French connection remains tenuous." He paused and then added: "Of course, we have Nazi money passing from Göring to Doriot and Göring to Villian."

"We reported our findings to Soucet, but what should be our focus for the near future?" I replied.

Hannibal sighed and lay back on the sofa. I waited while he gathered his thoughts. Finally, he said: "We did what we could in Germany."

He paused, took a deep breath, let it out and added: "The Nazi threat in Austria seems imminent. I think we should concentrate on helping Richter."

"Agree," I replied. "Our own observations show that meetings are being held among Nazis and opponents to the Dollfuss government." I paused, thinking. After a minute or so, I added: "The Nazis are planning something."

Hannibal looked at me intently and said: "Your intuition is usually accurate."

"Thank you," I replied, with a grim smile. "If the Nazis target the Dollfuss government, who will support Dollfuss? France? Britain? Italy?"

"Dollfuss is a fascist, so his best bet would be to seek help from Mussolini," replied Hannibal. "In the spring, the Italian newspapers had editorials that quoted Mussolini as saying that he supports Austrian independence."

## Friday evening, August 4

Hannibal and I met with Richter at police headquarters this morning. We three sat in his office, sipped coffee, discussed the results of our surveillance and outlined our suspicions.

After Hannibal and I finished our presentation, Richter was quiet for several minutes. Hannibal and I waited.

Finally, Richter said: "I will pass on your information to Chancellor Dollfuss."

## Friday evening, August 11

Shortly after we arrived at police headquarters, Richter looked in our office door and said: "Thanks to your warning, arrangements are in progress for a meeting between Dollfuss and Mussolini in Riccione, where Mussolini has a vacation villa."

Later, after Hannibal and I returned to our hotel suite, we sat in the parlor and discussed next steps.

Hannibal began by saying: "Dollfuss reacted as we expected. Mussolini is his obvious choice for international support."

"Humm," I responded. "We have a couple of friends in Italy. I wonder…"

Hannibal's eyes twinkled. "Do you mean Ruth Melzer and Annette Salicetti?"

"Old friends," I confirmed. "It's worth a few letters."

"Have at it," said Hannibal with a smile. "I'm fairly certain Ruth and Annette would like another adventure with the Cat in the Window." He paused and then added: "Do you know how to contact them?"

"Yes," I replied. "Ruth, Annette and I exchange letters and keep each other up to date. Ruth, whose maiden name is Canossa, visits her inherited Canossa estate in Tuscany regularly and vacations in Riccione. Annette has an apartment in Rome."

"Riccione?" said Hannibal. He grinned and added: "How convenient."

## Friday evening, December 8, 1933

In response to my letter of a few weeks ago, Ruth's Christmas letter arrived today. I was so glad to hear from her! Although we keep in contact by mail, our last time together was just after Hannibal and I married in June 1929, over four and a half years ago.

For the umpteenth time, Ruth invited us to join her at her estate in Tuscany. She also brought me up to date on her friends in Riccione.

In my November letter to Ruth, I described events in Vienna and the precarious position of the Engelbert Dollfuss government. I also hinted that Hannibal and I have more than just a passing interest in European political activities.

As I knew she would, Ruth read between the lines of my letter. She provided motherly advice about being careful, and she also provided details on Donna Rachele Mussolini and the Dollfuss family.

According to Ruth, Donna Rachele is Benito's second wife. Most of the time, she resides in the villa in Riccione with her five children. In return for a quiet, affluent lifestyle, Donna Rachele has acquiesced to her husband's continued infidelities and has created friendships, including Ruth, outside of the inner circle of Benito's fascist cronies, whom, for the most part, she dislikes.

Ruth also wrote about her observations concerning the very public meeting between Dollfuss and Mussolini in Riccione on August 24. After the meeting, Dollfuss sent his wife Alwine and their two children Hannerl and Eva from Vienna to Riccione for safety.

Alwine, Hannerl and Eva are guests of Donna Rachele at the Mussolini villa, and Ruth stays at the Grand Hotel a few blocks away. Ruth, Alwine and Donna Rachele have become good friends.

## Sunday evening, December 24

Christmas Eve, and Hannibal and I have been in Vienna for nine months. Art theft, mayhem in the streets, Nazi thugs and a plot against the Austrian Government. Our reports to Soucet certainly have variety.

We both know that danger lurks underneath the holiday festivities. However, for a little while, we have chosen to concentrate on the goodness promised with the season.

Hannibal bought some lovely holiday lights and decorations, and we found a small spruce tree at a nearby street corner market. Our suite looks very festive, thank you. The Ringstrasse has been decorated for the season and the view outside our window is what Christmas should be.

Hannibal and I have everything we need, so we exchanged small gifts. Hannibal gave me a beautiful, handmade Austrian jewelry box and I gave him fur-lined slippers. The gifts are perfect.

# 25

## MEAN STREET SNOOPING

*Friday evening, January 26, 1934*

Hannibal and I spend several days each week at the Schottenring Police Headquarters. As promised, Richter shares his steady stream of violent incident reports. Skirmishes continue between the Heimwehr and Schutzbund militias.

The Heimwehr is fascist but not pro-Nazi, and the Schutzbund, banned by the Dollfuss government but still a potent force, is socialist but not necessarily communist. Detectives and constables, including those with Nazi sympathies, carry out Richter's orders to keep the two militias apart, but the police are too few to have much effect.

So far, the Austrian Army has not intervened. The result is chaos in Vienna and other Austrian cities. In the meantime, the Nazis seem to be waiting on the sidelines.

Hannibal provides reports on the situation through Coulondre to Soucet. Our direction is to observe and report, nothing more.

*Monday evening, February 12*

Richter called a meeting in the squad room today at about noon. In addition to Hannibal and me, Lackner, Altman and Ritter attended. All other detectives were out on peacekeeping missions.

"I have a report from Linz," Richter began. "This morning, the Heimwehr, led by Emil Fey, searched the Hotel Schiff, a property owned by the Schutzbund. They found a cache of weapons."

Richter paused and looked at faces around the room. "The Schutzbund, commanded by Richard Bernaschek, put up an armed resistance at the hotel. Four Heimwehr and an unknown number of Schutzbund militia were killed."

"Has the violence spread?" Hannibal asked. Lackner, Altman and Ritter looked first to Hannibal and then Richter.

"Yes," responded Richter. I have reports from Steyr, Sankt Pölten, Weiz, Graz and several other cities. All report violent clashes."

"Vienna?" Lackner asked.

Richter nodded and replied: "According to local constables, Schutzbund militia have barricaded themselves in Vienna city housing estates in Gemeindebauten and in the Karl Marx Hof."

He paused and his face was grave. "I have been on the phone to the chancellor's office." He then added: "I recommended that the government call upon the army."

## Friday evening, February 16

For the last two days, the army shelled Karl Marx Hof and other socialist housing units in Vienna, killing hundreds of Schutzbund militia and civilians. The police, supported by the army, have begun a round-up of Schutzbund leaders throughout Austria.

Dollfuss has outlawed the Social Democratic Party as well as its Schutzbund militia. He rules with an iron fist. How long can this last?

## Saturday evening, May 5

At about 8:00 AM yesterday morning, Hannibal and I had breakfast at a restaurant near the corner of Königsklostergasse and Mariahilfer. We were watching for Taittinger, but I spotted Planetta and a companion as they walked by the restaurant window.

"Pay the bill and I will follow them," I whispered to Hannibal and pointed out the window. "Catch up when you can." Before Hannibal could respond, I was up and out the door.

Half a minute later, I was on the street and about half a block behind Planetta and his companion. They walked along Mariahilfer, talking in an animated fashion. I hurried to keep up.

After a couple of blocks, the pair walked up the steps to an apartment building. I crossed the street, stopped behind a parked lorry near an alley and watched. Planetta fumbled with a key, opened the apartment building door, and the two men went inside.

Hannibal arrived a few minutes later. "Planetta and his companion are inside that apartment building," I said in a low voice. "See the number 21 above the doorway?" I pointed discreetly.

Hannibal nodded and replied: "We're just a couple of blocks from Taittinger's place. Let's watch for a while."

As we watched, a few people passed by on the street. For the most part, they hurried on their way, avoiding eye contact with us and other pedestrians.

"Vienna has become a fearful city," I thought to myself. "People mind their own business."

Our surveillance paid off. About five minutes later, two more men arrived at building 21. One knocked, the door opened, and the two new men went inside.

"A meeting," I said in a low voice. "Planetta and three companions, but not Taittinger." Hannibal nodded.

The morning dragged on. At about 10:00 AM, the three unknown men exited the apartment building and without a word, walked off in three different directions. "Planetta's still inside," I mused. "Maybe he lives there."

"Humm," responded Hannibal. "Probably." He looked at me with a steady gaze. "Do you have something in mind?"

I grinned and said: "When Planetta's out, maybe I should go in."

Hannibal smiled, sighed and replied: "Breaking and entering is a crime, you know."

"Only if I'm caught," I responded. "Your job will be lookout."

Hannibal sighed again.

## Sunday morning, May 6

Busy night! Just after 10:00 PM, Hannibal dropped me off a block from Planetta's apartment building. Streetlights provided dim illumination, and lights glowed from windows. I could see people moving about, inside.

I wore ordinary street clothes, and I blended with the few furtive pedestrians on the street. Hannibal drove slowly down Mariahilfer; I could see our Duesenberg turn left about a block away.

I had a flashlight in my handbag, along with my Walther. My sheath knife was in its usual place. "Always be prepared," my thoughts concluded.

Hannibal and I had agreed that he would pick me up at the same spot in 30 minutes. My objective was outside reconnaissance. "Which apartment belongs to Planetta? Is there a back door?"

I slipped into the alley that passed behind building 21. Breaking and entering was reserved for a later night, after Hannibal and I had completed our preliminaries.

I had the filthy alley all to myself. "City services are intermittent, a consequence of the fighting," I surmised as I stepped gingerly around trash and stinky, raw garbage. Sleuthing can be less than glamorous.

I arrived behind building 21 after a few minutes. A light glowed from a rear window. I could see a figure as it passed by, just inside. It was Planetta. "Good luck," I thought with satisfaction. "He has the rear apartment on the first level."

I could see a railing and stairs leading down from the alley level below Planetta's window. I shined my flashlight down the stairs into the gloom. "Back door, basement level, below Planetta's apartment," I concluded.

I slipped down the stairs. A very dirty window, with bars, occupied the space on the left of the door. On the right of the door, I spotted a coal chute that led down from the alley.

I shined my flashlight into the pitch blackness inside the window. I could make out stairs and a pile of coal next to a furnace.

I then shined my light on the door latch. "Straight-forward," my thoughts continued. "Pick the lock, slip inside, go up the stairs, and do my thing."

I switched off my light and crept back up the outside stairs to the alley. "Time to return to my pick-up point," I muttered. "Hannibal will be waiting."

## Friday evening, May 18

For the past week, every afternoon and evening, Hannibal and I took turns watching Planetta's apartment building. Hannibal parked our car a couple of blocks away at a different location each day.

We walked along Mariahilfer, and one of us had Planetta's building in sight continuously. Our main spot for loitering was an unobtrusive alcove at the entrance to an alley across the street from building 21.

Our random comings and goings, combined with the strong tendency of Viennese to mind their own business, allowed us to go undetected, I think. "People are scared," I concluded. "They don't want to get involved."

Planetta kept an erratic schedule, except that he always left the building at 6:00 PM and returned at 7:30 PM, every day, as regular as clockwork.

"Probably goes out for his evening meal," I told Hannibal, as we headed back to the hotel at about 8:00 PM. "We have our window of opportunity."

"Agree," said Hannibal. "You should go through the back door, search, perhaps take photos and get out within an hour, tops." He paused, looked over at me and added: "I'll be nearby as back up."

I smiled and tucked my left arm under his right. "I know," I replied. "And yes, I will be careful."

## Saturday morning, June 2

We chose yesterday evening for my snooping expedition. We got more than we expected. How exciting!

We left our hotel at just after 5:00 PM in our Duesenberg. I wore black. My slacks, top, jacket, boots and gloves gave me a jaunty, as well as a practical appearance.

I carried my burglar tools, flashlight, camera and some odds and ends in a small bag that I slung over my shoulder. Of course, I also carried my Walther and sheath knife.

"One must dress the part," I said to Hannibal, as he turned left from the Burgring onto Mariahilfer.

He laughed and replied: "A formidable lady."

Hannibal turned left on Theobaldgasse, just a block past the intersection of Mariahilfer and Königsklostergasse, and left again into an alley that paralleled Mariahilfer. He weaved our car around trash and approached the cross alley that led out on Mariahilfer.

Hannibal stopped the car behind piles of trash, well-hidden from view by people on Mariahilfer. The alleys were deserted. We saw a few pedestrians on Mariahilfer, and an occasional lorry passed. Otherwise, we had the place to ourselves.

We could see Planetta's apartment building on the other side of Mariahilfer. I checked my watch. "Quarter until six," I said. "Planetta should be leaving any time now."

Sure enough, at just before six, Planetta exited the building and walked west along Mariahilfer. I gave him five minutes, and then got out of the car.

"You have an hour," Hannibal reminded me.

I moved quickly, crossed the street and slipped into the alley along the side of Planetta's building. Within minutes, I arrived at the cross alley at the back of the building. After a quick look around, I moved down the steps to the basement back door.

"Now pick the lock and get inside," I told myself. Soon it was done. I closed the door behind me. A dim light came in through the dirty window by the door, that was all. I put away my lock picks and took out my flashlight.

The stairs creaked a little as I climbed up to the apartment level. I opened the door at the top of the stairs slowly, carefully. Other than the creak of hinges, the place was eerily quiet.

The hallway was dimly lit from windows at the front of the building, so I turned off my flashlight. I could see doors to the right and left. "First door on the left will be Planetta's," I thought to myself.

Picking the lock was easy. I slipped inside and closed the door.

A small table lamp provided some illumination. I could see papers, maps, newspapers and note pads on the table in a small alcove dining room. More documents lay on a couch and on side tables.

I sensed movement across an interior doorway. "Oh!" I froze. "Meow," I heard. A yellow cat stepped out of the kitchen. The cat looked at me for a moment, then slinked across the room, minding its own business.

"OK," I muttered. "Nice kitty. Now get to work, Caroline." I put my lock picks away and took out my flashlight and camera.

The place proved to be a treasure trove. "Photos now, analysis later," I told myself. I managed to tie my flashlight to the stand of a desk lamp with string from my bag. Between the lamp and the flashlight, I had good illumination of document after document as I laid them on the desk under the light.

In less than an hour, I had photos of incriminating documents, maps, schedules and lists of names. The name 'Standarte 89' and the Nazi symbol 'SS' appeared everywhere. I filled three rolls of film.

Finally, I put away my equipment and looked around the apartment. Everything was as I had found it. I looked at my watch. "Seven o'clock," I muttered. "Time to leave."

As I was about to close the apartment door, the yellow cat walked over and sat down in the middle of the room. "Meow," it said. "Now don't tell," I whispered. The only answer was a soft purring.

Through the apartment door, lock it, down the inside stairs, out the back doors, fasten the lock and up the stairs to the alley. I breathed a sigh of relief as I topped the last step. Hannibal was waiting as I crossed Mariahilfer and got into the car. "Done," I said. "Let's go."

# 26

## CHANCELLOR'S END

### Sunday evening, June 3, 1934

Hannibal gave my three rolls of film to Coulondre in the Stadt Park this morning. Coulondre promised to return the developed prints and negatives by tomorrow noon. Although I had hurriedly read some of the documents while I took the photos, Hannibal and I need time to analyze and correlate the information.

### Monday evening, June 4

As promised, Coulondre delivered over 75 prints and negatives to Hannibal this morning. The photos were even better than I had imagined. Our analysis provides the blueprints for an internal power struggle between Rohm, the leader of the SA, and Himmler, the leader of the SS, and a Nazi putsch in Austria.

Hannibal and I are writing a report for Soucet on our findings. Hannibal will deliver it through Coulondre by tomorrow afternoon.

This morning, I sent a telegram to Ruth in Riccione through the hotel concierge. It read: 'Intrigue in Vienna. Berlin involved. Danger extreme. Warn your friends.'

Based on our earlier decision, Hannibal and I will also work with Richter to thwart the planned Nazi putsch. Hannibal thinks a nasty fight will happen, and the outcome is far from certain.

### Wednesday evening, June 6

Hannibal and I met with Richter in his office this morning. Hannibal gave a quick synopsis of our findings. Richter went to his door and looked around the squad room. Lackner was there, alone. In a calm voice, Richter said: "Detective Lackner, would you please join us?"

Soon the four of us made ourselves comfortable around the Richter's coffee table. Richter said: "Major Jones, please explain your findings." He smiled and added: "I will not ask how you obtained your information." I breathed a sigh of relief.

In his precise military manner, Hannibal briefed Richter and Lackner. When he finished, Richter leaned back in his chair. Lackner sat with his eyes wide and his mouth open.

Finally, Richter said: "Detective Lackner, please go to the chancellor's office, in person, immediately. Trust no one except the chancellor himself. Tell him that he is in extreme danger from the Nazis. Recommend that he call upon trusted elements in the army. We will provide more information as it becomes available."

He glanced at Hannibal and then me. He turned back to Lackner and added: "Do not reveal your source of information. I will call ahead and inform the chancellor's staff that you are on your way."

"Yes, Herr Chief Inspector," replied Lackner. He rose, nodded to Hannibal and me and departed.

Richter then turned back to Hannibal and stated: "I need your help in organizing a defense." He paused and asked: "How much time do we have?"

Hannibal took a deep breath, let it out, and replied: "I think events will unfold in Germany first. Himmler is the key, and he has to eliminate his SA rivals before he can act in Vienna."

"Suggest that we monitor radio broadcasts from Berlin," I added: "Hitler and perhaps others will make public announcements. If Himmler and his SS come out on top, Himmler will give direction to the SS Standarte 89 in Vienna."

"Agree," responded Richter. "He then turned to Hannibal and asked: "What's your assessment of Himmler's chances?"

Hannibal thought for a full minute. Finally, he said: "The evidence in the documents we found show that Himmler is a methodical political infighter." He paused and added: "I think the German generals will support Himmler; they don't like Rohm."

"Humm," responded Richter. "Since the danger in Vienna will come from the SS, our emphasis is clear. If Himmler succeeds in Berlin, we will know that SS Standarte 89 action in Vienna is imminent." The rest of us nodded.

### Sunday evening, June 24

Hannibal and I acquired a short-wave radio, and we monitor broadcasts from Berlin every day. So far, nothing, except the usual Nazi propaganda. Waiting can be frustrating.

### Monday evening, June 25

Rudolf Hess, Hitler's deputy, gave a speech in Cologne today. We picked up elements of the speech on the radio. Hess warned the German people about dangerous elements within the SA that are plotting 'a second revolution.'

"Such elements endanger national socialism," Hess stated. He concluded by warning of 'dire consequences.'

"Such a speech could only have been given with Hitler's approval," said Hannibal, as the broadcast faded into noise and static.

### Friday, evening, July 13

Hitler gave a speech to the Reichstag in Berlin today. We picked up most of it on Berlin radio.

Hitler stated that Ernst Rohm and 49 other high SA leaders were shot for plotting the imminent overthrow of national socialism and his own death. Another 27 SA and other officials were also killed in the subsequent purge. Hitler called the plot 'the Night of the Long Knives.'

## Monday evening, July 16

Hannibal obtained copies of *Le Temps* from Paris, the *New York Times,* and the *London Times.* We perused the newspapers as we relaxed in our hotel suite this evening.

Based on correspondents who attended Hitler's Reichstag speech, all three newspapers reported that Rohm and his 'mutineers' had been killed. According to the *London Times*, the Reichstag unanimously approved the Government's action and thanked Hitler personally.

"Himmler and the SS won, and Rohm is dead," I stated. "We can expect SS Standarte 89 to receive attack orders from Berlin any day now."

"Yes," replied Hannibal. "We can update Richter first thing in the morning."

## Friday evening, July 27

Early morning of July 25, the phone rang. Hannibal turned on the light on the nightstand and answered. I looked at the clock; it read 6:30.

"Right," said Hannibal into the phone. "We'll be there in thirty minutes." He hung up the phone, got out of bed and turned on more lights.

I rolled out of bed and headed for the bathroom. "Make it quick," I heard Hannibal say. "Dress for action. We'll meet Richter outside the Ballhausplatz, which houses the chancellery offices."

Fifteen minutes later, we were in our Duesenberg. Hannibal pulled out from the Hotel Wien and we sped down the Ringstrasse.

"No traffic," I observed as we raced toward the Burgring. I checked over my outfit and weapons.

I wore form-fitting black slacks, a pull-over black sweater, a black leather jacket and black leather boots. My Walther, with three clips of ammunition and a handful of loose shells, rested in a small purse with a shoulder strap. My sheath knife was strapped in its usual location. My hair was a bit of a mess, but that was OK; I was ready.

I glanced over at Hannibal. He was also dressed for action, with dark shirt and slacks, leather jacket and laced boots. His dark fedora hat rested lightly on his head. I could see the butt of his forty-five in its shoulder holster.

Hannibal turned right from the Burgring onto Heidenplatz, navigated the Michaelerplatz traffic circle and turned left onto Schauflergasse. We could see police cars at the next intersection.

The Ballhausplatz loomed in the early morning light about a block away on the left. I looked at my watch. "Seven o'clock, and I haven't had my coffee yet," I muttered.

Hannibal stopped near one of the police cars. We saw Richter and Lackner as we got out of our car. Richter was giving directions to several constables.

Lackner saw us as we approached, and he said. "One of our constables saw about 150 men dressed in army uniforms forming in the Volksgarten over there," and he pointed. I could see a group of men and a dozen trucks in the distance.

Lackner smiled grimly and added: "The constable was alert, and he recognized Detectives Altman and Ritter, both in uniforms for the chancellery guard."

"Ah," I responded. "Not right; the guard has army uniforms, and Ritter and Altman aren't entitled to wear them. I bet the others are also Nazis."

"Precisely," replied Lackner. "The constable called Chief Inspector Richter. Loyal units of the army are on the way."

"How soon will they arrive?" Hannibal asked.

"Late morning," responded Lackner with a frown. "We are on our own until then." He looked around and counted heads. "We have 15 men."

"No match," responded Hannibal. At that moment, Richter saw us, turned from giving directions to his small force and walked over.

"As your documents indicated, the Nazis will also attempt to take the radio station in the Heeresministerium on the Stubenring," Richter said as he approached. "I have already sent five constables to the station. However, the station is over two kilometers from here."

"We gave warning weeks ago," I said. "Didn't the chancellor take precautions?

"According to our contacts in his office, he tried," replied Richter. "I think he has traitors in his inner circle. They have delayed precautions at every turn, in spite of our efforts."

"The chancellor is a courageous man," said Lackner. "He refused to be intimidated and chose to remain at his post."

He grimaced and added: "I was on duty this morning at police headquarters. I called the chancellor's office when we got word from the constable. Apparently, Chancellor Dollfuss spent the night in a small apartment inside the Ballhausplatz. He's there now."

My mind raced. After a moment, I said: "We need to get inside the Ballhausplatz."

"What can we do?" Lackner said in a somewhat plaintive voice. "We are outnumbered ten to one."

"Fight!" I replied. I looked at Hannibal.

Hannibal took a deep breath and said: "A small force can fight a delaying action until help arrives." He looked at Richter with a steady gaze. "With your permission, I will lead."

Richter returned Hannibal's gaze. Finally, he said: "Yes." He thought a moment and added: "The Nazis will be watching the front, and they know we are here. Lead your force to the back of the building and try to slip unseen inside. Take a dozen constables." Hannibal nodded.

Richter continued: "I will remain here with three men to watch and coordinate with the army when they arrive." He paused a moment and added: "We may also get help from the Heimwehr."

He turned toward Lackner, but before he could say anything, Lackner said: "I will go with Major Jones."

Richter smiled and replied: "I know." He then turned to me and said: "Mrs. Jones, please stay with me. I will need your help."

"Not on your life," I replied firmly. "I go with Hannibal."

Richter smiled grimly and said: "I thought you would. However, I tried." He looked at Hannibal, smiled and added: "Good luck." Richter turned to the group of constables and began giving orders. Hannibal began checking arms and ammunition.

I turned to Lackner and said: "Stick with me. We'll give the Nazis more than they expect."

Lackner smiled and replied: "From what I have heard, I'm very glad you are on our side."

In his usual efficient manner, Hannibal organized his small force. "Let's divide into three squads of five persons each," he began. "I will lead one squad. Detective Lackner, you lead a second squad." He then looked at me with his steady gaze. "Caroline?" he said.

"Right," I responded. "I'll take the third squad." I paused a moment and then asked: "Guns and ammo?"

"The constables have rifles and 25 rounds each," replied Hannibal. "You, Lackner and I have pistols. I have 24 rounds." He looked at Lackner and then me. "I have 20," said Lackner. "And I have 32," I replied.

Hannibal then laid out his battle plan. "We'll take a wide circle away from the Volksgarten to the back of the Ballhausplatz. Each squad will move at 50-meter intervals. With luck, the Nazis in the Volksgarten won't spot us."

He looked around at each person in his force. "Once inside, our job will be to get as many people out of the building as possible, especially the chancellor and the other ministers. Afterwards, we will take up defensive positions. The Nazi assault can begin at any time."

He paused and then said: "Questions?" There were none, although several of the younger constables fidgeted.

"OK," Hannibal said, as he looked around. His confident smile and steady gaze inspired everyone. "What a guy," I thought to myself.

Hannibal continued his instructions. "Follow your squad leaders. Get people out. When the assault comes, pick your shots and conserve ammunition. Fight until relieved."

He looked at Lackner, then me and said: "Lackner, you follow my squad. Caroline, follow Lackner. Once we get inside, Lackner and I will gather the evacuees. Caroline, you hold the back door and guide people out."

He then looked at his watch and said: "It's now 8:00 AM. Check your watches." Both Lackner and I did so.

Hannibal then looked around at his squad and said: "First squad, follow me." He then took off at a steady, almost running, pace. His squad followed. Lackner and I led our squads at appropriate intervals.

We made it to the rear entrance of the Ballhausplatz without incident. When I arrived, Hannibal and Lackner were already inside. I heard loud voices.

I deployed two men inside the door and two outside. Disheveled, confused office workers and a few unarmed guards soon streamed down staircases and towards the door. I recognized Emil Fey, minister without portfolio, and Kurt von Schuschnigg, the foreign minister.

"Outside," I instructed, as people straggled up. "Constables outside will direct you to safety."

Emil Fey stopped by me and asked: "Is there a command post outside?" His gaze was steady, and I could tell that he wanted to be useful. "I am Heimwehr," he added.

"We need your help," I replied. "Chief Inspector Richter has a command post next to several police vehicles." I gave directions.

"Thank you," replied Fey. He smiled and added: "I have heard about you." He turned and headed out the door.

After about thirty minutes, the stream of people to be evacuated thinned out and finally ended. Hannibal strode up.

"Where is Dollfuss?" I asked.

"In his office," Hannibal replied. "He said that he will be the last person out. He is helping Lackner find people."

"Brave man," I said.

"Perhaps too brave," Hannibal replied. A couple of secretaries rushed up, and I gave directions. When I turned back, Hannibal was headed up a staircase.

I looked at my watch. "OK, 10:30," I thought to myself. "We've been here for over two hours."

A crackle of gunshots echoed from the front of the building. "The Nazis are coming," I muttered. My instincts told me that they would attack both front and back.

I raced toward the back door and shouted: "Windows!" My two inside constables quickly moved to the left and right windows near the door.

My peripheral vision caught the constable on the right. He fell just as he reached the window. Blood streamed from his head, and he didn't move. I heard rifle fire from my man on the left.

I could see my two outside constables through the right window as they raced toward the door. Neither man made it. Five uniformed men with rifles moved past their bodies.

The massive door opened. I dived to the floor and fired four shots as fast as I could pull the trigger. Screams. Three men went down in the doorway; their writhing bodies propped it open. The remaining two men retreated to a water fountain about twenty meters back.

I fired more shots at the men behind the fountain, and they returned fire with their rifles. Bullets clicked and whined as they struck the marble pillars and staircase steps behind me.

I had no cover on the floor, so I retreated to the side of the staircase. My remaining constable raced from his window to the other side of the staircase. I could hear shouts from outside as more men joined the two by the fountain.

My clip was empty, and I reloaded. My companion kept up a steady fire through the open door toward the fountain. More bullets struck the marble staircase.

"Oh!" My companion exclaimed. He slumped forward and fell on his face. I saw a bloody hole in the middle of his back from where a bullet had passed through. I was alone.

More than a dozen men ran from the fountain toward the door. "Can't stay here," my mind raced. I had a few seconds as the men were moving and not firing.

I jumped up and ran up the stairs, two at a time. I heard shots, bullet clicks and shouts, but I made it to the top. "Hide!" My thoughts continued. I saw an open office doorway, one of several along the open balcony. "Inside!" I found a desk and hid behind it; my Walther was ready. I could see back through the open doorway.

I heard shouts below. The Nazis had taken the lower level.

My heart pumped wildly as I tried to catch my breath. I heard firing from the front of the building. "Hannibal is still fighting," my mind firmly decided. I clamped down on thoughts that said otherwise.

I heard many men race up the staircase. One man was giving orders. I peeked from behind the desk. "Planetta!"

I heard a shout from further down the balcony. "Dollfuss ist hier im Kanzleramt!" Planetta moved out of my vision.

I then heard a high pitched but firm voice, speaking in German. As near as I can translate, the voice said: "Do what you like with me.

I am leaving the building now. If you want to shoot me, I shall die for the Fatherland!"

I then heard Planetta's voice: "Sehr gut. Sterben!" Two shots rang out in quick succession.

# 27

## VIENNA IN THE MIRROR

*Saturday morning, July 28, 1934*

I finally settled down to sleep at about midnight last night. Morning has arrived. It's time to continue my narrative about Wednesday, July 25, while my memories are fresh.

On that terrible day, the Nazis milled about outside the office where I was hiding. My four companions were dead, and I had shot at least five Nazis.

I had listened in horror as Planetta, the Nazi leader, shot Chancellor Dollfuss a few meters down the hall. We had saved many people, including at least two cabinet ministers, but we had not saved Dollfuss. Frustration!

Gunfire increased at the front of the Ballhausplatz, both inside and outside. I heard shouts of command and the words: "Ich sehe Armee Truppen! Sie schießen an den Nazis von außen!!"

It was Hannibal's voice. "Oh, thank heaven!" My thoughts raced. "Army troops are coming. How can I get to Hannibal?"

I heard shouts, including Planetta's voice. As near as I can translate, Planetta said: "Take him in the chancellor's office! Stay with him! He'll die soon."

I slipped out from my hiding spot and crept up to the door, my Walther ready. I heard voices down the hallway to the right.

The hallway was clear. Past the chancellor's office, I could hear men running down corridors leading toward the front of the building. Shots echoed.

276

"OK, Caroline, think! On this level, if I go left, I will find a corridor leading to the front of the building and Hannibal." I looked left and listened. "The Nazis went to the right," I concluded. "Go!"

I raced out and to the left. A corridor leading toward the front of the building loomed about twenty meters away. Just as I reached the corner, I heard a shout behind, then a fusillade of shots. Bullets hit the wall just as I turned the corner.

I dropped to my knees, swung my Walther around the corner and emptied the magazine. Two of my pursuers dropped. The remaining two retreated back into the chancellor's office.

"That will make them think twice about chasing me," I concluded with a sense of satisfaction. I reloaded with my third clip, jumped up and raced down the corridor.

Bodies lay in the corridor and staircase as I reached the front of the building. "Hannibal!" I shouted.

"Here!" I heard. I looked around the great entrance hall, both on my level and below. Shots from outside passed through broken windows and clicked as they hit the walls.

I spotted Hannibal on my level, near the balustrade at the top of the main staircase. He had three companions. Two constables were firing their rifles at fleeting figures on the lower level and outside the windows. One man lay next to Hannibal. A bloody, makeshift bandage wrapped around his chest. It was Lackner.

I raced toward Hannibal. Just before I reached his spot, a shot ricocheted off a near wall. Chips of marble and dust hit my face. I tripped and sprawled right next to Hannibal.

"Nice entry, Caroline," I muttered, as I brushed stinging chips and dust from my eyes with my left hand. My right still clutched my Walther.

"Caroline?!" Hannibal's voice sounded in my ringing ears. I felt strong arms pulling me to a sheltered spot by a pillar. I scrambled to a sitting position. Hannibal knelt next to me.

"I'm good," I replied. Hannibal's face had an expression of grave concern. "I'm good," I repeated. "What's the situation?"

Hannibal took a deep breath and let it out. He then glanced all around and then said: "Loyal army units are outside. A few Nazis are trapped at the front of the building and below us on the first level. Lackner took a bullet to his chest."

He paused and asked: "What happened at the back of the building?"

"We got everyone out except Dollfuss," I responded. "Planetta shot him. He's in the chancellor's office. I think he's dying. At least a dozen Nazis are in and around the chancellor's office."

"Humm," responded Hannibal. "Your constables?"

"All dead," I replied. I looked down at Lackner, who smiled wanly. "How are you doing?" I asked.

"I've been better," Lackner replied with a slight chuckle. He winced and softly exclaimed: "Oh!"

"Take it easy," I responded. I adjusted his bandage a little. It seemed to help.

Lackner motioned with his left hand toward the stairs and said in a weak voice: "I got Ritter and Altman before I was hit." I looked on the stairs. Both Ritter and Altman sprawled on their backs halfway up the staircase. Blood pooled underneath both bodies.

Suddenly, the firing stopped. The silence was eerie. I looked at my watch. "Almost five o'clock," I muttered. I looked all around. After a minute, I said: "Standoff."

"Yes," replied Hannibal. "The Nazis are vastly outnumbered." He paused and then added: "I think we'll be OK."

I thought a moment and then said: "We did good, in spite of losing Dollfuss. I counted at least fifty people who made it to safety out the back door."

"Yes," Hannibal replied. He looked around. "I estimate that over a hundred Nazis are dead or wounded here at the front of the building, plus more at your location at the back."

He paused, frowned, and his lips moved as he counted. "Our losses are ten killed and one wounded. I don't think the army lost many men." He glanced down at Lackner and smiled. "Our wounded will recover." Lackner smiled in return.

We waited another two hours before negotiations ended. At about 7:00 PM, Richter, Fey and an army colonel led a mixed force of at least fifty soldiers, Heimwehr, and police constables through the front door.

Hannibal and I stood up. Our remaining two constables joined us.

Richter and Fey saw us and smiled. Richter turned to the colonel and gave instructions. Within minutes, soldiers fanned out throughout the building.

Hannibal put away his forty-five and walked down to Richter. I stayed with Lackner.

After a quick conference, Richter sent a constable outside. The constable returned with two men and a stretcher. Within minutes, Lackner was on the stretcher and headed for medical attention.

About ten minutes later, soldiers led a disheveled group of about a dozen prisoners, hands over their heads, past us, down the stairs and out the door. I watched as Planetta passed, hands in the air. He gave me a venomous look. I suppressed an urge to shoot him. The battle was over.

## Sunday morning, July 29

I slept in this morning; I was exhausted. A slight noise from the hall to the door of our suite woke me up. I forced my eyes open and looked at the clock. It read 10:00 AM.

A figure stood in the bedroom doorway. I blinked several times and tried to focus. It was Hannibal, and he was fully dressed.

He smiled and said: "Good morning."

"You're right, it's morning," I replied in a grumpy tone. Hannibal chuckled.

"OK, OK," I responded. My mind slowly returned to the present. "What have you been up to?"

"I delivered a preliminary 'after action' written report to Soucet through Coulondre in the Stadt Park. I also verbally summarized our activities on July 25. Coulondre seemed grateful," replied Hannibal. "He also said Henri Taittinger has disappeared."

My mind finally focused. "You wrote a report already?" I responded. "Taittinger is gone?" I thought a moment, then added: "Not surprised, given the events on July 25."

"Yes," replied Hannibal. "More importantly, I ordered some coffee from room service. Want some?"

"Oh yes," I replied. I slowly sat up, stood, shuffled over Hannibal and gave him my warmest kiss. "You are such a nice man."

I then shuffled into the bathroom. After the usual, I splashed water on my face, brushed my teeth, ran a comb through my hair and put on my nicest white silk robe.

"Better," I mumbled to myself. I walked into the parlor and joined Hannibal. The coffee was waiting, and it tasted wonderful.

## Sunday evening, July 29

The hotel concierge delivered a telegram this morning. It read: 'Warning passed to my friends June 6. Events in Vienna on July 25 attributed to Berlin. Read *Il Popolo d'Italia*, Rome, July 26, *Travaso*, Venezia, July 27 and *La Stampa*, Torino, July 27 - Ruth.'

This morning, Hannibal bought all three Italian newspapers from the concierge, as well as the latest German *Völkscher Beobachter* and *Der Angriff*.

At about noon, we ordered a light room service lunch. We had salads, a couple of apple tarts and a nice tea service. As room service retrieved the dishes and portable table, we made ourselves comfortable in our parlor with the tea. We sipped and read the newspapers for a while.

Hannibal began the conversation. "According to all three Italian newspapers, Mussolini attributed the attacks in Austria to Hitler and the German Nazi Party."

I turned pages of *Il Popolo d'Italia* and found an editorial. "According to this, Mussolini personally informed Dollfuss' widow, who was a guest at his villa in Riccione, about the assassination."

I turned the page, continued reading and said: "He also put an airplane at the disposal of Austrian Prince Ernst Rüdiger Starhemberg, who had spent a holiday in Venice."

"Thanks to Ruth, Mussolini was prepared," I added.

"Humm," responded Hannibal. "According to the *Travaso,* the Prince flew back to Vienna and took charge of Heimwehr forces." Hannibal smiled and said: "I bet that was interesting, given that Emil Fey also considered himself in charge of the Heimwehr."

I found another article: "According to this, Mussolini mobilized a part of the Italian army on the Austrian border and threatened Hitler with war in the event of a German invasion of Austria." I continued reading and added: "Mussolini sent four divisions to the Brenner Pass."

"Let's see what *Der Angriff* has to say," responded Hannibal as he put down the *Travaso* and picked up the German newspaper.

After a moment, he chuckled and then said: "This article dated July 27 expresses regret over the assassination of Dollfuss."

Hannibal continued to read and then added: "According to Goebbels, the assassination was purely an Austrian affair."

"Humm," I replied. "I bet Himmler had to swallow hard when he read that one."

Hannibal leaned back on the sofa, looked out the window for a while and then said: "I think Mussolini's reaction over the Dollfuss affair surprised Hitler." He paused and then added: "Hitler does not want to fight Mussolini."

"Ruth did her job well," I said.

"Yes, she did," replied Hannibal.

## Monday evening, July 30

Hannibal and I decided to visit the Schottenring police headquarters this morning. As we drove away from Hotel Wien, I saw two sinister men watching us.

"Not good," I muttered and pointed. Hannibal looked, saw the pair and accelerated our car as we turned onto the Ringstrasse.

The streets were eerily empty of cars and workday civilians. Squads of soldiers patrolled major street intersections.

Fifteen minutes later, we pulled into the police parking lot. Army trucks and soldiers were everywhere. A no-nonsense army captain met us at the door. He was backed up by a sergeant and several soldiers.

Hannibal took out his passport, stepped forward and said: "I am Major Hannibal Jones. My wife and I are here to see Chief Inspector Richter." He showed the captain his passport.

The captain snapped to attention, saluted and replied: "I recognize you and Frau Jones, Herr Major." Your exploits on July 25 are well-known to all of us." Hannibal returned the salute.

The captain then smiled and said: "Please enter. The Chief Inspector will be happy to see both of you." He stood aside and motioned us to the door. One of the soldiers instantly opened the door for us.

"Wow!" I thought to myself. I didn't know how to react, so I just followed Hannibal.

When we reached Richter's suite, a dozen men in Heimwehr uniforms were in the squad room. As soon as they saw Hannibal, they snapped to attention. "As you were, gentlemen," said Hannibal, in a clear but soft voice.

The men relaxed a little, but they watched Hannibal with awe and respect. Several gave me an up and down look.

"I could get used to this," I thought to myself. I smiled and put on my best snooty expression.

Richter appeared in his office doorway, holding a cup of coffee. He smiled and said: "Please come in." He then turned to one of the younger Heimwehr and said: "Bring Major and Frau Jones some coffee, both black."

"Yes, Herr Chief Inspector," replied the young man, and he scurried off to the coffee bar.

We entered Richter's office. He motioned us to seats near the coffee table. Within a minute, two steaming cups of coffee rested on the table. Richter walked over and sat down. The young man left quietly and closed the door behind him.

"How is Detective Lackner?" I asked.

Richter smiled and said: "Always thinking of others." He paused and added: "Eric will recover. He will be in hospital for a while, but he should be out in a few weeks."

He then turned to Hannibal, then to me, and said: "Engelbert Dollfuss died of his wounds at about seven o'clock on the night of the 25." His face grew grim, and he continued: "According to his unrepentant assassins, it was a slow and painful death."

He paused and added: "President Wilhelm Miklas appointed Kurt Schuschnigg as the new chancellor."

"In addition to Planetta, who were the assassins?" I asked.

Richter pulled a piece of notepaper from his pocket and read: "Franz Leeb, Fridolin Glass, Josef Hackel, Ludwig Meitzen, Erich Worahb, Paul Hudl and Franz Holzweber were arrested. Others may have escaped the Ballhausplatz."

He looked up, his jaws tightened and he added: "There will be a trial, of course. However, the evidence is overwhelming. I'm certain all who were caught will be hanged."

"What about Anton Rintelen?" Hannibal asked. "He was involved in meetings with Planetta."

"Yes, he was," replied Richter. "According to Planetta during his interrogation and also the abortive Nazi radio broadcast, Rintelen was supposed to be the new Nazi chancellor."

He paused a moment and added: "During interrogation, Rintelen recanted. I don't know what will happen to him."

"What happened at the radio station?" I asked.

"Nazis forced an announcer to say that Dollfuss had resigned, and Rintelen was the new chancellor," replied Richter.

"However," he smiled and continued: "An alert telephone operator spread the alarm, and one of the station engineers cut the wires to the transmitter." He added: "About that time, my five constables showed up, along with two dozen Heimwehr."

"Other locations besides Vienna?" Hannibal asked.

Richter nodded and said: "In Carinthia, a contingent of Nazis tried to take over the state government offices, but Italian troops intervened. Reports are sketchy, but apparently the Nazis were overwhelmed and surrendered after just a few casualties."

He paused and added: "Reports are coming in from other locations, but it seems clear that Austrian government forces, in some cases aided by Italians from across the border, are in control."

The three of us were quiet for a while. Finally, Hannibal said: "All of the Nazis were probably members of the SS Standarte 89. How many escaped?"

"Several," replied Richter, and his expression grew grim. "Which brings me to my main concern at the moment. You and Caroline are in grave danger."

I gulped a little and asked: "How so?"

Richter responded: "During our interrogation of Planetta and several others, they expressed anger over 'two Americans' in the battle. They saw you both, and you were recognized."

He frowned and added: "They probably got their information from Ritter and Altman before they were killed. At any rate, during interrogation, Planetta said: 'We will have our revenge on the Americans.' His threat was backed up by several others in separate interrogations."

He paused and then continued: "We know that some Nazis got out during the battle. At least two were seen crossing the Bavarian border. Most likely, your names and exploits are known in Berlin."

Hannibal looked over at me. I returned his gaze, but then smiled and said: "Shall we go to Italy? I understand that Riccione is beautiful."

Hannibal chuckled and replied: "Good idea." He turned to Richter and said: "Caroline and I saw two men watching us this morning as we left the hotel. That, combined with your information, tells us that our Vienna days are drawing to an end."

"I understand," responded Richter. "Your service to Austria will be remembered."

He paused and added: "Plainclothes Heimwehr will provide security at your hotel for the remainder of your stay."

"Thank you," I responded.

Richter rose from his seat and offered his hand. Hannibal stood and the pair shook hands. Richter then turned to me, bowed formally, and said: "Madame Jones, I have never met anyone like you." He offered his hand.

I ignored his hand, stepped over, and gave him a hug and a big kiss on the cheek. I then stepped back. Hannibal burst out laughing. Richter smiled, blushed and put his hand to his cheek where I had kissed him.

## Tuesday evening, July 31

This morning, Hannibal informed Soucet, through Coulondre, with regard to our situation in Vienna. This afternoon, we received a telegram from Paris. It read: 'Agree with your suggested move. Contact me when you arrive at your destination. – S'

We visited Lackner in the hospital late this afternoon. He was in a cheerful mood, in spite of his wound. He will recover.

Tomorrow, Hannibal and I will ship our trunks to the Grand Hotel Riccione. The day after, we will drive toward the Brenner Pass. Vienna will be in the rearview mirror.

# 28

## SUN, SAND AND ESPIONAGE

*Thursday evening, August 2, 1934*

We checked out of the Grand Hotel Wien early this morning. "Eight days for our leisurely drive to Riccione," said Hannibal, as he turned our Duesenberg right onto the Ringstrasse. "I've made reservations for hotels along the way. We'll be in Salzburg tonight."

"Almost a year and a half in Vienna," I responded with a sigh. "So many changes!"

"Yes," replied Hannibal. "Schuschnigg is chancellor, and the Nazis are stopped, at least for a while." He paused for a moment and then added: "I gave Richter our new address in Riccione and told him about our contacts in Switzerland, if he ever wants to leave Vienna."

"Good," I responded. "What about Lackner?"

"The same," Hannibal replied. "Lackner is young, and he may decide to take my offer of a security position in a Swiss bank."

"I hope Richter retires to Switzerland," I mused. Hannibal nodded.

Our Duesenberg hummed along in a low, somber voice as we turned left on Mariahilfer and headed west. Hannibal accelerated a little on the straight road.

Somehow the sound of the car seemed in tune with my mood. Images of twisted death had intruded on my dreams last night, and they still live on the periphery of my awake mind.

I looked back through the rear window. "Richter was a good as his word," I said to Hannibal. "As far as I can tell, we aren't being followed."

Hannibal nodded and slowed our speed a little.

"OK, Caroline, think positive," I told myself, as I buried thoughts of blood and battle. "We did what we could in Vienna." I took a deep breath, let it out, looked over at Hannibal and asked: "How far is it to Salzburg?"

"About 298 kilometers," replied Hannibal. "We should arrive late this afternoon." He returned my glance and smiled. I know he sensed my desire to change the mood. He added: "The drive is beautiful this time of year."

"Where are we staying tonight?" I decided to pretend we were on holiday.

"Hotel Auersperg," replied Hannibal. "We'll have a nice view of the Hohensalzburg Castle on the hill." He added: "I'll give you a tour of the town the next day, including the Mirabell Palace gardens."

"Lovely," I responded. I then snuggled a little. Hannibal has a way of making me feel special.

### Saturday evening, August 11

After our two-night stay in Salzburg, our route took us to Innsbruck, near the border with Italy. We spent two nights in the luxurious Hotel Schwarzer Adler, located on Kaiserjägerstrasse. Innsbruck was picturesque, with many little shops. Hannibal was very patient when I tried to visit them all.

On August 6, we departed Innsbruck. Our route took us over the Brenner Pass. An automobile road was planned, but in places, the ancient Roman Via Raetia was still only a footpath. Hannibal made arrangements for loading our Duesenberg on a railroad freight car, and we booked first class passage.

"OK, Caroline," I thought to myself. "Concentrate on the beauty of the Alps and the hospitality of the train staff."

The views were spectacular. Like a typical tourist, I oohed and ahhed over scenes of dairy cattle grazing in alpine pastures, with snow-capped mountains in the background. I chattered on and on about my observations. Midday, we enjoyed a sumptuous lunch and tea.

Hannibal smiled in response to my chattering. I know he was pleased that I was trying to put the memories of our recent experiences in Vienna under wraps, at least for a while.

Near the top of the pass, we crossed the border into Italy. Customs was tedious, but we had no problems. Hannibal, in his usual way, had everything in order.

In Trento, we picked up our car and spent the nights of August 7 and 8 in the Hotel Venezin, located on the Piazza Duomo. On the 8th, Hannibal gave me a tour of the Cathedral of Saint Vigilius. We also walked around the Buonconsiglio Castle. Fascinating!

On August 9, we drove to Bologna and stayed at the Hotel Corona d'Oro, located on the Via Guglielmo Oberdan. Hannibal took me on a walking tour through the old city. I still marvel at the tilted Garisenda Tower; why it hasn't collapsed is beyond my understanding.

We left Bologna on August 11 for the final leg of our journey. The distance was only 126 kilometers, so we arrived just in time for lunch at the Grand Hotel Riccione on Viale Antonio Gramsci. Casually dressed tourists on holiday were everywhere.

"Ah," I said, as we drove up to our hotel. "Sun, sand, a luxurious hotel and beautiful people."

Hannibal laughed. I laughed in return; memories of our dark days in Vienna are now firmly under control.

"And you are beautiful, Mrs. Caroline Case Jones," Hannibal replied. He leaned over and kissed me on the cheek.

"Humm," I whispered in his ear. "I think I will have pleasant dreams tonight." I returned his kiss, with added emphasis.

Check-in at the Grand went smoothly, and we have a lovely suite with a view of the beach. Ruth is also at the Grand; we left a message for her right after check-in. Hannibal also sent a telegram to Soucet.

## Sunday evening, August 12

What a wonderful reunion! Ruth's hair is all silver now, but she is still a lovely, sophisticated lady. Her mind is as sharp as ever. Even Hannibal joined in the conversation as Ruth and I prattled on about old times over lunch in the Grand dining room.

Ruth also gave us the lowdown on Mussolini's presence in Riccione. "Donna Rachele and her children stay at their villa at Viale Milano 31 full-time," said Ruth. "Benito visits occasionally, but spends a great deal of time in Rome."

Ruth smiled knowingly and added: "Benito maintains a communications center on the third floor, here in the Grand." Her voice turned to a whisper, and she leaned toward me. "I know a young lady who works in the communications center."

Hannibal heard, and his eyes widened a little. He said: "You are full of surprises, Ruth."

"Indeed," I thought to myself. "How much does Ruth know about our activities?" To Ruth, I said: "I hope to meet your friends in Riccione, especially the young lady that you mentioned."

Ruth caught on immediately. "I will arrange it," she whispered. "Her name is Carmen Olmi. She is the daughter of the caretaker of my villa in Tuscany." Her smile increased slightly and she added: "We can meet in a purely social setting, of course."

She placed her old hand on mine and continued: "I don't know the particulars, but your adventures as described in your letters over the past few years left lots of clues. The Dollfuss episode confirmed what I have suspected for a long time. You are involved in espionage." She giggled and whispered. "How exciting!"

My mouth dropped open. As I recovered, I glanced at Hannibal. He was smiling. I whispered to Ruth: "We have friends in France."

"Humm," replied Ruth. "I thought as much." Her smile turned into a slight frown, and she added: "I do not like what is happening in the country of my ancestors. The Italian people deserve better." She paused again and continued: "I will help as much as I can."

"So, there it is," I thought to myself. "We have a new partner." To Ruth, I smiled and said: "Welcome to our little team." She giggled and patted my hand in response.

## Monday evening August 13

Early morning was beautiful, so Hannibal and I decided to walk north on Viale Milano, turn right toward the beach and then back along the beach toward our hotel. We had coffee and a sweet roll before we left our room; we planned to have breakfast after we had worked up an appetite.

We looked like typical tourists. I wore a light print Chanel summer dress and matching white sandals. Hannibal had white slacks, a light blue shirt with an open collar and white shoes. Where did he get the shoes? Neither of us had hats, it was fun to feel the sea breeze as it ruffled our hair.

I marveled at the palm trees that lined the streets; we hadn't seen palms since our visits to Florida six years ago. So different compared to Berlin and Vienna! I reveled in the sunshine.

After a couple of blocks, Hannibal said: "Based on photos in the local newspaper, I believe that is Mussolini's villa." He pointed discreetly.

I looked. About half a block away along Viale Milano, I saw a white, three-story building, with arches around the ground floor. A gravel drive wound through a manicured lawn that bordered the street. The property was surrounded by a tall wrought-iron fence. I glanced around and spotted a street sign that read: 'Viale Latini.'

"Nice," I replied. "Donna Rachel lives in style." Hannibal nodded.

"Oui, Madame," said a soft voice behind us. "Allons-nous marcher ensemble vers la plage?"

I jumped a little and turned. I saw a portly gentleman in white, with a straw boater hat and a walking cane. "Soucet!?"

After we passed Mussolini's villa, the three of us turned right on Viale Parini and headed toward the beach, a short distance to the east. On our left, we paralleled a breakwater, a small boat harbor and a canal that led through the beach to the sea.

When we reached the beach, we turned right and headed back toward our hotel in the distance.

Soucet began the conversation. "Your work in Berlin and Vienna was most valuable, and you both have earned the thanks of the French Republic."

He chuckled a little and added: "And your fee, of course. I added a substantial bonus."

Since Soucet was looking at me, I smiled and replied: "Thank you, I wish we could have done more." I gave Soucet a wry expression and added: "We left just ahead of our pursuers."

Soucet frowned and responded: "Yes. But to use your phrase, the 'bad guys' will eventually find you in Italy." His frown turned to a slight smile. "For the moment, I think you are reasonably safe in Riccione."

We walked in silence for a while. Seagulls gave their raucous calls overhead, and the surf sighed and rolled in slow rhythm to our left. A few cars moved along the Viale Milano in the distance to our right.

After a few minutes, Soucet looked over at Hannibal and added: "However, beware. Villian and others may now have more than a watching brief."

Hannibal nodded in response; no words were needed.

I gulped a little. Villian's sinister face rose out of my memories and rested in my conscious thoughts for a few moments. Finally, the face faded. I gave a sigh, looked at Soucet and asked: "What is our mission in Riccione?"

"Ustaše," replied Soucet. "They are a Croatian terrorist group. Also, the Internal Macedonian Revolutionary Organization, commonly called the IMRO. We think that Mussolini funds both groups, and they both have fascist ideologies. However, we need confirmation and actionable evidence."

He paused and added: "Alexander I, the King of Yugoslavia and a French ally, may be in danger."

I drew a blank. I had not heard of either the Ustaše or the IMRO. I vaguely understood that Yugoslavia included Croatia and regions of Macedonia, and I also knew that Yugoslavia had a king, but that was about it. I looked over to Hannibal and then Soucet with a quizzical expression.

Hannibal nodded toward Soucet and responded: "Mussolini wants to dominate the Balkans, including Yugoslavia." He paused and added: "Unrest against the Yugoslavian government serves his imperial interests."

"Precisely," replied Soucet. "We also have the problem of Henri Taittinger. He may have moved to Italy."

"Oh?" I responded. "While we were in Vienna, we discovered that he had a relationship with his cousin Pierre and Jacque Doriot in France, as well as the Nazis in Vienna. Is there more?"

"Possibly," replied Soucet. "All we know is that the Jeunesses Patriots, headed by Pierre, may have Italian Fascist as well as German Nazi affiliations. We need to discover if Pierre gets funds from Mussolini."

"Humm," responded Hannibal. "We do have connections here in Riccione and elsewhere in Italy." He paused and added: "We will do what we can."

"Good, good," replied Soucet. "Send me coded telegrams when you can. I will be back in Paris." He paused, smiled, tipped his hat and added: "I will leave you now."

He turned right and walked back towards Viale Milano. Hannibal and I watched as he turned the corner by a building and disappeared from view.

We continued our walk back towards the Grand Hotel Riccione in silence. We had lots to think about. The seagulls and surf continued with their background sounds, as if to emphasize the beginning of a new direction for our espionage mission.

# 29

## SECRETS

*Tuesday evening, August 14, 1934*

Ruth arranged for us to have tea late yesterday afternoon. Carmen had just finished her shift in the Mussolini communications center at the Grand. We met in a small, open tea patio adjacent to a restaurant about a block from the hotel. Sounds of surf and seagulls provided background, and the sea breeze ruffled our hair. The setting was lovely.

After introductions, Ruth ordered high tea, which included cucumber sandwiches, an assortment of little hors d'oeuvres, scones and chocolates. The waiter soon left with our order. We settled in for girl talk, with espionage overtones.

As the waiter departed, Carmen smiled coyly and said in a low voice: "Ruth told me about you." Her eyes twinkled. I could tell that she was enjoying her introduction to being a snoop.

Her smile changed to a frown and she added: "Benito Mussolini treats women who work in the center as his harem. I don't like him. How can I help?"

"Good personal motive," I thought to myself. I raised my eyebrows a little and replied: "Your activities on our behalf could be dangerous."

Ruth nodded, reached over and patted Carmen's hand. She said: "Caroline is right, Carmen. Things could go badly if you are caught."

Carmen nodded, took a deep breath and responded. "I know." She looked at Ruth intently and added: "I don't like the fascists. In the communications center, I have seen how they have forced our country into a dictatorship." She paused and then concluded: "I have seen orders to kill people."

"I understand," I replied. We were all silent for a minute or so. The waiter arrived with our high tea. After we had a few sips of tea and couple of hors d'oeuvres, I added: "We are concerned about the Ustaše and the IMRO."

Carmen put down her teacup and replied: "Both have training bases in Italy. Mussolini pays for it. I have seen orders to pay go out to banks."

"Wow!" I thought to myself. "Carmen will be a gold mine of information." We settled in for an hour as Carmen related detail after detail.

Late Monday evening, I briefed Hannibal on what I had learned. I was stuffed from the afternoon tea, and Hannibal said that he had grabbed a bite after he stopped by several local banks, so we didn't order dinner. Instead, we chose to sit on our balcony, discuss our findings, listen to the surf and watch the stars come out.

I began the conversation. "A Bulgarian named Vlado Chernozemski, a member of the IMRO, seems to be a key player in Mussolini's schemes." I paused and added: "According to Carmen, he receives regular payments from Mussolini's staff."

"Humm," responded Hannibal. "Is Chernozemski in Italy?"

"Yes," I replied. "Carmen said that he is an instructor at a Ustaše training camp in Borgotaro. Apparently, the IMRO and the Ustaše work together."

"Borgotaro is a village near Parma, about 200 kilometers from here," responded Hannibal. "Parma has several big banks." He paused and asked: "Do Mussolini's funds go to any banks in Parma?"

"I'll ask," I replied. "Carmen also said that she regularly sent coded telegrams from Mussolini's staff to Chernozemski while he was in a Ustaše camp in Janka-Puszta, a town in Hungary."

"Carmen is a wealth of information," responded Hannibal. "Any other names?"

"I'll try to pronounce the names right," I replied. "Carmen said that Mijo Krali, Zvonimir Pospišil and Milan Rajic also show up frequently in messages."

We both gazed to the east for a while, as the sky grew black out over the sea. Stars brightened and filled the heavens. "Beautiful," I thought to myself.

Hannibal broke the spell by saying: "I established several contacts in a local bank today." He chuckled a little and added: "My transfer of a million Swiss francs from our account in Geneva seemed to break the ice."

"Humm," I responded. "Enough for tonight. Can we watch the stars now?"

Hannibal replied: "Of course." He leaned across from his seat and kissed me. I kissed him back. Much later, I fell asleep with pleasant dreams.

## Wednesday evening, August 15

This morning after coffee, I planned a walk on the beach. Hannibal stayed in our suite, going over finances in preparation for a visit to our new Riccione bank. He said that he intended to go to the bank after I had returned from my walk, and we had finished breakfast.

As I returned from my walk, I passed through the hotel lobby. I saw a sinister-looking, heavy-set man arguing with the clerk at the hotel check-in counter. The man wore casual attire, including a short-sleeved shirt.

I discreetly stepped behind a nearby pillar, picked up a lobby magazine from an end table, pretended to read and eavesdropped.

The man spoke in broken Italian. I couldn't make out everything, but he was upset about an opened envelope that contained 'most secret' information. "Who opened my mail?" he snarled.

The clerk didn't appear intimidated. "No one at this counter, I assure you," replied the young clerk in a smooth voice. "I put the envelope in your box just as I received it from the government communications center upstairs. They may not have sealed it."

The heavy-set man raised his right arm in a threatening gesture. The clerk stepped back from the counter, but didn't lose his composure.

As the man raised his arm, I spotted a tattoo on the inside of his right forearm. It had a skull, crossbones and the letters 'VMRO.'

Apparently, the man decided not to be violent, lowered his arm, put the envelope in his pocket, and stormed off.

"How interesting," I thought to myself. "The letters don't match 'IRMO,' for the terrorist group." I paused in my thinking process. "Still," I concluded, "I'll follow up with the clerk."

I put down my magazine and walked over to the counter. I had met the young man during check-in and several times afterwards. His name was Fredo Rendesi, and we were on friendly speaking terms. Fortunately for me, Fredo tended to gossip a little.

Fredo looked up, smiled as I approached and said: "Buongiorno, signora Jones, posso aiutarti?"

"Buongiorno, Fredo," I replied in a voice just above a whisper. "I overheard your conversation with that rather nasty man a few moments ago. Who is he? Is he a guest at the hotel?"

Fredo looked around; no one was close by. His expression changed to a grimace. He said in a confidential tone: "His name is Vlado Chernozemski, and yes, unfortunately, he is a guest." He raised his eyebrows a little and said: "Why do you ask?"

I looked at Fredo intently for a few seconds. I decided to take a chance and responded: "I'm a private investigator. Chernozemski may be a person of interest." I held my breath and waited.

Fredo smiled with a knowing expression. He looked around again, pointed discreetly toward the ceiling and responded: "By arrangement with the government people in the communications center upstairs, Chernozemski picks up messages every few days at this counter."

"How interesting," I replied. "Are there others like him? I couldn't place his accent."

Sometimes he is accompanied by others," Fredo replied. "He is Bulgarian."

"Humm," I replied. I didn't want to arouse suspicions about my interest in the communications center, so I changed the subject: "You handled the situation very well, Fredo. Perhaps you should be a diplomat."

Fredo laughed and said: "Grazie, signora, but that would be a demotion from my current position." He paused, acquired a mischievous look and added: "Being a private investigator would be much more interesting."

We both laughed. After a few more pleasantries, I said goodbye to Fredo and walked over to the elevator. "Hannibal will be very interested," I mused as the elevator hummed its way up to the floor with our suite. "But what is 'VMRO?'"

Hannibal had finished his accounting calculations and was sipping a cup of coffee when I walked into our parlor. I poured myself a cup from the pot on the coffee table, turned to Hannibal and said: "I had an interesting encounter downstairs." I then related the incident with Fredo and Chernozemski.

"One of our persons of interest," responded Hannibal. "Good work."

"But I don't understand the letters VMRO," I replied. "Is there another organization besides IMRO?"

"Chernozemski is Bulgarian," responded Hannibal. "Bulgarians have a southern Slavic language. They use the Cyrillic alphabet. The letter 'V' is an 'I' in Bulgarian."

"Oh, I see," I replied. How does Hannibal know such things?

## Thursday evening, August 16

I decided to go for a walk again this morning at about quarter until eight. Hannibal was busy coding a telegram for Soucet, as I prepared to leave our suite. "Breakfast at nine-thirty?" I asked.

"Sounds good," replied Hannibal with a smile. He looked at his watch. "I'll be finished by then."

On my way through the lobby, I spotted a familiar face from the past. Henri Taittinger was standing at the check-in counter. My mouth dropped open. I put my hand to my mouth and turned away. "What is he doing here?" My thoughts raced.

I walked slowly across the lobby and slipped out the door that opened towards the beach. "I don't think he saw me," my thoughts continued. I looked at my watch. "I'll wait ten minutes and then go back and tell Hannibal."

The ten minutes seemed like an hour. I fidgeted, paced, but waited. Finally, I slipped back through the door into the lobby. Taittinger was nowhere in sight. I walked slowly to and entered the elevator. It moved slower than molasses in January as it hummed its way to our floor.

Finally, the door opened. I exited and rushed towards our suite. I stopped before our door, smoothed my dress, took a deep breath, used my key and entered.

Hannibal looked up from his work with a surprised expression. "That was quick," he said.

"Henri Taittinger is here," I said in as calm a voice as I could muster. "I saw him in the lobby. I don't think he saw me."

## Friday evening, August 17

The bad guys are everywhere. Early this morning, I decided to bring Ruth up to date. I called her room and made arrangements to go for a walk on the beach.

Hannibal understood. "After I finish this paperwork, I'll go to the bank and see what I can find out about transactions involving our persons of interest." He eyed me carefully. "Be careful and stay in public places."

I smiled. Hannibal's eyes said more than his words. "I will," I replied.

Ruth and I met in the lobby at about quarter until eight. We were both dressed in resort casual, with stylish light print dresses and sandals. We carried purses on shoulder straps.

Ruth also had an 'old ladies' straw hat and her ubiquitous cane. The hat gave her a rather comical 'country matron' look.

I grinned in spite of myself when I saw the hat.

Ruth observed the direction of my stare. She sniffed, tossed her head back, gave me an imperious look and said: "Very chic, don't you think?" She reached back and tilted her hat forward into a jaunty position on her silvery hair.

I burst out laughing. Ruth joined in. "It prevents sunburn," she said in a mock defensive tone. "You should try one."

"Never!" I responded between giggles. "Anyway, I want a light tan first."

Our little repartee was a good start to what we intended as a pleasant walk along the beach.

At just before eight o'clock, we headed north, along the water's edge, in the direction of Mussolini's villa. I could see the breakwater and the masts of private sailboats in the boat harbor just beyond the villa.

I turned to Ruth and asked: "Will you be OK if we walk to the breakwater and back?"

Ruth gave me a determined glance. Her eyes twinkled and she replied: "Of course. Do you think you can keep up the pace?" With that, she took a couple of exaggerated strides and waved her cane in the air. We both giggled.

We walked in silence for a while. The surf and seagulls provided pleasant background sounds. My thoughts turned to our espionage work. I recalled Hannibal's question about Parma banks.

I turned to Ruth as we walked and asked: "Do you know if Mussolini uses Parma banks to pass funds to the Ustaše training camp in Borgotaro?"

Ruth was silent for a moment and then replied: "I'll ask Carmen. I will see her tonight."

"Thank you," I responded. "Hannibal has banking contacts, and he will follow up based on Carmen's information."

I thought a moment and added: "We need to know who, how much and how often." Ruth nodded.

The breakwater was much closer now, and we could see Mussolini's villa just to the west. As we continued to walk, I explained our concerns about Henri Taittinger.

Ruth was quiet for a few moments and then replied: "I observed a man who spoke with a French accent at the villa during my visit a couple of days ago. He was talking to one of Benito's aides."

She paused in her walk, turned to me and asked: "What does Taittinger look like?"

I stopped walking, opened my purse and took out the photo of Henri Taittinger that Coulondre had given Hannibal while we were in Vienna.

Ruth squinted her eyes, looked at the photo and then at me. "That's him," she stated matter-of-factly. She was silent for a moment and added: "I'll see what I can find out from Donna Rachele."

I put away the photo, and we continued our walk. The breakwater was close now. I was about to suggest that we turn around and head back towards the hotel, when Ruth stopped, pointed with her cane in the direction of the breakwater and asked: "What's that?"

I looked in the direction indicated by her cane. My mouth dropped open. After a moment, I closed it and then said: "A body."

"Oh!" responded Ruth. "Shall we investigate?"

# 30

## ASSASSIN'S STRIKE

*Saturday morning, August 18, 1934*

Friday morning, Ruth and I examined the dead body. It lay face down in the sand, parallel to the surf line. The head was toward the breakwater, which bisected the beach about three meters away.

We approached slowly, taking care not to disturb two sets of footprints in the sand.

"Humm," I muttered. "The man is fashionably dressed in white trousers, light blue shirt and white slip-on shoes."

"His right leg, foot, arm and hand are being washed by the incoming tide," responded Ruth. She paused, stepped back a little, observed and added: "The body, left leg, arm and hand are dry."

I turned and looked back south, along the surf line. "Left footprints from down the beach up to the body," I stated. "The footprints match the man's left shoe. The right footprints have been washed away by the incoming tide."

I paused, observed and continued: "A second set of footprints start at the breakwater, walk up to the body, then turn right along the breakwater back toward the Viale Milano."

"What time is it?" Ruth asked.

I looked at my watch. "Eight-nineteen," I replied. "We arrived less than five minutes ago."

I walked up close, leaned over and gently lifted the man's left arm. "No rigor mortis," I stated. "Also, I see a bullet hole in the back of the man's head."

"I have a camera in my purse," responded Ruth.

"Ruth is full of surprises," I thought to myself. "Oh good," I uttered.

Ruth grinned as she saw the expression on my face. "I had planned to take photos of beach scenes, but this body is much more interesting," she said.

I recovered my poise and responded: "Good idea."

Ruth's grin broadened a little as she laid her cane in the sand and extracted a small camera from her purse.

She took photos of the body from several angles, the footprints in the sand next to the body and the footprints along the surf line. I laid my purse along one of the footprints from each set for scale. Ruth immediately understood, and snapped two more photos.

I marveled at her clinical attitude and efficiency. To Ruth, I asked: "Have you have done this before?"

"Humm," responded Ruth. She smiled again. She clambered up on one of the rocks in the breakwater and took another photo of the body and both sets of footprints, with a larger field of view.

"OK, Ruth," I thought to myself. I suppressed a chuckle. "Keep your little secrets."

To Ruth, I said: "If you are ready, I will turn the body over. I want to see if there is an exit wound from the head shot."

"Ready," replied Ruth. She remained on her rock perch, with her camera set.

I turned the body over, to the left, away from the water. Sure enough, the bullet had exited through the man's forehead. The sand where the face had rested was soaked in blood, but I spotted a tiny hole. Ruth snapped a couple of photos.

I stood, opened my purse and extracted a small wooden spatula, a set of surgical gloves and two small paper bags.

It was Ruth's turn to look surprised. She asked: "Do you always carry those things in your purse?"

"Usually," I said with a bland expression on my face. I didn't mention the Walther handgun and three clips of ammunition.

Ruth recovered quickly and replied: "Did you notice the bullet hole in the chest?" She paused and peered down from her perch. "It probably pierced the heart."

"Humm," I responded. "Since there was no exit wound in the back, the bullet is still inside the man's chest." I looked up at Ruth with a grin. "We'll leave that one for the coroner." I paused and then added: "However, we might find one in the sand."

I got down next to the place where the man's face had been, put on my gloves and began to dig in the bloody sand with the spatula. About 20 centimeters down, I found a bullet.

"Bullet from the shot through the back of the head," I stated matter-of-factly. I held the bullet up so Ruth could see and then dropped it in one of the paper bags. "7.63 millimeter," I added.

I stood up, took off my gloves and put them, along with the spatula, in the second bag. Ruth stepped down from her perch on the rock. We were silent for a few moments, as we both thought about the evidence so far.

Ruth began. "The victim was walking north along the beach before the tide came in. The footprints show that he didn't stop before he was shot."

"Yes," I responded. "The first shot was from the front, into the chest, while the man was walking toward his assailant."

Ruth nodded and said: "The second shot through the back of the head was a coup de grâce, while the victim was face-down in the sand."

"The victim saw his assailant," I mused. "Since he didn't stop walking until he fell, the shot was unexpected."

"The assailant and victim may have known each other," Ruth stated. She looked around. "The shot was straight-on, and the breakwater limits how far back the assailant was standing when he pulled the trigger."

"Humm," I responded. "A 7.63-millimeter bullet means that the gun was probably a rather common semi-automatic handgun," I responded. "Let's look for shell casings."

I climbed up on one of the breakwater rocks and looked around. Ruth bent over and peered in the sand next to the body.

After a couple of minutes, I spotted a shiny object between two rocks at the very edge of the breakwater. "7.63 x 25-millimeter shell casing," I said. I carefully added the shell casing to the paper bag with the bullet.

I also examined the footprints next to the two rocks. I peered closely, then said: "The assailant stood here and shot the victim as he approached."

"Here's another shell casing," stated Ruth. She pointed down in the sand not far from the body.

I walked over toward Ruth, taking care not to disturb the assailant's footprints. I carefully added the second shell casing to my paper bag with the bullet and the other shell casing.

"I'll take more photos," responded Ruth. Soon it was done.

"Let's check the victim's pockets," I said. We found a receipt from the Hotel Milano e Ungaria, Viale Milano 2, Riccione, and some Italian lire in coins and paper. I put the receipt and money in my evidence bag.

"No identification," I mused. "Still, the hotel front desk might be able to use one of our photos and the receipt to provide an identity and some information about the victim's activities at the hotel."

"Did you notice his right forearm?" Ruth asked. I hadn't; I had concentrated on the bullet wounds. I looked at the forearm.

To my surprise, I saw the VMRO tattoo. "Good observation," I said. Ruth beamed.

I stepped back and surveyed the scene. "Anything else?" I asked.

Ruth was quiet for a full minute. Finally, she said: "I don't think so, except for the fact that the tide is still rising."

"Yes," I replied. I looked at my watch. "Nine o'clock precisely." I looked at Ruth with a bemused expression and said: "Time to call the cops."

"Yes," replied Ruth. She shaded her eyes with her hand and looked at the gleaming white Villa Mussolini nearby. "I am known at the villa, and carabinieri policemen are always on duty."

I thought a moment and then said: "I can wait here with the body. Would you also call Hannibal at the Grand from the villa?"

"Of course," replied Ruth with a smile. She walked over the sand, picked up her cane and turned toward the villa.

"Oh," I said: "You needn't go into detail to the police about our preliminary investigation, especially about the photos."

Ruth looked over her shoulder, smiled, nodded and then started her walk toward the villa. I sat down on a nearby breakwater rock and watched as she covered the distance in about five minutes.

I could see her as she approached the beachside gate in the fence around the villa. A uniformed man stepped out of a guard post. The two talked. I could see Ruth as she pointed in my direction. After a minute or so, the guard let her pass, and she disappeared inside.

I looked at my watch. "Nine-ten," I thought to myself. Minutes passed. I looked around. I could see a few people along the beach in the distance. Seagulls gave out their raucous calls as they wheeled overhead.

I glanced over at my dead companion. "OK," I muttered; "Who shot you and why?" The only replies were the sounds of the surf and the seagulls.

Two uniformed men left the villa through the beach gate and headed across the sand in my direction. I looked at my watch, and it read nine-thirty. "That took a while," I thought to myself.

Movement near the breakwater back toward Viale Milano caught my eye. A Duesenberg turned on Viale Parini and stopped. Hannibal got out, shaded his eyes with his hand and looked in my direction. He arrived at my location before the two policemen.

"That was quick," I said as Hannibal strode up.

His eyes swept across the scene. After a few seconds, his gaze rested on me. "You've been busy," he said. His expression showed concern. "Are you OK?"

"Of course," I replied, as I stood up from my rock. "We have a male murder victim. He was shot twice. He has a VMRO tattoo."

"Humm," responded Hannibal. He looked intently at the body. "Ruth said over the phone that a man was murdered and gave your location. She also said that the police had been notified." He looked back toward the villa. The two policemen had covered about half the distance.

I gave Hannibal a quick summary of Ruth's and my crime scene activities. I finished just as the policemen arrived.

The two policemen stared at the body and then turned to Hannibal and me.

After introductions, Hannibal stood quietly while I explained what Ruth and I had discovered.

"The poor man was face down in the sand when we found him," I said in my best innocent voice. "I turned him over to see if he was alive." I gave out a big sigh, looked down and sniffled a little.

"Of course, signora," replied one of the policemen in a solicitous voice. "I understand completely."

A voluble conversation between the two policemen followed. I remained silent and sniffled a little more. Hannibal did his best to stifle a chuckle. I gave him my best brave smile.

I heard the title 'Maresciallo' and the name 'Antolini' several times. After about five minutes of excited discussion, one of the policemen scurried back toward the villa. The other stood guard in his best officious manner.

Hannibal, the remaining policeman and I waited patiently. Finally, at about ten-thirty, we observed a police car as it pulled up by our Duesenberg.

After another five minutes, a middle-aged, portly policeman in a resplendent uniform arrived at the crime scene. He was followed by two younger policemen in less resplendent uniforms. The two young men joined the policeman from the villa.

Hannibal stepped forward and said: "I am Hannibal Jones." He nodded in my direction and added: "My wife Caroline and her friend signora Ruth Meltzer discovered this body at about eight-fifteen this morning. Signora Meltzer is currently at the Villa Mussolini."

"And I am Inspector Adolfo Antolini, a Maresciallo of the Carabinieri," responded the portly policeman. He handed Hannibal a card with his name, title and phone number.

He turned away from Hannibal, glanced at the body, turned to one of his subordinates and gave a series of curt orders, including one to go fetch a camera from the car and another to call for an ambulance. The subordinate ran back toward the police car.

One of the remaining two policemen started walking all around the body, taking notes and obliterating footprints. Antolini turned, saw and exclaimed: "Idiot! We must preserve the crime scene!"

The man stopped taking notes, walked back from the body, stood by the other police subordinate and hung his head. Antolini muttered curses and glared at both policemen. Hannibal and I looked at each other. "Oh my," I thought to myself.

"We will wait for the camera," Antolini announced.

He then turned to me and said: "In the meantime, signora Jones, would you tell me what you observed when you and signora Meltzer found the body?"

Before I could begin, he added: "Please accept my deepest condolences concerning the distress you must feel after such a terrible experience."

Hannibal turned away and stifled a chuckle.

My attitude toward the bumbling Antolini softened a little. "He's being considerate of my feelings," I thought to myself. "That's nice."

Hannibal turned back around and watched me with a twinkle in his eyes. I gave him a snooty look and turned to Antolini. I presented a complete, concise verbal report, including times, my observations about the body and the fact that Ruth had taken photos of the body and footprints.

I then took the evidence bag out of my purse, gave it to Antolini and said: "The bag contains a 7.63-millimeter bullet that I dug from the sand under the face of the deceased. It also contains two 7.63 x 25-millimeter shell casings that we found near the body and the contents of the victim's pockets."

Antolini's eyes stared and his mouth was open. It took him half a minute to recover after I had finished my presentation. I waited patiently.

Finally, Antolini asked: "When may I have the photos?"

"Good question," I thought to myself. To Antolini, I said: "Signora Meltzer and I should be able to have the film developed and prints to you tomorrow."

I paused and then added: "As I explained earlier, two shots were fired, and one bullet most likely remains in the victim's chest. Major Jones and I are private investigators, and we would appreciate it if we could see the autopsy report in exchange for the photos."

Antolini raised his eyebrows and said: "Private investigators? What is your interest in this death?"

"Signora Meltzer is a friend of Donna Rachele Mussolini," I stated blandly. "I can have signora Mussolini contact your superiors if you feel that such a phone call would be necessary."

Again, Antolini's eyes widened and his mouth opened. No words came out. Finally, he stuttered: "I, I don't think that will be necessary."

He turned to Hannibal. After a long pause, his expression brightened, and he added humbly: "I would appreciate your assistance in this investigation." Hannibal nodded.

Antolini turned back to me.

"Happy to help," I replied with a smile.

I looked over at Hannibal. His expression said: "Well done." I smiled sweetly in return.

I heard the sound of an old car in the distance. I glanced back along the breakwater. A chattering, decrepit-looking ambulance had driven up behind Antolini's police car.

Soon two attendants with a stretcher and a policeman hurried toward us. I could see a camera in the policeman's hand. "Better late than never, I suppose," I thought to myself.

## Saturday evening, August 18

I used our portable film processing supplies and equipment to develop Ruth's film this morning. The bathroom is a mess, but we have negatives and three sets of prints.

Hannibal and I will keep the negatives and one set of prints and deliver two sets of prints to Antolini, along with a suggestion that he forward one set to the medical examiner.

Hannibal called Antolini at the phone number on his card. Antolini said he would send a policeman to pick up the prints.

The policeman was prompt, and he told Hannibal that Antolini expressed thanks. He also invited us to meet him at the Hotel Milano e Ungaria at 9:00 AM on Monday morning.

# 31

## EVIDENCE TRAIL

*Monday evening, August 20, 1934*

Ruth and I made arrangements for lunch today. Hannibal dropped me off at a restaurant on Viale Milano, not far from the Villa Mussolini.

Hannibal planned to drive to the Hotel Milano e Ungaria, meet Inspector Antolini and follow up on the receipt I found in the victim's pocket. He also carried a couple of photos of the victim's face.

As we pulled up to the restaurant, I said: "I will return to the hotel after lunch. See you this evening."

Hannibal smiled and replied: "We can compare notes over wine." He then drove off.

Ruth and another lady were waiting just inside the quiet, elegant-looking restaurant. Ruth introduced me to her companion. "Caroline, please meet Donna Rachele," she said. "We have lunch here often."

I observed Donna Rachele Mussolini. "A strikingly beautiful, middle-aged matron," I surmised to myself. I said my hellos in a friendly, yet reserved manner.

I glanced around, but I didn't see any obvious signs of security guards. "Interesting," my thoughts continued. "Either Donna Rachele does not have guards, or they are very inconspicuous."

After the hellos, Donna Rachele said: "I gave Chef Louis several of my hometown recipes some time ago, and he has been a friend ever since." She paused, smiled and added: "I look forward to lunch and our time together."

I liked Donna Rachele instantly. My thoughts continued. "How could such a nice person be married to a dictator?"

As the Maitre'd seated us at a quiet corner table, Ruth said: "Donna Rachele is the expert here. Shall we let her select our lunch?"

"Wonderful," I replied. "Perhaps Chef Louis will prepare one of your recipes."

Donna Rachele smiled. After we settled in, she ordered a healthy-sounding spinach salad, tiny rye bread slices with an herb and olive oil dipping plate, a delicious-sounding chicken piccata with lemon, butter and capers, and later, Italian-style carrot cake and coffee.

The lunch was light and simple. It reminded me of lunches that I had in Chicago's Little Italy. "Delicious," I said as we sipped our coffee. "Especially the chicken piccata."

"Donna Rachele's recipe," responded Ruth with a twinkle in her eyes. Donna Rachele beamed.

A minute passed. Donna Rachele's expression clouded a little. I watched over the rim of my coffee cup as I sipped. Finally, she said: "Ruth told me about the body on the beach." She paused and then added: "So close to home, and I am concerned about my children."

"The man had a VMRO tattoo," Ruth stated softly. "It's the Bulgarian version of IMRO."

"Oh my," exclaimed Donna Rachele. She then whispered: "I overheard my husband talking to his staff about payments to the IMRO. The money goes to a bank in Parma." She paused and then added: "I think the IMRO wants to overthrow the King of Yugoslavia."

"Wow!" I thought to myself. "Why is she telling us state secrets?" I'm sure my expression revealed my thoughts.

Donna Rachele watched me for several moments as she sipped her coffee. Finally, she put down her cup and said: "Benito ignores our children, except for publicity purposes. I know he sees other women."

"Rejected wife, philandering husband," I thought to myself. To Donna Rachele, I simply said: "How very sad." I continued with my coffee.

Tears formed in Donna Rachele's eyes. She picked up her coffee cup again and sipped quietly.

After a few moments, Ruth ventured: "Caroline is an accomplished private investigator. She has an interest in the murder of the man on the beach last Saturday."

I picked up on Ruth's lead. "Adolfo Antolini is the local carabinieri inspector."

Donna Rachele eyed me for half a minute as she sipped her coffee. Finally, she said: "I know Luca Barreto, the carabinieri superintendent for Riccione."

She smiled and added: "His men provide my security." She raised her eyebrows a little and gave a quick nod toward two men in suits, sitting at a table across the dining room. "You may have noticed."

I took a discreet look at the two men. They looked in my direction. "I missed that one," I thought to myself.

I turned to Donna Rachele and smiled.

"I will tell Luca about your interest," she stated. "I'm sure Inspector Antolini will cooperate."

We finished our lunch at about 1:30 PM. Donna Rachele's expression changed to a frown, and she said: "Benito sent word this morning that he would arrive later this week, and I must make preparations."

"And Ruth and I should return to the Grand," I said, as I finished my third cup of coffee. "My husband, Ruth and I want to compare impressions concerning the murder on Saturday." Ruth nodded.

"I'll call for my driver, and he can take you to your hotel after he drops me off at the villa," replied Donna Rachele.

She smiled and added: "This has been a very enjoyable experience." She looked over at the two men at a table across the room and nodded. One got up and walked out through the dining room door.

Half an hour later, Ruth and I were alone in the back seat of Donna Rachele's Mercedes town car. An internal dividing window separated us from the driver.

"A most informative lunch date," I ventured to Ruth, as the driver weaved in and out of traffic on Viale Milano on the way to the hotel.

After a few minutes of silence, Ruth responded: "Yes. Donna Rachele's comment about the Parma bank matches what Carmen told me the evening of the 17th. The name of the bank is Banco di Roma. It has a branch office in Parma."

I gave Ruth a long, searching look. "You have demonstrated amazing skills in our investigations," I replied.

Ruth was quiet for a full minute. As our car pulled up the hotel, she said: "Since 1932, I also have friends, like yours, in Paris."

"I see," I replied. I didn't know what else to say.

We got out of the car and went inside the hotel. Before we parted company in the lobby, Ruth said: "Be careful about your judgement of Henri Taittinger. There is more to him than his association with Nazis and Fascists."

With that mysterious comment, Ruth smiled and patted me on the shoulder. Her eyes twinkled. She added: "Wonderful lunch. See you later." She turned, left me standing in the lobby and walked slowly to a nearby open elevator.

I stood in the lobby for several minutes, collecting my thoughts. "OK, Caroline, what's next? We have a murder to solve." I saw Fredo behind the check-in desk as he finished up with a hotel guest.

"Aha!" My thoughts continued. "Chernozemski is a guest at the hotel. Fredo might know something."

I walked over to Fredo, smiled and asked: "Have you seen Vlado Chernozemski since your encounter on August 15?"

"Good afternoon, signora Jones," Fredo replied. "Yes. He checked out of Room 207 at 6:30 AM on August 17." Fredo smiled and added: "Thank goodness." Fredo turned the register around so I could see the entries.

"Early in the morning on the same day that Ruth and I discovered the body," I thought to myself, as I looked at the entries for the 17th. "Not just a coincidence."

Fredo leaned across the counter and whispered: "I was on duty when Chernozemski checked out. His suit looked as if he had dressed in a great hurry."

I looked intently at Fredo and asked: "Is Room 207 still vacant?"

Fredo turned to his wall of mail boxes with room keys, took out the key to Room 207, turned back to me, smiled knowingly and said: "Given your interest in Chernozemski on the 15th, I thought you might be back with more questions."

He paused and then whispered: "I put the room on the maintenance list. It hasn't even been cleaned."

I'm sure my expression said more than words. I grinned wryly and replied: "May I visit the room?"

Fredo turned around, peered into the office behind the counter and said: "Alberto, please attend the counter while I run an errand." A young man emerged from the office and stood dutifully behind the counter.

Fredo turned back to me, grinned and said: "Follow me."

Within a couple of minutes, we arrived at Room 207. Fredo looked around; we were alone. He unlocked the door, and we stepped inside. Fredo quietly closed the door behind us. The room was quiet, almost spooky.

I looked around the room, noting details. "Rumpled unmade bed, lampshade askew, sand on the floor, drapes pulled shut, wardrobe door open, no clothing on the hangers and one hanger on the floor," I quickly surmised. "Messy, and he left in a hurry."

I walked into the adjoining bathroom. "Towels on the floor, more sand and an odd odor," I observed.

I thought about the odor for a moment. "Ahah! It's the smell of gun oil." I looked down and saw the source. "Oil on a hand towel. Someone wiped down a gun."

A bath towel caught my eye. I bent over and straightened it out on the floor. I could see the outline of a shoe and more sand. "Not a footprint, but enough of an outline to take measurements," I concluded.

I opened my purse, took out one of my evidence bags and put the oily hand towel in the bag. I carefully folded the bath towel and tucked it under my arm. Carrying my purse, bag and bath towel, I returned to the bedroom.

Using another bag and a sheet of paper from my purse, I collected a sample of the sand from the floor.

As I finished, I glanced at Fredo. He stood there in wide-eyed silence. I looked around the room for a full minute. I smiled at Fredo and said: "All done."

Fredo opened the door and looked out into the hallway. "All clear," he said. We stepped out of the room, and Fredo locked the door.

I looked at Fredo's face with a steady gaze. "Thank you," I said in a soft voice. "You have the instincts for a career as a detective."

Fredo replied with a smile. "Glad I could help."

Later in my suite, I organized and labeled the evidence from Room 207 and finished my notes for all of the day's activities.

As I put down my notebook, I heard a key in the door. Hannibal had returned.

"Busy day?" He asked, as he entered.

"Yes," I responded. "But your story first." Soon we were comfortably seated in the parlor.

"OK," responded Hannibal. "I met with Inspector Antolini at the Hotel Milano e Ungaria. We talked to the desk clerk and showed him the victim's photo and the receipt from his pocket."

Hannibal paused and continued. "The clerk recognized the man in the photo and retrieved a passport from the hotel safe. The victim is Dimitri Kajic. He is from Bulgaria. Antolini kept Kajic's passport."

"Humm," I responded. "Chernozemski and Kajic may have known each other."

"Quite likely," said Hannibal. "The receipt from the victim's pocket was from the hotel dining room. Antolini and I checked with the Maitre'd, and he recognized the receipt and the passport photo."

Hannibal continued: "The Maitre'd recalled that Kajic and a companion had dinner the evening of August 16. He also said that Kajic and his companion argued."

"Humm," I mused. "If we ever get a photo of Chernozemski, we should re-visit with the Maitre'd."

"Yes," replied Hannibal. "We also inspected Kajic's hotel room. Since he had not checked out, we found a few interesting items."

Hannibal paused for a moment and continued: "We found a used train ticket from Parma to Riccione for August 15 and an unused ticket from Riccione to Milan and on to Geneva for August 21."

"Kajic was skipping town," I hypothesized.

"Possibly," replied Hannibal. "I will check with my banking contacts in Geneva and find out if Kajic had a Swiss account."

"How about fingerprints in the room?" I asked.

Hannibal grinned and said: "I dusted the room while Antolini watched. He seemed fascinated."

"I bet," I replied. "Any luck?"

"I found two sets. One is probably Kajic's. We'll have to check the autopsy report. The other belonged to a hotel maid, which I verified by taking prints of the maid assigned to Kajic's room."

We were silent for a minute or so, while Hannibal let me digest the information. Finally, I asked: "Anything else?"

"Just one item," responded Hannibal. After Antolini and I finished, we said our goodbyes in the lobby. As Antolini walked toward the door, I noticed a well-dressed man seated nearby who watched us intently. When I returned his stare, he quickly picked up a newspaper from a nearby table and pretended to read."

I shifted a little in my chair and waited. Hannibal had a way of creating anticipation.

Hannibal continued: "I walked over to Antonio Basilone, the front desk clerk, whom I had met earlier. I pointed out the man seated in the lobby. Antonio recognized the man as a hotel guest. I asked Antonio to pull the man's passport from the safe."

"He did, and I checked the passport. The man's name is Petre Zivkovic. He is from Yugoslavia." Hannibal grinned and added: "I returned the passport to Antonio along with a substantial tip. He agreed to do a little snooping."

"Humm," I responded with a mischievous smile. "Well done. Our list of players is getting longer." Hannibal nodded.

We were both silent for a while. Finally, Hannibal asked: "So, how was your day?"

I gave him a complete verbal report. Afterwards, Hannibal phoned for a room service dinner, including a bottle of chianti. "We earned the wine," I said as Hannibal returned to the parlor.

Hannibal laughed. "I have my motive," he replied. "I plan to ply a beautiful woman with strong drink."

"Humm," I replied. I pulled him down and gave him a warm kiss. "You don't need the wine."

# 32

## ROOT OF EVIL

Rain pattered on the window of our bedroom this morning, as I slowly slipped into the awake world. Hannibal had a way of making pleasant dreams happen, and I reluctantly let them fade into my memories for future reference. I rubbed sleep from my eyes, got out of bed and toddled into the bathroom.

As I emerged a few minutes later, I saw Hannibal, who was standing in the hall between the bedroom and the parlor. I focused my eyes. He was fully dressed and had a steaming cup of coffee in each hand.

"No walk on the beach today," I mumbled. "It's raining."

Hannibal smiled and said: "How about a cup of coffee instead?"

I padded over to Hannibal, kissed him, and started to snuggle. "Careful, you'll spill the coffee," he said with a chuckle.

"Hummf," I responded and stepped back a little. I looked at the coffee cups and sniffed. The aroma was good. I then replied: "You have coffee, so you are forgiven." Hannibal's eyes twinkled as he handed me a cup.

We walked into the parlor. My white silk robe was waiting for me across one of the soft easy chairs by the window. I set my cup on the coffee table, put on my robe, made myself comfortable in the chair and picked up my cup.

Hannibal sat in the chair next to me. Soon we were sipping coffee and listening to the rain outside.

"We got a phone call this morning while you were still asleep," said Hannibal. "It was Luca Barreto, the carabinieri superintendent for Riccione."

"Oh?" I replied, as I tried to focus my mind on the implications.

"Barreto said he had received a phone call from Donna Rachele Mussolini," Hannibal continued. "He assured me that Inspector Antolini would deliver Kajic's autopsy report and the ballistics report to our hotel suite, personally, at our convenience."

Hannibal paused and grinned: "I told Barreto that noon today would be fine." Hannibal looked at his watch and added: "It's now eight-forty-five. Room service breakfast will be here at ten. Antolini will arrive at noon. Think you can be dressed by then?"

"Hummf," I responded, and slowly sipped my coffee for emphasis.

At just before noon, I was fully dressed and ready for Antolini's arrival. I wore my form-fitting white Chanel slacks with billowy lower legs, a beige, slightly daring blouse and mid-heeled matching beige shoes. A yellow and blue silk scarf tied around my neck added a splash of color. Of course, my hair was fully coiffed.

Hannibal, who was dressed in white slacks, casual light brown shirt and slip-on brown shoes, said: "You look very stylish."

"Thank you," I replied, and I gave Hannibal my best snooty look. He laughed.

We made ourselves comfortable in the parlor. Hannibal moved a third chair from the bedroom to the parlor for our expected guest. A silver coffee service, china cups and saucers rested on a side table. Light steam rose from the spout of the pot.

At precisely noon, we heard a light knock. Hannibal walked into the entryway and opened the door. I got up and stood in the hallway where I could see our arriving guest.

Antolini stood in the doorway. He was slightly damp from the rain. He had a large envelope in one hand and a folded, dripping umbrella in the other. "Buongiorno, Major Jones, Signora Jones," he said. "I have the reports."

"Please come in, Inspector," said Hannibal.

I put my hand to my mouth to hide my smile. After a moment of recovery, I said: "We have hot coffee in the parlor. Just leave your umbrella in the hallway, and join us." I stepped aside and motioned to the doorway that led to the parlor.

Antolini gave a big sigh, stepped into entryway, leaned his wet umbrella against the wall and replied: "Grazie, signora."

Soon we were seated in the parlor. I poured Antolini a cup of coffee. After he dried out a little, he spread the autopsy and ballistics reports out on the table. I could see a third report in his envelope.

"Let Antolini set the agenda," I thought to myself. "He'll get to the third report."

"The autopsy confirms what we already know about the cause of death," said Antolini. "The medical examiner removed a second 7.63 caliber bullet from the body."

After a couple of sips of coffee, he added: "However, due to the rapidly changing ambient temperatures of the air and sea, he was not able to determine a window for the time of death."

"I can help with that," responded Hannibal. "I checked the Riccione tide tables for August 16 and 17. Low tides occurred at 6:32 PM on August 16 and 5:17 AM on August 17. High tides occurred at 1:02 AM and 10:49 AM on August 17. The tide was rising and had just reached the body when Caroline and Ruth arrived at the crime scene at 8:15 AM on the 17th. I also visually checked the high and low tide line marks on the beach."

Hannibal paused, looked at Antolini with steady gaze and then continued. "The last high tide receded past the crime scene at 3:39 AM on August 17. The victim therefore fell to his position on the beach after 3:39 AM and before 8:15 AM on August 17."

"We can reduce that end time to before 8:00 AM, because I could see the breakwater next to the crime scene from the time Ruth and I started our walk on the beach," I added. "No activity."

"We have an approximate four hour, 21-minute window for the time of death," Hannibal concluded.

Antolini sat with his mouth open and eyes wide for half a minute. Finally, he recovered his composure, retrieved a notepad and pencil from his pocket, and scribbled. After he finished, he said: "I will tell the medical examiner."

While Hannibal was reciting his time and geometry narrative, I scanned the ballistics report.

After Antolini finished taking notes, I said: "According to this ballistics report, the 7.63 x 25-millimeter bullets and shell casings were used in a Mauser C96 semi-automatic pistol, which leaves distinctive firing pin and rifling marks."

I recalled my training lessons in Paris and continued: "The C96 was used extensively during the world war. Many are still available."

"Yes," responded Antolini. "The IMRO and Ustaše are known to use such guns."

I raised my eyebrows a little. "Antolini probably knows that Mussolini sponsors the IMRO and the Ustaše," I thought to myself. "Yet he showed no sign of hesitation in his statement about the possible source of the murder weapon."

I glanced over at Hannibal. I could tell from his expression that he had reached the same conclusion.

Antolini set his cup down, took the third report out of the envelope and said: "Superintendent Barreto said that you would be interested in this report." He laid it on the table and added: "It is most secret."

Hannibal and I scooted our chairs to a position where we could both read. After a few minutes, Hannibal looked at Antolini and asked: "Does Benito Mussolini know about this investigation into the IRMO and the Ustaše?"

Antolini took a deep breath, exhaled, gave Hannibal a steady gaze and replied: "Not all of us in the Carabinieri are fascists." He looked at me and added: "Your reputation precedes you."

I returned Antolini's gaze and said: "Still, you and Superintendent Barreto are taking a risk."

Antolini shrugged and replied: "We appreciate your help."

After Hannibal and I finished reading the secret report, Antolini quietly returned it to its envelope. He rose from his seat and said: "This has been a most interesting day. I know you both have work to do." He smiled and added: "Thank you for your hospitality."

After Antolini departed, Hannibal looked at me and said: "The report shows that Kajic handled the money transfers from the Mussolini government to the IMRO and Ustaše."

"Follow the money," I replied. Hannibal nodded.

### Wednesday evening, August 22

Hannibal visited our Riccione bank and the Hotel Milano e Ungaria today. After my usual walk on the beach and a visit to Fredo, I stayed in our suite, had a light lunch and wrote a coded report for Soucet.

Hannibal returned at about 5:00 PM. As he walked into the parlor, I said: "Dinner will arrive at 6:30. Picking items from a room service menu was hard work. I hope you like my selections."

Hannibal laughed and said: "I hope you also ordered wine. We have much to discuss, and wine seems appropriate."

"The wine has already been delivered," I responded, as I pointed to an ice bucket, a bottle of Italian pinot grigio and wine glasses on the side table.

"Perfect," replied Hannibal. "You pour while I spread my notes on the coffee table."

Within a few minutes, we were seated by the coffee table with glasses of wine in hand. "So how was your day?" I asked.

"Most interesting," replied Hannibal. "My banker friends found out that Kajic has a substantial personal account in a Geneva bank. He is also listed as an authorized agent on the IRMO account in the Parma branch of Banco di Roma."

He paused and added: "A large sum in Italian lire arrived by inter-bank transfer to Kajic's Geneva account on August 16. The amount matched precisely the amount that transferred out of the IRMO account in the Banco di Roma branch in Parma on August 13. The transfer took four days to clear."

"Kajic was embezzling money from the IRMO," I responded. "Motive for murder."

"Yes," replied Hannibal. "And Chernozemski is a known IRMO member. He could be their hit man."

"Even though Chernozemski is our prime suspect, we do not have proof."

Hannibal nodded and said: "My friend Antonio at the Hotel Milano e Ungaria gave us another suspect."

"Oh?" I responded.

Hannibal replied: "Antonio searched Petre Zivkovic's room. He found several incriminating telegrams and a Mauser C96 pistol. One of the telegrams was from a staff member in the royal household of the King of Yugoslavia."

"Humm" I responded. "Does Zivkovic know that his room was searched?"

"No, according to Antonio," replied Hannibal. "Zivkovic was out when he searched. He took detailed notes from the telegrams and did not touch the pistol. He left the room just the way he found it."

"Good," I replied. "Your Antonio seems to have good snooping skills. Tell me about the telegrams."

"They were written in the Serbian language, and Antonio copied them verbatim," responded Hannibal. "I don't yet have a translation, but the telegrams mention Kajic, Chernozemski and King Alexander."

"Given that one of the telegrams is from the royal household, Zivkovic is probably an agent of the King, with a mission here in Riccione," I mused.

"Most likely," replied Hannibal. "Since the IRMO wants to kill the King, Zivkovic has a motive for killing Kajic."

"How about shoes?" I asked.

"None in the room," replied Hannibal.

"Strong motive, how about opportunity?" I asked.

"The hotel register shows that Zivkovic arrived on August 12. He's still here." Hannibal replied.

I thought a moment and then said: "We need to compare Zivkovic's pistol rifling and firing pin to the bullets and shell casings that killed Kajic."

"Yes," Hannibal replied. "We can give our information to Antolini. He will have enough evidence to issue a warrant to search Zivkovic's room, confiscate the pistol and make comparisons."

"He can also compare Zivkovic's shoes to Ruth's photos of footprints," I responded. "Antolini has a set of Ruth's photos."

"As I recall," Hannibal added with a smile, "You used your purse for scale in the photos of footprints. Antolini can make accurate comparisons. I'll call him tomorrow."

After a few moments of silence, I said: "I had Fredo do some snooping this morning with regard to Henri Taittinger's room."

Hannibal looked at me and waited.

After a moment for suspense, I said: "Taittinger checked into the Grand on August 14. He's still here. He therefore had opportunity to meet and kill Kajic on the beach early on the 17th."

"Did Fredo have any luck in the room?" Hannibal asked.

"Based on my instructions, Fredo searched for and found shoes with sand on them," I replied. "He took measurements."

I paused and then continued: "Afterwards, Fredo and I compared the shoe measurements to Ruth's photos of footprints. The shoes don't match the photos."

"Did Fredo find a Mauser C96?" Hannibal asked.

"No," I replied with a wry smile. "He found a Walther, very much like mine."

"OK," said Hannibal, "Unless you found something incriminating, Taittinger had no motive, except that he and the IRMO compete for Mussolini's money."

"Pretty weak motive," I agreed. "Opportunity, but weak motive and no murder weapon. Taittinger is not our killer."

"We are left with Chernozemski, who skipped town at 6:30 AM on the day of the murder, and Zivkovic, who has a Mauser C96 pistol," Hannibal concluded. "After Antolini does his work, we can meet him at a convenient location."

# 33

## DEATH AHEAD

*Saturday evening, August 25, 1934*

By pre-arrangement, Antolini visited Hannibal and me in our suite this morning. After the usual preliminaries, we adjourned to seats in the parlor. I had arranged for coffee and sweet-rolls from room service.

After a couple of bites of sweet-roll washed down with half a cup of coffee, Antolini relaxed a little.

I began the conversation. "Any results with regard to Zivkovic's Mauser pistol?"

"We confiscated the pistol and test-fired it in our laboratory," replied Antolini. "The grooves in the bullet and the point on the firing pin don't match the grooves on the bullets and the firing pin impact marks on the shell casings from the Kajic crime scene."

"What about footprints?" Hannibal asked.

"Zivkovic's shoes do not match the crime scene footprints," replied Antolini.

"Zivkovic is not the killer," stated Hannibal. "Still, he is an agent of the King of Yugoslavia."

The three of us sipped coffee for a while. Antolini finished his first sweet-roll and eyed the others still on the tray.

I looked at Antolini and said: "I gave you a towel with shoe imprints from Chernozemski's room. How did the imprints compare to the crime scene footprints?"

"Inconclusive," replied Antolini, as he reluctantly turned his attention from the sweet-rolls to me. "The measurements are approximately the same, but the towel was smudged."

"We don't have a murder weapon, and we can't match shoes to footprints, but Chernozemski is our only remaining suspect for the murder of Kajic," I said.

"I agree," Hannibal added. "He had motive and opportunity, and he skipped town immediately after the murder. Unless someone else turns up, he was most likely the killer."

Antolini brightened a little, and he said: "On August 19, Chernozemski had to show his passport when he bought an airline ticket in Rome for a flight to Budapest."

He paused, picked up a second sweet-roll and continued: "After the sale, the ticket agent recognized the name from a list of arrest warrants. He notified Superintendent Barreto."

After washing down a bite from the second sweet-roll with a couple of sips of coffee, Antolini continued. "Our carabinieri were too late to catch Chernozemski in Rome, but Barreto immediately sent a telegram to our agent in Budapest."

Antolini finished the remainder of the second sweet-roll, used a napkin, sighed contentedly, leaned back in his chair and said: "The agent was able to surreptitiously meet the airplane when it arrived. He followed Chernozemski by car to Nagykanizsa."

"The Ustaše have a training camp in nearby Janka-Puszta," responded Hannibal.

"Beyond the reach of the carabinieri?" I asked.

"For now," responded Antolini. "Mussolini supports them. However, there's more. Our agents spotted Mijo Krali, Zvonimir Pospišil and Milan Rajic, all known IMRO agents, as they arrived in Nagykanizsa on August 20, 21 and 22, respectively. All are suspected assassins."

I thought a moment and then said: "The IMRO is planning something."

Antolini turned to me and replied: "That's our conclusion. Four suspected assassins arriving at a Ustaše training camp at about the same time is highly unusual."

We were silent for several minutes. I re-filled everyone's coffee cup.

Finally, Hannibal said: "We should follow up with Zivkovic. As an agent of King Alexander, he is in Riccione for a reason."

A moment passed and Antolini responded: "After we questioned him and tested his pistol, we had no reason to detain him. We returned his pistol. He's still staying at the Hotel Milano e Ungaria." He gave Hannibal a quizzical look and added: "What is your interest?"

"The gathering of IMRO agents in Janka-Puszta is ominous," replied Hannibal. Zivkovic might shed light on the situation."

Realization dawned in Antolini's expression, and he said: "Please keep me informed." Hannibal nodded.

Antolini rose from his seat, turned to me and said: "You are a most gracious hostess. Thank you for the coffee and sweet-rolls."

I rose from my chair, smiled and replied: "There is one sweet-roll left. Would you like to take it with you?"

Antolini quickly replied: "Si signora, Grazie."

I leaned over, wrapped the sweet-roll in a napkin and handed it to Antolini. Hannibal smiled at the exchange.

After the usual goodbyes, Antolini departed. Hannibal and I were alone. "Let's contact Zivkovic," Hannibal stated.

"Agree," I responded, as I thought about the implications.

## Monday evening, August 27

Hannibal and I visited the Hotel Milano e Ungaria late this morning. Hannibal checked with his friend Antonio at the front desk while I found an unobtrusive seat in the lobby.

Hannibal soon returned from his errand with Antonio, sat next to me and said in a soft voice: "Antonio saw Zivkovic as he entered the dining room half an hour ago." He pointed discreetly to the dining room doorway.

Hannibal looked at his watch. "Eleven-thirty," he said. "Zivkovic is probably having an early lunch. Let's wait."

Zivkovic emerged from the dining room at about noon. He immediately spotted Hannibal. He stopped and stared. Hannibal rose from his seat and walked toward him. I followed.

"I'm Hannibal Jones," said Hannibal as he approached Zivkovic. "We may have a common interest." He offered his hand. With a tentative move, Zivkovic shook hands.

Hannibal turned to me as I stepped up and said: "My wife Caroline. We are private investigators."

Zivkovic gave me a quick glance, nodded and said: "Signora." He returned his attention to Hannibal and said: "You are Americans. I have heard about you." He looked at me again.

"The IMRO and Ustaše are planning something in their camp in Janka-Puszta," I said. "We have information." I then told him about Chernozemski and his three companions.

Zivkovic's eyes widened. After several moments, he said: "Shall we go for a walk outside?" He then looked at Hannibal.

Hannibal nodded, and the three of us walked across the lobby and outside onto Viale Milano. Zivkovic led us north to a street crossing and turned right toward the beach. After about a block, he turned in at an open-air coffee bar. We found seats and ordered coffee.

We all sipped quietly for a few minutes. Zivkovic watched first Hannibal and then me. Finally, he asked: "You know about the IMRO and Ustaše?"

"We know that they are a threat to your King," Hannibal replied.

Zivkovic nodded and said: "We of the royal household have vowed to protect the King." He paused and asked: "Do you have information about a specific threat?"

"No, just knowledge about suspicious activity in Janka-Puszta," replied Hannibal. "Chernozemski is a known assassin."

Zivkovic sat quietly for a while. Finally, he said: "I will relay your information to my colleagues in Belgrade."

His face acquired a deeply troubled look and he said: "King Alexander has planned a trip to France. He will meet with Foreign Minister Louis Barthou."

In a slow and measured response, Hannibal said: "I would advise against such a trip. Security for your King would be difficult."

Zivkovic replied: "Yes. I will pass the word."

I thought a moment and then said: "Your agents in Janka-Puszta should observe Chernozemski and his colleagues. If they leave Hungary for France, action will be imminent."

Zivkovic looked at me for a moment and then said: "Our agents will observe."

Silence reigned again. Finally, Zivkovic put money on the table for the coffee, rose from his seat, smiled at me and said: "Arrivederci, signora Jones." He then turned to Hannibal.

Hannibal rose from his chair and the two men shook hands. Zivkovic turned and walked away. Hannibal sat back down and sipped his coffee.

After about a minute, I said: "We did what we could." Hannibal nodded.

We both rose from our seats and walked along the street towards the beach. We turned at the surf line and headed toward the Grand. Later that afternoon, Hannibal sent a coded telegram to Soucet.

## Saturday evening, September 1

While Hannibal worked on reports this afternoon, I arranged to meet Ruth at our previous open-air tea patio.

As I walked up to the patio check-in counter, the Maitre'd recognized me. "Signora Meltzer and her companion are already seated, he said. "I will escort you to their table."

"Companion?" I puzzled to myself. "What has Ruth been up to?"

As I approached the table, I saw Ruth, who was facing me. A man sat at the table with his back toward me. Ruth saw me and smiled. The man stood and turned. I recognized Henri Taittinger.

I stopped in my tracks. I'm sure my mouth was wide open in surprise. I looked at Taittinger and then Ruth.

Ruth smiled and said: "Please join us, Caroline." She added: "I believe you know Monsieur Taittinger."

I closed my mouth. After a moment, I replied: "We've never actually met." I looked at Taittinger, who gave me a wry smile.

"Ah, signora Jones, I have heard so much about you," said Taittinger. "I saw you and your husband from a distance in Vienna."

"Please sit, Caroline," said Ruth. "We have much to discuss."

Taittinger pulled back a chair for me. I sat down and scooted my chair a little toward Ruth.

The waiter arrived and we ordered tea and scones. After he left, Ruth said: "Monsieur Taittinger has friends in France."

Taittinger continued to smile, and he said: "The French government has many branches and constituencies. The different groups are often at odds, and they do not share information."

"You made some interesting contacts in Vienna," I responded. "They were not French."

"So did you," Taittinger replied. "We each have our methods of getting information."

"Some at the French Embassy had a different view of what you were doing," I retorted. "Were they mistaken?"

"To some extent," replied Taittinger. "Sometimes our interests overlap, sometimes they do not."

"Why are you here?" I asked.

"To warn you," Taittinger replied. "Villian is in town. Another man, with a prosthetic right hand, is also here. His name is Raeder. He and Villian may or may not be working together. You should leave immediately."

My mouth dropped open again, and I gave an involuntary shudder. Villian's sinister face, scar and all, popped into my conscious mind. Raeder, with a contorted, screaming face and bloody right hand, joined him.

Finally, I closed off the memories, concentrated on the present, and replied: "Why are you telling me this?"

Taittinger's face acquired a mysterious expression and he said: "In this case, our interests overlap."

The waiter arrived with our tea and scones. Taittinger took a couple of sips of tea and said: "I will leave you now. Enjoy your tea." He stood, looked at Ruth and said: "Adieu Madame." He turned, and without another word, walked quickly out of the tea patio.

I watched him leave. I then turned to Ruth. I'm sure the question was apparent in my expression. "Double agent," said Ruth. She then sipped her tea.

We both were quiet for a while. I tried to nibble at a scone, but I had no appetite.

Finally, Ruth said: "I think you should heed the warning. I plan to depart for my villa in Tuscany tomorrow. I will take the train from Riccione to Bologna and then to Florence. Carmen will come with me; her position here has become too dangerous."

She smiled wistfully and added: "I would love to have you and Hannibal as my guests at the villa."

I gave a big sigh. The scones looked better. I nibbled and sipped my tea. I then said: "I will tell Hannibal." I looked into Ruth's eyes and added: "Thank you."

The afternoon passed. We both returned to the Grand and parted company in the lobby.

I took the elevator to the floor with my suite, unlocked the door and interrupted Hannibal as he worked on reports. He looked up as I entered the parlor.

In a soft voice, I said: "I have something to tell you."

## Very early Sunday morning, September 2

Hannibal and I will be on the road again right after breakfast. Hannibal made all of the arrangements, including shipping most of our luggage by rail and moving our money from the bank in Riccione to the Banco di Roma branch in Florence. He also sent a telegram to Soucet and made a phone call to Antolini.

The banking transaction was tedious on the weekend. Hannibal called the home of the bank president, who promised to complete the transaction on Monday morning. He said that he was sorry to see us leave, but wished us well.

We have a 260-kilometer drive to Ruth's villa. Instead of the long route through Bologna on the main roads, we will use secondary roads and traverse a pass across the Apennine Mountains directly to Florence. Hopefully, the bad guys won't follow us.

# 34

## STEALING TUSCANY

*Monday evening, September 3, 1934*

On Sunday, our Duesenberg chugged dutifully over the Apennine passes, through the town of Romagna and into the valley of the Arno River. The drive was picturesque, bumpy and without modern conveniences. We stopped for lunch and petrol in Arezzo. As best that we could tell, we were not followed.

Ruth had provided accurate driving directions to her estate. She told us that her villa rested on a little hill at the end of a two-kilometer gravel driveway that branched to the east from the main road, halfway between Florence and Siena.

We by-passed Florence on the south side and headed toward Siena. "We'll visit Florence later," said Hannibal.

We found the turn-off from the main road. It was marked with a stone sign that was engraved with Ruth's maiden name 'Canossa.' The white gravel driveway was lined with well-kept olive groves and vineyards.

"Lovely," I said, as Hannibal drove slowly toward the cluster of buildings on the hill in the distance.

The driveway ended in a circle in front of the two-story main house. A white marble fountain with multiple sprays of bubbling water rested in the center of the circle, and it was surrounded by a manicured lawn, multicolored flowers and four marble walkways. The walkways radiated like spokes of a wheel, symmetrically arranged from the edge of the fountain to the driveway.

The façade of the main house was made of beige-colored limestone. Pale red limestone accented many tall, multi-paned windows. White marble steps led to a broad landing and a grand set of main entryway double doors.

A caretaker's cottage, garages and servant's quarters rested amid hedge-lined gardens on both sides of the main house. Reddish tile formed the roofs of all of the buildings.

Hannibal drove halfway around the circle and parked just past the grand entryway. I could see an active winery not far from the main house; grapes were being processed.

White barns and other outbuildings gleamed in the sun about fifty meters behind the main cluster of buildings. Tractors and other equipment, as well as horses, dotted the pasture nearest the barns.

"A working country estate, ancient of days, yet with modern equipment," I thought to myself.

As Hannibal and I got out of the car, the entryway door opened. Ruth stepped out on the white marble landing at the top of the stairs. She was followed by a middle-aged couple and Carmen.

Hannibal and I walked up the steps. I hugged a smiling Ruth. Not to be outdone, Ruth turned and gave Hannibal a big hug. "You are too tall to kiss," said Ruth with a mischievous grin, as she looked up at the towering Hannibal. Hannibal blushed, and I laughed.

Ruth turned to her smiling companions and said: "Hannibal, Caroline, please meet Carlo and Maria Olmi. Carlo manages the estate, including the olive groves and the vineyards. Maria supervises the household. You already know Carmen, their lovely daughter."

We exchanged warm greetings. I instantly liked Carlo, and especially Maria. She looked like everyone's concept of a warm, loving Italian mother.

Several servants filed out of the doorway and unloaded our car. As Ruth led us into the house, Carlo said: "Your main luggage has arrived at the train station in Florence. I will send someone to pick it up tomorrow."

The entryway opened to a spacious parlor on the left and a library on the right. The library was lined with books from floor to ceiling. A ladder on rails provided access to the higher levels of books.

Both rooms had a golden ambiance. Comfortable chairs, coffee tables and lamps formed groupings for reading and intimate gatherings. Baroque frescoes decorated the ceilings. Tall window let in lots of light.

"Wow!" I thought to myself. "Ruth lives in style."

At the back of the entryway, a grand staircase led up to balconies and rooms on the upper level. Straight ahead on the ground level, a double hallway on both sides of the staircase led to more rooms at the back of the house.

"Your bedroom is upstairs," said Ruth. "It has a nice view of the fountain and an en suite bathroom. After you have settled in and freshened up, please join our little family in the parlor. We'll have tea at three o'clock, and we can catch up on our affairs."

At about 3:00 PM, Hannibal and I dressed appropriately for afternoon tea and descended the stairs. As we entered the parlor, I saw a maid setting a tea service and sweets on a coffee table. She finished and left discreetly as we entered the room.

The room was cool, in spite of the afternoon sunlight that streamed in the windows. "Fall in Tuscany," I thought to myself. "My memories touched on other fall seasons, ranging from small town Indiana and the Wabash Valley to Chicago, New York and finally, to Europe. "So many changes," I mused to myself.

Ruth, Carlo, Maria and Carmen were already seated. Ruth, as hostess, motioned us over to two chairs next to hers. "Please join us," she said with a warm smile. "How do you like your tea?"

After Ruth poured tea and we were all settled, Ruth began the conversation: "Enze Salicetti, our neighbor, has a problem." Ruth paused; I could tell she was choosing her words carefully. "Enze and his two sons, Alceu and Marcu, are being harassed by Mussolini's Blackshirts."

As I heard the familiar name 'Salicetti,' I immediately thought of Annette Salicetti and her Mafioso grandfather Ange. I looked at Ruth and then Carlo. I sipped my tea and asked: "How so?"

Carlo responded: "Enze owns over two thousand acres of olive groves and vineyards. He employs over 100 workers. The estate is a major producer of sangiovese grapes, fine Chianti Classico wine and olive oil. It is one of the richest estates in Tuscany."

He paused and added: "The estate has been in the Salicetti family since the time of Napoleon."

"The Blackshirts are trying to force Enze to sell at a bargain price," said Ruth. "Enze has been accused of having Mafia connections."

"Humm," I mused. "Is Enze related to Ange Salicetti from Corsica?"

Ruth smiled and replied: "Enze and Ange are brothers."

To myself, I thought: "And so my friend Annette is Enze's grand-niece." To Ruth, I said: "I can see how the Blackshirts have made a Mafia connection."

"Yes," replied Ruth with a wry smile. "We are aware of Ange's nefarious background." She sipped her tea for a moment and then said: "We think Salvatore Neri is behind the attempt to confiscate the Salicetti estate."

I drew a blank at the name 'Neri.' I'm sure my face had a puzzled look.

Carmen placed her cup and saucer on the table, looked up and said: "I saw messages between Neri and local Blackshirts while I worked in the Riccione communications center. Neri often vacations in Riccione. He has a mansion in Florence."

"During the 1920s, Neri was a lieutenant of Cesare Mori, the former Iron Prefect of Sicily," Carlo added. "He persecuted Mafia families in both Italy and Sicily."

"Ange Salicetti is based in French-controlled Corsica, but he has operations in Italy, said Hannibal. "His operations would have been affected."

"Is Enze a Mafioso?" I asked.

"No," responded Carlo. "I have known both Enze and Ange since I was a child. Ange moved to Corsica and began a new life. Enze was the eldest, and he stayed on the Tuscan family estate."

"Ah," I responded. "The eldest son inherited the estate, and the youngest had to make his own way, probably with some cash to start." I paused and asked: "I take it that Enze has remained legal in his business dealings?"

"Yes," replied Ruth. "Enze and I have had minor disagreements over land access and water rights, but we have always worked them out. As far as I know, his business activities are all legal and above board."

I gave Ruth a long look and asked: "Have you been harassed by the Blackshirts?"

Ruth smiled wryly and responded: "No. The local fascists are well aware of my friendship with Donna Rachele Mussolini."

"Humm," responded Hannibal. "So, Neri is using the Mafioso excuse to obtain a very valuable estate in Tuscany."

"Precisely," replied Ruth. "We landowners don't know how to stop him. Others besides Enze, not as well-connected as I am, have also been affected. Harassment has become widespread. Tuscany's long-established society is being threatened."

We were silent for a while as everyone sipped tea and sampled the sweets.

Finally, Ruth smiled and said: "Anyway, we are happy you are here."

"So are we," replied Hannibal. "Riccione had become dangerous." Ruth and Carmen both nodded.

"You are safe here," said Carlo. He paused, grinned and added: "Besides, Maria promised an excellent Tuscan-style dinner." We all laughed; the change of subject pleased everyone.

I then looked at Maria and asked: "So what's for dinner? Laughter continued as Maria gayly explained every dish.

### Saturday evening, September 8

The past few days have been filled with sun, long walks in the countryside and relaxation. On Friday, Ruth hosted a small dinner party at the villa. She invited the Salicetti family.

Of course, Hannibal and I were also invited. Aside from a pleasant evening, I think Ruth wanted Hannibal and me to hear the Salicetti story of fascist persecution first-hand.

Enze was a handsome, white-haired, vigorous-looking man in his 70s. His face was bronzed by the Tuscan sun and his hands had the calluses of hard work.

Enze's wife Sophia could have been Maria Olmi's elder sister; she was the epitome of Italian motherhood.

Alceu and Marcu were younger editions of their father. They were also tanned and fit; both showed the effects of working the land. Their wives Alma and Celeste, respectively, were classic, dark-haired, beautiful Italian women.

"In Hollywood, these two females could be movie stars," I thought to myself. "What a fine-looking family!"

After social pleasantries and a scrumptious dinner, everyone relaxed with glasses of fine Chianti Classico, supplied by Enze. The conversation turned to the Blackshirts. The Salicetti men confirmed what we had been told by Ruth, Carlo and Carmen, with the addition of new names.

"The Blackshirts have harassed and threatened my workers in the groves and vineyards," said Enze. "They beat several of our junior managers and tried to get them to say that we were involved in black market schemes to avoid taxes on our products." He paused and smiled grimly. "Our managers remained loyal."

Alceu then said: "The Blackshirts were led by Capo Manipolo Vincenza Molazana and Capo Squadra Adolfo Badia."

I drew a blank on the titles. Marcu saw my expression and explained: "In American terms, a capo manipolo is a lieutenant and a capo squadra is a sergeant. Both are fascist Blackshirt titles."

I recovered my composure and asked: "Did Molazana and Badia threaten you directly?"

"Last month, the pair visited our home," said Alceu. "They threatened my father with arrest as an 'enemy of Italy,' unless he gave up our estate and left Tuscany."

"Fortunately, my sons were present, along with Giovanni Montieri, our master viticulturist, and several servants," Enze added. "Molazana and Badia left after their threats, and no violence occurred."

The faces of the Salicetti men hardened. "They are re-living memories of the event," I surmised to myself. "I wouldn't want to mess with this trio, even on their own without backup." My thoughts continued: "They look as tough as nails."

Alma and Celeste rescued us from further dark discussions. The pair walked over, and Celeste said: "Come, let's have another glass of wine." Alma added: "The moon through the west windows is lovely. Let's go watch it for a while."

I followed Alma and Celeste, and the four men followed me. Alma was right, the moon bathed the Tuscan countryside in a pale, silvery light.

Along the driveway by the fountain, a sporty little car gleamed in the moonlight. "Nice car," I said, as I pointed.

"Thank you," said a voice behind me. I turned and saw Alceu's smiling face. "It's my new Alpha Romero. In the sunlight, you can see the bright red color."

"Just my style," I mused. Hannibal looked at me and smiled.

I shifted my thoughts to the overall scene and said: "Beautiful moonlight." Several other voices replied: "Yes." Ruth, Maria, Carmen and others joined us at the window. Our more serious previous discussion moved to the background of my mind, at least for a while.

## Tuesday morning, September 11

As Hannibal and I descended the stairs to dinner Monday evening, Carmen rushed to greet us. Her face expressed intense consternation, and she said: "Enze Salicetti phoned. Two men were murdered on his estate earlier this evening. He asked if you would investigate."

"Of course," I blurted, without thinking. Hannibal raised his eyebrows and gave me a quizzical look. His expression said: "So soon?"

I then realized that less than a month had passed since the murder of Dimitri Kajic in Riccione.

Hannibal turned to Carmen and asked: "Who? Do you have names?"

"Vincenza Molazana and Adolfo Badia," Carmen replied. "They were found along the driveway to the Salicetti villa."

# 35

## MURDER ON THE ESTATE

*Wednesday evening, September 12, 1934*

After Carmen's announcement of murder, Hannibal and I raced back upstairs to our room and changed to casual attire.

I wore my Chanel black slacks, a stylish, form-fitting light gray pull-over cashmere sweater, black leather jacket and sensible, laced walking shoes. Of course, I carried my purse with a shoulder strap and my ubiquitous Walther pistol. My sheath knife was in its usual location.

Hannibal wore dark slacks, an open-collared shirt, laced boots, his old, worn leather jacket and a fedora hat. His forty-five rested in its shoulder holster. We were ready.

Hannibal grabbed our leather case with a low-light camera and our other crime scene equipment. We headed back downstairs. Ruth and Carmen waited for us at the entryway.

Ruth had a paper sack and Carmen had a thermos. "Sandwiches and coffee," said Ruth. "Eat when you can." She handed me the sack.

Carmen handed me the thermos and said: "Turn left toward Siena at the end of our driveway. Go two kilometers. The Salicetti driveway is on your left. It's marked with a sign that says Salicetti."

Ruth added: "Alceu will drive his car and meet you at the crime scene. It's along the Salicetti driveway, about a kilometer from the house."

"Right," I replied, as I juggled the sack and thermos. "See you later."

I waited on the steps as Hannibal retrieved our Duesenberg from a garage on the far side of the caretaker's cottage. Soon we were driving at moderate speed toward the main road.

As Hannibal concentrated on driving, I looked behind. "No dust cloud," I mused. "We had a rain shower earlier this afternoon." I looked to the west. Clouds obscured the sun low in the sky.

We found the Salicetti turn-off with no problem. As we turned, I looked at my watch. "Six forty-five," I said. "Look for Alceu's car."

Hannibal nodded, drove slowly and peered ahead in the fading light.

I spotted Alceu's red Alpha Romero ahead on the grass on the right side of the driveway. It was parked about 20 meters behind a black Fiat sedan. Both the driver and passenger doors of the sedan were open.

Alceu stood by his car, watching us, as Hannibal pulled in behind. I looked at my watch. "Seven o'clock," I muttered. "With the cloud cover, it will be dark soon."

Hannibal and I walked along the gravel toward Alceu and the Alpha Romero. I could see two bodies, one in front of the sedan and the other a few meters away towards an olive grove.

As we approached, Alceu had a grim expression. He said: "I was driving home from Siena in my Fiat 15 truck. I found the sedan and bodies at about 5:15 PM, as you see them. That's Molazana near the front of the sedan. Badia is over there, a few meters away." He paused and added: "Except for farm trucks, I didn't see any vehicles on the road from Siena."

"What did you do when you saw the bodies?" Hannibal asked.

"I pulled over behind the sedan, got out and walked on the gravel to the front of the sedan. I could see from the driveway that both men were dead. I recognized their faces and uniforms. I then returned to my truck and drove to the villa."

He paused and added: "When I reached the house, I called the carabinieri in Siena. My father called Ruth. I then returned to this spot in my car to wait for you and for the carabinieri."

He looked at his watch and continued: "The carabinieri should arrive in less than an hour. It's over a 25-kilometer drive from Siena."

Hannibal, Alceu and I walked on the gravel towards the sedan. "The sparse grass and damp, soft earth along the driveway will be good for tire tracks and footprints," I said softly.

Hannibal heard and responded: "I was writing reports next to the window in Ruth's library when the rain stopped in the area between one and two o'clock this afternoon."

As I approached the rear of the sedan, I saw two sets of tire tracks. One belonged to the sedan, and the other turned off the gravel onto the grass and then back on the gravel just behind the sedan.

I looked at Alceu, pointed to the second set of tracks and asked: "Are those the tracks of your truck?"

"Yes," replied Alceu. "There is another set of tracks in front of the sedan, along with some footprints."

"Alceu has a good eye for detail," I thought to myself. "He also speaks very carefully. Why?"

The three of us continued on the gravel to the front of the sedan. I could see Molazana's body sprawled face up in front of the car. Blood covered the front of his Blackshirt uniform just under the sternum. His face had a wide-eyed, surprised expression.

I stared at the wound. "Doesn't look like a gunshot wound," I stated softly. "Knife?"

"I think so," responded Hannibal. "Do you see the footprints?"

I looked carefully. One set came around from the driver's side of the sedan and ended in a confused set at the victim's position. Another set led from the passenger side to the second body some distance away.

I could discern three other sets. Two were made by small shoes with narrow heels and one was made by larger shoes.

"Three people besides the two victims were present," I said. "The two smaller sets of footprints were probably made by females, and the other by a male."

"Very likely," replied Hannibal. "One set of smaller footprints leads to Molazana and the other smaller set leads to the passenger side of the sedan."

He paused a moment and added: "The larger footprints lead from and to the gravel by the front of the sedan. The person, probably male, stopped in front of the sedan and then returned to the gravel."

I looked ahead along the driveway. After a moment, I said: "Let's look at the tire tracks just ahead of the sedan." I pointed.

We walked forward on the gravel and studied the tire tracks. After a couple of minutes, Hannibal said: "A vehicle pulled off the road and stopped. It did a U-turn and headed back toward the main road."

"Two sets of small footprints lead from the passenger side of the tire tracks to the sedan and then back to this vehicle," I responded.

"Yes," replied Hannibal. "I also see two large footprints on the driver's side of the tracks, one going and one returning as the person stepped to and from the gravel and the vehicle."

Hannibal walked back to the front of the sedan and then back to the tire tracks. "The footprints of the three persons who got out of the other vehicle match the non-victim footprints near the sedan."

I turned to Alceu, who still stood on the gravel driveway. He was wide-eyed and in apparent awe at our performance. "You are very good," he said.

I smiled and replied: "Please wait here." Alceu nodded.

I walked over to the second body. A blood trail led from the sedan passenger side to the body. I looked carefully at the body and said: "The victim's throat was slashed. The carotid artery was cut on the left side."

I studied for a moment and added: "The killer approached the victim from behind, reached around with a knife in his or her right hand and sliced the victim's throat from left to right. The killer was right-handed."

Hannibal walked up, stood beside me and said: "Agree. The victim's throat was cut as he stood over by the passenger door of the vehicle. He staggered over here and collapsed. Death occurred within seconds."

"Our two killers knew exactly what they were doing," I mused. "I think we are looking for two females. But who was the unknown male?"

"Good question," replied Hannibal. He thought a moment and then added: "Time to take photos. I'll get the camera and a ruler for scale."

"OK," I responded. "While you are doing the photos, I will walk a big circle to see if I can find other tracks that lead to or from the crime scene."

Hannibal looked over at Alceu and said: "Please walk back to your car and wait for the carabinieri. When they arrive, ask them to park behind our car. Tell them who we are and what we are doing."

He smiled and added: "If they are experienced, they will understand and wait for us to finish."

Alceu nodded and returned to the Alpha Romero.

Hannibal had finished with the photos, and I had completed my circle of the crime scene, when I spotted a car approaching from the main road. Its lights were on. As it approached, I could see that it was a police vehicle.

I looked at my watch. It read seven forty-five. Hannibal walked over and stood next to me. I pointed to the arriving car. Hannibal nodded.

I then said: "There are no footprints leading to or away from the crime scene. The killers arrived and left either by car or truck."

I thought a moment and then said: "The tire tracks and footprints are fresh. Also, the bodies were dry, except for blood. The murders occurred after the rain had stopped by about 2:00 PM. If Alceu's statement is correct about his arrival at the crime scene, the murders occurred before 5:15 PM."

My thoughts continued, and I added: "We need temperatures of the ground beneath the bodies, the air and the bodies themselves to determine an independent time window for the deaths."

"Yes," replied Hannibal. "We also need autopsy reports, comparisons of relevant photos to vehicles and shoes and identification of murder weapons." He paused a moment and then added: "The carabinieri may have files. Who knows what might turn up?"

Our conversation was interrupted by the arrival of the carabinieri. Alceu properly directed the driver to park behind our Duesenberg. Two men got out of the car. Both wore police rather than Blackshirt uniforms. "A good sign," I thought to myself.

After a short discussion with Alceu, the two grim-faced carabinieri walked over toward Hannibal and me. Alceu got in his Alpha Romeo and drove off toward the Salicetti villa.

"I am Chief Inspector Luigi Grassi," said the first man as he approached. He turned slightly toward his companion and added: "This is Sergeant Armand Solari." Solari nodded in response.

Grassi turned back to Hannibal and continued: "Senore Salicetti told me about you. I was already aware of your reputation." He looked intently at Hannibal. His expression changed from grim to a slight smile. He offered his hand.

After the two men shook hands, Grassi turned to me. His smile broadened. "Ah, signora Jones," he said. "I was told that you are talented. I see that you are also beautiful."

I offered my hand. Grassi bowed slightly, took my hand and kissed it. He released my hand gently, straightened but continued to smile. I liked him immediately.

I glanced at Hannibal, who was doing his best not to chuckle. I gave him a snooty look, turned back to Grassi, and smiled coyly.

However, a thought of caution crept into my consciousness. "What if Grassi is a fascist?"

Grassi turned back to Hannibal and said: "Now to business. Tell me what you have discovered."

In his typical military fashion, Hannibal briefed Grassi on our activities and findings. He also outlined the importance of temperature measurements to determine an independent window for the time of the two deaths.

Grassi looked at our leather case, which rested on the edge of the driveway nearby. "Do you have the equipment?" He asked.

"Yes," replied Hannibal. "Perhaps Sergeant Soleri will assist, and we can complete the measurements while we still have light."

"Of course," responded Grassi. He turned to Solari and gave a nod. Hannibal walked over to the case and extracted the necessary equipment. Soon he and Solari were at work.

Grassi watched for a while, then turned to me and asked: "Why are you and Major Jones interested in these murders?"

I thought a moment and then answered truthfully: "Hannibal and I are guests of Ruth Canossa Meltzer, who lives at a nearby estate. Enze Salicetti, who owns this estate, called Ruth and asked us to investigate after his son Alceu discovered the bodies."

Grassi's eyes did not waver. After a moment, he said: "I see." His expression changed to an enigmatic smile and he added: "Your help is most welcome."

I returned Grassi's gaze. "OK, Caroline," I thought to myself. "Time to change the subject." To Grassi, I asked: "When will the bodies be picked up and taken to autopsy?"

Grassi smiled as if he understood my ploy. "An ambulance is on the way." He paused, took out his pocket watch, looked at the time and added: "I notified the medical examiner before I left Siena. The examiner said that he would be able to send an ambulance with attendants late this evening."

Grassi's smile broadened a little, as he looked intently into my eyes.

"He anticipates my next question," I thought to myself.

After a moment, Grassi's said: "I would appreciate your review of the autopsy reports when they are done and other reports that I have in my files."

"OK, Caroline," my thoughts continued. "He knew that I was going to ask to read the autopsy reports. Who is playing whom?" To Grassi, I smiled and replied: "Glad to help."

As we finished this last exchange, Hannibal and Solari replaced notes, thermometers and other equipment in our equipment case. Solari had a grim expression; the task had not been pleasant.

He and Hannibal walked over to Grassi and me when they finished. "Done," Hannibal said.

The sound of a vehicle chattered in the distance. I looked down the driveway toward the main road and saw headlights. Grassi said: "Most likely our ambulance."

A few minutes later, an ambulance with two attendants arrived. The crime scene work was finished shortly afterwards.

As the ambulance prepared to leave, Grassi looked at me and then Hannibal and said: "I will call you at the Canossa estate by noon tomorrow. Will you have the photos ready?"

"Yes," replied Hannibal. "We look forward to working with you." The two men shook hands.

Grassi turned to me, bowed slightly and said: "Good evening, signora Jones." He turned, said a few words to Solari and the pair got in their police car.

One of the ambulance attendants got in the victim's sedan, did a U-turn, and drove off. The other attendant followed in the ambulance with the two bodies.

Hannibal and I were alone. Darkness had fallen, and clouds obscured the moon. We stood for a moment as the sound of the police car, the sedan and the ambulance diminished in the distance. In the quiet that followed, the crime scene was spooky.

Hannibal broke the silence by saying: "You had a long conversation with Grassi while I took temperatures. Tell me about it as we drive back to Ruth's estate."

We got in our Duesenberg, and Hannibal started the engine. I looked at my watch in the dim light of the instrument panel. "Ten o'clock," I said.

Suddenly, I realized that I was ravenously hungry. I got out Ruth's sandwiches and carefully poured a cup of coffee from the thermos. We ate sandwiches and shared the coffee as Hannibal drove. Between bites, I told Hannibal about my conversation with Grassi.

As we turned into Ruth's driveway, Hannibal said: "Grassi is very different than Inspector Antolini in Riccione."

"Yes," I responded. "He is much more perceptive. I like him, but we have to be careful."

## Thursday evening, September 13

Grassi called at noon today. We have an appointment at nine o'clock tomorrow morning at Carabinieri headquarters in Siena. Hannibal and I will bring prints of our photos from the crime scene. Grass promised to provide autopsy and other reports related to the murders.

Hannibal and I spent the afternoon at the Salicetti villa. We interviewed Enze, Alceu, Sophia, Anna, Celeste and the villa staff.

The interviews revealed a tale of Blackshirt harassment, led by Molazana and Badia, going back several years.

Marcu and Giovanni Montieri, the viticulturist, were not at the villa. According to Enze, the pair have been on a business trip to Florence since the morning of September 9, the day before the murders. "Marcu and Giovanni deal with our suppliers and distributors," Enze said. "They often travel to Florence and beyond."

We finished our interviews at about 4:00 PM. As we drove away from the villa on our way to Ruth's place, I said: "The Salicetti's certainly have motive for murder."

Hannibal nodded and replied: "But did they have opportunity?" He paused and then added: "We need to compare our photos to shoes, including the ladies. We also need to compare photos to tires on Salicetti vehicles."

I thought a moment and responded: "Let's let Grassi make those comparisons. We can suggest a plan for him at our meeting tomorrow. If we do it, the Salicettis will be offended."

"Good idea," replied Hannibal. "We will get more information if we remain on good terms with the Salicettis."

# 36

## MAFIA CONNECTION

Friday evening, September 14, 1934

This morning, Hannibal and I dressed in business attire, left our guns and knives in our room and drove nearly 30 kilometers to Siena.

The town was lovely, with its cathedral, red-tiled roofs, narrow cobblestone streets and broad, picturesque piazzas. We found the carabinieri headquarters at Piazza di San Francisco 11 with no problem.

Grassi and Solari were waiting. After the usual greetings, Grassi said: "My superior wants to meet you. Please follow me."

"OK," I thought to myself. "Why?"

Grassi led us into a spacious office suite, with baroque décor, elaborate frescoed ceilings and an aristocratic-looking man behind a huge, ornate desk.

The man rose from his seat as we entered the room. He smiled, and his startlingly blue eyes had a steady gaze.

Before Grassi could make introductions, the man stepped forward and said: "I am Aldo Fabri, the Carabinieri Superintendent for Tuscany."

He paused; his eyes twinkled, and he added: "And you are Major Hannibal Jones and the talented and beautiful signora Caroline Case Jones." He offered his hand to Hannibal.

After the two men shook hands, Fabri turned to me, bowed slightly and said: "Welcome to Siena, signora."

I offered my hand and said: "A pleasure to meet you, senore. I hope we can be of service."

Fabri bowed again, took my hand, kissed it formally and stepped back slightly. His smile broadened.

"I could get used to this," I thought to myself. I gave Fabri a reserved smile.

Fabri escorted us to a large conference table by a huge window. I could see the spires of the Siena Cathedral and the Torre del Mangia in the distance, outlined against a clear blue sky.

I shifted my tourist daydreams to the background of my mind and re-focused on business. Fabri was offering coffee.

After we settled in, Fabri said: "Chief Inspector Grassi has reports for you to read, and I understand that you have photos."

"Yes," said Hannibal. He opened his briefcase and took out a stack of prints. As he arranged the photos, Solari laid several reports on the table.

Hannibal rose from his seat and explained the photos. Fabri, Grassi and Solari stood, peered intently at each photo and listened.

When Hannibal finished, I said: "Suggest that Chief Inspector Grassi and Sergeant Solari visit the Salicetti villa. During the questioning process, Sergeant Solari can compare the footprint photos to the shoes of everyone in the household, including the females."

Fabri nodded. He turned to Grassi and said: "Follow up with the tire track photos as well as footprints. Check every Salicetti shoe and vehicle."

"Yes," that would work," responded Grassi. "We might be able to either implicate or eliminate the Salicettis as direct participants in the murders." He turned to Solari and said: "Please make an appointment." Solari nodded and left the room.

Fabri looked at me, raised his eyebrows a little and said: "Are you friends with the Salicettis?"

"We met socially," I replied. "Hannibal and I can be more effective if we gather information from them in friendly social settings."

Fabri eyed me carefully and said: "I expect that you plan to pursue other avenues of investigation."

"Yes," I replied. "We want to know more about Molazana and Badia."

"You can begin with the reports on this table," replied Fabri. "They include autopsies and files on local Blackshirt depredations." Fabri's comment ended with a slight frown.

"How interesting," I thought to myself. "Fabri doesn't like Blackshirts." I glanced at Hannibal. His expression indicated that he also caught the nuance of Fabri's comment.

Fabri continued: "I have meetings to attend. Please feel free to use this table to review the reports. Take as many notes as you like." He paused and then added: "This case has larger implications and should remain most secret."

After Fabri and Grassi left the room, Hannibal and I spent the remainder of the day reading and writing at the table. A secretary kept us supplied with coffee, and she brought sandwiches at noon.

## Sunday evening, September 16

Hannibal and I spent Saturday and Sunday mornings at Ruth's villa, reviewing our findings. Hannibal and Carlo drove to Florence and back Saturday afternoon. "Banking business, a telegram to Soucet and other errands," said Hannibal. Other errands? Hannibal didn't elaborate.

On Sunday afternoon, the sun was hot for September, so Hannibal and I relaxed in the shade on Ruth's verandah at the back of her villa. Ruth joined us, and a servant brought iced tea. Hannibal and I had our notes.

Hannibal began the conversation. "Based on Alceu's statements, he found the bodies and the sedan at 5:15 PM on September 10."

"I timed our drive from the turn-off from the main road to the crime scene at about 15 minutes," I added. "Alceu said that other than farm trucks, he didn't see any other vehicles on the road from Siena, and he saw none on the driveway."

Ruth sipped her tea, set her iced tea glass down and said: "That means Alceu turned from the main road onto the driveway at about 5:00 PM. Since he didn't see any non-farm vehicles on the road, the vehicle with the killers had already passed the turn-off and had headed towards Florence."

I did some quick calculations in my head and said: "The killers had to have left the crime scene no later than 4:45 PM."

Hannibal then said: "During our interviews at the Salicetti villa on the 13th, Enze told us that on the 11th, some of his workers stopped at the villa. They told him that on the 10th, they were harassed by a dozen or more men, most dressed in Blackshirt uniforms, while they worked in the olive grove near the junction of the driveway and the main road."

"Time?" Ruth asked.

"According to Enze, the workers told him that the men arrived in four sedans at about 3:00 PM," responded Hannibal. "They were led by Molazana and Badia."

Hannibal flipped through his notes and continued: "One sedan stopped momentarily, but then headed on toward the villa."

"Did the workers see who was in the car that headed toward the villa?" Ruth asked.

"No," replied Hannibal. "A worker who had stood near the driveway said that the car that continued on was a Fiat 527. It had a license plate with an 'F' for Florence. He didn't get the number, and he couldn't see who was in the car."

Hannibal paused and added: "The workers said that the Blackshirts who remained accused the Salicettis of having Mafia connections. They beat several workers."

Hannibal flipped through his notes and continued: "At about 4:00 PM, Molazana and Badia said they were going to the Salicetti villa. They took one sedan. The others headed toward Florence in two sedans. The workers left a little later in their farm truck and also headed toward Florence."

"Molazana and Badia had to have arrived at the crime scene at about 4:15 PM," mused Ruth. She leaned back in her chair and concluded: "The murders had to have occurred between 4:15 and 4:45 PM."

"Very good," said Hannibal with a smile. "The autopsies confirm a time of death between 4:00 and 5:00 PM."

Ruth smiled, took another sip of tea and said: "Alceu's story checks out." Her smile disappeared. She looked at me and asked: "Murder weapons and method?"

"Knives," I replied. "Molazana was stabbed once under the sternum and into the heart with a long-bladed, double-edged knife, probably a stiletto. He died almost instantly. He had no defensive wounds."

I paused and added: "The autopsy confirmed that Badia's throat had been slashed from left to right, severing the carotid artery under his left ear. The killer attacked from behind and was right-handed."

"What about footprints?" Ruth asked.

"Grassi called this morning," replied Hannibal. "He and Solari visited the Salicettis yesterday. The footprint photos do not match the shoe sizes of any of the Salicettis, male or female. Grassi said Solari checked all of the shoes of everyone in the villa."

I then said: "During our interviews of the Salicetti villa staff on the 13th, we confirmed that Enze and the Salicetti women were at the villa during the time of the murders. We know that Alceu was on his way to the villa when he discovered the bodies."

Ruth asked: "What about Marcu Salicetti and Giovanni Montieri, the viticulturist?"

Hannibal flipped through his notes and said: "According to Enze, Marcu and Giovanni left for Florence on the 9. They have not yet returned."

"A loose end," I muttered. Hannibal and Ruth nodded.

Ruth's face acquired a steely look. She said: "The Salicetti's could have hired assassins. They certainly have motive."

I looked at Ruth and thought to myself: "In spite of her friendship with the Salicettis, Ruth retains her objectivity." I glanced at Hannibal. His expression indicated that he had the same thought.

We three were silent for several minutes. I finally turned to Ruth and said: "When we arrived, you mentioned that you and others suspect that Salvatore Neri was behind the Blackshirt harassment. The carabinieri reports that we read yesterday confirmed your suspicions."

"According to the newspapers, Neri and Cesare Mori were the scourge of the Mafia in Sicily and elsewhere," responded Ruth. She paused a moment and then added: "It's interesting that the carabinieri would track Neri's activities in Tuscany."

"Yes," responded Hannibal. "According to one of the carabinieri reports, since the mid-1920s, Mori and Neri have employed brutal tactics against the Mafia in Sicily and mainland Italy. Their depredations are widespread. Tuscany is just a more recent center of activity."

I added: "According to the report, in Sicily alone, over 11,000 alleged mafioso have been arrested. Thousands more have been arrested in mainland Italy. Many died in prison. Mori and his henchmen confiscated property and sold it to prominent fascists at bargain prices."

"Oh my," responded Ruth. Her expression hardened. "Mori and Neri must be stopped." She paused and then asked: "But how?"

I replied: "Given the investigative reports that we read, there is more to Fabri's carabinieri organization than we know," I stated. "I suspect that Fabri, Grassi and Solari have an agenda."

"Perhaps," responded Ruth, with a wry smile. "But unfortunately, the Blackshirts have the backing of Mussolini."

I thought a moment and said: "The Salicettis have a Mafia connection through Enze's brother Ange."

Ruth leaned back in her chair, sipped her tea and looked at me intently over the rim of her glass. After a moment, she set the glass on the table and asked: "What do you know about Ange Salicetti?"

I told her about my relationship with Annette, Ange's granddaughter.

Ruth's eyes widened as I explained about Annette. "Oh," she responded.

After my explanation, I added: "I think I will contact Annette. She lives in Rome."

I grinned and continued: "Perhaps Annette can help with regard to Neri and other elements of this case." I thought a moment and added: "Of course, I will be completely truthful with her about our involvement and findings to date."

Hannibal said: "Good idea about Annette." He paused and added: "We have three basic questions: Who killed Molazana and Badia? Who ordered the hit, and why?"

"Agree," I replied. "Right now, our only suspects for ordering the hit are the Salicettis. Are there others?" I thought a moment and added: "Annette will have an incentive to clear the Salicettis from any involvement."

"Still, her special skills and input will be valuable," responded Hannibal. He paused and added: "We three, in cooperation with Fabri and company, can provide objectivity."

"So, what's your plan?" Ruth asked.

I thought a moment, smiled mischievously and replied: "Neri has a mansion in Florence. I bet he keeps records. Let's find out. Annette and I have experience in such matters."

"Oh my!" Ruth exclaimed, as she discerned my meaning. She smiled wistfully and added: "Too bad I am so old."

Hannibal and I laughed.

# 37

## FLORENCE INTERLUDE

*Tuesday evening, September 18, 1934*

My morning began with a planned routine for a leisure day: out of bed at eight, breakfast at nine and work on correspondence until noon. The throaty growl of an automobile changed everything.

"What's that racket?" I mumbled as I poked my head out of the bathroom door. My hair was a mess; I held my toothbrush in my hand, and my mouth was full of toothpaste. Further, I had just stepped out of the shower, and my clothes were all on the bed. "What time is it?"

My two questions were greeted with silence, except for the car outside. Somebody was revving the engine. "Hannibal?" Again, no answer.

"OK, OK," I muttered. "I'll speak to Maria about the noisy car when I go downstairs." I finished brushing my teeth, more or less combed my hair, shuffled to the bed and got dressed. The clock on my nightstand read 8:30.

I was still tucking my blouse into my pants as I navigated the stairs. The house was strangely quiet, except for the noise of the revving car outside. I made my way to the front door and opened it.

"Surprise!" a multitude of voices exclaimed. I blinked in the morning sunlight. Hannibal, Ruth, Carmen, Carlo, Maria and the entire household staff stood on the landing just outside the door.

As if by signal, they parted to either side. There, on the white gravel of the driveway, sat the most beautiful red sports car convertible that I had ever seen. A young, raven-haired woman, dressed in high-fashion sports clothes, sat in the driver's seat.

The young woman revved the engine one last time, shut it off, got out of the car and motioned me to the car door. It was Annette, and she grinned from ear to ear.

I was speechless for I don't know how long. I'm sure my eyes and mouth were wide open. "Annette!" I finally exclaimed. "How?"

Everyone around me burst into laughter. Hannibal slipped up behind me, kissed me on the neck and said: "I hope you like your new Alpha Romeo. It comes with an expert chauffeur."

Annette's musical voice rose above the laughter. "I will drive only until you learn to drive it yourself." She ran up the steps and gave me a big hug. "Wonderful to see you!"

After everyone settled down, Annette and Hannibal explained.

"I knew something was up from your letters," began Annette. "Hannibal contacted me in Rome two weeks ago. We met in Florence last Saturday."

I looked at Hannibal, who smiled in his enigmatic way. He said: "I told Annette everything. I also ordered your new car two weeks ago. Carlo and I picked it up in Florence on Saturday. Annette volunteered to drive it over today for your surprise."

I looked around at everyone. "You, you rascals," I sputtered. "I had no idea!" My words and expression elicited another round of laughter.

Accompanied by Annette, I hurried down the steps to my new car. Hannibal followed, and said, in his precise military manner: "Alpha Romeo, 1934, Model 8C-2300." Annette laughed and added: "For us girls, it's a Spider Zagato."

The red color gleamed in the morning sunlight, and the brown leather interior looked soft and inviting. "How beautiful," I replied. I got in on the driver's side. Annette joined me as a passenger.

After Annette explained the controls, I started the engine, carefully put the car in gear and drove triumphantly all the way to the main road and back. What fun!

Later, after a merry breakfast, Ruth, Annette, Hannibal and I had coffee on the verandah, enjoyed the late morning sun and got down to business.

Ruth began the conversation. "Enze phoned this morning. Marcu and Giovanni returned from their business trip yesterday. According to Enze, they were unaware of the murder of Molazana and Badia."

She paused and added: "Marcu said that he and Giovanni visited Antonio Baldi, a buyer and distributor of Chianti Classico. The trio had made a trip to Genoa together to set up shipping arrangements. Baldi, his secretary and several others can vouch for their whereabouts from September 9 through the 17."

"I will follow up on Marcu's alibi," responded Hannibal. He looked at Annette, then me and continued: "I expect that you two will work out a plan with regard to Neri."

"Oh yes," responded Annette. "I have already done some homework." She turned to me and added: "I know several clerks in the Florence city planning office, and I have already reviewed the architectural drawings for Neri's estate."

I opened my mouth to say something, but drew a blank. I'm sure that my expression was comical. Ruth and Hannibal both chuckled.

"I'm still in business," Annette said with a mischievous grin. "The mansion was originally built in 1910, but Neri had it renovated in 1932. The drawings are very detailed."

"The best cat burglar in Italy, I'm sure," I thought to myself. I recovered my poise and responded to Annette: "Just like old times in Paris." Annette giggled.

### Wednesday evening, September 19

Annette and I had an exciting drive to Florence this morning in my new Alpha Romeo. Fortunately, most of the drive was outside the city, and I had a chance to acquire a 'feel' for the car.

Once in the city, it was white-knuckle driving all the way. I dodged lorries, other cars and even donkey carts. Annette laughed as I alternately swerved, shifted gears, accelerated, braked and said a few un-lady-like words.

We checked into the Excelsior Hotel Italie on the Piazza Ognissanti. After a calming lunch at a ristorante on the piazza, we planned our reconnaissance of Neri's villa. We returned to our room and changed into sporty slacks, blouses, leather jackets and hiking shoes.

"The villa rests halfway up a hill in the most exclusive suburb of Florence," said Annette, as we roared out of the hotel parking lot in second gear. I finally shifted into a higher gear and the roar diminished.

"Go southeast along the Via Lungarno Soderini to the Pont alla Carraia, which crosses the River Arno. Cross the bridge, continue south on Via Serragli and through the gate in the old city wall," Annette continued. "I'll keep track of street signs and tell you when to turn."

I tried to keep it all straight as we rumbled along the cobblestones.

After we passed the old city wall, Annette said: "Follow Via Serragli to the traffic circle where it joins Via Senese, Via de Poggio Imperiale and Via Machiavelli. The villa is on Via Senese near its junction with Via del Campora."

"How do you remember all of this?" I asked, with obvious awe.

Annette grinned and replied: "I know the neighborhood from previous visits."

We rumbled along for half a kilometer before Annette exclaimed: "Oh! Turn right into this empty lot!"

I slammed on the brakes, double-clutched, down-shifted and swerved right.

"Not bad," Annette said with a giggle, as I brought the car to a halt just centimeters from a tree. "That tree jumped right out in front of you."

"Very funny," I gasped as my heart pounded. After a minute to regain my composure, I asked: "What's next?"

"As I recall from the site layout drawing, we can see down into Neri's estate from the top of that wooded hill up there," and she pointed.

Annette rummaged through her voluminous purse for a few moments, pulled out a set of binoculars and said: "Let's go snooping."

Not to be outdone, I reached in a bag under my seat and pulled out my new camera with a long telephoto lens. "OK," I said smugly. Annette's eyes widened.

We climbed the hill above Neri's villa. We found a hidden spot where we could observe the comings and goings from the estate, which was below us and about 100 meters away. In the distance, we could see the Florence Cathedral and other beautiful Renaissance buildings.

"Quite a view," I said softly.

"Uh-huh," responded Annette, as she looked through her binoculars. "I have spent hours on this hill. We can see many rich mansions."

I smiled; my remark had referred to the cathedral.

I shifted mental gears and concentrated on Neri's place. The main building was a two-story mansion, set among lovely gardens. I recognized boxwood hedges, a rose garden and a fruit orchard.

A white gravel driveway passed through an ornate gate in a high, surrounding wrought-iron fence. The driveway ended in a circle in front of a grand entrance to the mansion. A smaller lane branched off and led past a garage to the back of the mansion.

"For deliveries," I thought to myself. I took a notepad from my pocket and scribbled. "There must be a back door."

Annette noticed my scribbling and said: "The drawings at the planning office showed that the whole estate encloses 6,000 square meters. The main mansion has two floors above ground and a full basement. It has a total of 700 square meters of floor space."

Her eyes twinkled, and she added: "I have memorized the interior layout. On previous trips to this hill, I noticed that except for some sinister-looking household staff, there is no security, not even dogs."

I smiled at Annette and replied: "Very good." We both returned our attention to the side doors and windows of the mansion. "OK, Caroline," I muttered. "Concentrate on breaking and entering."

After about thirty minutes, my thoughts were interrupted by a taxi, as it passed through the open gate and pulled up to the mansion. Two young, raven-haired women got out.

I took a couple of photos. The door to the mansion opened, and a sinister-looking man in butler's attire motioned the women inside. The taxi pulled ahead a little and parked.

As the two of females entered the front door, Annette said: "The Santini sisters, Rosa and Rita. They are Sicilian. In my grandfather's circles, they are known as competent, well-paid assassins."

I looked at Annette carefully. She smiled, shrugged and said: "I met them once, in a social setting."

"OK, Caroline," I thought to myself. "Leave that one alone." I turned my attention back to the mansion.

Rosa and Rita stayed inside for about thirty minutes. I took more photos as they exited the front door and got into the taxi.

Shortly after the taxi left, a chauffeur-driven Mercedes pulled out of the garage and up to the front door of the mansion. The butler and another servant carried out several suitcases and other baggage.

When the loading was done, two well-dressed men came out of the mansion door. I recognized them from photos in Fabri's file. "Neri and Mori," I said softly. "How interesting." I snapped a couple of photos. "Away for a trip."

"Maybe the household staff will take the night off," said Annette. "There is a festival in the main piazza near the cathedral."

"Then tonight is our night," I decided. "Let's go back to the hotel and prepare."

"Right," responded Annette. Her face took on a sober, professional expression. "Just like old times."

## Late Thursday morning September 20

Success! But not without several intense moments. Annette and I arrived at our secret spot on the hill above Neri's estate just before midnight. A half-moon provided dim, silvery light.

We dressed in stylish black for the occasion, and we both had backpacks with our burglar equipment, including lock picks, flashlights and a low-light camera.

I looked down the hill to the mansion. Except for an outside light at the main door, the place was totally dark. "The master is gone, and the servants are asleep," I whispered.

"Or at the festival downtown," replied Annette. "We have to be careful about possible late returnees."

"Humm," I responded. "Let's go. You know the layout, so lead the way."

We silently crept down the hill and arrived at a tree next to the wrought iron fence. Annette took off her backpack and pulled out a knotted rope. She slipped her backpack on and draped the rope over her shoulder.

We climbed the tree and found a sturdy branch that hung over the fence. Within a couple of minutes, we slipped down the rope to the garden inside the fence. "Our escape route," whispered Annette, as she gave the rope a little tug.

I nodded in response. "Shall we find a back door?" I whispered.

"Right," replied Annette. "Follow me."

We moved stealthily through the gardens and to the back of the mansion. I spotted a service door in the dim moonlight. "Our entry point," I whispered. Annette nodded. I took off my backpack, found my lock picks and put my backpack on.

Within a couple of minutes, we were inside. The place was quiet, almost spooky. Moonlight through a couple of windows illuminated the room. We were in a kitchen. "Where are the offices?" I whispered.

Annette glanced around for a moment and then replied: "We have to go through that doorway." She pointed.

"A hallway leads past a dining room and several parlors," she continued. "A grand staircase rises near the main front entrance, and a smaller staircase leads down to the basement and servant's quarters. We have to go up the staircase to the library and office suite on the upper floor."

We waited a few moments to make sure no one was awake. "Down the hall and up the stairs," whispered Annette. We crept up the staircase. "In here," she whispered again, as she opened a door. We entered. Annette closed the door and switched on her flashlight.

I looked around. The office has several filing cabinets, chairs and a large mahogany desk. I started with the filing cabinets. Annette stepped over to the desk.

After a minute or so, Annette whispered: "Over here." I looked. She held up a ledger. I walked over. Annette held the flashlight as I leafed through the pages.

"We've hit the jackpot," I whispered. "Names, addresses and payments made and received." I took off my backpack, fished out my camera and laid it on the desk.

Two names stood out for payments made: Rita and Rosa Santini. "Look at that," said Annette, and she pointed. Payments of 5,000 Swiss francs were made on September 8 and again on September 19. An address was written next to the names.

I peered at the entry next to Annette's finger. It was a scribble of 'mafioso' beside the names Rita and Rosa. "How interesting," I whispered. "Anti-Mafia Neri knew who he was dealing with."

I flipped more pages. As expected, we found entries for monthly payments to Molazana and Badia. "Our murder victims," I whispered. Annette nodded.

We also found the name 'Cesaré Mori' and the names of several other high-ranking Fascists. Next to each name, columns with monthly receipts were listed. "Neri is being financed by Mori and others on a monthly basis," I said. Annette nodded again.

Using a flashlight and the low-light camera, we took dozens of photos of ledger pages.

When we finished, I packed up my camera while Annette returned the ledger to its proper place. We looked around to make sure everything looked undisturbed, shouldered our backpacks and soundlessly left the office.

"There's a master bedroom suite on the other side," whispered Annette, and she pointed across the space next to the grand staircase landing.

I thought a moment and then whispered: "Let's look for shoes." Annette acquired a puzzled look. "We have photos of footprints from the crime scene," I added. Annette's expression showed that she understood.

We entered the master bedroom. As expected, no one was there. I looked for and found a neat row of men's shoes in a closet. I looked carefully at the soles of each pair. Finally, I found a pair with a distinct pattern on the sole.

"This pattern matches the pattern of a set of footprints at the crime scene," I whispered. I took my camera and a ruler out of my backpack. Annette held the light while I took several photos. "I think we have a match," I whispered. "I'll compare measurements later to be sure."

I took a couple of photos of the shoes in situ and back further to show the closet in the larger setting of the bedroom. Annette held the flashlight and watched. Her face showed fascination.

I looked closely at the shoes again. I saw traces of mud. "Humm," I thought. "The carabinieri lab can compare this mud to the mud at the crime scene."

I took out a small paper sack from my backpack and took some scrapings. I placed the sack and camera in my backpack. "Evidence," I whispered. Annette nodded.

We looked around, made sure that we left no traces of our activities and departed the bedroom.

I thought a moment before we descended the stairs. "Let's visit the garage," I whispered. "Maybe we can find a car with tire tread that matches our tire tread photos from the crime scene."

Within a couple of minutes, we were downstairs in the kitchen. As Annette was about to open the door, we heard a rambling, singing baritone voice just outside.

"Oh, boy," I uttered in a soft voice. "Hide." Annette and I looked frantically around. She slipped into a pantry and closed the door. It was too small for both of us. I scrambled and hid in a small space behind the kitchen stove and an adjacent wood box.

I heard the sound of a key in the door lock. The door opened and the kitchen light switched on. I caught a glimpse of the butler, dressed in casual attire. I made myself as small as possible behind the stove. The mumbling, singing voice continued. "Drunk," I concluded.

The drunken butler weaved with uncertain steps to an ice box cooler on the far side of the kitchen. I raised up slightly and watched. He got out the makings of a sandwich and a pitcher with a brown liquid. He turned, and I ducked down. I listened as he rummaged around.

I heard the tinkle of liquid being poured into a glass and a chair scraping on the floor by the table. "Sandwich and ice tea," muttered the butler. "Needs mustard," the voice continued. The chair scraped again, and I heard footsteps.

I peeked over the stove top and watched in horror as the butler staggered over to the pantry. "Annette!" My thoughts raced. The butler opened the door and took a jar of mustard from a top shelf.

I ducked down again as he closed the pantry door. Footsteps creaked on the floor as he made his way back to the table. The singing continued intermittently between the sound of noisy drinking and eating.

The butler gave no indication that he saw anything in the pantry except the mustard. "How in the world?" My mind explored the possibilities.

The midnight snack continued for ages. Finally, the butler finished. I listened as he left the table, put his glass in the sink, switched off the light and staggered out of the kitchen. I could hear him singing as he navigated the hallway to the stairs that led to the basement.

I stood up from behind the stove. Annette stepped out of the pantry. Moonlight shined through the window. I whispered hoarsely: "He didn't see you."

Annette grinned and replied: "I made myself invisible. Shall we go to the garage?"

For a moment, I didn't know how to respond. "OK," I finally uttered.

We left the mansion and made our way to the garage. I picked the lock to a side door. We entered into the garage and closed the door behind us. Annette switched on her flashlight. I saw a car in the shadowy darkness and two empty spaces for other vehicles.

A staircase led to a balcony and rooms on a second floor. "Chauffer's quarters," whispered Annette as she pointed up. She put her forefinger to her lips. I nodded.

I pointed to the car and whispered: "A Fiat 527 sedan. The license plate begins with F." I took the camera out of my backpack.

Using the low-light camera and a flashlight, we took photos of the tires and license plate. We finished, put away our equipment, exited the garage and retraced the trail back to our vantage point on the hill. I looked at my watch. "Three in the morning," I said softly.

Annette grinned and replied. "I had a wonderful time. How about you?"

I gave a big sigh, smiled, and said, with all the aplomb I could muster: "Me too. We'll have to do it again sometime." Annette laughed.

We made our way back to the Alpha Romeo and drove to the Excelsior Hotel. I was exhausted. Developing photos, writing a narrative of our observations and planning follow-up actions can wait until much later in the morning.

# 38

## ITALIAN JUSTICE

*Thursday evening, September 20, 1934*

Annette phoned from her room about 10:00 AM this morning. After I rolled out of bed, showered and got dressed, she joined me for a late room service breakfast.

Afterwards, we used the bathroom to develop our photos with my portable equipment. We reviewed the prints and made some hurried notes. I will write a thorough report later.

"The Santini sisters are of particular interest, and we have an address," I mused, as both Annette and I sipped coffee and looked at the photo of the pertinent ledger page. "According to this ledger, the sisters are staying in Florence."

Annette studied the address for a moment and replied: "I know the neighborhood. Via Maffia 20 is an apartment building not far from the Sagrestia di Santo Spirito, a small Renaissance church."

I looked at Annette intently and replied: "You certainly know Florence."

Annette smiled, shrugged and responded: "Let's take a taxi from our hotel to the church and then walk to a small café just across the street from the apartment building. We can watch the apartment from the café." Her smile broadened, and she added: "I know the proprietor."

"How?" I thought to myself. "Careful, Caroline," my thoughts continued: "Best not to know." To Annette, I replied: "Sounds good."

We arrived at the café at about three this afternoon, just in time for tea. The proprietor, a small, middle-aged man with a luxuriant moustache, smiled knowingly at Annette, seated us at a table by the window and brought tea and pastries.

He then nodded in the direction of two burly men, dressed in non-descript workman's clothes, sitting at another window table across the room. Annette gave me a nudge under our table and nodded in the direction of the two men.

I glanced quickly in their direction and then back to Annette. I'm sure my eyes were wide in surprise. I whispered: "The butler and chauffeur from Neri's estate. Why are they here?"

Annette took a deep breath, let it out and said softly: "Same as us. They are watching the apartment building."

I sipped tea, discreetly watched the two men and tried to read lips. By unspoken agreement, Annette continued to watch the apartment building. I couldn't catch all of the men's conversation, but I did discern the name 'Neri' and the phrase 'uccidi il mafioso.'

I made the connection. "Neri's butler and chauffeur have additional duties," I concluded to myself. I turned to Annette and whispered "Those two are after the Santini sisters."

Annette nodded and replied: "Neri wants to eliminate ties to those who could point a finger. Besides, the Santinis are Sicilian." She paused a moment and added: "I would wager that it was similar with Molazana and Badia; they knew too much."

I thought a moment and then said: "Motive for murder." Annette nodded.

We continued to watch the two men and the apartment building. The proprietor kept us supplied with tea.

At about 5:00 PM, I spotted Rita and Rosa as they exited the apartment building. The pair walked leisurely down the street.

I looked at Annette, who nodded in response. I then glanced quickly at the two men across the room. They were intently watching the sisters.

I turned my attention back to Rita and Rosa. They entered a small grocery store about a block away.

I glanced back at the two men. They stood up. One dropped a few lire on the table, and they moved quickly out the café door. They crossed the street and entered the apartment building.

I looked at Annette. Her eyes were wide, and she whispered: "Ambush. I've seen it before."

My thoughts raced. Something deep inside, something primitive, rebelled against the thought of two men killing two women from ambush. It didn't matter what the women may or may not have done.

I made a decision. "We have to warn them," I stated, as I looked intently at Annette.

Annette returned my look. In a few seconds, she nodded and said in a firm voice: "Yes. Let's go."

I dropped some lire on the table for our bill, and we headed for the door. I saw the proprietor as he watched us with a look of fascination. I could tell that he knew a drama was about to unfold. "Buona caccia," he said softly, as we passed him on our way out.

We walked down the café side of the street and crossed in front of the grocery store. As we reached the curb, Rita and Rosa came out of the store. They each had a bag of groceries.

Their eyes widened as they both recognized Annette. They glanced at me with expressions of suspicion.

Annette stepped forward and spoke to the sisters in an urgent but calm voice. Rita glanced toward the apartment building and then returned her attention to Annette.

The conversation was over quickly. Rita and Rosa nodded to me, smiled, turned and walked in the opposite direction from the apartment building. Annette and I watched as they disappeared into an alley.

After a minute or two of watching, Annette and I walked to the Sagrestia di Santo Spirito, caught a taxi and returned to the Excelsior Hotel.

Our mission in Florence was finished. We packed, checked out of the hotel and loaded up my Alpha Romeo. We were mostly silent as we headed back to Ruth's villa.

## Sunday evening, September 23

Ruth, Annette, Hannibal and I had tea and scones on the villa verandah this afternoon. Hannibal and I were satisfied that we understood who, why and how with regard to the Molazana and Badia murders. Ruth and Annette agreed to critique our findings before we briefed Fabri and Grassi.

I began the conversation: "No one from Enze Salicetti's estate committed the murders."

Ruth gave sigh of relief. Annette said: "My great uncle Enze has always traveled a legitimate path." Annette smiled knowingly at me. I smiled back. I'm sure we had similar thoughts.

To Ruth, I said: "I'm reasonably sure that we can trust Fabri and Grassi." I paused and asked: "What do you think?"

"I know Fabri's family," Ruth replied. "They are strong supporters of King Victor Emmanuel and the House of Savoy." She smiled enigmatically and added: "The royal family often has a different agenda compared to transitory prime ministers."

I'm sure my eyes widened in surprise. After a moment, I responded: "Perhaps they have concerns about Mussolini and his Blackshirts."

"Yes," replied Ruth, as she raised her cup for another sip. "And you can trust Fabri and Grassi."

We were all silent for a while. Hannibal broke the silence by saying: "I visited Marcu's and Giovanni's contacts between September 9 and 17. Their alibis check out."

Hannibal looked at Annette and then me. His eyes twinkled and he said: "You two had some exciting adventures."

"Humm," I responded. Annette giggled and sipped her tea.

Hannibal continued: "We have enough documentation for the carabinieri to arrest Neri. Mori will certainly remain under suspicion." He frowned a little and added: "Whether or not arrests are politically feasible remains to be seen."

"I'm unsure of the sequence of events on the day of the murders," said Ruth. She looked at me and asked: "Would you please explain?"

"Neri drove his Fiat 527 sedan to the crime scene on the Salicetti driveway before 4:15 PM on September 10," I responded. "We matched his shoes and his Fiat 527 tire tread to the footprints and tire tracks at the crime scene."

Hannibal picked up the narrative. "The Santini sisters were most likely in the car with Neri. Although we were unable to confirm that their shoes made the footprints at the crime scene, the footprints were almost certainly female."

I then said: "They were joined by Molazana and Badia in their own car sometime after 4:15 and before 4:45. Neri, Molazana and Badia had probably arranged beforehand to meet and then continue on to the Salicetti estate."

Hannibal added: "Based on Molazana's statements at the olive grove confrontation with workers shortly before 4:00 PM, Molazana and Badia had certainly planned to drive to the villa. From the evidence at the scene, they stopped behind Neri's car halfway to the villa."

I then said: "Molazana and Badia knew Neri, and had no reason to be on guard. The Santini sisters probably slipped up close and used their knives before the victims had a chance to defend themselves."

Hannibal concluded the narrative: "Neri and the sisters then departed the scene, drove down the driveway and made the turn north toward Florence before Alceu arrived at the crossroads at about 5:00 PM."

We were silent for a few moments before Ruth responded: "You can place Neri at the crime scene at the proper time, but not the Santini sisters." She smiled, looked at Annette and added: "How nice." Annette returned the smile with an innocent look.

## Tuesday evening, September 25

Hannibal phoned Grassi Monday morning. He made an appointment for ten o'clock today at Carabinieri Headquarters in Siena.

Hannibal and I left for Siena in the Alpha Romeo at about eight o'clock. I drove, and Hannibal courteously avoided critiquing my driving abilities. I was still getting used to accelerating, shifting gears and braking.

Fabri, Grassi, Solari, Hannibal and I were seated at Fabri's conference table precisely at ten. In his usual military manner, Hannibal presented our findings and gave Grassi our completed report.

After Hannibal finished, Fabri and Grassi conferred for a couple of minutes. Grassi looked at me and then Hannibal. He stated: "You have provided sufficient evidence to justify an arrest warrant for Neri. However, we don't have enough to arrest the Santini sisters."

"Agree," I said. I thought a moment and then asked: "What about Cesare Mori?"

"He is a Senator now," replied Grassi.

"Understand," I replied. "Insufficient evidence and political influence."

As I finished my comment, we heard a knock at the door. "Come," said Fabri. A clerk entered and handed Fabri a single sheet of paper.

After reading the sheet, Fabri looked up and said: "Neri was found dead in his home this morning. So were his butler and chauffeur. Apparently, all three had been stabbed while they were asleep in bed."

Fabri looked back at the sheet. After a moment, he looked up and added: "The investigating team didn't find any evidence to identify a killer or killers. The other servants seemed frightened, but assured the investigators that they didn't see a thing until they discovered the bodies at about 8:00 AM." He looked intently at Hannibal and then me.

Hannibal and I looked at each other for a moment and then back to Fabri. "The Santini sisters," I thought to myself. Hannibal smiled slightly.

Fabri caught Hannibal's smile, leaned back in his chair, smiled and said: "I think we have covered enough ground on this case."

Grassi also smiled, looked at Fabri and said: "But then we have the other matter."

"Yes," mused Fabri. "Let's wait a few days while we put together a file." He then looked at Hannibal and said: "Would you and Signora Jones be willing to take on another case? It would involve travel."

Hannibal looked at me. I raised my eyebrows. That was enough for Hannibal, who turned to Fabri and said: "Perhaps. We are staying at the Canossa villa."

Fabri turned to Grassi and asked: "How much time do you need for your research?"

Grassi leaned back, thought a moment and replied: "About two weeks."

Fabri looked at a calendar on his desk. He then turned to Hannibal and said: "Would you and Signora Jones visit us here at headquarters on October 9?"

Hannibal looked at me. I took a deep breath and said: "Annette and I are going shopping in Rome, but we should be finished before the 9."

The three men laughed. Fabri said: "It's a date. See you both at ten o'clock on October 9."

# 39

## COLONIAL INTRIGUE

*Sunday evening, October 7, 1934*

On October 2, Annette, Carmen and I took a train from Florence to Rome, the eternal city. We stayed at Annette's apartment near the Piazza del'Orlogio.

Annette lives in style. Her apartment occupies a corner suite in a four-story apartment building that had been renovated in 1932. To the east, I could see the Vatican and the Castel Sant'Angelo from my bedroom window, across the Tiber. The Pantheon was a short walk to the west.

We did more sight-seeing than shopping; Annette was the best tour guide ever. She has connections, and we visited the Sistine Chapel in Vatican City. We also took taxis to the Trevi Fountain, the Spanish Steps, the Coliseum and the ancient Roman Forum. The sights were fantastic. I took lots of photos.

I was surprised that Rome has little private automobile traffic. However, streetcars ply most major thoroughfares, taxis are available and lorries make deliveries. Ubiquitous military vehicles with Blackshirt occupants park at many street corners.

I also noticed that pedestrians are less well-dressed than in Paris, Berlin and Vienna. Annette said that Italy has been hit hard by the world-wide economic depression. She also said that costly colonial wars in Italian Libya, Eritrea and Somaliland have limited the money available for public works to boost employment.

"The people are poor, but the trains run on time, and Mussolini has his empire," Annette said with a wry expression. "Fascists control the newspapers, and editors enthusiastically trumpet about another impending war in far-away Ethiopia."

After a tearful goodbye to Annette on Friday, Carmen and I caught the train back to Florence. Hannibal met us at the train station. I miss Annette, but not fascist Rome.

## Monday evening, October 8

While Hannibal and I were having breakfast with Ruth this morning, Hannibal got a phone call from the Banco di Roma in Florence. He took the call in the library. After about ten minutes, he returned to the breakfast table with an expression of concern.

"Problem?" I asked, as Ruth and I looked intently at Hannibal.

Hannibal returned my gaze and said: "The Nazis have taken over the German Reichsbank. My contact at the Banco di Roma said that a man from the Reichsbank arrived on Friday. He had proper credentials. He asked another manager at the bank about us."

Hannibal paused and then added: "My contact overheard the conversation. The man from the Reichsbank now knows about our money transfer from Geneva to Riccione on August 14 and our transfer from Riccione to the Banco di Roma in Florence on September 3."

I'm sure my eyes expressed dismay, and I replied: "The Nazis know we are in or near Florence."

"I think so," said Hannibal. He smiled ruefully. "Like us, they followed the money."

He looked at Ruth and added: "We need to leave before they trace us to your villa."

Ruth let out a big sigh; she had been holding her breath. After a moment, she replied: "I understand. I will be so sorry to see you go." A tear formed in the corner of her eye. She tried to smile as she looked at me. I reached over and held her hand for a moment.

Breakfast ended. Hannibal and I have much to do, including a visit to Carabinieri Headquarters in Siena tomorrow morning.

## Tuesday evening, October 9

Today's meeting with Fabri and Grassi had surprises for everyone. Hannibal and I arrived at just before 10:00 AM. We were immediately escorted into Fabri's office. I sensed urgency in the expression on Fabri's face as Fabri, Hannibal, Grassi and I took our seats at the conference table.

Fabri began the conversation. "Crown Prince Umberto just returned from a state visit to Mogadishu in Italy's Somaliland Colony." He looked intently at Hannibal, then me and added: "The local carabinieri and army troops foiled a potential assassination attempt."

Grassi's face was grim. He said: "King Victor Emmanuel will visit Mogadishu on November 3. He will tour the city and participate in ceremonies and dinners for an entire week."

He paused and continued: "Security will be comprehensive, but the King has enemies."

Hannibal leaned back in his chair, took a deep breath and responded: "Newspaper accounts say that Italy's colonies in Africa have experienced rebellions by native tribes." He paused, looked at Fabri intently and asked: "Why?"

Fabri and Grassi looked at each other for several moments.

Finally, Fabri replied: "You have touched on a subject that greatly concerns us. From 1928 until last year, we received many anecdotal reports of brutal repression and killing by Italian and colonial troops in Libya."

Grassi added: "The troops were commanded by Marshal Emilio De Bono, General Pietro Badoglio and General Rodolfo Graziani. All three are now in Eritrea and Somaliland."

"Invasion of Ethiopia?" I asked. I then added: "It's in the newspapers."

"They are waiting for an incident to justify invasion," replied Fabri. "An assassination would do it."

Grassi added: "The House of Savoy supports colonization, but it may be their undoing." He paused and continued: "Facts about the brutal aspects of colonization may change the King's mind."

I looked at Hannibal for a long moment. I could tell that we were having similar thoughts. Hannibal turned to Grassi and asked: "Do you want us to investigate repression and killing in Italy's African colonies?"

Grassi responded: "Your reputation for gathering evidence is well-known to us." He smiled and added: "We also know about your French connection." He looked at Hannibal and then me.

"Oh, good heavens!" I'm sure my face expressed surprise. I took a deep breath, held it for a moment and let it out slowly. I looked at Grassi and then Fabri.

Fabri returned my gaze and said: "In this situation, your French colleagues and our small anti-fascist group have compatible objectives." He paused, smiled enigmatically and added: "Capitaine Inspecteur Soucet and I have worked together in the past."

"Whether or not Fabri knows Soucet, he certainly knows about us," I concluded. I looked at Hannibal.

Hannibal returned my gaze for a moment. He then turned to Fabri and said softly: "We will check with Soucet."

"Of course," replied Fabri. He turned, looked at me and waited.

I returned his gaze for a moment. His eyes remained steady; there was no lie in them.

I then looked at Hannibal and said: "I've always wanted to see Africa."

Fabri and Grassi both smiled and looked from me to Hannibal.

Hannibal replied: "The timing is fortuitous." I could tell from his expression that we both were thinking about the Nazis, who were hot on our trail. Leaving Florence was necessary in any case.

Another thought crossed my mind. "Cover story?" I asked. "European art collection won't work in Africa."

"True," replied Hannibal. He was quiet for a while. Fabri, Grassi and I waited. Finally, Hannibal said: "My banking partners in Geneva are always looking for investment opportunities in developing countries. Italy's colonies might be of interest."

"Humm," I responded. I turned to Grassi and then Fabri. "When do we leave?" I asked.

Fabri and Grassi both breathed sighs of relief.

Fabri's smile changed to an all-business expression. He looked at me and answered: "As soon as possible. Ala Littorio Airlines has experimental flights from Rome to Benghazi and from Benghazi to Tripoli, Asmara, Mogadishu and even Addis Ababa."

He looked at Hannibal and said: "As an investment banker, you could spend time in all four colonial cities without raising suspicion. For now, even trips to Addis Ababa in Ethiopia are possible."

Grassi added: "You will need guides. They can escort you to wherever you need to go. There are many garrisoned agricultural stations, run by Italians, scattered across the colonies."

He smiled and added: "All have prime opportunities for investment." He turned to Fabri and waited.

Fabri nodded, looked at Hannibal and said: "Trust no one in the colonial administration. Almost all are dedicated fascists." His expression showed distaste. He then added: "I will give you a list of names of people you can trust. Most are lower-level Catholic clergy"

Silence reigned for several minutes as we all digested the implications of our plans. "Wow!" I finally concluded to myself.

"I have secret reports on Libya, Somaliland, and Eritrea that you might like to read while Grassi and I attend to arrangements," said Fabri. He looked at Grassi and asked: "How long?"

Grassi looked at his watch. "We should be done by two o'clock. The airline will take the longest. We also need to do visas and letters of introduction."

The two men left, and a secretary brought in a stack of files. Hannibal and I began reading.

After pouring over several reports, I said: "Lots of anecdotal reports, mostly from Catholic priests, about atrocities."

"Humm," responded Hannibal. "They reported second-hand rumors of vast concentration camps, but did not present direct evidence."

"We know what to look for," I replied. "I will write down names of the priests in the reports and compare them to Fabri's list. Most are based in Benghazi, but there is one in Mogadishu."

Fabri and Grassi returned just after two o'clock. Hannibal and I looked up from our reading.

Fabri broke the silence. "I arranged for a lunch a few minutes ago. My apologies for running well past noon. I can have my secretary bring it in." He looked at me, smiled and asked: "Are you hungry?"

My tummy growled audibly in response. I quickly added: "Yes, thank you." Hannibal suppressed a chuckle.

As we were all eating sandwiches and drinking tea and coffee, a young man opened the door, peeked in and said: "Please excuse me, senore Fabri. I have an urgent message." He shuffled his feet in great agitation.

"Yes," responded Fabri. He held out his hand. The young man walked over and gave Fabri a single sheet of paper. Fabri read; his eyes widened, and he stood up from his seat. Hannibal, Grassi and I stopped eating.

Fabri looked around at our faces. In a slow voice, he said: "King Alexander I of Yugoslavia and French Foreign Minister Louis Barthou were assassinated in Marseilles, France about an hour ago. The assassin, a Bulgarian named Chernozemski, was killed by a mob at the scene."

Grassi's face expressed horror. He responded in a voice just above a whisper: "King Alexander was our Crown Prince Umberto's first cousin."

Hannibal and I exchanged looks. "Chernozemski," I mused softly. "We tried." Hannibal nodded.

### Saturday evening, October 13

Hannibal and I left Ruth's villa last Wednesday. Grassi had booked us on a flight from Giovan Battista Pastine Airport in Ciampino to Benghazi this morning. He arranged to meet us in Ciampino.

Before we left Ruth's villa, Hannibal transferred the title of our Duesenberg to Carlo and the title of my Alpha Romeo to Carmen. With the help of a friendly clerk in the Florence municipal government, Hannibal also eliminated the paper trail.

"It's the least we can do in return for their hospitality and help with regard to our investigations," I said to Hannibal.

"Yes," he agreed. "We can always get you a new sports car later."

I smiled in return; I will miss my toy.

After tearful goodbyes to Ruth, Maria and Carmen, Carlo drove us to Florence.

We packed light. In addition to our weapons, cameras, binoculars and forensics gear, we each had one formal and several casual outfits. Carlo hid our trunks of clothes and other belongings from the Nazis in one of his warehouses.

Hannibal said that we could buy suitable clothes for wear in the colonies when we arrive in Benghazi.

Hannibal also exchanged coded telegrams with Soucet on Wednesday. His responding telegram said: 'Association with Fabri confirmed. Plan approved. Strong interest in Italian activities in Africa. Your account in Geneva has been credited with a substantial fee.'

We spent Wednesday night in the Excelsior Hotel in Florence. Hannibal closed our bank account in Banco di Roma Thursday morning. Most of the money was returned to our bank in Geneva, but Hannibal kept a large sum in cash for our adventures in Africa.

"Italian lire, Swiss francs and gold coins," said Hannibal. "Banks in Africa might be a problem." We divided the money into several money belts and other hidden places.

On Thursday afternoon, we caught a train from Florence to Ciampino, just southeast of Rome. The trip took only about two hours.

With his usual foresight, Hannibal booked a room at a small family-run hotel on Via Ovidio in Ciampino for Thursday night. The hotel was just a kilometer from Giovan Battista Pastine Airport.

Grassi met us at the hotel Friday morning for breakfast. He had our visas, airline tickets, a list of contacts and letters of introduction. "Be careful and good luck," said Grassi, as we parted company. "Africa is dangerous." He and Hannibal shook hands.

Grassi turned to me and said: "Arrivederci, signora Jones. I have never met anyone like you." He bowed and formally kissed my hand. I shall miss him.

Hannibal and I arrived at the airport early Saturday morning. We cleared customs and made it to the gate just before 10:00 AM. At 10:15, we were invited to board our flight.

Hannibal explained our route as we walked to our Savoia-Marchetti S.73 trimotor airplane.

"We will fly from Giovan Battista Pastine to the land runway at l'idroscalo Orbetello aerodrome, about 120 kilometers northeast of Rome. At Orbetello, we will board a prototype CANT Z.506 float plane for a flight to Siracusa De Philippis aerodrome in Sicily."

"Prototype?" I asked, with a cautious expression.

"Yes," replied Hannibal with a grin. "The Z.506 won't be in full production until next year."

"Oh my," I thought to myself. To Hannibal, I tried to smile with confidence. It didn't work.

Hannibal's eyes twinkled and he continued: "At our stop in Syracuse, we will re-fuel, rest overnight and then fly to Benghazi. We'll be at the aerodrome in Benghazi tomorrow afternoon."

My recollection of the geography of our flight was vague, so I asked: "Is the flight mostly over water?"

"Yes," replied Hannibal. "We will be about a kilometer above the Mediterranean."

The pilot greeted us as we boarded. "Welcome to our experimental flight," he said. "We hope to start regular service next year." He smiled brightly and added: "Our accident rate is very low, less than 20 percent."

I gulped a little and looked at Hannibal. He just smiled. We found our seats and stored our hand luggage.

"Off to Benghazi on an experimental airplane, over water, with a 20 percent chance of going down," I thought to myself. I looked out the window as we raced and bounced down the runway. Our three motors roared. I vibrated all over. "Oh, good heavens!"

# 40

## DESERT COLONY

*Sunday evening, October 14, 1934*

This morning, we made it to Orbetello and transferred to our float plane. Within minutes, we roared across the lagoon in the midst of a huge spray of water.

The plane finally lifted from the surface with a sudden surge. My butt pressed firmly down with the heavy force of the liftoff, and my fingernails dug into the arms of the seat. I was petrified.

I looked over at Hannibal. He sat there, eyes closed, with no expression of fear.

"OK, Caroline," I thought to myself. "You can do this." I took a deep breath, let it out slowly, and said to myself: "No fear, no fear, no fear..." The engines roared on and on.

After an eternity of flight, we splashed down in the water, skidded sideways for a while, and finally coasted to a dock and a seaplane ramp.

Hannibal opened his eyes, looked at me and said in a matter-of-fact tone: "Welcome to Syracuse." He unbuckled his seat belt, stood up and offered his hand.

I unbuckled, got up slowly and took his hand. My whole body felt weak and unsteady. I gave Hannibal my best smile, considering the circumstances. His eyes twinkled.

He then said: "Ala Littoria booked us at the Grand Hotel Ortigia on Viale Mazzini. They will provide transportation."

As I collected my hand luggage, he added: "We can have a nice dinner at the hotel." My stomach churned at the thought. I gave him a venomous look.

I wobbled off the plane, walked slowly along the dock, found dry land and headed toward a waiting limousine. Hannibal was at my side, ready to steady my progress. I was nauseous and in a bad mood. The situation was infuriating.

## Monday morning, October 15

Last night, check-in at the Grand Hotel passed in a haze of confusing images. Hannibal took care of everything, while I crash-landed in a soft chair in the lobby.

To my addled senses, the lobby chair moved around and around. Closing my eyes made it worse, so I opened them and focused on a nice landscape painting across the room. The technique helped a little.

Our suite was nice enough. Hannibal ordered a light room service dinner while I took a much-needed bath. Like the chair in the lobby, the tub kept moving around. I focused my eyes on my toes sticking above the bath water.

My nausea gradually subsided. Refreshed, I got out of the tub, dried with a luxuriant towel, combed my damp hair and put on a soft robe supplied by the hotel.

I felt much better. I heard Hannibal in the parlor; room service had arrived. I suddenly felt hungry.

I toddled into the parlor. Hannibal was sitting next to a portable table covered with white linen and several covered dishes. A pot of tea rested on a side table. Hannibal looked up and smiled.

"Feeling better?" He asked as I approached.

"Yes, thank you," I replied. Hannibal is such a thoughtful man.

I don't remember what I ate, but it tasted good. Afterwards, Hannibal took a bath while I slipped into bed. Later, he joined me. We snuggled. My senses returned to normal.

This morning, light filtered through the window way too early. I focused my eyes and my mind at about the same time. Hannibal was out of bed; I heard him in the parlor.

"Ah, yes," I thought to myself. "We are in Syracuse. Today we fly to Benghazi."

The thought of another float plane ride caused the room to move around. "Oh boy," my thoughts continued. "Concentrate, Caroline." I wrote these notes in my diary, and it helped. My mind is prepared, I think, for another flight.

## Tuesday morning, October 16

Yesterday, at Hannibal's suggestion, we had a very light breakfast of toast, oatmeal and tea. The Ala Littoria limousine picked us up at 9:00 AM.

We boarded the float plane at the dock in the harbor at about 10:30. "Off into the wild blue again, and eight hours to Benghazi," I mused to myself.

This time, I managed much better on the flight. Most of the time, I followed Hannibal's example, closed my eyes and dozed. I even had a light meal, sipped lots of tea and made frequent trips to the lavatory.

After a grueling eight hours in the air, we splash-landed in the Benghazi inner harbor. The plane taxied to the dock at the Idroscalo. After collecting our luggage and checking through customs, Hannibal hailed a taxi.

The driver, who was Italian, recommended the Hotel Berenice, which, he said, was located just across the street from the new Benghazi Cathedral.

"Great," I thought to myself. "Our first contact is Father Leonardo, who is assigned to the cathedral."

The driver navigated the Via Comte Giacomo on our way to the hotel. The buildings were new along the route, and they had a very European architecture. Most pedestrians appeared European.

I was surprised. I expected more exotic buildings and darker people consistent with a North African culture. I looked at Hannibal and asked: "Where are the natives?"

"From what I have read, Benghazi has a large Italian population," Hannibal replied. "Most of the native population lives in the older quarter of the city." He smiled and added: "We are passing through Mussolini's showcase."

I watched out the window. After about a ten-minute drive, we turned left by a new telephone exchange building and continued for another block. We stopped right in front of the beautiful Hotel Berenice.

A tall, dark man in a white uniform opened the taxi door, bowed and motioned me toward a doorman, who was also in uniform. As usual, Hannibal handled tips, check-in and other details.

I found a seat in the lobby and looked around. The place was cool, comfortable and very new. "Welcome to colonial Africa," I mused to myself.

We had a corner suite on the top floor. Hannibal opened the gauze curtains, and we looked out. A beautiful sunset glowed in the west, and I could see a lighthouse to the north by the seashore. To the east, across a piazza, a cathedral bathed in golden light.

"The Agan'd Lighthouse, the middle harbor, the Gulf of Sidra, the Maydan El Catedracya and the new Benghazi Cathedral," Hannibal said softly. "You can also see the Via Vittoria on the other side of the cathedral." How does he know such things?

## Wednesday evening, October 17

Hannibal and I dressed in summer business attire this morning. After breakfast, we walked across the piazza to the cathedral.

The main nave was still under construction, but we saw several priests, dressed in plain habits, near a side door. One of the priests, a young man with a fringe of sandy hair, saw us and smiled as we approached.

Hannibal handled the introductions in Italian. "Pardon, Father, I am Hannibal Jones, and this is my wife, Caroline. We are looking for Father Leonardo."

The priest nodded and replied: "I am Bernardino. Father Leonardo and I are both members of the Franciscan Friars Minor of Genova." He turned slightly, nodded toward the side door and added: "Leonardo is inside."

He turned back to Hannibal; his brow furrowed a little; his smile broadened, and he said: "You are American."

Hannibal chuckled and replied: "Yes. I suppose my Italian has an American accent."

Bernardino nodded graciously, looked at me and said: "Welcome to Benghazi, signora Jones." He raised his eyebrows a little and asked: "How is it that two Americans are in Benghazi?"

I didn't quite know how to respond. After a moment's hesitation, I did a slight curtesy and said: "In Rome, our friends suggested that Father Leonardo could guide us on our visits to Libyan towns and villages." I paused and added: "We have a letter of introduction."

Bernardino raised his eyebrows a little more and responded: "Shall we go inside?" He motioned to the door.

After the door closed behind us, Bernardino led us down a long, dimly lit corridor. After about 20 meters, he opened a door on the right and motioned us inside.

I saw a spacious, brightly lit, yet spartan office. Several men in habits sat at desks, working on documents or reading texts.

Bernardino looked at a young priest at the far end of the room. In a soft, clear voice, he said: "Father Leonardo." The priest looked in our direction, got up from his seat and walked silently toward us.

Bernardo opened the door and the four of us stepped outside. He closed the door. We were alone in the corridor.

The young priest looked at Bernardino, then Hannibal and finally, me. "I am Leonardo," he said in a low voice.

Bernardino introduced us. Hannibal took a sealed envelope from his jacket pocket and handed it to Leonardo, who opened it, took out a letter and read for a few moments.

Leonardo then folded the letter, returned it to Hannibal and said: "A missive from my old friend Aldo Fabri." He paused, smiled and added: "Aldo speaks very highly of you both."

He then turned to Bernardino and said: "Major and signora Jones are on a mission." He paused and added: "We have common interests."   Both men turned to Hannibal.

"Caroline and I would like to know more about the military response to the Senussi rebellion," said Hannibal. "Superintendent Fabri suspects that it was brutal."

Leonardo grimaced and replied: "I reported to Fabri what our Muslim contacts reported to us. We have rumors, some first-hand witness testimony but no evidence."

I looked intently at Leonardo and asked: "How might we obtain evidence?"

Leonardo and Bernardino exchanged glances. After a moment, Leonardo said: "We know a man you should meet. His name is Amed al Mukhtar. He lives in the Arab quarter near the mosque and the old marketplace."

I was about to ask directions, but Leonardo smiled as if he anticipated my question. "You will never find him unless I guide you." His smile broadened a little and he added: "We will have to change clothes."

"Amed is Muslim?" Hannibal asked.

"Yes," responded Bernardino. "He is also a scholar among his people. In spite of our differences in religion, we have common interests in archeology and African cultures, including Bedouin, Berber and other ethnic groups. We have become friends."

His face expressed a wry smile and he added: "Just don't tell Bishop Domenico Moro."

"Hannibal returned the smile and said: "Not a word.""

I thought a moment and then said: "You mentioned changing clothes."

Leonardo and Bernardino exchanged glances again. After a moment, Bernardino replied: "Westerners are not welcome near the Mosque. When we visit Amed, we dress in local garb."

Leonardo nodded, looked intently at me and said: "Would you mind dressing and acting as an Arab male? Women in Muslim society have certain roles that may be a disadvantage in your efforts to gather evidence."

My mouth dropped open. I'm sure I blushed. All three men did their best to suppress chuckles. Finally, I recovered my poise and said: "Why not?" It was a good response.

I decided to go on a verbal offensive. I looked at Leonardo, then Bernardino and said: "Apparently, your secret Muslim friend would be frowned upon by your superiors. Why are you doing this?"

After a moment, Leonardo took a deep breath, let it out and replied: "Fair enough." He gave a sigh and continued: "We believe that genocide, whether it's Muslim or Christian, is against the teachings of Christ."

Bernardino then added: "For political reasons, our local superiors support the government. For reasons of faith, we do not." He looked at me, and his eyes watered a little. "At least, that's how we justify to ourselves our sins of secrecy and disobedience."

"Other members of the Franciscan Order in Rome are sympathetic to our concerns," Leonardo added. "Someday, we hope to present our case to the Holy Father."

Silence reigned for quite a while. Finally, Hannibal said: "Others, not part of the church, also have concerns. We work on their behalf." He paused, looked intently at Leonardo and added: "As you said earlier, we have a common interest. Let's find the evidence."

Leonardo and Bernardino looked at each other for a moment. Bernardino nodded.

Leonardo looked intently at Hannibal and said: "Agreed." He then looked at me, smiled and said: "I know a lady who can help you dress as an Arab male."

I blushed again. To recover, I did one of my classic sniffs, looked squarely in Leonardo's eyes and replied: "I hope she has a sense of style, even if it's male clothing."

All three men laughed. It was a good ending to a very productive meeting.

## Saturday evening, October 20

Hannibal and I spent yesterday shopping along the Via Roma for appropriate European colonial dress.

Hannibal found a tailor who agreed to produce a white linen suit and several khaki trousers, shirts and a bush jacket. He also bought a pair of desert boots and a khaki-colored pith helmet.

I settled for a couple of white dresses, a simple matching hat and white shoes. For the desert, I bought tailored khaki outfits, tall desert boots and a pith helmet similar to the one selected by Hannibal.

All of our European clothing was scheduled for delivery to our hotel suite next Wednesday.

Our Arab dress was a different matter. At the direction of Leonardo, I found Fatima in the back of a tailor shop on a side street near the Hotel Berenice. It was a dimly lit place, but neat and clean. I soon had suitable Arab male clothing, with certain hidden modifications.

Fatima insisted that I wear a hijab, a traditional headdress and veil, pulled down around my neck so that it could be lifted up to cover my head and face, just in case. She helped me wind a turban and don other male clothes to hide my hair, the hijab and my feminine features.

I also made modifications to hide my Walther handgun, knife and spare ammunition clips. Fatima's eyes widened as she saw my weapons. "May Allah protect you," she finally uttered.

Due to his size, Hannibal had more trouble getting fitted. Omer, the tailor and Fatima's husband, finally succeeded in making him look like a rather large Arab.

## Wednesday evening, October 24

Our new colonial clothing arrived this morning. I look pretty good in khaki, if I do say so myself. I pirouetted for Hannibal, who laughed and gave the appropriate compliments.

Leonardo left a message at the hotel front desk this afternoon. We will meet him tomorrow evening, after sunset, at Omer's tailor shop. His message told us to change clothes inside Omar's place and wait for transportation.

## Friday morning, October 26

Last night, Hannibal and I met Leonardo at Omer's tailor shop. We all dressed in Arab clothing. Outside, Yusuf, our driver, waited in a rickety-looking old automobile.

Leonardo noticed my stare at the car. "Don't let the exterior fool you; the engine is finely tuned and powerful; the suspension has been modified for desert driving and the tires are new."

Leonardo and Yusuf talked for a few minutes in a language that I didn't understand. Finally, Yusuf pulled out into traffic. Leonardo was right, the engine purred.

Yusuf navigated the well-lit streets of the Italian quarter along the seaside Promenade with confidence. I watched for street signs. We turned right on Via Margherita.

After our turn, the street lights became few. Although traffic, mostly lorries, was light, Yusuf slowed down.

For a while, buildings included shops and light industrial complexes. Most were totally dark. After a couple of kilometers, we turned right on Via Czio and then left on a narrow, dark side street.

I couldn't see a sign. Here and there, lights gleamed from apartment windows.

As we crept along in the dark, I detected a unique, somewhat sour odor. Leonardo noticed my sniffing and wrinkled nose.

"Welcome to the smell of an ancient African town," he said. "The marketplace is not far away. Also, the lack of sanitation, combined with the odors of animals, the market and cooking, produces an odor mixture hard to describe, but one you will never forget." He was right.

"So different than the new Italian quarter," I thought to myself. I squinted and tried to make out details in the dim light.

We passed small fires in grates along the street. Women moved by the fires.

Leonardo noticed my glance and said: "Cooking dinner. Most cook outside to avoid burning down the buildings."

"What do they eat?" I asked.

"Lamb, goat or fish when they can get it," replied Leonardo. "They also eat vegetables, rice and an unleavened bread called lavash, or a variant that originated in the middle east, called chapati."

He looked at me, smiled and said: "Locals use the bread as a wrap for meat and vegetables. The cuisine is quite good."

I look closely at one of the fires, and asked: "What do they use for fuel?"

"Charcoal, if possible," answered Leonardo. "But charcoal is expensive. More often, little girls have the job of making patties from animal dung, drying them in the sun, and supplying them to their mothers for cooking fires."

Yusuf turned right into an alley and stopped. "We have arrived," said Leonardo. "It's time for you to meet Amed al Mukhtar."

# 41

## THE CAMP

*Friday evening, October 26, 1934*

Thursday night, Yusuf, Leonardo, Hannibal and I reached our destination in the heart of the Arab quarter. Yusuf remained with the car, and Leonardo led us to the door of a plain looking, mud-brick building.

A white-haired man in traditional Arab clothes opened the heavy wooden door as we approached. Light from lamps gleamed out into the darkness of the street.

Inside, I could see a sparkling fountain in an enclosed courtyard. Decorative tiles covered the walls, and exotic plants grew in a small, manicured garden that surrounded the fountain. "Plain exterior, beautiful interior," I thought to myself. "So different compared to Europe."

Our greeter bowed courteously to Leonardo and then to Hannibal and me. "As salaam alaykum," he said, in a soft, melodious voice; "ahlan bik."

Leonardo put his hands together, bowed and replied: "Alaykum assalam."

I didn't know how to react, so I followed Leonardo's lead. I bowed slightly and repeated Leonardo's response. Hannibal did the same.

Our greeter smiled and motioned us inside. As I passed, he gave me a curious look. I was dressed as a male, but I could tell that he sensed that something was not quite right.

He looked at Leonardo, bowed again and silently disappeared through the back of the courtyard.

Leonardo turned to Hannibal. In Italian, he said: "You have been welcomed with a traditional Arab greeting, usually reserved for believers. Such a greeting is an honor."

I'm sure my face expressed bewilderment.

Leonardo looked at me and said: "Abdul Azim, whom you just met, serves my friend, Amed al Mukhtar, the master of this house." He paused, smiled and added: "Amed is fluent in both Italian and French."

I gave a sigh of relief. I glanced at Hannibal, who nodded politely to Leonardo. He gave no sign of confusion. His manners are so polished. How does he do it?

Abdul appeared from the shadows. He bowed and motioned us to an enclave at the back of the courtyard. I discreetly slipped off my turban and pulled up my hijab.

Leonardo led the way. As we entered the enclave, I saw intricate carpets on the floor, hanging tapestries and oil lamps that gave off dim light. I sniffed and detected jasmine.

"Exotic and lovely," I thought to myself.

At the back of the enclave, I saw an elderly, bearded, turbaned man in rich flowing robes. He rested comfortably on embroidered cushions. He was reading a book through wire-rimmed spectacles. Several books and scrolls lay among scattered cushions.

The man looked up, laid his book aside and took off his spectacles. "Ah, peace be upon you and welcome to my house," he said in soft, perfect French. "My friend Leonardo has told me about you. I am Amed al Mukhtar."

He motioned us to sit on cushions in front and to the side. Leonardo bowed and found a seat. Hannibal and I followed his lead.

After we were seated, Leonardo said, in French: "Amed, may the blessings of Allah be upon you, please meet my good friends Major Hannibal Jones and Madame Jones."

As Leonardo made the introductions, I carefully observed our host. His eyes twinkled. He looked first at Hannibal, nodded and then stared into my eyes.

"You wear the hijab nicely, Madame Jones," he continued in French. "Thank you for observing our custom."

I nodded politely and returned his gaze. After a moment, I replied: "I am new to your customs; please forgive me if I make errors."

Amed nodded graciously and said: "Your exploits in Europe are known to us."

I looked at Hannibal and then Leonardo. I was glad the veil hid my expression of surprise.

Leonardo smiled and said: "You are known as the malakat alqital al'amrikia, the American fighting queen."

Amed added: "Islam has a long tradition of fighting queens. Our history includes Khawlah bint al-Azwar, our queen who fought the Romans, and Nusaybah bint Ka'ab, who saved the Prophet Mohammad, peace be upon him."

Amed paused and then added: "My tribe welcomes you to our common cause." He turned to Hannibal and continued: "You are most fortunate to have such a life companion."

"Yes," replied Hannibal. She is my right hand, and wields a mighty sword in our cause."

Again, my veil hid my astonishment. I thought: "How does he always know what to say?" To Amed, I nodded and said: "May the blessings of Allah be upon you for your kind words."

"Oh heavens, let my response be appropriate," I thought to myself. I waited for a reaction. Apparently, it was appropriate; all three men smiled.

Silence reigned for a while. Finally, Hannibal asked: "How is it that Father Leonardo and you are friends?" He paused and then added: "Christian and Muslim?"

"We both revere Abraham, peace be upon him, as our common spiritual ancestor," replied Amed. "Muslims also honor and respect Jesus as a messenger of God."

Leonardo added: "We have more in common than our differences." He paused, smiled and continued: "Aside from questions of divinity, there are many paths to God."

"We should all learn from your example," replied Hannibal. He looked intently at Amed and asked: "Would you tell us about the conflict in your country?"

Amed's eyes misted, and he was quiet for several minutes. Finally, he said: "The Italians hanged my brother Omar, September 16, 1931." He paused and added: "Omar, may Allah's blessings be upon him, was the spiritual leader of the Senussi rebellion."

I saw the pain in Amed's eyes. I perceived that his emotions were raw underneath his kindly face. I said softly: "I am so sorry for your loss."

Amed gazed at me for a long moment, smiled wanly, and replied: "Omar was one of many, many thousands from Cyrenaica and elsewhere in Libya who were killed by the fascist Italians. I believe your term is genocide."

"Do you have evidence?" I asked. "Proof would help others justify action against those who committed this terrible crime."

Amed lay back against his cushions, closed his eyes and in a voice just above a whisper, said: "From 1928 through 1932, the fascists operated 16 concentration camps."

After a pause, he continued: "Substantial remnants of the largest six: Soluch, Agedabia, Abyar, El Agheila, Marsa Brega and Sid Ahmedel Maghrun, still exist, along with mass graves and scattered survivors."

He opened his eyes, looked intently at me and then Hannibal and said: "Abdul can take you there." He smiled wistfully and added: "I am too old for such an arduous journey."

"Yusuf could drive," mused Leonardo. He looked at Hannibal.

Hannibal turned to me; the obvious question was in his eyes.

I nodded, turned to Leonardo and said: "When can we start?" Leonardo smiled.

Amed gazed into my eyes and said: "You will have my countenance among the tribes. I will send word."

Amed rose slowly from his seat, bowed and added: "May the blessings of Allah be upon you."

## Friday evening, November 2

According to the local Italian newspaper, King Victor Emmanuel will arrive in Mogadishu tomorrow. I wish him the best; given the unrest in the colonies. Assassination is an ever-present danger.

Hannibal and I will take a different journey. We will accompany Leonardo, Yusuf and Abdul on a clandestine visit to scenes of alleged genocide in Cyrenaica.

We will begin by driving about 60 kilometers to Soluch. According to Leonardo, Omar al Mukhtar was executed at the Soluch camp. We will look for remnants of the camp, take photos and attempt to locate survivors.

Yusuf will drive his decrepit-looking but finely tuned car on the dirt road between Benghazi and Soluch. We will carry food, water, extra petrol, cameras, binoculars, bedrolls and weapons.

Hannibal and I discussed our plans this evening over dinner. Hannibal began the conversation: "A railway parallels the road from Benghazi to Soluch, but it is used almost exclusively by Italians. The road is available to native travelers."

"Danger?" I asked.

"Probably," answered Hannibal. "Senussi rebels have attacked road travelers and even trains along the route. Trains and government truck convoys are protected by Italian colonial troops, and there is a garrison in Soluch."

"I hope Amed gets the word out to the tribes about us and our trip," I responded.

"Our native clothes will help mask our identity as Westerners," Hannibal responded. "However, we may need to explain ourselves if we encounter tribal groups."

He looked at his watch and added: "Better go to bed early; we have to meet Yusuf at Omer's tailor shop at five o'clock in the morning."

## Saturday evening, November 3

We are camped halfway between Benghazi and Soluch. Yusuf built a small fire from dry sticks and what Leonardo said was dried camel dung. Dinner consisted of goat, lentils and rice wrapped in lavash. Yusuf seasoned everything with pepper. The mixture was quite tasty.

I am wrapped in my blankets; the desert is cold at night. I made these diary entries by firelight. Just before dusk, I heard the sound of a train several kilometers in the distance.

Except for the occasional cry of some distant animal or a night bird, we have the desert to ourselves. The stars are very bright away from the lights of the city.

## Late Sunday morning, November 4

I woke up before dawn this morning to the sound of several men speaking Arabic. I also heard animal grunts and groans and the shuffles of many large feet. I sat up with a start. In the pre-dawn light, I saw huge beasts not ten meters away.

I focused my eyes. Camels! I looked wildly around. Hannibal, Leonardo and Yusuf were surrounded by a dozen men in desert attire. I rubbed my eyes. I could see rifles and bandoleers of ammunition. I put my hand on my Walther beneath my clothes.

A man walked over and peered intently at me. His head and face were wrapped in dark cloth; I could only see his eyes. "Malakat alqital al'amrikia," he stated. He then bowed, backed away and returned to the group of men.

More men and camels came up. I lost count at fifty men and at least that many camels.

I got up, covered my head and face with my hijab and walked over to Hannibal. Leonardo was serving as interpreter. Abdul and Yusuf stood by him. Both had looks of awe tinged with fear. A tall man swathed in desert robes appeared to be the leader of the newcomers.

After a minute or so of discussion in Arabic, Leonardo turned to Hannibal and me. "Bedouin from the deep desert," he said. "This is Sheikh Bajes Salah Mohammed abu Rabia of the Al Heuwaitat. His band is from the borderlands near Egypt. He is leading a rescue mission."

Leonardo smiled at my confused expression. "You may call him Sheikh Bajes Salah, his noble title and given name. The rest refers to his ancestry and tribal affiliation."

I looked up at the Sheikh, who was nearly as tall as Hannibal.

He returned my stare with dark, intense, appraising eyes. After a moment, he said: "Malakat alqital al'amrikia, salaam alaykum." He nodded in an aristocratic manner.

"Alaykum salaam," I responded, and bowed slightly deeper than the Sheikh.

Several of the Sheikh's companions chuckled at my pronunciation, but the Sheikh nodded courteously, turned to Leonardo and said: "Tahadath bishakl jayid."

Leonardo turned to me and said: "Well done."

"Rescue?" I asked.

Leonardo turned to the Sheikh, and a long discussion ensued.

After several minutes, Leonardo looked at Hannibal, then me and said: "Sheikh Bajes Saleh and his men are on their way to Soluch. Many of their tribe were captured and taken to the Soluch concentration camp four years ago."

He paused and continued. "Remnants of the tribe thought all had died. Two months ago, a survivor made it to the homeland oasis. Some women and children are being held as slaves by the traitors who work for the Italians."

I looked at Hannibal. Words were unnecessary. I turned to Leonardo and said: "Ask Sheikh Bajes Saleh if we may join him."

Leonardo turned to the Sheikh and translated. Several of his companions heard the conversation. I heard them say: "Alhamd lilhi!"

The Sheikh turned to his companions. After a brief discussion, he turned back to Leonardo smiled and nodded.

Leonardo turned to Hannibal, then me and said: "You are most welcome."

Hannibal, Leonardo, Abdul, the Sheikh and several others began a council of war. I tried to follow the Italian part of the conversation, but got lost in the details. I was able to discern that Yusuf would remain with and hide the car. We would ride camels across the sands to Soluch.

"Saves time, and we will approach the town from an unexpected direction," explained Hannibal. "We will stop a few kilometers from Soluch this afternoon, approach the town at night and be in place by midnight."

"Oh boy," I thought to myself. "Riding a camel?" I looked over at one of the huge beasts. It stared right back and spit in my direction. I recoiled instinctively.

Hannibal saw my expression and chuckled. "Abdul will show us how it's done." Abdul heard, saw my apprehensive looks at the camels, grinned and nodded.

"The Sheikh has a guide with first-hand knowledge of the concentration camp," said Hannibal. "He is that boy over there." Hannibal nodded in the boy's direction. I looked. The boy couldn't have been older than twelve.

The boy saw Hannibal's gesture and smiled.

Hannibal continued: "His name is Salim Baddar. He was the survivor who made it home. He answers to Salim."

The council of war continued. Salim was invited to join. He found a stick and drew a map in the dirt. I watched carefully, along with the Sheikh, Hannibal, Leonardo and several others. I made out the town and a large rectangle nearby.

Leonardo explained as Salim filled in details. "The town is here," he said; and he pointed. "The large rectangle represents the old concentration camp."

He pointed and explained details. "Living huts, guard posts, commandant's house, headquarters building, barracks and mass graveyard."

He paused and then continued: "According to Salim, the garrison occupies the barracks, headquarters and commandant's house. The slaves live in a few nearby huts. The remaining huts are empty."

"What happened to the people?" I asked.

"Except for the slaves, all are dead," replied Leonardo.

"How many slaves?" I asked Leonardo. He turned to the Sheikh and a discussion in Arabic ensued. Leonardo then turned to me and said sadly: "Salim told him that fifty were there when he left. That was two years ago. There may be fewer now."

"How many went to the camp?" I asked.

Leonardo turned to the Sheikh and conversed again in Arabic. After a moment, he turned back to me. His face was ashen, and he said: "According to Sheikh Bajes Saleh, over 20,000 were taken."

I was stunned. I looked at Hannibal. I could see that he had the same reaction. "We must take photos of the mass graveyard," I said softly.

Hannibal nodded and replied: "We also need to look for camp records."

Silence reigned for several minutes. Finally, Hannibal turned his attention to Salim's map and asked: "Where is north?" He looked up into the night sky for a moment, and then pointed to the north star.

Leonardo began a discussion with Salim. The boy had seen Hannibal' point to the sky, and I could see that he understood.

"Probably navigates the desert by the stars," I thought to myself. I watched as Salim drew an arrow in the dirt next to his map. "Bright boy," I concluded.

"How many soldiers in the garrison?" I asked.

Hannibal replied: "According to Salim, about two hundred. However, that was two years ago." He paused and added: "Given the unrest among the tribes, more may have been added."

The Sheikh had fifty experienced desert warriors. Within an hour, the council had settled on a general plan. Details would come later.

The attack and the rescue effort would begin simultaneously. The camels would be kept back in the dunes, and they would be the rendezvous point. Ten warriors would serve as a rear guard as the others escaped into the desert.

I thought a moment and then asked: "When did Salim get to the home oasis?"

Leonardo sighed and said: "Two months ago. The oasis is over eight hundred kilometers from here. Salim spent almost twenty-two months making his way home. If she's still alive, his mother is one of the slaves."

# 42

## BATTLE OF SOLUCH

*Tuesday evening,* November 6, 1934

We are in the sand dunes, about ten kilometers northeast of Soluch. Pre-dawn light tinges the eastern sky. My hands are so cold as I write these words by firelight. Scenes of battle and death sear my memories, along with sinister faces from my past.

Just before midnight yesterday, our band of fighters slipped silently across the sands to a rock outcropping overlooking Soluch, the garrison and the concentration camp. Ten warriors remained with the camels hidden in the dunes. Stars filled the sky, and a full moon shone near zenith.

The warriors moved silently; nothing rattled or clattered in the night. I saw rifles, daggers and a few curved swords. The only sound was the hiss of a breeze across the sand.

I shifted my equipment a little to make sure that I did not disturb the silence. My Walther rested in a holster on a belt at my waist on my right side. My long knife and extra ammunition clips were in a sheath and pouch on my left. I had a small pack on my back with a flashlight, a low light camera and a leather flask of water.

Hannibal moved silently a few steps ahead. He had his forty-five in a shoulder holster. A flashlight, another camera and a water flask were in his backpack. The Sheikh had offered him a rifle earlier, but he declined. He did accept a curved dagger, which he tucked in his belt.

411

Hannibal, Leonardo and the Sheikh lay on the rocks and peered through binoculars over the rock outcropping. They were accompanied by little Salim, who whispered and pointed out details in the scene below.

I looked past Hannibal. Lights from Soluch glowed half a kilometer to the right. The garrison and abandoned concentration camp spread out just a few hundred meters directly in front and below.

The garrison included an occupied barracks, a headquarters building and what appeared to be a commandant's house. Lights were on in the barracks and house; the headquarters building was dark.

A two-and a half-meter-high mud brick wall surrounded the garrison buildings, forming an enclosed compound. I could see a step for riflemen on the inside of the wall on the far side. A few sentries paced back and forth near corner guard posts and postern doors in the wall.

The concentration camp was a vast, ordered array of huts adjacent to the garrison compound. A few lights gleamed in huts near the wall by the barracks, the rest were dark. "Slave quarters," I concluded. "The focus of our rescue effort."

I squinted my eyes and looked intently at a large building between the garrison and the town. Lights gleamed around a freight yard, and I spotted a locomotive and a string of passenger and freight cars. Light glowed through the windows from one of the passenger cars. I moved forward, nudged Hannibal and pointed.

Hannibal nodded and whispered: "Probably visitors to the garrison. The freight cars carried supplies; I can see loaded carts at the siding."

Sheikh Bajes Saleh assigned his warriors to three battle groups. Ten were assigned to Leonardo, Salim and me for the rescue effort.

Hannibal, Abdul and five others would silence the sentries. After the sentries were down, Hannibal would use his flashlight to signal the Sheikh. Hannibal and his men would then enter the postern doors and slip into the headquarters building. Inside, they would look for records.

After the signal, the Sheikh would lead the remaining twenty-five over the wall and prepare for an attack on the barracks and commandant's house.

Leonardo, Salim and my group would follow the Sheikh's group and go to the slave huts outside the wall. If we were lucky, my group could get the occupants of the slave huts out before any alarm.

I would signal with my flashlight once we were out, and the Sheikh would attack. If an alarm happened during the rescue or during the occupation of the headquarters, the Sheikh would attack immediately.

Once the slaves left the camp, I planned to return with Salim to visit the mass graves. With luck, we could use my camera and flashlight to take photos.

Everyone would rendezvous at the location of the camels. The camel guard would cover our retreat and join the main group in the desert as soon as they could.

Such was the plan. However, events turned out differently.

At midnight, Hannibal and his men moved silently down the rocky hill. I could see them as they used the sparse cover to approach the sentries just outside the compound wall.

Soon it was done: swiftly, silently and deadly. Hannibal signaled with his flashlight.

The Sheikh and his men were next. I marveled at how efficiently they scaled the wall or entered the postern doors.

We were next. Salim led the way. I tried to be as silent as the little boy; who flitted between rocks and sand dunes. I succeeded, more or less. Leonardo followed, along with my ten warriors.

Within a minute, we were at the wall. The nearest hut was fifty meters beyond, across open ground.

"If Hannibal and his men got all of the sentries, we should be OK," I thought to myself. I turned, gave a hand signal and then ran across the open space. Salim ran in front. Leonardo and the men followed. Leonardo joined me; the others fanned out to the nearest dozen huts.

A light flickered through a window in the nearest hut. Salim made it through the rag-covered doorway first. I followed. I heard him exclaim: "al'umu al'iinath!" as he scurried about in the shadows. I blinked and focused my eyes in the candlelight.

I glanced around the room. I saw a firepit, a few pots, items of clothing and a dirt floor.

Within seconds, I heard a scuffling sound and a clatter of something falling. Someone moved in the shadows. A voice responded to Salim's outcry. "Salim!"

Leonardo stepped up beside me and said hoarsely: "The boy has found his mother!"

I heard frantic voices outside. Leonardo looked back through the doorway. He turned back to me and said: "Our men have entered the other huts. They are gathering women and a few children outside."

A woman, dressed in rags, moved from the shadows inside my hut. Salim helped her; she moved unsteadily. Her face, once beautiful, was drawn and haggard. She saw me, and her eyes opened wide. Other faces appeared out of the shadows.

Salim looked up at me, tried to smile and said: "al'umu al'iinath."

Pop, pop, pop! Pistol shots! I recognized the heavy sound of Hannibal's forty-five. A fusillade of rifle fire followed. Shouts of command rang out. The firing became general, punctuated by screams of agony.

"Come with me!" I shouted in Italian. I waved to the doorway. Leonardo translated. Six women joined Salim and his mother.

I drew my pistol, moved through the doorway, turned and motioned urgently to Salim and the women.

I turned again and faced the compound. The firing from inside the compound became a steady roar. Bullets clicked and whined as they struck the mud brick walls of the huts.

Leonardo joined me, followed by Salim and the others. Above the din, I shouted: "Tell five of the men to find women and children and take them to the rendezvous point. Five stay with me!" Leonardo translated, and the men obeyed.

Aided by five warriors, at least thirty women and a few children stumbled and scrambled toward the rocks and dunes.

I turned to my men. They looked at me expectantly. One exclaimed: "Almalika!"

I motioned for them to spread out and pointed toward the postern door in the compound wall. Without a spoken word, they understood. Within seconds, they formed a firing line, ten paces apart, facing the door.

We didn't have a long wait. I heard shouts of command inside the compound. The words were Italian. "There are more outside! Through the door and over the wall!"

Dozens of men in colonial uniforms streamed through the postern door and over the wall. Two officers came through the door, waving swords and firing their pistols in my direction.

I ran forward to a position slightly in front of my firing line, dropped to one knee and began firing. Pop, pop, pop!

Men fell, including one of the officers. My warriors fired, and more men dropped. Some screamed and rolled in the sand. Others lay silent.

I glanced side to side. Two of my warriors dropped without making a sound.

At least two dozen soldiers closed the gap. There were too many.

No time! I emptied my pistol and shoved it in my holster. I drew my knife and assumed a knife fighter's stance.

I faced three men running toward me. Others swarmed to my left and right. The fight became a general, deadly melee'.

The remaining officer closed and swung his sword in a sweeping arc. I ducked and brought my knife up and into his abdomen. He groaned and dropped.

In front, a rifle with a bayonet entered my vision. I parried with my left arm and slashed with the knife in my right hand. Blood spurted from the man's face, and he fell back.

The third man had better luck. His bayonet pierced my robe and hit my ammo pouch. I pivoted counter-clockwise to my left and slashed with my knife. Blood spurted. The man screamed and staggered away.

I glanced frantically around. All of my men were down, including Leonardo.

True to his calling, Leonardo was unarmed. Yet he bravely followed me into battle. "Why?" My thoughts raced. "Later, Caroline," my thoughts concluded.

Leonardo rose to his knees. Blood dripped from his wounded left arm.

For a moment, our remaining opponents busied themselves bayoneting my fallen warriors. I saw my chance.

I grabbed under Leonardo's right arm with my left hand and pulled up. He rose unsteadily.

"Run!" I shouted. Leonardo nodded and we ran and stumbled around the side of the hut and out into the rocks and sand dunes.

For the moment, we were alone. As we ran, I shoved my knife into its sheath, pulled a fresh ammunition clip from my pouch and reloaded my pistol.

We made it into the dunes. I heard a shout behind; we were being chased.

I spotted two figures in the sand near some boulders just ahead. It was Salim and his mother. I could see that the mother had fallen, too weak to rise.

Salim stood in front, protecting her. He had a dagger. His face expressed both fear and fierce determination.

"Salim!" I shouted. He recognized me, and his face broke into a smile.

He shouted back: "Almalika!" He lowered his dagger.

Shouts from behind grew closer and louder. I looked back. Six colonial soldiers appeared from the dunes. Several fired rifles and pistols. Bullets whizzed by.

"Oh!" I turned to the sound. Salim sprawled on his back. He didn't move. His mother screamed.

"Take the mother!" I shouted to Leonardo.

Leonardo reached around the mother's waist with his good arm and the pair stumbled off into the dunes.

I turned and faced my opponents. A blood-red film descended over my vision. I gave out an animal scream and charged.

Time stood still. I emptied my pistol as I ran. Men fell. I drew my knife and slashed.

Silence. I looked around. Six men were down. Several moved and groaned, others lay still.

Thoughts crept up through my slowly ebbing fury. "What have I become?" I saw a dark abyss, and I was falling. I closed my mind's eye and forced my thoughts to the present. The red film over my vision slowly cleared.

I looked at Salim, lying on the sand. Leonardo and the mother were gone. The firing from the compound had stopped. Then, Salim moved.

I ran over and knelt beside the boy. He opened his eyes, groaned and moved his hand to his chest.

I pulled back his clothing and peered intently. I saw a thick leather pouch on a string around his neck. The pouch had a bullet hole.

I turned the pouch over, no exit hole. I opened it. A thick book, about ten centimeters square, lay inside. A pistol bullet had penetrated about halfway through the book. The bullet fell out.

I looked at Salim's bare chest. He had a nasty bruise. I looked at his face. He smiled wanly and uttered: "Almalika."

I returned the smile. Tears formed in my eyes.

I heard sounds in the dunes. I rose and raised my pistol.

"Caroline!" It was Hannibal's voice. Hannibal, Abdul and the Sheikh strode into view. I holstered my pistol and sheathed my knife.

Hannibal's face expressed intense concern. "Are you hurt?" he asked.

I took a deep breath and let it out slowly. "No," I finally replied. My mind cleared. "I lost five of my men," I added.

Hannibal looked down at Salim, who rose unsteadily to his feet. Hannibal turned back to me and said: "You saved thirty-five women and children."

I tried to smile. I thought a moment, then asked: "Our casualties?"

Hannibal thought a moment and then said: "Fifteen dead, including your men. We also have ten wounded, including Leonardo." He smiled and added: "All will recover."

"Evidence from the camp?" I asked.

"Records and photos," replied Hannibal with an expression of satisfaction. He smiled and added: "Since you were busy, I also found the mass graveyard and took photos." He motioned to Abdul and concluded: "Abdul held my flashlight. I think the photos will be good."

I looked over at Abdul and the Sheikh. They were staring at the six bodies in the sand around me. The Sheikh turned his gaze to me, bowed and said: "Almalika," in a tone of deep respect.

"The garrison?" I asked.

"I estimate that over 150 died," replied Hannibal. "Some were wounded, but the Sheikh and his men finished them." He sighed and added: "About fifty ran to the train station. We didn't follow."

I looked intently at Hannibal's face. I could tell that there was something else. "And?" I asked.

After a moment, he replied: "I saw Raeder on the well-lit train station platform. He was in a German uniform. Along with Italian officers, he organized a defense, including machine guns. We had the cover of the garrison walls, so they didn't fire."

He paused and then added: "Raeder was watching us through binoculars."

"Oh!" I exclaimed.

"There's more," said Hannibal. "I saw a scar-faced man on the step at the back of one of the passenger cars. I looked through my binoculars. It was Villian."

### Saturday evening, November 10

The events following the battle of Soluch blur in my mind. I remember an endless walk alongside camels through the sand, groans of wounded on litters and voices of grateful women and children. Somehow, we made it to Yusuf and the car.

Hannibal, Leonardo, Abdul, Yusuf and I parted from Sheikh Bajes Salah Mohammed abu Rabia of the Al Heuwaitat and his band when we reached the car.

The Sheikh came over to me, stood quietly for a moment, then said: "Malakat alqital al'amrikia, salaam alaykum," as he gestured with his hand and bowed. His eyes said more than his words.

"Alaykum salaam," I responded. I put my right hand over my heart and bowed in return.

Little Salim stood by the Sheikh, grinning from ear to ear. He had a well-earned dagger in his belt.

The Sheikh looked down, smiled and said: "salaa allah ealayh wasalam."

Leonardo, his left arm in a sling, stepped up by me and said softly: "The Sheikh said: 'May God bless him and grant him peace.' I think Salim is his grandson."

I knelt in front of Salim and opened my arms.

"Almalika," Salim uttered. He stepped forward and threw his arms around my neck.

Tears came to my eyes, and I sobbed for a moment. I could see Salim's mother on a litter behind Salim and the Sheikh. She smiled, put her hands together in a prayerful fashion and nodded.

I stood up. Salim ran to his mother. The Sheikh was already among his men, giving orders. The camels were packed and litters arranged. Men moved about with efficient, quiet purpose. A long journey lay ahead.

Hannibal and Leonardo joined the Sheikh near the camels. They had a long discussion. I really didn't care; I was exhausted.

With as much dignity as I could muster, I walked unsteadily to the car. Yusuf helped me get into the back seat. He put a robe under my head for a pillow and another over my body.

I don't remember anything about the drive back to Benghazi, except for fitful dreams of scar-faced Villian and snarling, intense Raeder.

# 43

## PRELUDE TO VENGEANCE

*Sunday morning, November 18, 1934*

I woke up to the sound of church bells. I opened my eyes. Light streamed through white gauze curtains over the bedroom window. The room was cool but comfortable. I heard Hannibal's voice, speaking to someone. Comprehension came slowly.

"We arrived at the hotel from the desert last Thursday," my thoughts began. "I hear the bells of Benghazi Cathedral, so it's Sunday."

Recent events in the desert seem like a dream.

Hannibal appeared in the doorway. He was fully dressed in colonial khaki. "Coffee's ready," he said with a smile. "So is room service breakfast."

I took a deep breath, stretched, blinked and smiled. "Wonderful," I said. "I'll be out in a few minutes." Hannibal nodded, turned and walked back into the parlor.

I rolled out of bed and walked slowly into the bathroom. It took a while, but I did all of the usual. I dressed in form-fitting khaki pants, high-topped boots, a white blouse and a stylish bush jacket. A knotted yellow silk scarf around my neck added a jaunty look.

"So different than my clothes in the desert," I mused. Visions of the battle tried to surface, but I firmly decided to concentrate on the present. I sauntered into the parlor, showing off my new outfit.

Hannibal was sitting in an easy chair, sipping coffee. He looked up, smiled and said: "Very nice." He lifted his cup and asked: "Want some?"

"Yes, please," I responded. I walked over, kissed him on the cheek and then sat on the nearby sofa. Hannibal poured coffee and brought it over.

After a few sips, I smelled eggs, toast and fresh fruit. I looked over at a portable table with white linen and two chairs. Orange juice and covered dishes rested on top of the linen.

Hannibal saw my glance, got up and pulled back a chair. I rose from the sofa, walked over and sat down. Breakfast was delicious. Afterwards, we adjourned to the sofa with coffee.

Hannibal began the conversation. "I delivered our hand-written report and photos to the French Consulate last Thursday morning. It left for Paris and Soucet in a diplomatic pouch that evening."

I thought a moment, then asked: "What about a report to Fabri in Siena?"

"Already done through Leonardo," replied Hannibal. "I provided an edited version of our report to Soucet, including photos of the mass graves." He paused and added: "Leonardo added his own narrative and sent a package directly to Fabri."

"Good," I responded. "Any local news about the fight at Soluch on November 5?"

Hannibal nodded and replied: "The Benghazi Italian newspaper carried a second page article about Soluch." He smiled and added: "The King's visit to the colonies made the headlines."

"Details on the battle?" I asked.

"Sketchy," said Hannibal. "The raid was attributed to Senussi rebels. According to the article, the raid was beaten off with light casualties. There was no mention of the slaves."

His smile broadened, and he added: "The article did mention that international visitors to Soluch, including a German officer, helped organize the defense of travelers at the railroad station."

"Raeder!" I exclaimed.

"Yes," replied Hannibal. "Apparently, he was a hero."

I sipped my coffee for a while. Finally, I asked: "Do you think Raeder and Villian recognized us?"

Hannibal thought a moment and then said: "I doubt it. We were wearing native clothing, it was night, and we were at least 200 meters away in the dark."

"Still, they know we are in Benghazi," I replied.

"Most likely," agreed Hannibal. "Anyway, we accomplished our mission here."

He paused and added: "I picked up a telegram from Soucet this morning at the hotel front desk." He took a piece of paper from his bush jacket pocket and handed it to me.

Soucet's telegram read as follows: 'Excellent work. Evidence forwarded to appropriate authorities, including British. Leave Benghazi immediately. Risks very high.'

I put the telegram on the coffee table and said: "Soucet is reacting to our reference to Raeder and Villian in our report. Interesting that the French informed the British." I paused, looked at Hannibal intently and asked: "Shall we continue to Mogadishu?"

Hannibal returned my gaze and said: "We do have unfinished business." He raised his eyebrows and waited for my response.

"Let's do it," I replied. "When can we leave?"

"Tomorrow morning," responded Hannibal with a smile. "I anticipated your response. I contacted Al Littorio Airlines on Saturday."

"OK, Smarty," I replied. "I'll pack after we finish our coffee."

I took another sip of coffee, thought a moment and asked: "Raeder and Villian?"

Haven't seen them since Soluch," replied Hannibal. He thought a moment and then added: "They are bound to turn up here soon. The quicker we leave, the better."

"Maybe they won't expect us to go to Mogadishu," I said tentatively.

"Perhaps," replied Hannibal with a frown. "Eventually, they will check with this hotel and then Al Littorio."

"Yes," I mused. "We could follow up with the priest in Mogadishu whose name is on Fabri's list." I thought a moment and then added: "Italian plans for colonial expansion in Ethiopia should be our focus."

"Agreed," replied Hannibal. "According to the Benghazi Italian newspapers, King Victor Emanuel finished his visit to Mogadishu November 11. He left safely. The fascists will need another propaganda excuse for invasion."

### Monday morning, November 19

I have a few minutes to make entries in this diary. Hannibal and I leave for the airport in an hour for a flight to Mogadishu.

We have stops in Cairo, Wadi Halfa, Khartoum, Cassala and Asmara. With stopovers, the trip will take five days. In addition to Al Littorio, several legs of the journey will be on British Imperial Airways.

The route is still experimental, but all of our airplanes will be land-based trimotors, thank heaven. I don't want to experience another water landing with a floatplane.

Hannibal scouted the lobby before our light breakfast. He returned to our suite and reported that according to the front desk clerk, no one had asked about us.

"We may get to the airport and our flight without being spotted by Raeder and Villian," he said.

### Saturday afternoon, November 24

Hannibal and I arrived at Mogadishu Patrella Airport this morning. The flights and stopovers took forever. After customs, we took a taxi from the airport to the new Albergo Croce de Sud Hotel.

As usual, Hannibal handled the check-in. Our suite is very nice, and I am exhausted. Hannibal said he will go on a scouting expedition around town while I make these diary entries and take a nap.

## Sunday evening, November 25

Yesterday, Hannibal bought the Friday and Saturday editions of the *Somalia Fascista*, the Mogadishu Italian newspaper. We read them over coffee this morning in our room. The newspapers had a series of articles on what the editors called: 'the Welwel Incident.'

Hannibal looked up from his reading and said: "According to this article, on November 23, 500 Italian colonial troops at the Welwel Oasis fort were attacked by 1,500 Ethiopian troops. The battle is on-going, and casualties are mounting on both sides."

"Humm," I responded. "This article says that the battle is being observed by British commissioners tasked with surveying the boundary between British Somaliland and Ethiopia."

I paused, read more and then added: "The British are encamped at Ado, about 30 kilometers away from Welwel."

We both read in silence. After a while, I looked up and said: "This newspaper editor clamors for war." I paused and then added: "The Italians have their propaganda incident."

"So, it would seem," Hannibal responded.

Hannibal was quiet for several minutes. Finally, he said: "The French, and now the British, have our evidence about Italian atrocities in Libya."

"Yes," I replied. "Also, Marshal De Bono, General Badoglio and General Graziani, the main leaders with regard to the Libyan atrocities, now lead troop concentrations in Italian Eritrea and Somaliland."

"The stage is being set," mused Hannibal. "Italian invasion of Ethiopia is just a matter of time."

"I wonder what the French and the British will do," I replied.

"If they oppose Mussolini's Ethiopian adventure, they risk pushing him toward closer relations with Hitler," answered Hannibal.

"Humm," I responded. "I wonder if preparations for war include concentration camps in Italian Eritrea and Somaliland?"

"It's worth checking out," replied Hannibal. "Perhaps Father Francesco, our Mogadishu contact, can shed light on the subject."

### Tuesday morning, November 27

Hannibal and I met with Father Francesco at the new Mogadishu Cathedral yesterday. The gothic-style building has triple arches and identical twin towers on the front. The façade is made from mottled brown stones that seem to glow in the morning sunlight.

"Beautiful," I said, as Hannibal and I approached through the surrounding manicured gardens, palm trees and lawns.

"The largest Roman Catholic cathedral in Africa," responded Hannibal. "Like Benghazi, the place is run by the Franciscans." He paused and added: "Another Mussolini showcase."

We went inside. Hannibal asked an accommodating attendant for Father Francesco. The man bowed, turned and walked silently down a long corridor parallel to the main nave. He turned a corner to the left and disappeared.

We waited just inside the main door. The place was cool and dimly lit from stained glass windows above. I shivered a little, but not from the cold. Somehow, the place seemed artificial in this exotic African country, like the rest of Mussolini's colonial additions.

A few minutes later, a middle-aged priest approached. "I am Father Francesco," he said. "How can I help you?"

Hannibal handled the introductions and gave Francesco a letter from Fabri.

Francesco read the letter, smiled and said: "We have much to discuss. Please follow me."

He led us down the corridor. We turned the corner to the left and entered an administrative wing. We arrived at a small, private office. Francesco opened the door, smiled and motioned us inside.

I looked around. The office had sparse furnishings but lots of books on shelves. Francesco had a desk, a few comfortable looking chairs and religious hangings on the walls. Light streamed in from two windows.

"Simple, functional and not ostentatious, unlike Europe," I thought to myself. Francesco's office, at least, felt genuine, not artificial.

Soon we were seated. Francesco offered us tea, which he fixed from hot water and loose tea in a pot and tea strainers on our cups.

After we were comfortable, I observed our host. I could tell that he was also appraising us. Finally, he said: "I received a letter from Father Leonardo just yesterday. I know what you accomplished in Libya."

Hannibal took a deep breath, let it out and said: "We need your help with regard to concentration camps in Eritrea and Somaliland." He paused and added: "Fabri and others need evidence."

"I have heard of a camp on the Island of Nocra," replied Francesco. "Also, some of my parishioners work in construction, and they told me about plans for a camp at Danane, which is a town on the coast about a hundred kilometers southwest of Mogadishu."

"A new camp?" I queried.

Francesco looked at me for a moment, sighed and replied: "It's one of many preparations for war."

"If I remember my geography correctly, Nocra is in the Red Sea, over 80 kilometers off the coast from Massawa," said Hannibal.

"Yes," replied Francesco. "Except for Italian officials and prisoners, a trip there would be nearly impossible."

"How about Danane?" I asked.

"Accessible by dirt road along the coast," replied Francesco. "I know someone who could take us there. His name is Abram, and he is a native Christian. He worked at the camp earlier this year. He quit when he discovered its future purpose."

I looked at Hannibal. After a moment, I said: "We could collect evidence of its intended use."

"Humm," responded Hannibal. "Site construction papers might somehow become available." He looked at me and grinned. "We can also take photos."

We both turned to Francesco, who smiled and said: "Let's work out the details."

# 44

## SHE-DEVIL

*Saturday night, December 1, 1934*

Another diary entry by firelight: Hannibal, Francesco, Abram and I have a hidden camp just off the coastal dirt road. We passed the town of Oreale, and I can see the lights of Marka, a seaport town, just ahead.

I can hear the surf of the Indian Ocean, about a hundred meters to the east. The temperature seems moderate, but the wind off the sea is cold and damp. My fire consumes a few sticks of wood and dried dung. The odor is indescribable. Still, heat is a good thing.

Francesco told us that the port in Marka supplies construction materials to the Danane camp. Lorry convoys travel from the port to Danane, which is about forty kilometers southwest along the coast.

No accommodations for travelers exist between Mogadishu and Danane. We are a self-contained and fully-supplied unit, and we are ready for clandestine operations.

We have a decrepit-looking Fiat 521C for transport, bedrolls, food for five days, cans of water and petrol and of course, weapons and ammunition. In addition, Hannibal and I have backpacks with low-light cameras, a telephoto lens and flashlights.

According to Abram, the Danane site has a cluster of buildings under construction and about a hundred tents for workers. The site is littered with stacks of materials and supplies, and a motorpool area has dozens of lorries and construction equipment.

The camp occupants include Italian administrators, engineers and skilled workmen. It also has local laborers and a few colonial troops for guards.

Abram said that security was lax when he worked there; the guards were mostly concerned about theft of supplies by the native workers.

Abram also said that Danane is an arid, inhospitable place. The landscape has sparse scrub trees, dense bushes and no fresh water, except seasonal tributaries to the Shebell River, which is about 30 kilometers north of the site. Water, kept in large tanks, requires constant re-supply from the port.

We will pass west of Marka before dawn and hide in the scrub. Our immediate objective will be to observe the convoys from the port to Danane and take photos. After nightfall, we will continue on to Danane.

Once near the site, we will reconnoiter the camp and take photos. Under the cover of darkness, we hope to sneak into the camp, enter the administrative tents and buildings and take photos of documents.

Once we have our information, we will use the cover of darkness to head back past Marka. Afterwards, we hope to be on the road back to Mogadishu.

## Tuesday morning, December 4

Success! We have photos of convoys and the layout of the construction site. Most important, we have photos of documents that provide details on construction and intended use for the site.

We obtained photos when we burglarized the headquarters tent Sunday night. The workers had all gone to bed, even the guards.

However, as Hannibal and I slipped out of the camp, lights came on in the headquarters tent. We heard a cry of alarm, but we made it to the car and escaped down the road in the dark.

*Saturday evening, December 15*

On December 5, our trip back toward Mogadishu became a nightmare. The nightmare lasted ten days, and I am just beginning to sort out events in my tortured mind.

That morning, dawn was beginning to show pink at the horizon out over the ocean. We stopped about five kilometers from Oreale and pulled off the road into the scrub. The sea pounded below a thirty-meter cliff behind our camp.

We could see the road. The best view was from a hidden spot at the top of the cliff.

Nothing moved. Satisfied, we settled in for the daylight hours. We planned to pass around Oreale the following night. It didn't turn out that way.

Abram was first on watch. He found a spot near the top of the cliff. Hannibal, Francesco and I settled in our bedrolls next to the car. We were all exhausted.

Gunfire! Bullets struck the car and the bushes all around. I heard "Ahee!" from the top of the cliff. I rose to a sitting position. I saw Abram rise up and fall.

"Take cover!" Hannibal yelled. "Ambush! Rifle fire!"

Abram continued to scream in agony. Hannibal scrambled through the bushes toward Abram. Francesco and I flattened ourselves behind the car, which continued to take hits from the rifles.

I peered around the edge of the car for a couple of seconds, then ducked back. Many men appeared in the bushes across the road.

My mind raced. "Two hundred meters; my pistol won't be effective," I surmised. I looked over at Francesco. He was wide-eyed and muttering prayers to Saint Mary. "Stay down!" I yelled.

I turned toward Hannibal on the cliff. I saw him pull Abram up and half-drag him toward boulders at the cliff edge. More rifle fire, and both men fell over the edge.

"Hannibal!" I screamed. I rose up and raced toward the cliff. Rifles cracked, and bullets clipped bushes all around. In seconds, I made it to the boulders, got behind them and peered over the edge of the cliff.

I wasn't hit, but I didn't care. "Hannibal!" I yelled. "Oh God, no!"

I saw Abram sprawled, face up, on the rocks thirty meters below. Blood smeared on the rocks behind his head.

I looked frantically around. Surf pounded and thundered in the rocks. Hannibal was not there.

Bullets clipped and whined on the boulders. I heard distant commands. I peered between two boulders toward the road. I saw a man in Nazi uniform and a dozen colonial soldiers.

Raeder! He saw me. His face twisted into demonic grin.

I looked again. The soldiers were streaming across the road, firing as they came. Raeder was directly behind them.

I looked over toward the car, just in time to see Francesco rise up a little. He was instantly hit with a fusillade of rifle fire. He fell back and lay still. I was alone.

I scrambled to the right, parallel to the cliff edge, for a hundred meters. Bushes hid me from the view of the soldiers; at least I couldn't see them. I stopped and crouched behind some bushes.

I heard the voices of the soldiers as they reached the cliff. Much yelling occurred. Rifle fire continued. Raeder's voice rose above the noise. The firing stopped.

I forced myself to think. "Hannibal is gone." The thought boiled to the surface, along with an anguished moan. "Not now!" I forced my thoughts to the present. Rage took over, and red film covered my vision.

"Get behind them, get close and attack," I concluded through my rage. I had no thought of escape or risks. "Oh Hannibal," I moaned. Again, I forced my grief down. I wanted to kill.

I rose up slightly. The road seemed clear. I scrambled, crouching, through the bushes. As I crossed the road, I saw another car in the distance, perhaps 500 meters in the direction of Mogadishu.

I ran up a small hill where I could see down to the road and over to the cliff.

I watched the soldiers as all but two returned to the road. They gave no indication that they saw me. "They think I fell over the cliff," I guessed. "Good. I have an advantage."

Two lorries came into view from the direction of Danane. They stopped, one behind the other. The soldiers gathered around.

The car in the direction of Mogadishu stopped. I watched as it pulled off into the bushes about two hundred meters away.

The sun peeked above the ocean horizon. Through my vision, the sun seemed blood red. "Time for inventory," I thought to myself. "I have my pistol, a pouch with three extra loaded clips, and my knife."

My thoughts continued: "Attack while they are off guard."

My mind made up, I slipped through the bushes, down the hill, toward the road. The soldiers, including Raeder, were milling about the two lorries. Raeder was trying to calm his excited companions, with limited results.

"They think they have won," I thought to myself. I felt a grim smile distort my face. "They are about to find out differently." I took my Walther out of its holster and loosened the snap on my knife sheath.

I moved through the bushes parallel to the road, to the right, for about fifty meters. I then ran to the bushes a dozen meters from the lorries. I crouched and listened. Laughter continued from the direction of the lorries. "Not spotted," I concluded. "Time to get close."

In a silent rush, I made it to the back of one of the lorries. I had my pistol in my right hand and an extra clip in my left. On my right, two soldiers sauntered around the lorry.

They saw me. Their eyes widened. It was their last sight. I fired twice. Both dropped like stones. I ran around the lorry to the left. Four soldiers and two drivers stood at the back of the second lorry. Just as they turned, I fired four times.

All four soldiers fell. One screamed in agony. I ejected my empty clip, slammed in the second and fired once. The screaming stopped. The two drivers fumbled for pistols in their belts. I shot them both.

"Eight down, six to go, plus Raeder," my thoughts raced. My rage boiled as I ran around the side of the second lorry. Raeder was there, with four soldiers. He saw me and yelled. All four soldiers raised their rifles. Raeder fumbled for his pistol with his left hand.

"Right hand no good," my thoughts continued with satisfaction. "Thanks to Hannibal's shot in Berlin."

I ignored the raised rifles, dropped to my knees, smiled at Raeder, and fired.

Raeder dropped his pistol, clutched at his shoulder, screamed and ran toward the cliff.

Bewildered, his four soldiers glanced at their fleeing leader, then back to me. Two of them fired. I heard a 'snick' as one of the bullets whizzed past my left ear. The other shot went wild.

They missed, I didn't. Two shots and two men down. I reloaded with my last clip and shot the last two soldiers by the lorry. I looked up toward the cliff. The remaining two soldiers stood there, mouths open, as Raeder ran toward them, shouting in German.

"Good," I thought with satisfaction. He forgot to speak in Italian." I raced up the hill after him.

I fired one shot at the two soldiers, and they ducked behind the boulders near the edge of the cliff.

I had three shots left. I ran toward the cliff. Raeder reached the cliff, turned and fell back against the nearest boulder. His face expressed wide-eyed terror.

The remaining two soldiers stepped out from the boulders, their hands in the air. Their faces expressed abject terror. I'm sure they thought they had met a she-devil incarnate. They were probably right; a dozen of their companions lay dead.

"Resa! Resa!" They exclaimed.

"Surrender is a very good idea," I translated in my mind. I glanced back at Raeder, who cowered against the rocks, and then at the two terrorized soldiers. I kept my pistol aimed at Raeder.

"Fuggire!" I uttered. The two soldiers looked at me, then Raeder and finally at each other.

"Since I told them to run, I won't shoot them," my thoughts continued. The pair turned and scrambled through the brush. I didn't care where they went.

I concentrated on Raeder. His face had a pleading look. His good left hand clutched his bleeding shoulder. I slowly put my pistol in its holster and drew my knife.

I held my knife point up so Raeder could see. My rage boiled, and the red film across my vision grew more intense.

I thought of Hannibal as he fell over the cliff. The faces of the dead Francesco and Abram flashed in my vision. I imagined slashing, stabbing and cutting Raeder's hideous face. I stepped forward.

Raeder cried out: "No! No!"

Bang! Bang! Raeder's face dissolved into a bloody mess. He slumped down and fell over.

I spun around. Villian stood there, pistol in hand.

# 45

## BACK FROM THE ABYSS

Events on December 5 are slowly coming into focus. Villian had just shot Raeder, and I stood, staring, trying to comprehend.

Villian had the advantage; his pistol was out and ready. Going for my pistol in its holster would be fatal. I had my knife in hand, but I was too far away for knife fighting.

Villian smiled grimly. In perfect, formal English, he said: "We meet at last, Mrs. Caroline Case Jones." He paused, put away his pistol and added: "I have followed your exploits since Berlin."

I didn't know what to say. I dropped my knife. Finally, I stuttered, and in a plaintive voice cried out: "Hannibal!" I felt utterly alone and defeated. I fell to my knees and sobbed uncontrollably.

After several minutes, I regained control; wiped tears on my sleeve and rose to my feet. Villian was still there, watching. I looked into his eyes, and they expressed sympathy.

I took a deep breath, let it out slowly and asked: "Why?"

Villian said: "Good question." His smile broadened a little, and he added: "The answer is complicated." He glanced toward the cliff, then turned back to me and said: "Shall we find your husband first?"

An image of Abram's shattered body on the rocks below the cliff leaped into my consciousness. I focused my thoughts on Hannibal. "He wasn't on the rocks below the cliff," I said. "But I saw him fall."

"Let's find him," responded Villian. His eyes held steady; there was no malice in them.

I picked up my knife, put it in its sheath, rose up and made my way past Raeder's body toward the cliff edge. I paid no further heed to Villian. I had to know about Hannibal.

I lay down at the cliff edge and stretched out as far as I could without falling. Abram's body was gone; the rising tide had washed it away.

I felt Villian's presence as he slipped up beside me and looked down.

"Abram was there," I said as I pointed. Waves surged over the rocks below. I inched out a little further and looked down the face of the cliff. Bushes and small trees grew here and there. The long branches of one tree, directly below, moved slightly.

"See?" I exclaimed.

Villian responded: "Yes. We need to get down there."

"How?" I asked.

Villian was quiet for a minute or so. Finally, he said: "I saw a winch on the front of one of the lorries. I have used them before."

My thoughts raced and a plan formed. "Let's drive the lorry as close to the cliff edge as we can. I don't know how to operate a winch, so you will have to lower me over the cliff on the winch cable."

Villian nodded, and I could see that he understood what I had in mind. Without another word, we hurried down toward the lorries by the road.

I forced my mind to ignore the bodies strewn around the lorries. Within a few minutes, Villian had driven the lorry with a winch, with many bounces, stops, retries and lurches, to within a few meters of the cliff edge.

Villian got out of the lorry cab. He left the engine running. Over the noise of the engine, he said: "The engine turns a generator, the generator charges batteries and the batteries run the winch DC motor."

The end of the winch cable had a steel hook. Villian reached over to the winch, flipped a lever, and the cable released and spun off the spool a little. Villian pulled the cable out a few meters and wrapped it around my waist twice. He then slipped the hook over the cable and pulled the cable snug.

He flipped the lever again and engaged the motor. "Ready," he said.

Villian operated the winch, and I lowered slowly over the cliff's edge.

About ten meters down, I found Hannibal caught at the base of a tree against the cliff face. I could see that he had struck the sturdy top limbs during his fall, and the limbs had guided him to the cliff face.

I yelled up to Villian: "Stop!" My body stopped in its descent, and I swung gently back and forth.

Hannibal was wedged tightly, but his body moved spasmodically, and he groaned. "Alive!" I exclaimed. Relief and joy caused my entire body to tremble.

Villian answered, but I didn't heed the words. My attention focused on Hannibal. He appeared semi-conscious. I saw blood. He groaned.

I swung myself back and forth and finally over to Hannibal. I grabbed the tree and found a perch.

After I made myself secure, I yelled: "Slack!" Villian responded, and soon I had a couple of meters of slack cable. I then unwrapped the cable from my body and secured it around Hannibal's lower body and then his chest, under his arms.

I slipped the hook on the cable so that it pulled on his body above his center of gravity. I checked my work, held on to Hannibal and the cable and called out to Villian: "Ready! Pull us up!" Slowly, with many bumps and swings, we inched up the cliff.

Villian helped me at the top. We unfastened the cable and half-carried, half-dragged Hannibal down to our disheveled camp site. For the moment, I ignored Francesco's body and our bullet-riddled car and concentrated on the severely wounded Hannibal.

Hannibal had a nasty gash on his forehead and blood seeped from a bullet wound through his left shoulder. I checked both sides; the bullet went clean through. Other than bruises, he had no other wounds.

Villian peered over my shoulder and said: "I have a first aid kit." He then disappeared through the bushes.

While Villian was away, I collected bedrolls and fixed a bed for Hannibal. I had him as comfortable as possible and was in the process of removing his bloody shirt when Villian returned.

Villian knelt beside Hannibal and inspected his wounds. "Find water," he said.

I got up and returned with a water tin and a couple of shirts. I used my knife and made wash cloths and bandages from one of the shirts. Together, Villian and I cleaned Hannibal's wounds.

As we worked, Villian said: "I have medical training. Bullet wound first."

Villian opened the first-aid kit and laid out an array of fairly sophisticated equipment on a clean white cloth. His kit included antiseptics, salves, sutures, needles, probes, long forceps and scissors.

I watched, with a combination of awe and emotional turmoil.

Villian peered closely at the entry and exit wounds and said: "Jacketed bullet, no expansion or fragmenting."

He cleaned the external bullet wound, front and back, with liquid antiseptic. He used a sterilized probe and forceps to remove bits of cloth from the bullet path inside the shoulder. He then coated the probe with antiseptic salve and pushed it through the entire path of the bullet.

"Clean, with a coating of antiseptic salve," said Villian, as he inspected his work. "No arteries were cut, so I'll stitch up the entry and exit. The wound should heal nicely." Soon it was done.

Villian turned his attention to the gash on Hannibal's forehead. "Nasty gash, lots of blood, concussion, but no fracture." He paused and then added: "Probably hit his head on the rock face of the cliff." He washed out the wound with liquid antiseptic and began stitching.

As he finished, he said: "A dozen stitches, and it will heal." He looked up and added: "He'll have a scar to remind him of how close he came to dying."

A lump rose in my throat as I comprehended Villian's words.

Villian saw my expression and said: "OK, nurse, take care of the bandaging."

I understood the intent of Villian's comment; he had given me something constructive to do. I looked into his eyes and replied: "Yes." Villian moved aside and busied himself cleaning his instruments. Soon we both finished. Hannibal rested comfortably.

I looked at my watch and then the sun in the sky. I was surprised. Although it seemed like forever, the time from the ambush to the present had only been three hours.

Villian saw me check my watch. He checked his own and said: "We have a little time. The two soldiers who escaped were on foot, and Orleale, the nearest town, has no telegraph or phone service."

He glanced around. "I have my car; yours is damaged beyond further use. The two lorries would be conspicuous. We can wrap, load and fasten the priest's body on a running board. Your husband can rest in the back seat, and you and I can sit in front."

He thought a moment and added: "We'll take extra petrol, water, first-aid kit, your equipment and weapons, nothing else. Driving straight through, we should be in Mogadishu before dawn tomorrow."

We both sat on the ground near Hannibal and rested our backs against the trunks of scrub trees. After a few minutes, I looked intently at Villian and asked, for the second time: "Why?"

Villian smiled and said: "Men working for Director Louis Du Bellay caught me at the border of France and Spain in July 1930."

His smile disappeared, and he stared into the sky. His face acquired a pained look. He then looked back at me and added: "I was taken to Paris. Du Bellay gave me a choice: either be shot as a spy or serve as a double agent."

I thought a moment and then asked: "Did Captain Inspecteur Soucet know?"

Villian smiled wryly and said: "No. Du Bellay is a very complex man."

He paused and then continued: "My first assignment was you. I was told to stay on good terms with Herman Göring, but protect you and your husband. I found opportunities to give Raeder and his thugs false leads."

I didn't know what to say. I stuttered: "I, I thought you were my enemy."

Villian's stare seemed to penetrate to my inner being. "We have much in common," he replied.

His reply stunned me for a moment. "You are a paid assassin," I finally blurted.

"And you have killed many men as a paid espionage agent," Villian quickly responded. "Tell me, is there a difference?"

Villian's response cut deep. I closed my eyes. Faces of dead men surfaced in my mind. "No," I muttered. I couldn't respond with a difference. Thoughts brought anguish. "What have I become?"

I opened my eyes and looked at Villian. He returned my look with a steady gaze. Tears formed and I choked on a stifled sob. "No," I muttered again.

Villian's face acquired a look of sympathy, but it faded into one of pain. He said: "I have fallen into the abyss; there is no return for me." He let out a sigh. After a long pause, he added: "For you, there is still time. Back away from the abyss, and go home."

I felt a hand touch mine. I looked over for the source. Hannibal was looking at me with his steady gaze. I tried to smile as he held my hand.

Thoughts of relief mixed with joy pushed back the darkness. "I almost lost what I value most," I concluded. To Hannibal, I said: "Villian is right. We should go home."

The ride back to Mogadishu seemed endless. We passed a few natives going about their business, but no vehicles.

At just before dawn on December 7, we pulled up next to the Mogadishu Cathedral. I went inside. Villian and the now conscious Hannibal waited in the car.

I found several nuns inside the main chapel. They looked at me in amazement. I hadn't thought about my disheveled appearance until then, but I'm sure I was quite a sight.

"I am Sister Agnes," said an older-looking nun. She spoke in Italian and eyed me carefully. "May I help you?"

"I'm Caroline Jones," I replied in as controlled a voice as I could muster. "My husband is outside in a car. He is severely wounded." I paused and added: "Father Francesco is also in the car. He is dead."

"Oh!" Exclaimed Sister Agnes and several others. I led the way back to the car. Villian was gone.

Sister Agnes was a model of efficiency. "Father Francesco told us about you before he left," she said, as we helped Hannibal walk into the cathedral side door. "We will help you."

I didn't know what to say. I'm sure my face expressed a pleading look, combined with thanks.

Sister Agnes smiled and added: "Fortunately, the French warship *Jeanne d'Arc* is in the harbor." Her smile broadened a little. "Capitaine

Andre Marquis is a devout Catholic, and he stops here often during his regular port of call visits."

Events passed quickly. Francesco's body was taken inside, our equipment was removed from the car, and the car disappeared. Within an hour, Capitaine Marquis arrived with several sailors.

"Your mission is known to us," said Capitaine Marquis, as Hannibal and I were escorted from the cathedral to a waiting car. "Capitaine Inspecteur Soucet sent a message that alerted us that you might need help in Mogadishu."

I marveled at Soucet's efficiency and anticipation of our needs. "Merci, Monsieur Capitaine," was all that I could manage.

As I close these notes, Hannibal and I are cleaned up and safe aboard the *Jeanne d'Arc*. Capitaine Marquis said that we will pass through Suez in a couple of days, and we will be at the port of Marseilles before Christmas.

Hannibal is better, and we will compile a report of our findings at Danane later during the voyage. Soucet sent a radio message to the ship. Among other things, he said: "France owes you profound gratitude for your services."

My inner demons are under control for now. The events since December 5 seem like a dream.

Villian disappeared, back into the shadows. I think he knows how grateful I am for saving Hannibal, and me, from the abyss. Perhaps my gratitude will be some solace as he continues his tortured journey.

Hannibal and I agree, it's time to go home. I wonder if Saks Fifth Avenue in New York will have the latest fashions from Paris? I plan to find out.

# EPILOGUE

## Sunday, January 20, 1935

A new year, and Hannibal and I have concluded our affairs in Europe. Our four and a half years there brought adventure, accomplishment, comedy, tragedy and knowledge of a world so different than hometown America. We may return someday.

We have our old suite aboard the *Isle de France,* and we sail into New York Harbor tomorrow. I look forward to seeing the Statue of Liberty again. Hannibal promised that I could shop in New York to my heart's content.

Over breakfast this morning, we discussed the future. "We could go to a little ski resort in upstate New York that I know about," said Hannibal, as we sipped coffee. "It's called Lake Placid. What do you think?"

"Sounds wonderful," I replied. "We need to rest, and you need to heal." I thought a moment and then added: "I wonder if they have murders there?"

# ABOUT THE AUTHOR

*Frank and Linda Gertcher enjoying Alaska*

Frank L. Gertcher was born in Clinton, Indiana and raised on a small farm in Sullivan County. In addition to publishing many papers in scientific journals, he co-authored two successful textbooks and authored six novels and a book of poems. He is an active member of the Mystery Writers of America (MWA). Frank and his wife Linda live in the Shell Point Retirement Community near Fort Myers, Florida, and they travel the world doing research for Frank's books.